THE GIRL IN PARADISE

A.J. RIVERS
& THOMAS YORK

The Girl in Paradise
Copyright © 2023 by A.J. Rivers & Thomas York

PROLOGUE

Lafrenière Park
Metairie, Louisiana
May 18, 2008

A COOL SUMMER WIND BLEW THROUGH THE RED CURLS OF ISABELLE Walker's hair as she skipped down the sidewalk on her way home. She pushed back the tangles, trying to keep her crimson locks from getting caught in her school bag. It was the end of the school year, and the fourteen-year-old was excited about a well-deserved vacation. She'd just made her way off the school bus happily with a few of her neighbors. Holding her book bag snug tightly on her shoulder, she waved goodbye to her friends for the summer break as the bus passed.

"Maddie, don't forget to call me later!" she yelled, adjusting her bag as the bus grinded and rocked past.

A pale girl in the middle section of the bus answered her from a window as Bella walked by. "I will, Bella. We could go down to the mall and shop!"

"Okay!" Bella waved and continued her walk home.

Even from forty feet down the street, she heard the bus door as it creaked closed. Bella made her way down the half-block to her house, smiling as she caught a glimpse of children running in the adjacent Lafrenière Park between the towering emerald bushes shrouding the park's borders with the street.

Memories floated through her as she heard the peals of laughter and the shrill cry of someone shouting, "You're it!" in a game of hide and seek. Bella thought for a moment that she might want to join them. It hadn't been long ago at all that she had been one of the children throwing dodgeballs and chanting, "Red Rover" in this very park. But she was going to be in high school soon, and it was time to stop playing such silly games.

That was one of the things she loved about her little town of Metairie, Louisiana. It was abuzz with sunshine, laughter, and joyous children at play.

Bella made her way up to her family's porch, but before heading inside, she wanted to take one last look out at the park. That tiny spark of childhood won out over her teenage self-seriousness. With a day this beautiful and cool, she just couldn't stand being indoors. Maybe she could play a little bit. Her friends wouldn't have to know.

Unknown to her, as she walked up to the park watching a mother and son play catch, Bella was watching a tragedy about to unfold.

On that fateful day in Lafrenière Park, as the cool winds blew to stifle the blazing heat of a mid-afternoon sun, Bella spied a gray-dirt baseball field. The field seemed to glimmer in a rippling wave of heat and emerald grass as Bella glanced at two people throwing a ball. She recognized one of them—the famous Representative Marsha Martin, who they'd just done a lesson about in social studies. The second—a boy half Bella's age—resembled Marsha. Bella watched them, shaking her head as the Congresswoman wiped the sweat from her face and reached awkwardly with a baseball mitt to catch a ball tossed to her. The curly, blond-haired boy's arm held all the intensity—if not the athletic prowess—of a seasoned major league veteran at the tender age of possibly seven years old.

The blue-eyed boy sheepishly grinned and kick the ground with a cleated foot. His mother called a stern warning over the other sounds of the park. "Tommy Maxwell Martin, don't you throw too hard, mister. You'll bruise my hand, son."

Bella caught the boy's mischievous giggle as he apologized, "I'm sorry, Mommy."

But both mother and son laughed and shook their heads at each other's throws.

"A few more throws then frisbee, okay?" Representative Martin pleaded as her son groaned in protest and paced waiting to receive the next thrown ball.

"Okay, Mom. But promise me you'll catch the next one like I taught you. You have to open the glove wider and use both hands to catch like Coach Joe told us," Tommy scolded, showing her the proper technique.

Marsha sent the ball back in a weird, lopsided toss. Tommy ran up to catch the ball before it landed on the grass. He dove and made an incredible grab to the delight of his mother.

Congresswoman Martin, red-faced from her errant baseball throw, laughed and cheered despite the embarrassment. "Thanks for the lesson, sweetie. I hope I didn't throw it too hard to you."

"Mom, I'm not a baby anymore. You can really sling the ball to me now," Tommy declared proudly. He chopped his feet to show Marsha that he was ready for any throw she had.

Bella had seen enough sports and laughter by this point. She prepared to turn from the happy mother and son. But then she heard a cell phone ring and watched the congresswoman turn over baseball duties to another woman. Marsha shrugged her shoulders at her son and walked away to take the call. Bella felt bad, but not bad enough to go play with him. Bored, she left the park, ready for a snack at home. Her mother was probably waiting for her with a peanut butter and jelly sandwich.

While Bella was eating her sandwich and watching Scooby-Doo in the safety of her home, she glanced out the window toward Lafrenière Park. An unmarked van had just pulled up to the spot she'd been standing in not five minutes before. As Bella poured herself a glass of milk, she frowned as she saw two men wearing purple feathered Mardi Gras masks getting out of the vehicle.

"Weird," she said to nobody in particular. She glanced over to her mother, who was chatting on the phone in the other room and hadn't seemed to notice.

The men moved cautiously toward Tommy Martin and his nanny as they continued throwing the baseball. One of the masked men strolled behind the nanny, making comical gestures, which caused Tommy to laugh. Bella shook her head, thinking the two men were funny as well. She couldn't hear what they were saying, but the shocked look on the woman's face told her that it was probably full of bad words. As the woman turned to scold the man, Bella was shocked to see the second man ran up behind Tommy and grab him. He clamped a hand over the boy's mouth and made a beeline for the van. The first hit the nanny in the face, knocking her to the ground and then the men got into the van and sped off.

Bella screamed. "Mommy, some men in masks grabbed the congress lady's son! They just hit a woman too!"

The warble from the other room paused momentarily, like Bella's mom hadn't quite caught the gist of what she was saying. She yelled louder. "Mom!"

What Bella and her family would later learn is that something terrible happened that day to poor Tommy Martin and his mother. Bella and everyone in her community were shocked by the incident. Police and politicians were outraged that such a high-profile kidnapping could occur in Metairie. Everyone was terrified another kidnapping could occur. Police were under massive pressure to find the child.

It was two days after the kidnapping that Bella saw the police were using her once safe park, her place of sunshine and laughter, to map their plan to find Tommy Martin. Representative Martin and a team of police and reporters were in and among the staged area surrounded in yellow police tape. Bella could even smell the food trucks and coffee vendors who were positioned down her street preparing meals for the exhausted police officers.

"What the heck are you doing outside, young lady?" came the growling yet concerned voice of Bella's dad from behind her. Both her parents were wide-eyed and nervous. "Tommy Martin was kidnapped just two days ago. You can't be out here. The maniac might still be around here."

Bella looked down and found herself out on the sidewalk. She hadn't even realized she'd been so drawn to the scene that she'd left the safety of her home.

"Isabelle Lauren Walker! What were you thinking? You have scared your father and me half to death," Bella's mother bellowed. Bella was sure she'd be grounded for this stunt. At a minimum, no phone for the foreseeable month. At a maximum, no video games or outside for a month... maybe more. So much for summer vacation.

She hung her head down. "I—I just had to know how the case was going. I just had to."

"You get inside right now," her father demanded.

She looked back to her father. Then Bella turned to glimpse one more time the throng of police and specialists trying to find Tommy Martin. Her shoulders shrugged, saddened by all that she was witnessing. Bella mumbled, "Tommy, I hope you're safe. I just know they'll do everything to find you soon."

There was an endless barrage of scoldings from the minute she stepped inside. The outcome was just as bad as Bella had assumed—no video games, no phone, and no outside for a month.

But, understanding her obsession with the lost boy, they did allow her to watch TV in the family room—as long as both parents could keep an eye on her.

"Mom, do you think they'll find him?" she asked as they watched the news on WDSU. The sixty-inch screen illuminated the polished fleur-de-lis tiles of the floor. Bella always enjoyed the way the floor glimmered like polished bronze.

"I don't know, Bella," her mother admitted. "There's a lot of good people looking though. They're highly trained investigators who specialize in abductions, just like your aunt. They know how to find people who have been taken. Or people who don't want to be found."

"And there's the full political weight of the congresswoman's friends making sure they catch the kidnapper," her father added.

"Dad, who's the lady way back in the corner? That sure looks like Aunt Natalie. But she's supposed to be on vacation in Scotland or something, right?" Bella strained her eyes to see a tall woman wearing an FBI forensics shirt, with her auburn hair pulled back in a ponytail.

He frowned. "No, it couldn't be…"

A tired Metairie police chief—Paul Arcadio, the screen read—smiled. "The city of Metairie is proud to announce that we have found Tommy Martin, after an exhaustive seventy-two-hour search. The kidnappers have been apprehended and placed in custody, but more importantly, Tommy Martin is back with his loving mother, Representative Marsha Martin. The boy is in excellent health but wants a Big Mac and extra large fries. I guess he's a little hungry."

People in the room laughed, and the Walkers chuckled too.

"There is no way we could have captured these scumbags without the invaluable resources and additional manpower of the Federal Bureau of Investigation." Chief Arcadio turned and gestured to the auburn-haired lady in the back whose face was as red as her hair, obviously embarrassed for being put in the spotlight. "I'll say this as clearly as I can with absolute humbled thanks. Without the help of the FBI's forensic psychology expert, Dr. Natalie Roberts, this case may have had a different outcome."

There were laughs of surprise when Bella's aunt's name was mentioned by the chief. There were cheers and hugs, then all went quiet as Natalie reluctantly stepped up to the podium.

"That's my godmother for you!" Bella whooped with pride. "She's supposed to finally be taking a vacation. But there she is on TV around the corner catching that kidnapper."

She watched in awe as Aunt Natalie walked up to the rickety wooden podium, scanned the audience with her green eyes, and adjusted the microphone to reach her towering height to speak.

"A loving mother had her child taken from her in a beautiful community park where families build memories of love and laughter. We, and I mean every law enforcement officer in this room working together, caught these monsters and stopped their plan to ransom poor Tommy and extort his mother.

"Now, I ask you to promise our community, this state, and our country to never let the monsters win. Don't let what they did frighten you to not use the park. Never let them ruin your hope, your love, and the laughter of your park and this wonderful place of happiness—ever."

A flurry of questions rose from the crowd before Natalie pointed out one reporter. The cameras focused on him then back to Aunt Natalie, "Dave Landry, WBRZ. Why did this monster, as you called him, Dr. Roberts, decide it was a good idea to steal a congresswoman's son in an open park in broad daylight? Surely, there had to be a reason?"

Natalie shrugged. "Money. Money was the reason. Harold Armand craved wealth beyond his wildest dreams, and all the perks that went with it—power, respect, and revenge. Apparently, he'd been laid off from Congresswoman Martin's marine division down in Port Fourchon and wanted more than his hundred-thousand-dollar severance package. Greed and stupidity to extort money from a powerful congresswoman drove this man and his accomplice to take and tie up an innocent child and pawn him off like common cattle." Aunt Natalie leaned back from the podium and adjusted her jacket. Bella could see her aunt was ready to turn the microphone back to Chief Arcadio.

"One more question, Dr. Roberts." Before Natalie could say no, the reporter bellowed, "Is this the last one, Doc? You've been catching the baddies for quite a while. And you certainly have trained some experts out there to take over for a well-deserved rest."

"Great question, Tony. After thirty years, the answer to your question is… we'll see."

Laughter and applause echoed on the TV and in the Walker home as well. And when Aunt Natalie stopped over later to spend the night, the applause and hugs continued a little longer. "I wanted to tell y'all I was in town, but we didn't want to tip off our perp. My apologies to you."

"No worries, there, Natalie. We understand." Bella's dad took his sister's coat and led her to sit in the dining room to enjoy a large pepperoni pizza ordered in her honor by Bella.

"I knew if they called you that you would catch him," Bella beamed. Natalie greeted her with a warm hug.

"I didn't catch him alone, Bella. There were a lot of people who worked together to stop Harry Armand." Aunt Natalie sighed and paused before saying, "Some paid a heavy price to catch him."

Bella didn't understand her aunt's cryptic words. All she knew as a precocious fourteen-year-old was that her aunt was a real hero. She'd beaten evil, and the world was a safe place for the innocent once more. But Bella wouldn't be satisfied with the accolades of her aunt. Bella Walker, inspired by her Aunt Natalie's heroics, wanted to be an admired hero too.

And like her Aunt Natalie, one day in the future, when Bella had indeed become an FBI forensics psychology expert, she'd feel the burden that comes with being a hero. It would be during the worst case of her career.

Her mentor, her partner, and closest friend, Ray Mandola, would fall as heroes sometimes do to save others. As her hands lay across Ray's heaving, dying chest, she would cry in rage. The same hands that were clotted with her partner's blood, would fire a shot to stop a maniac who'd attacked her team.

And on some nights, when the world was long asleep, Bella would awaken and remember Ray's eyes. He had the bluest eyes. The kind that carried all the shimmer of the ocean, that saw the world in wonder like a child playing under a starlit night.

But then that sick monster, The Harbinger, ambushed us and stole the light forever.

Tears would fall like a towering, rushing waterfall splashing down her face to the darkness of the cold floor. In those moments of sadness and angst, Bella Walker would look back and recall her aunt's cryptic words.

Some paid a heavy price to catch him.

CHAPTER ONE

Western North Shore
Waianae Mountain Range
Eastern Valley Near Mount Ka'ala
Oahu, Hawaii
July 16, 2023

FBI FORENSIC INVESTIGATOR RACHEL GENTRY WIPED THE SWEAT off her brow and caught the pungent smell of damp earth and bananas as she maneuvered down a slope into a pristine rainforest surrounding the North Shore. Colorful birds with all manner of caw and birdsong annoyed Rachel and her team of officers on their journey. They weren't on a pleasant hike on this walk into the dense, humid jungle. This was a dark sojourn of discovery for their investigation into a string of horrific deaths. And today, while nature remained in balance and beautiful on the island of Oahu, brutal slayings in this valley of emerald green said otherwise.

Rachel was running lead on the case and directed her forensic specialist accordingly. Since taking over, she had been at her wits' end trying to deduce a motive or catch a break on any of the thousand leads. She wasn't alone in her frustration with the case. The Honolulu Police Department was underbudgeted and underresourced; in a last act of desperation, with fear mounting and the pressure at a blistering boil in the community, they'd requested her office's assistance—a request that Rachel gladly accepted to serve and protect the jungles of her childhood home.

Rachel squatted next to a tired, semi-athletic man who yawned repeatedly while sealing ziplock bags with pieces of bloody cloth. It almost sounded callous to say, but the body they'd discovered brutally murdered didn't even rise to the level of alarming anymore.

"Make sure you bag everything with the proper seals," she ordered. "I want dates on everything and times. We don't want a repeat of the ordeal we had in that Maui missing person's case."

"No worries. I'll triple-bag them and keep the labels inside the bag. You know how the humidity out here ruins paper... and runs the ink." He pointed to six of the bags he had sealed with labels properly transcribed. Wiping sweat from his shirt sleeve, he continued, "You know, that Maui case was destined to get axed anyway. Too many major players with skin in the game were working against us."

Both agents stood, and Rachel turned her head and gave a narrowed stare to her second-in-command. "What's that supposed to mean, Agent Makani? Am I missing something?"

Billy Makani put out a tanned hand and pointed in the direction of the nearby town. "Rachel, you know what we're up against. Don't play stupid. This location, the fact the locals didn't see or hear anything—and the ones who most likely did—won't say a word. It reeks of something. This state of ours is as corrupt as they come."

"I know the score, Billy. For every crook we catch, two more show up thinking they're the next big underworld boss. We don't have the resources or funds to watch everyone, and these thugs know it." Rachel grimaced and kicked a dried-out coconut husk by her foot. "They use the old tools—fear, intimidation, and bribes. Some go further and use the Hawaiian folklore to literally put the fear of a god in them."

Billy shrugged his shoulders and picked up his bags of labeled evidence. "Well, when you put it that way, why bother? We just do like some of our veteran colleagues did, I guess. File the reports, keep up the image of investigating, and maybe solve a crime or two if we're real lucky. Maybe we get an envelope of cash on our desk for looking the other way. Maybe we don't. Either way, we let our conscience be our guide."

Rachel sighed and looked out at the sprawl of a massive coffee plantation out toward the western North Shore. "If I ever get to that point, Agent Makani, I'll go home and run the family business. C'mon. Let's get this stuff back to the lab."

They advised the coroner's team to finish evidence recovery and had only just started back to the car when the sporadic ringing of her phone startled them both. In the mountains of the remote North Shore of Hawaii, it was rare to get a text message, much less an actual phone ring. "It's not showing the number, but it's ringing through. That's weird."

"You gonna answer?" Billy asked as they headed up the hill to their vehicles parked up on the dirt road.

Rachel stopped on the red dirt road seventy feet from their off-road vehicle and answered. "Gentry."

"Ra—is that you—I just—"

"Sorry, you're cutting out," Rachel said.

"—landed in Honolulu," the voice finally came through a little clearer.

"Bella?" she gasped.

The familiar voice of an old friend finally came through, if only for a moment. "Rachel, where are you? I just got—"

She cut out again before Rachel could answer. Excited, Rachel blurted out her location to Bella. She repeated herself several times on the phone to make sure Bella got the directions accurately. "Bella, if you can hear me, I'm on a call near a valley by the Waianae Mountain Range. Take H-1 up to Route 93. Text me when you're close, and I'll meet up with you."

"You're as giddy as a schoolgirl having a sleepover, Agent Gentry. What gives?" Billy cracked.

Rachel grinned as they piled into the SUV. "The best forensic psychologist the FBI has ever produced next to Natalie Roberts and Candace Wren."

"Big talk," Billy mused. "This Bella Walker must really be something."

Rachel turned on the ignition as Billy got into the passenger's seat. The coroner's team was just now making their way out to the parking area. Both grimaced as they watched them lift the body bag into the unmarked, white van and then place a smaller bag carrying a head inside too.

Rachel turned the vehicle south to rendezvous with Bella and shook her head free of the image. "All those FBI legends were great detectives, dummy. But do you get what I'm saying? Somehow, Bella heard about my urgent request for her assistance. Despite somebody in our front office, or theirs, trying to shelve three requests for her help. Now that Bella Walker is here, we might be able to solve this booger of a case."

—·—

Bella Walker pushed back a curl of her auburn hair and groaned. It had taken the customer service desk almost a full hour to rent her a car that sat collecting dust in the adjacent parking lot. She stared with her emerald eyes out at the lone rental, then checked her watch again as if it would make the time pass any quicker.

"They sure aren't in any kind of hurry in Hawaii," she grumbled under her breath.

It was only adding to the mounting frustration she'd been feeling for the last few hours. What was supposed to be a fun visit to her best friend Rachel and maybe some time on the beach had quickly turned sour. Finding out midflight from her trusted boss that Hawaii's field office had tried to shelve Rachel's three requests for assistance from her made Bella's blood boil. Not to mention that Rachel had apparently been called away on the case and so hadn't been able to pick her up. It left her feeling discombobulated and on the wrong foot; and despite the beautiful weather and bright sun, she felt a cloud over her mood.

Thankfully, it wasn't too much longer before the attendant returned with the keys to her rental, and before she knew it, she was on H-1 and then Route 93, enjoying the splendor of the towering verdant mountains and beautiful tropical menagerie. Where she was headed, of course, wasn't going to be nearly so pleasant.

She rounded the corner to the address Rachel had texted her and broke into a bright grin as her best friend came into view.

"Did you check into a hotel or something, Bella?" Rachel jabbed as she rushed forward to give Bella a hug the moment she stepped out of the car.

"Hey, ain't my fault your island folks love to take their sweet time," Bella countered, though she still bristled a bit. She hated to be late for anything.

Rachel and her partner, a tall, gangly Pacific Islander with raven black hair, threw back their heads and laughed.

"I like her," he told Rachel. He reached out a hand for her to shake. "Aloha. Agent Billy Makani. I've read and heard a lot of great things about you, Agent Walker. I—"

"Just call me Bella, if you don't mind," Bella interrupted, watching how Billy reacted to her request. He seemed a little out of sorts being interrupted in his obviously prepared introduction. It echoed a lot to Bella.

Billy continued with a red face and embarrassed smile, "Okay, Bella."

Finally, she lifted her hand to shake his and immediately sized him up.

Rachel's partner is a rookie. She's working with a second-year agent at best in one of the most remote and corrupt places in the U.S. next to Alaska and the bayou. How did this kid pull a lush assignment like this fresh out of the academy at any rate?

With formalities out of the way, Bella broke into a smile. "I had the opportunity to use your fine rental establishment at Honolulu Airport since I had no ride waiting for me. I must say they're as prompt and efficient… as a *snail.*"

"Wait, I had someone scheduled to pick you up and give you a car to drive up." Rachel smiled, then sarcastically added, "Oh, wait a minute. I'm sorry; we had to pull them for the multiple homicides up on the North Shore."

Bella wiped the sweat from her brow and then walked back to her rental for a bottle of water. Even though she was used to it, growing up in Louisiana, the humidity was always a killer. She huffed. "How dare a murder investigation get in the way of travel arrangements to get me up here to… well, a murder investigation. I heard on my flight over that you've been trying to get me to Hawaii for quite a while."

"Yeah, I guess today sums up my requests. What took you so long?" Bella and Rachel laughed while Billy shook his head at the inside joke between the two of them.

"I'm here now. That's all I can say. And this case is already starting weird with your office shelving—oh, I mean—having difficulty approving your request."

"The field office said it had been sent on three separate occasions to yours," Rachel said in her typical sarcasm. "So, you mean the beacon of FBI integrity lied to a desperate field agent begging for your services in several murders? The scandal, dear lady, is more than I can bear."

Bella smiled but was already tired of the banter and ready to get to work. "Well, this beautiful island is starting to have that scummy feel of New Orleans. How about we go check out what y'all found?"

"Follow me, Bella," Billy offered. He and Rachel climbed back into their off-road vehicle. They showed Bella where to leave her car parked off to the side of the road in a gravel parking area. Then Rachel waved her into the passenger's side of the vehicle, and Rachel maneuvered into the back seat.

Bella frowned. "Are you sure you don't want me to sit in the back?"

Rachel chuckled while putting her seatbelt on behind Bella. "With the way Billy drives up in these mountains, I could use a break from the terror."

Twenty minutes later, Billy parked the vehicle, and all three agents climbed out of the gray SUV. Bella went to the edge of the red dirt road as some tropical bird cawed just above her head in a nearby tree. She looked down a steep decline of mountain at least one hundred feet into a valley of trees and banana groves that moved as an ocean of green.

The three agents maneuvered between tree roots, mud puddles, and rocks to reach the area marked off with yellow police tape. Before even ducking under the tape, Bella scanned her surroundings closely in a grid check of the entire crime scene, all the while noting the rest of the forensic investigators putting a decapitated woman into a body bag.

"How many bodies so far?" Bella asked as she continued to walk and check the right side of the marked-off perimeter.

Rachel wiped her left brow and swatted a mosquito. "Five. All decapitated, staged sitting up with their knees bent and feet under their buttocks. It was as if they were praying. Then there were these weird statues in front of each praying victim. I'll show you the photos when we get back."

"Do we know who the victims are?"

"Identification remains to be seen, but if it follows the patterns of the previous kill sites, these will almost certainly be some of the wealthiest people on the islands. Elites."

"Sounds like they have enemies," Bella mused. It wasn't so dissimilar from a case she had handled long ago: the Harbinger Killer case. Bella could see why her old rival had called her in.

"And you'd be right, Agent Walker," Rachel replied. "But the trouble is, that only *expands* our suspect pool. An operation as meticulous as this wouldn't just be some disgruntled employee or someone trying to strike back at the one percent."

"I'm inclined to agree," Bella replied.

Bella continued to circle the scene, practically tiptoeing to avoid damaging any additional evidence that might be found. She stooped down low to examine some footprints. "I recognize most of these footprints as military or police issue footwear."

"Pretty common on the islands," Billy supplied. "Lots of folks use the Army surplus stores for their main shopping. Probably more popular than Jordans out here."

Bella nodded. "But these smooth ones, to the left of each place where the victims were, are curious. Definitely not military grade. The left big toe in each instance pivots inward, with the foot perpendicular to the back right foot. As if someone were swinging something with purpose. Something like a bat, or—"

"A machete or ax." Rachel rubbed her chin and walked over to look. "That would explain the beheadings. Think we'll get anything off the boots or footprints other than the obvious?"

Bella stared intensely at the footprints before answering, "Well, the size of the foot for starters is someone of a small stature. No treads, or recognizable treads anyway, also means possible imported footwear—maybe India, China, or elsewhere. But Hawaii imports pretty much everything but coffee, bananas, macadamia nuts, or coconuts. There again, a killer wearing imported, smooth-sole shoes, could be a dime a dozen. These prints may mean nothing at all."

The team continued looking for clued when Bella paused and asked, "What about these?"

Billy followed her pointing finger to a small cluster of shiny, black rocks and chuckled. "Those are the tears of Pele."

Bella frowned. "Who?"

"*Ka wahine 'ai honua.* The ancient fire goddess. She created these islands long ago, and her spirit still lives on in the lava and steam from the volcanoes here."

"It's glass, Agent Walker," Rachel chimed in. "They're solidified lava drops that cool into this form. See? It looks like a tear. You can find them all over the mountains."

She stooped down to pick one up, admiring the way it shined in the light. But then she heard thunder and looked up at an oncoming thundercloud moving swiftly from the west and headed in their direction. The towering thunderhead cracked lightning blasts of brilliant white light from the billowing purple cloud. Fluorescent blue and emerald arcs were etched in the upper levels of the storm.

"Crap. Just what we needed," Bella muttered as a second thunderous roar trembled the mountain.

"Storm's moving in fast, Bella. It looks like we're done for today." Rachel advised Bella, then turned to her team of investigators. "Time to wrap it up, folks, before we get caught in a mountain washout. I don't know about you, but I'd like to skip that kind of fun today."

They nodded and hurried to take as many photos and gather as much evidence as they could of the scene before it became a muddy mess. Bella was just about to turn and join Rachel when something caught her eye. She lowered to a squat and took a photo with her phone before reaching into her pocket for a pair of gloves.

"Can someone pass me a bag?" she asked.

"We're out of bags. What is it, anyway?" Rachel furrowed her brow and stooped to look just as the rest of the team packed up.

"It looks like some kind of weird statue." Bella had it in hand now and was turning the statue and checking the intricacies of the design. She noted how the reddish-black statue with humanlike renderings carved into it was only six inches high and four inches wide. To Bella, it looked like a screaming man with a banana leaf lion's mane. "Is this the kind of statue you mentioned?"

Rachel nodded as she ushered Bella out of the wind and back down the mountain. "Looks just like it. That's a bad rendition of a Hawaiian war god. By bad, I mean it is a horribly inaccurate depiction, made of the worst clay material, and a crudely fired paint job. This is something you might find for ten bucks in one of those tourist traps down by the Oahu Mall."

"Yet here it is."

Bella tapped the statue with her nails. There was something rattling inside the war god. She shook the statue to confirm that there was an object within. Carefully, she inverted the statue, and a white, waxen stick with a gold band fell to the ground just as the first drops of cold rain fell on her skin.

Bella stopped to pick up the stub of a candle and recoiled in disgust. "Dear lord!" she gasped.

"What is it?" asked Billy.

She picked it up and showed them. "It's a severed finger."

CHAPTER TWO

BELLA TOOK A DEEP BREATH AND INSPECTED THE FINGER CLOSELY, willing her stomach to settle. The gold band on it had indeed been a small ring. The finger itself was a pinky, but to which side, she couldn't determine. "Well, there's one for the books."

Rachel wasn't even fazed. She turned her head harshly to snap at the forensic investigators booking it out of the rain. "Which one of you specialists dropped a victim's finger? Check all the evidence bags back at the morgue," she growled. "I swear, this lab, Bella."

But Bella couldn't even respond. The rain was falling faster in big, fat drops that splashed heavily on the palm trees, and before they knew it, the pitter-patter had become a full rainstorm. Bella quickly shoved the finger back inside the war god and tried to cover it with her hands as she transferred custody to Rachel.

"I'll explain later," Rachel shouted over the storm. "I'll give this to the tech—you head up to the car."

Scrambling and half slipping to make the summit, Bella finally reached the road just as the rains unloaded into a deluge. Within minutes, water was cascading from the upper climes of the mountains. "You weren't kidding about washouts, were you?"

"No, we need to get out of here now. Hawaii is notorious for freak waterfalls or vehicles getting swept off the road." Rachel climbed into their vehicle, and Bella followed suit. "Billy, we'll get Agent Walker to her car tomorrow. For now, we stop, and you run and get her bags. Then we bring her to the hotel. I'm sorry about your car, Bella. But in this weather, we always look out for each other."

Bella looked down at her soaked shirt and shook off the droplets from her auburn hair. "A warm hotel sounds good to me. Do you guys keep a towel or two handy? This rain did a number."

"Oh, I think I left it out on the beach," Rachel joked. "You know, I was out there all morning soaking up the sun."

"No wonder this case is taking so long," Bella countered. Rachel turned with a knowing grin. Bella smirked right back.

The drive from the North Shore to Honolulu took about an hour and a half due to the torrential rain. In between the constant drone of the windshield wipers and the blast of the heater, Bella and Rachel caught each other up on their lives over the last couple of years.

"You liking Colorado?"

"It's quiet. Small. Cold."

Rachel let out a single chuckle at that.

"But it's not so bad. Telluride is a cute little town, and it's away from everything. Tons and tons of old-style, miner-forty-niner types, and it's not too bad of a drive up to Denver if I want to hit the big city. I was hoping to have time to ski up on those pristine mountains, but the job has been hectic, as you know."

Rachel nodded. "Oh, everyone knows your schedule is booked since you nabbed The Harbinger. That one made Jeffrey Dahmer look like a choir boy cooking at Popeyes. Though I wouldn't want to know Dahmer's secret recipe for fried chicken."

Everyone heard Billy Makani's stomach growl at the mention of the latter. "You had to mention Popeyes, Rachel. Really?"

"You love that chicken, huh?" Rachel cracked. The women both laughed hysterically as Billy's stomach groaned even louder a second time. The sound was like a groaning large dog. The sound was so hilarious that Bella giggle-snorted. Upon hearing her giggle-snort, all conversations paused for a moment in the vehicle. All that was heard for a few seconds was the drone of the windshield wipers and the storming rain. Then everyone bellowed with laughter to the point tears fell from all.

———•———

Alohilani Resort
Waikiki Beach
Honolulu, Hawaii

They arrived at Bella's hotel and dropped her off to check in. Rachel rolled down her window and nodded, "We'll see you in the morning. Don't do anything I wouldn't do."

"I would never." Bella smiled and turned to leave, then glanced back once she took in the fullness of the place from ground level. "How do you guys afford such extravagance on a meager FBI budget? This place must be three hundred a night."

Rachel got out of the vehicle and walked over to Bella. She leaned in and whispered, "I requested your help, Bella. For that, I spared no expense, even my own, to make sure you have everything you need while you are here. Don't hesitate to call me for anything."

"Room service? If I need a midnight pizza?" Bella cracked without missing a beat. Both women laughed.

"You better hope I don't come in and take a slice for myself." Rachel turned, waved her off, and climbed back into the SUV. "I set up the room for tonight on the fly. I was lucky to get it for one night. This place is always booked. So we'll check out tomorrow morning. And you'll have—"

Bella already knew what she was going to say. "A slum at the coffee plantation, Mrs. Gentry? Whatever will the neighbors say? This scandal could—"

"Funny, Bella. But you knew I'd never let you stay in a hotel, right? Besides, you can finally meet Mr. Right. As in he thinks he's always right."

They giggled while Billy shook his head in protest. "You had to use my joke. You just flipped it around and made the dude Mr. Right, didn't you?"

"Come on, Billy. It's still funny either way." Rachel waved good-bye for the night, and Bella waved in return as they headed to the office to close out for the evening.

Bella pulled her luggage and walked past the spacious white seating adorning the port cochere of the Alohilani Resort. On her walk, she spied tall coconut palms landscaping near the pool and lounge areas. As she walked up to the front desk, she stared wide-eyed at a towering, luminescent white plaster wall piece showcasing all the islands of Hawaii.

After check-in, Bella nearly gasped at the lobby's centerpiece: an immense two-hundred-eighty-thousand-gallon lobby oceanarium sporting all manner of fish and corals in striking colors of crimson, violet, orange, and yellow. For the briefest moment, Bella recalled snorkeling trips with her parents in the turquoise waters out in the Florida Keys, and another hair-raising scuba adventure with a bull shark near an oil platform off Grand Isle—the latter culminating in Bella not getting in the water for a while.

She continued to pull her bag to the elevator, refusing the bellhop's offer to handle her luggage. She'd always been cautious of strangers touching her things, a quirk that she and her famous FBI aunt both shared. It wasn't paranoia but a precaution. And having seen some of the things she had, Bella was always sure to take precautions.

The door of the elevator chimed as she stepped out of the elevator and onto the third floor and headed down the hallway. The card key clicked her door open, and she stepped into the opulent room. She left her bags by the ultra-comfortable, goose down bed and proceeded to walk out onto her balcony for a view of the beach. It certainly was better than the Overlook Hotel. And even in the downpour, the view was gorgeous.

Bella opted for a steaming hot shower after the jungle rains of the Waianae Mountain Range. Letting the heat soak in loosened the nagging aches and pains of muscles and joints that plague all veteran agents, and Bella was no exception. After the shower, and in warmer night clothes and robe, she prepared for the best night of sleep she'd had in days. She wrapped up in the lavender fragrant comforter and blanket and rolled over to turn off the lamp.

Then Bella paused and looked at her cell phone by the lamp. The finger in the war god statue intruded her thoughts like a bright beacon in the darkness, and she couldn't ignore it. With her eyes heavy from jet lag and a cloud of fatigue blanketing her mind, Bella picked up her phone to review the pictures one last time before going to sleep. She pined over each picture and felt the dread of déjà vu. It was that uncanny feeling that she had been through this before. Had it been a year ago? *Could it have been two years since the d—*

She still couldn't think about what happened when things went south with The Harbinger—the case that had made her a legend also demanded a sacrifice for such fame. Yes, the feelings, the needs, and the obsessive drive were all back... and it frightened Bella. For there had been one lesson she had learned in stopping The Harbinger: obsessively solving a case at all costs had indeed been a price too high for her to pay.

Like a ghost haunting her on a cold nights when a gust of howling wind down a chimney might do more than extinguish the red coals of a dying fire, Bella would hear those warning words from Aunt Natalie again.

Some paid a heavy price to catch him.

She clicked off the lamp and lay in the dark room. She closed her eyes and tried rubbing her temples to relax her mind. Her thoughts initially were like a rushing ocean wave—tumultuous and churning, they raced into a black, ragged shore of recalled memories. It was that inevitable crag of shoreline where ultimately, they crashed and exploded into a cloud of mist—or in Bella's case—tears.

But as she twisted and turned in her bed, struggling to sleep, fighting to put the past back into its bottle, she relented and focused again on today's scene and its similarity to another horrific case she solved. With the suppressed memories released, Bella's memories of the past—her failures, her ghosts—erupted as a thunderous, fiery volcano blasting back her safeguards to forget. The clues, the potential suspects, the motives, the solutions, or speculations, sweeping in to drive her to find sanctuary and solitude from their deadly meaning.

Bella recalled the horrific case that had brought her the fame she had so long ago craved. Something about the amputated finger—its symbolic nature, its preparation, and the ritualistic manner of its murdered owner—followed similar patterns to the Harbinger Killer case. To understand this case, she would have to dig up the past to figure out why everything had eerie similarities.

CHAPTER THREE

Denver, Colorado Field Office
FBI File NO. 89-231671: The Harbinger Killer Case
July 14, 2018

I T WAS INITIALLY BELIEVED THE HARBINGER KILLED RANDOMLY. In appearance, there was no rhyme or reason in his victim selection. Patterns and predictive computer modeling had been a bust. The murderer's behavior ran counterintuitive to the databases of law enforcement. Notably, he killed wealthy people and *then* switched to killing the poor—a highly unusual order of choice according to every profiling expert the Bureau had on hand.

Supervisory Special Agent Henry Worrell, with his graying hair and hardened face, would grumble to Bella, "Usually, these psychopaths start practicing their carving with prostitutes or the homeless. Then they move up to the average lonely housewife or traveling salesman in a dive hotel. Finally, they might escalate to killing a family or high-profile celebrity. Usually, by then, the compulsion makes them sloppy. Many of these maniacs want to be caught in the end, most having secured their horrific legacies."

"I can tell by the bags under your eyes that this one is different, huh?" Bella asked.

"You're telling me, kid," he groused.

She never wanted to become that obsessed with her own work. Henry would not be long for this world if he kept up that kind of pace, and she thought the pressure would be unbearable.

A defining moment—a break in the case—struck like a meteor falling from the skies. And it was those very star-studded night skies that revealed all. While surveying the Harbinger's latest kill site in a valley not far from the Rockies, Bella stumbled onto the motive of the killer and his complicated selection of victims. Looking at the placement of four dismembered bodies, she looked up and found her answer.

"Henry, is that Polaris or Aldebaran positioned directly above us?" Bella studied the celestial stars whose heavenly glimmer was at odds with the crimson, dismembered carnage in the valley's dark field.

"Say that again, Bella? Alde—what? And did you just mention a fictional star?" Puzzled, Henry looked up with two other agents scratching his head.

"Polaris is a real star, Henry. It's the North Star." She moved out into the valley to get a clearer view of the stars, double-checking her trajectory with the twinkling lights in the sky.

Henry followed suit, straining his eyes to look up and then back down to the victims. "You don't say? So, you're saying the bodies all line up with the current constellation above us, Bella?"

"Yes. Wait, you already knew that when we got here? How did you figure the Harbinger would place their parts this way?" Bella squinted and flashed her flashlight back in the direction of the forensic team setting up more lighting to recover evidence.

Henry stooped to study one of the hands of the victims—a woman in her twenties, not much younger than Bella herself. The thought sent a shiver through her as Henry waved to a forensic tech passing by to get a sample he'd found under the woman's nails. "Well, yes and no. It was a hunch. I had exhausted all other avenues. From age to social standing to birth dates, I had become frustrated and went for a stroll to clear my head."

"And that's when you looked up to the night sky and figured it out," Bella finished for him.

"No. But it cleared my head enough for me to go back inside to read. I was wanting to immerse myself in something different. To put my mind elsewhere but on the case for a few hours. I decided, totally by chance mind you, to read the short H.P. Lovecraft story 'Polaris.' It was certainly an incredible concept regarding the reality of dreams." Henry stretched and cracked his neck, then grimaced.

"And this led you to the stars being the key... how?"

He chuckled. "I'm getting there. Never been the stargazing type. But I've been looking up a little more lately. I did take note of it when we got here but wasn't sure of myself."

"And now I've had the same thought."

"Two is a pattern." Henry took a ragged, painful breath. The rattle of his breathing and a fluidic cough unnerved Bella. The years of Winston cigarettes and all-night booze benders had wreaked havoc on Henry Worrell's aged body.

"Henry, are you okay?" Bella leaned in to whisper. "This case will kill you, if you let it."

He bristled, but she insisted. "You've been running yourself ragged. Why not let someone else take over for a bit?"

"Bella..." But he couldn't protest any longer before coughing again.

"Two is a pattern," she echoed. "Come on, Henry."

Henry stood and groaned. "Alright, you win. We do the bag and tag, and I'll take some time off to heal up the crummy cough." Then Henry gave her a devilish smile, "But if anyone is taking over, it's you."

"Are you serious?" Bella looked at her supervisor, stuttering in disbelief. "Why not request Crawdad Crawford or Fae Wren to take over?"

Henry coughed and then pointed to the team bagging another body. "They're okay, at best, Bella. Maybe in a few more years they catch the Harbinger. Maybe by then, he'll be bored and ready to give up... with a pile of bodies under his belt."

"Why are you putting me on lead?" Bella couldn't figure out why he'd put her on such a high-profile gig, much less now lead. She'd only been out of the academy six months. If she took the case, veteran FBI agents, men and women who had put in years to be lead investigators, would be enraged. Her appointment might jeopardize the case. "You know this will piss everyone off, right?"

"I'm dead serious, Walker. We need to shake things up if we're going to catch him. No one else has come close to understanding the Harbinger Killer. You've been undaunting and relentless in trying to figure out what makes this maniac kill. Tonight, you showed me the why. The Bureau will come around."

Bella shook her head. "Yeah, they'll come around alright. The first chance our 'professional' colleagues get to stall the forensics, set me up with a gag or two, or send me out chasing my tail, will get everyone laughing. They always screw with the rookies, you know."

"I don't care about their feelings or yours for that matter. You put aside these petty emotions, or you'll never be the agent I know you can be." He ran his hands through his graying brown hair as they walked underneath the blazing tower lights of the forensic site. Both watched the technicians making last-minute labels and packing away the final bags of evidence. "Never let your pride or emotions get the better of you. If you get out of control, mistakes get made, and people will die."

"Wow, who gave you such wise words, sensei?" Bella laughed and patted Henry's back gently.

"Oh, a wise expert in the field. One of the true greats in criminal psychology—Dr. Natalie Roberts." He cleared his throat, and yet again, it turned into a rattling cough. "She also told me that cigarettes and booze would kill me. You know her or something?"

"I might have met her once." Bella shrugged her shoulders and didn't offer any more on the subject.

"Don't worry, kiddo. Everyone knows she's your aunt."

And the next morning, Henry Worrell trudged off to semiretirement. He took a well-deserved sabbatical and sought the finest treatment in his home state of Virginia. A month passed, and then two, and then three, and while the Harbinger's bodies piled up, Bella felt they were getting closer and closer with each new murder.

Finally, they had a break in the case. She was risking a lot on her theory, but she knew—just *knew*—they were right on his tail. Hours before they were set to catch him, Bella called Henry. His rasping voice unnerved her.

"We're getting close, Henry. I think the Harbinger knows it too."

"Bella… this is a dangerous time. The Harbinger is a cornered animal. Those are the worst kinds. Expect anything from any direction. He may use the team against themselves or set you up. Be prepared."

"We got a jump on the where and when. He'll try to mimic Thuban next; I just know it. It was the previous North Star in the constellation Draco the Dragon. He won't resist that kind of immortal sacrifice."

She waited for a minute for him to reply, but he said nothing. Didn't even cough. "Henry?"

A different voice came through the phone, and it held all the iciness of a reptile.

"At the time the Egyptians built the pyramids, Thuban was their lord and blood, the avatar they gave freely. This pile of rotting meat that was chasing me is dying. The universe calls us all home one day, Agent Walker."

Bella's blood ran cold. She could hear the rhythmic breathing of the voice, waiting like a panther to lash out.

"I can't use this man for the next ritual. But I will leave him something to remember me."

"Don't hurt him! He's been through enough... Harbinger." Bella calmed her nerves and tried to rationalize with the maniac. "Besides, you'll ruin the celestial energy for your reincarnation."

The sinister voice chuckled. "You surprise me with your knowledge of the stars, Agent Walker. You are the all-seeing, leering eye winking down from your monstrous FBI vault. You are the insane eye—not me!" he screeched maniacally.

Bella had to think but had no time. She had pulled over while coming back from another of the Harbinger's kills. On the side of the road across from a gas station, with mere minutes before the Harbinger might do his worst to the ailing Henry Worrell, she made a move. She did her best to roll down her window, unlatch her seatbelt, and climb out of her vehicle without making a sound. Opening the door would set off the alarm and tip off the Harbinger, who might still kill Henry.

She pushed herself out the window and fell onto the asphalt of the road. Spouting nonsense to distract the Harbinger, Bella ran toward a coffee shop for help. "You don't know if you are in a dream, right?" Bella said into the phone.

"I don't believe you understand the meaning of Polaris," the Harbinger hissed. "It was never about dream sequences or Lovecraft. It was never about some third-rate author of fantasy. I summon demons to serve me using The Keys of Solomon from the ancient Ars Goetia."

Bella darted into the coffee shop, grabbed a pen from her pocket, and wrote down Henry's address and a note to call the FBI and authorities. She added the Virginia FBI field office as well to the note. When the barista gave her a puzzled look, Bella flashed her badge and pointed to the note which read, *I have a killer on the phone about to kill an FBI agent. I'm distracting him. Please call now!*

The young server stumbled back and ran to a side office to call, nodding and giving a thumbs-up when he had done so. Bella nodded and mouthed her thanks.

It took an hour—the longest hour of Bella Walker's life—for the team to get to Henry Worrell. She hadn't been able to stall the Harbinger for the entire time. She'd babbled as much as she could, but eventually, he unceremoniously ended the call and disappeared.

Her phone rang again, and she pressed it to her ear in panic. "Is he alive? Did the Harbinger hurt him?" she practically shouted into the phone.

"He's fine, Agent Walker," came the voice of Tony Robillard, one of the supervisory agents out in Virginia.

"Oh, thank God." She breathed the world's biggest sigh of relief.

"The Harbinger must be getting soft. Do you want to talk with him?"

"If you don't mind."

Robillard handed over the phone, and Henry cleared his throat. "Hey, kid."

"Hey, yourself. You really had me worried there."

"Yeah, it's time to retire when a scumbag breaches my high-dollar security. The guys will never let me live… it down." They both laughed at Henry's terrible pun. And, as they laughed, Bella wiped a grateful tear. She'd cry more tears in her next tangle with the Harbinger.

The net narrowed to catch the beast. Bella raged in frustration, desperately trying to prove to the veteran team that her methods were working. No matter what she tried, it didn't work, and every inch of progress she thought she'd made turned out to be completely bunk. Her drive and anger were on full display for many of the agents to see and shake their heads.

The worst part came when the Harbinger sacrificed an innocent family on a crag in the White Mountains. The rumors of criticism that had been previously held in whispers were now said out loud. Nobody trusted Henry's choice to put the rookie in charge. Even her partner, Ray Mandola, was starting to doubt if she had what it took to get the job done.

She didn't blame him. She had the same doubts herself.

"We've been at this for close to six months, Bella. He made us look like fools with the attack on Henry. Actually, he made Henry seem sloppy and out of touch."

"Don't remind me," she muttered.

"Now everyone—including the best criminal minds in the business—swear this must be a cult leader. Personally, I believe the Harbinger is a Jim Jones-like messiah ordering his followers to kill without impunity. But Terry and Joe over there are certain he's imitating Charlie Manson and his family. At this point, whoever or whatever he is…" Ray paused, shrugging his shoulders with his palms out, while looking at Bella's obvious astonished wince and narrow stare. "Yeah, there's bets he might be a rougarou or werewolf or something, pulling the puppet strings for his minions of death."

Bella shook her head and palm slapped her forehead. "Yeah, we'll need a gris-gris and conjure man before this one's over. How did these clowns get through the Academy?"

"You want to hear the latest on the astronomy professor's findings?" Ray passed her a file from the University of Tennessee.

"Why, I sure would. What's the latest on the longitude and latitude points I asked you to follow up on?" Bella leaned in on her desk to take some notes on a yellow pad. She'd been waiting on the professor's star map review of over fifty stars brighter than Polaris.

Ray flipped open his notes and pushed back his raven-black hair before beginning, "Well, the averages he found were between 35 to 45 degrees for the longitude. They were between 80 to 120 degrees on the latitude. Adjusting for the time of year as you asked, the most likely mountain the professor figures would be the Cascade Mountain Range. He figures the Harbinger will choose a spot just below Mount Rainier. So, what's this maniac's recent obsession with all these mountains?"

"I'm assuming he wants to be closer to his god. That's my best guess. Or he's playing more games to divide and conquer the FBI." She scribbled a few more notes on the yellow pad and turned to a satellite map on her tablet. "We need a team to land here and set up a perimeter by what I'm seeing is a cave system."

Ray picked up the tablet and glanced over the map. He cut his eyes to her for just a second and shifted his mouth like he wanted to say something, but then turned away.

"What?" she asked.

"It's nothing."

"*What?*" she pressed. "Come on."

He sighed. "You're right, but I don't like the look of that area. We'd be in a bad way if he has friends in those caves or traps. That's thick, arboreal terrain to track through carrying arms. We might need local law enforcement to lend a hand and some local trackers."

Bella was actually surprised. He was trying to undercut her for once. She let out a silent whoop and nodded. "We are bringing the full force of the FBI into that location with some of the most trained officers on the planet. Locals for sure, and we'll call the park rangers too. Vet all the trackers you can for the area."

Ray grinned. "With all that in place, we surround this butcher and bring him in. What could go wrong?"

The smooth flight to get to the Cascade Mountain Range took about two hours. The late summer weather was tranquil, and the plane landed without a bounce. As Bella watched their descent, she caught the full view of Mount Rainier looming in the shadowed distance. Shards of blazing white sunlight spread across its peaks. As the plane parked and the various agents filed out, Bella took one more glance at the swaying pines at the base of the mountain and the shadows haunting Mount Rainier's ghostly forest and shivered.

There was a monster in those woods. And now they were about to catch it.

She pulled her go-bag out of the compartment and headed down toward the vehicles waiting for them, whispering a mantra.

"We've planned for everything. We've planned for everything," she told herself. She knew the map couldn't cover all the details and they might hit a hurdle or two on the trek. But that's the breaks sometimes.

Later, when all hell had broken loose, Bella would come to regret her overconfident words.

———•———

Bella paused her thoughts of the past. Her mind back in the Alohilani Resort, she climbed out of the soft warmth of her bed. She went to the minifridge and opened it for a cold bottle of water, though, now that she was thinking about the Harbinger case, she almost opted for the small bottle of Jack Daniels instead. Remembering she'd have a full, hot day investigating in the jungles of Hawaii, Bella thought better of it.

Bella's voice wavered, and tears fell as she spoke to the darkness of her room, "Some paid a heavy price to catch him."

She sipped her water and continued to recall that fateful night in the Cascades four years ago.

———•———

It was an unusually cool night as they moved in for the capture of the Harbinger. Chilling night winds caused the towering pines and birch to creak and sway. Onward, as the gusts blew through the canopy of the forest, Bella's team stalked and surrounded the location where the Harbinger was set to stage his next murders. They moved as silently as wraiths and as cautiously as mountain lions through the dense undergrowth.

Two local trackers had advised the team that they saw distant campfire light at the mouth of a cave on a winding peak. In the upper climes, they signaled to Bella they were going in to inspect. As the rest of the team proceeded cautiously up and around the rocks of the cave, it became evident that there was indeed a roaring, orange campfire illuminating stony walls. Ray hand signaled a second time—for radio chatter might tip off the Harbinger—that they were going to move to their right and then circle. The former Marine reconnaissance sergeant turned FBI agent signaled his group to maneuver and surround the Harbinger. Bella watched with bated breath and hope beyond hope that this would be a quick capture.

Those hopes were dashed instantly. Blinding white and orange explosions lit up the night sky to her right where Ray and his team had gone, sending billowing plumes of smoke into the air. Before she could even react, there were secondary explosions to Bella's left where another team, run by veteran agent Hank White, had entered.

"Damn it," she roared into the radio. "Regroup! Get out of here!"

The voices of injured agents screamed in pain and terror in the aftermath of each explosion. She resisted the immediate urge to rush in to help as they, too, would be ambushed. Going in blindly would just get more people hurt. Better to get bomb specialists here as soon as possible. With sweat pouring from her brow and her heart thundering, she screamed on her radio and phone to their base of operations.

"Agents down! I repeat, agents down! Mobilize medical and extraction teams! There's been an ambush! We need you here now!"

Remembering her training, and realizing the Harbinger had set traps, she cautioned all and pointed to the ground.

"Nobody steps anywhere without triple-checking for traps. Incendiary or worse. Watch your step, the trees, and where you place your hands. He's got the whole place booby-trapped."

Bella and everyone stepped cautiously and swiftly looking for trip wires. They edged foot by foot in tense silence, looking below, around, and above for anything to set off a grenade, pipe bomb, or whatever the Harbinger had staged.

"Got one here," one of her team reported.

"Eyes on it," Bella ordered. "Mark the location for the bomb squad when they get here, then go around it."

Thankfully, most of the set traps could be disarmed, and the team could move forward to the Harbinger's lair. Sure, proceeding toward the mad killer in this manner was beyond risky. And most agents would have stood down to wait for bomb specialists. But an obsessed and enraged Bella Walker was not about to let the Harbinger slip away and kill more innocent people. She could not—she would not—let the maniac get away. Better to be suspended or fired for stopping him.

She gripped her gun tightly and ventured forth into the darkness, vowing that no matter what happened to her, this monster would be put away.

Back in the moment listening to the roar of the Hawaiian surf, Bella spoke to the rolling waves. "I was such a fool."

She idly rubbed a hand under her shirt over the jagged scar on her right side. It didn't hurt anymore, not physically. But it was always on her mind.

The next part of her reverie was more of a blur, proceeding in rapid flashbacks that bombarded her senses—frantic moments and images she couldn't unsee. She recalled regrouping with her team and delving into the cave. She recalled more blasts going off, gunfire echoing in the night, and the eerie starlight in the trees. She wasn't quite sure what she recalled; the whole situation was so chaotic that it blended together in the madness of the night.

She recalled the gurgling of what sounded like jelly through a straw and knew the truth was more horrific than she could bear.

"B—Bella," choked the voice.

Fire blazed all around, and the radio chatter reached a cacophonous din; but Bella was focused instead on the horrific sight of Ray lying there, covered in blood, with half his chest gone.

She darted to his side and removed her windbreaker to try to staunch the blood. "Stay with me, Ray," she begged.

"Little late for that, kid," he replied with a caustic laugh. His eyes were already glassing over.

"No. *No!* I'll get you out of here. The EMTs are already on their way up. They'll—"

With what little strength he had left, he shook his head. "Get this bastard for me, Bella."

"Ray…" she whispered.

He managed to look down at his mangled torso and let out a final wheeze. "What could go wrong…"

And then he became fixed and lifeless with one final breath.

Bella would find out later that Ray's careless step had kicked off a trip wire, springing a bouncing betty bomb. Shrapnel and bearings had blasted out, shredding the entire team. Ray caught the brunt of the blast, sparing most of the rest of the team, but their injuries were so severe that they couldn't possibly complete the mission now.

A shadow darted at her with a large knife and stabbed her in the side. Bella screamed in fury and pain and was only barely able to push the darkness away before it was able to make another stab at her.

She fired blindly, hoping it would hit her assailant but knowing it wouldn't. She fought to get to her feet and ignore the torrent of blood flowing down her side.

"I hadn't expected you so soon, Bella Walker," came the reptilian voice from the shadows, clearly pleased with his work. It was like the darkness itself split wide into a grin, the flames its mouth and the stars its eyes.

But it was not a monster; it was merely a man. He stood perfectly still, silhouetted by the flames, as if he were the devil himself, welcoming the damned into hell. A cloud shifted, and moonlight poured into the clearing; and finally, after so long, Bella Walker came face to face with the Harbinger.

The towering shadow held the youthful face of a schoolteacher or a Wall Street trader. Hell, he might have been a Sunday school teacher. "Seems you'll have a funeral or three this week when we're done."

The shadows took over his face, and once again he was the monster that had plagued Bella's nightmares for so long—and would continue to do so for the rest of her life.

With every second that passed, she lost a little more blood and a lot more sanity. But she had to stay alert. She couldn't be his final victim. Not now. Not after the price she and others had paid.

She recalled the team regrouping, closing in on her location. She recalled scrambling back away from the crazed man, his eyes even sharper than the knife he brandished. She recalled kicking dirt and rocks up into his face to slow his approach. She recalled twisting to one side, then another, desperately trying to claw to her feet and gain some space.

She didn't recall emptying her clip into the Harbinger's legs, making him collapse to the ground. She didn't recall that she'd somehow straddled him and unleashed a flurry of blows so severe they broke every bone in the man's face. She didn't recall that she'd nearly fought off the bystander who'd found her and staunched her bleeding side.

But she was debriefed on all that later in the hospital.

It was only then that she truly understood what her Aunt Natalie had once warned. The price had been too high. Could she have planned better? Of course, and the investigation into the debacle would report such findings. Should she have brought in the bomb specialists before the assault on the Harbinger's hideout? It was over, but now fingers were pointing everywhere to assign blame for the chaos.

Would she lose her job or be benched to desk duty for the remainder of her career? No, of course not. She was the newest poster child of the FBI. She made the media rounds just like her aunt and was immediately heralded as a rising young star in the Bureau. She was a hero.

Her mistakes and losses were forgotten only because the Harbinger lay in a cold cell under the tightest security that the federal government could offer.

But she never felt like a hero, and she never forgot.

The sea winds were picking up. Bella decided to go back inside. The glowing, green numbers on the clock told her that it was past time for bed, but she already knew she couldn't sleep with all her racing thoughts. Maybe a run and swim were in order. She got dressed again and trudged down to the fitness center. Setting the treadmill on four to warm up, she quickly advanced the speed to eight and the incline to a modest four. She set the time for one hour, a duration guaranteed to clear her head.

The hour passed too quickly, and Bella ended her workout and headed back to her room. There would be plenty of time tomorrow to get a real run on the beach or in the pristine mountains to help her rest. And, possibly... for a little while... forget.

After a second hot shower, Bella clicked off the lamp and buried herself into the covers, whispering, "I'm sorry, Ray."

CHAPTER FOUR

S HE WOKE AT DAWN, GLAD THAT SHE SLEPT RELATIVELY WELL. SHE got dressed in her standard work attire: a simple button-down shirt, black slacks, her standard-issue boots, and her holster. Already starving after last night's run, she decided to make a morning coffee in the room before the hotel restaurant opened. With her hot coffee nearly burning her hand, she headed down to sit in the lobby and wait for the place to open. She figured it would be a good time to catch a better view of the lavish oceanarium and all those red, purple, and orange fluorescent fish.

Bella hadn't slid into the cold seat for more than fifteen minutes— and two refills of coffee from the lobby machine—when Rachel walked up and interrupted her thoughts.

"Wow, you recover from a thirteen-hour flight something fierce." Rachel shook her head and smiled. She slid into a seat across from Bella and pushed back her brown hair with her right hand. "What's your secret for preventing jet lag?"

"Running for an hour before bed and lots of coffee. Seems to keep me jazzed." Bella showed her a full coffee cup. "So, I see you got here early before Billy. That's curious."

"I didn't think you were up yet. I planned to have breakfast ready for you and catch up." Rachel looked out a clear window, and Bella followed her stare. The two watched the molten orb of golden sun just breaking the horizon. "I wanted to ask you something you're not going to like."

Bella huffed. "Shocker."

Rachel pressed her lips into a fine line and looked at her sympathetically. "I was just concerned about you."

"Aw, that's sweet," Bella cracked. "And here I was thinking you only called me over for help on the case."

"It's just… you kind of disappeared from the face of earth. What gives?"

"It's simple. I've been busy."

"But since the Harbinger—"

"My team and I caught a very bad man. That's all there is to it." Bella gave Rachel a knowing nod. It was sharp enough in tone to convey that Bella didn't want to discuss anything further.

"Bella, don't pretend that we haven't been friends for years or that we weren't like sisters at the Academy and beyond. If something was bugging you, you always called. Even if I didn't always agree with your decisions."

Rachel was being animated with her hands, and Bella caught the usual dramatic antics that had always annoyed Bella in their conversations. Bella was truly glad for their friendship, but she always thought Rachel made more of things than they were. She was the type to make a mountain out of a molehill—if they had moles in Hawaii.

"I agree." It was the best method to diffuse Rachel. Agree that she's right and move her back to the case. This was the reason she was here, after all. "You deserved to hear from me more often. We were friends. Scratch that, I mean, we still are friends. I should have reached out when Ray—"

Rachel sighed. "How many times do I have to tell you, Bella? I know you'd argue with me until kingdom come. But I'll say it to your face." Rachel leaned in to stare into Bella's eyes. Rachel's brown eyes were red and certainly bloodshot, most likely from the pressure of her current case.

Bella already knew, but had no choice but to play along. "And what's that?"

"The Harbinger was the person responsible. *He* killed Ray Mandola. It was not you." Rachel leaned back and continued to watch Bella.

"I agree, Rachel. If he hadn't killed so many people, the FBI wouldn't have been up in the Cascade Mountains getting ambushed. I made my peace with Ray and the others who got hurt. But you don't know what it was like to have to see it happen." She said it matter-of-factly—not judging, not condescending, but merely stating the truth.

The restaurant had finally pulled the velvet rope away from the entrance, and Bella stood up. "This is a dangerous job going out to solve murders and catch bad people. Every time, and every day, we put our lives on the line to save as many people as we can. There's no room for regret. Now come on. Let's get breakfast."

"Now, this sounds like the Bella Walker who kicked my butt in self-defense class." Rachel smiled and badly faked a martial arts move with her hands. Bella laughed uncontrollably.

"If I remember correctly, I smoked you in the obstacle course and run times too."

They walked up and each grabbed a plate for the breakfast buffet. Bella's stomach growled at the opulent spread of buttery biscuits, sausage, bacon, peppered eggs, and fresh pastries.

Rachel's brow furrowed as she loaded up her plate with fruit and a bagel. "Ha ha. I'd have whooped you if I hadn't twisted my right ankle two days before the testing. Do you want a rematch, madame?"

Bella finished plating her breakfast and grinned as they made their way to a table with a beautiful view of the beach and rising orange sun. "I'll pass. These days a tortoise could probably take me in a run. Anyway, you managed to come back home to save the island of Hawaii from all the gangs and crooked politicians. How's that been working out for you?"

"As you can guess, since I put in three requests to get you here, not so good." She took a bite of her eggs and chewed diligently before continuing. "I mean, seeing Mom and Dad has been great. I'm especially grateful to have gotten the time with them. They're aging and declining from years of running the coffee plantation. But never tell them that. Dad's as stubborn as ever."

Bella nodded. "I remember how his eyes lit up as he discussed the 'little coffee farm' with my folks. Some people just do what they love to do and make it a success no matter what." Bella took a sip of orange juice and then her coffee.

Rachel put out her hand and showed Bella the latest ring from her husband. "And you do recall, I got hitched. I sent your invite and begged you to be a bridesmaid, but you were stuck up on another mountain solving a case." Rachel comically overextended her bottom lip in a frown.

Bella put her head down, red-faced with embarrassment. "I sincerely apologize for that, Rachel. I did everything I could to try and be here for your wedding. But the Blue-Eyed Banshee had taken another kid, and we had to act fast."

"What's with the names these guys give themselves?" Rachel asked through a mouthful of pineapple. "The Blue-Eyed Banshee?"

Bella shrugged. "He had blue eyes, I guess."

After breakfast, Bella went back up to her room, brought down her belongings, and dropped her key off at the front desk. The maître d', a tall, rail-thin young man who looked paler—and gaunter—than a skeleton, asked the usual questions. "How was your night, Miss Walker?"

"It was excellent, young man. Thank you." Bella shook the young man's hand, feeling distinctly like he was some sort of Halloween ghoul.

"We truly hope you had a pleasant stay. Please visit us again soon." The eccentric man printed her hotel receipt, which Bella immediately gave to Rachel for reimbursement with the Bureau.

The ladies made haste to leave with Bella whispering to Rachel as they exited the hotel, "That one put off a strange vibe with me, Rachel."

"Oh, Carl? He's harmless. He's quite a curiosity, though, on the island. He can talk for hours about various species of snails and insects. If you need a question answered about bugs, he's your guy." Rachel opened the hatch to load Bella's suitcase into the trunk of her Lincoln Town Car.

They got into the car, but before Rachel turned on the ignition, she held her breath for a second too long, like she was preparing herself to ask something.

"Out with it," Bella demanded. "You should know by now I know your facial expressions."

"Alright, alright," Rachel griped. "One thing is troubling me about the Harbinger case. How did you manage to outmatch that maniac? You were in the dark; you couldn't have known he was right behind you. You were alone, surrounded, your team got caught. How did you get him?"

Bella rubbed her temples. "I will tell you, Rachel. But don't ask me any more about it, okay? I'm here to stay focused on your case."

That was a way out-of-line question, even for her, Bella thought. *Somehow, I feel she gets off on my pain from the ordeal. I really should tell her to mind her own business. The Harbinger has been locked up for years.*

"A mind like the Harbinger had a flaw." Bella wanted her words to register clearly about the case and its off-limits nature. Also, she wanted Rachel to understand that her question had been a little too intrusive.

Rachel turned the ignition and made her way out of the parking lot. "The Harbinger had a flaw. What was it? How could that psychopath have made a mistake?"

"His arrogant and insane need to watch his victims die. He had to watch me pull my shirt to stop Ray's bleeding. Like a vampire, he had to draw all his energy from the innocent blood that poured out of Ray's body." Bella paused and gritted her teeth holding back her fury. "So, after all the extensive research, the countless hours going over reports from agents who had lost their lives tracking him, I figured him out. I gave him what he wanted."

They had stopped at a red light. Rachel stuttered to ask the next question, "And what exactly did you give the Harbinger to catch him?"

"I let him stab me, Rachel. I let him think he was an all-powerful god, killing his sworn enemy by a starlit ritual. I let him have his pound of flesh."

"You..." Rachel trailed off and looked down at the spot where the scar was. "You never told me that part."

"I never told anyone that part. But I knew I had to be there alone. I knew it was a risk—that it was my life or his. But he wouldn't have come out if I hadn't put my life out there. I had to make that sacrifice, even if it meant I could die."

Stunned, Rachel murmured under her breath. "Remind me to keep my mouth shut next time about one of your cases." She turned her head and raised a brow inquisitively at Bella. She drove a little farther as the sun shimmered on the road's asphalt. "You do know that letting a maniacal serial killer stab you is the kind of behavior that's a few fries short of a Happy Meal?"

"This is Hawaii, Agent Gentry. You mean a few fries short of a spam burger." Bella rolled her eyes and grinned to ease her friend's troubled mind. Even if it couldn't ease her own.

CHAPTER FIVE

Nimitz Beach
Oahu, Hawaii
July 17, 2023

"I THOUGHT WE WERE HEADED TO THE OFFICE?" BELLA FURROWED her brow and pointed at the black shimmering glass FBI building that Rachel had just passed.

"The teams are still getting the last of the evidence organized and tagged. As you were getting your beauty sleep—needed, I might add—we worked through the night going over everything, including the finger gods."

Bella snorted. "Really? You labeled the dismembered finger 'finger god'?" Bella shook her head as Rachel made a turn off Enterprise Street onto Kapolei Parkway then headed west. "Of course, you did."

"There were several fingers. Each one of those ugly statues held one," Rachel explained as she turned up a long driveway that twisted slightly up a hill. Bella noted a cascading waterfall near a beautiful turquoise pool adjacent to a large bungalow.

"Now, that's curious. Each person killed had a finger and head offered to a Hawaiian deity."

Bella looked around the lavish wood-framed home with its spacious porch. There were several Hawaiian masks and a surfboard adorning the front of the home. Large iron torches lined both sides of the home and extended in unison with a towering, concrete-poured fence. "This place is lavish, I must say. And the security is practically impregnable, Rachel. Who's the witness we're interviewing? Gotta be some rich—"

Rachel laughed. "No, dummy. This bungalow is your home away from Colorado while you're here."

Bella's mouth dropped open. She closed it, and then opened it again, not knowing what to say.

"Oh, your face reminds me, there's a fishing dock out back."

"Rachel, I'd have been fine down at the FBI temporary quarters. This is way too much. An agent could easily get dis—"

"Nonsense, Bella. In all the years we have known each other, that's one thing you will never let happen. You are too dialed in on a case to ever get distracted." Rachel took off her seatbelt, and they both opened their doors to get out. "You have a great view of the beach, a waterfall by your pool, and all the room you will ever need to bring every file we have on the case here."

"And, what if I skip the dogged pursuit of justice and rigorous reading of a thousand case files for a *party*?" Bella snickered and emphasized the last word in a singsong voice.

"Are we discussing the woman who spent her days and nights at the Academy memorizing all the files front to back, to not just graduate, but write thousand-word dissertations on every serial killer ever caught by the Bureau? I highly doubt you'll throw a luau or even a lobster bake." Rachel rolled her eyes and grimaced while escorting Bella up to the creaking porch.

Bella giggled and stopped pulling her suitcase. She put her hands out in an appealing gesture. "You got me there. I'm one hundred percent guilty of being a boring workaholic. I have no social skills whatsoever."

"Finally, something we can agree on." Rachel unlocked the door and tossed Bella the key as they entered.

Bella whistled at the marvelous sight. The floors were antique teak wood, and the ceiling was made of an intricate, ornate plaster that held casted scenes of turtles and tropical birds. The bay windows and walls were immaculately clean. As the two agents walked farther into the house, Bella saw a lava rock fireplace in the center of the living room prepped with wood if needed. Not that it would ever be lit in the balmy ninety-degree heat of Hawaii.

"A fireplace in a jungle, Rachel? Now I've seen it all." Bella stooped down to further inspect the oddity.

"It's for those grand parties you plan on throwing between all those fun forensic files. Besides, maybe you get lucky on one of your surfing adventures and meet Mr. Wrong." Rachel pointed to a winding, white sand trail leading from the back of the pool down a sand dune to a massive beach with the bluest water Bella had ever seen. "Anyway, the beach is down that path if you get bored and want to take a swim."

"With all the turtles and … tiger sharks? No thanks." Bella had been shaken since her family adventure with Mom and Dad scuba diving by the Gulf of Mexico oil rigs. A bull shark had decided that day to go after her. If her father hadn't acted quickly with a spear gun, Bella would have been the shark's dinner. But since the incident, she'd had a sort of aversion to water—for the best of reasons.

"You still have it, huh?" Rachel was asking another one of those personal, intrusive questions that drove Bella up a wall. She was staring at Bella's right, shirt sleeve-covered shoulder. "The scar. It's clear as day you still hate the water."

"Yes." Bella got the question out of the way. Again, that eerie feeling that Rachel was feeding off her past pain was there. It was just another odd question that grated on Bella's mind like nails scratching on a chalkboard. She pulled her sleeve to show the bite scar. It didn't sting in her mind nearly as hard as the one down her right side, but it was much more visible. "Dad did a good job bandaging my arm that day. And I don't hate water. In pools, I swim like a fish. I'm just a little… extra cautious of the ocean."

"Anyone in your situation would be." Rachel beamed a brilliant smile and continued her tour of the bungalow. "So, to our left is the rainforest shower, sauna, and jacuzzi all in the same area. The second and third bathrooms are to the rear and right of the place. Washer and dryer as you saw were adjacent to the kitchen." Rachel paused scanning the whole house one more time. "Did I miss anything?"

"Is the fridge stocked like the hotel?" Bella grinned and pointed to the driveway. Rachel had forgotten a critical item that Bella needed— her rental car they left up on the North Shore. "I saw the store was seven miles—"

Red-faced with embarrassment, Rachel palm slapped her forehead. "How the heck did I forget to get your car to you? Well, it looks like a road trip to the North Shore again. I'll call Billy to let him know."

Bella looked out toward the jagged, emerald mountains of the North Shore then back to Rachel. "We can get the car later. I want to see the evidence and begin reading all the case files. I'd like to start with any of the witnesses we have turned up."

Rachel looked at Bella and then back toward the North Shore. "You don't want to leave a rental up near Waianae Mountain Range. The gangs up there are notorious for stealing or burning vehicles. Think of the Wild West. Only it's a wild Hawaiian west. Leave your horse around desperadoes up there, and they will steal it, sell every part of it, and burn the rest. Even if you are law enforcement."

"You and Billy might have mentioned that when we left it near a ravine." Bella gritted her teeth. "Good thing I took the keys."

Rachel led the way to her vehicle for the haul up to get Bella's rental car. "They don't need k—"

"I know that. I was being sarcastic," Bella interrupted, shaking her head in disgust. "This is going to take all day, isn't it?"

"Probably. But just think of the gorgeous tropical views on our drive." Rachel laughed as Bella groaned. The inefficient way Rachel was approaching this case was extremely aggravating.

———•———

Western North Shore
Waianae Mountain Range
Eastern Valley Near Mount Ka'ala

The shadows between the forested valleys on Rachel and Bella's journey seemed to have their own life. Bella leaned against the window watching the mysteries of the North Shore mountains and canopies pass by. As the winds of the jungle gusted and swayed the oceans of green, ochre, and magenta, Bella watched their undulations, shaking her head in wonder.

"Beautiful sight, isn't it?" Rachel asked.

Bella nodded. She situated herself upright in the seat and tried to focus her mind on everything she'd seen at the crime scene yesterday.

Making mental notes she went over each minute she had been at the crime scene.

They were staged in a circle. Heads lopped off with an extremely sharp blade. What I saw of the cervical spine and flesh was too smooth a cut for a machete— too clean a cut, for sure. The decapitations remind me of that Celtic case I heard about in Scotland. It was a broad ax that did the victims in. This has that ritualistic feel to it. And that might be the point. The person or people delivering the killing blow were incredibly strong, and efficient too. Not a splinter of bone. This is a strange one for—

"What are you thinking about?" Rachel interrupted Bella's train of thought. They were making good time to her car with hardly any traffic or rain.

"I was thinking this kill site was staged." Bella narrowed her eyes and watched Rachel's response. It was a habit of hers to always study everyone—including the lead agent on the case.

Bella hated to admit it, but after twenty-four hours of observing Rachel and her team, she was sorely disappointed. Her friend was getting too relaxed and sloppy. It was a bad combination when dealing with dangerous killers. They should have sent a rookie to get Bella's car so they could be at the station researching and reviewing evidence.

You don't send the senior agents up to the North Shore to get their vehicles. I'm going to press her on why this is occurring. This isn't the by-the-book Rachel Stein I remember from the Academy.

Looking out the window at a large sugar cane plantation, Bella conveyed the obvious: "Rachel, what's going on? We should've sent rookies for my vehicle. Senior agents stay back and look over gathered evidence, statements, and reports. That's standard protocol for a lead investigator and the forensics expert. We don't do car recovery, normally."

"We have a mole, Bella." Bella's eyes went wide with surprise. She hadn't expected Rachel to say the obvious. "Someone got the inside track on one of our confidential informants. He's one of the victims you saw yesterday. Right after, Billy found bugs in our offices too."

"Now it makes sense. I couldn't figure out the hotel or the whole extravagant bungalow tour. Usually, you would have dropped me off and come back to pick me up or something." Bella sighed with relief as their vehicle slowed at a red dirt road.

"I thought you'd figure it out when I put you up at the most expensive hotel on Oahu. I guess jet lag did get the better of you." Rachel pointed to Bella's car, "Sorry you had to rent a car. We had to debug a few of our office vehicles too. This was some high-tech and high-dollar surveillance on us."

Bella unlocked her seatbelt as the vehicle came to a stop. "Well, that's a clue in and of itself, Rachel. Bugging an FBI building isn't the typical petty criminal's modus operandi. This—"

"MO. I went to the same school and class as you, *Agent Walker.*" Rachel grinned as she interrupted.

Bella closed her eyes. "I know; I get carried away with the lingo. So, we can limit our search field." It was at that moment that Bella paused and turned back to Rachel. She had realized another ploy and grimaced. "And the car on the roadside? I could have taken my car yesterday to go back, huh?"

Rachel nodded pulling off the red dirt road to where Bella's vehicle was parked. Rachel continued to explain: "I didn't want to chance it until we got you secured and eyes watching you. If the inside guy or gal—I'm not sure of the who just yet—leaked your location, then we'd have bigger fish to fry. That's part of why I brought you in in the first place. Yesterday marks the third informant in the last two months that this murderer or cult killed."

Bella gently slugged her friend. "Well, on a positive note, when they're trying to kill off your confidential informants and you, then you might be getting close. In my opinion, after yesterday, the murderer is sending a message to scare you and your team off their trail."

Rachel stopped the vehicle, and they got out of the Lincoln. The dense, tropical jungle just past the road glimmered from yesterday's downpour. Bella stood, leaning on the car, and said, "Collecting any evidence in that heap must be a huge pain at times."

"You have no idea, Bella. The humidity and the jungle have squashed many of our cases. I can't tell you how many judges have tossed our cases despite the best evidence recovery we could manage." Rachel pointed to a nest of six-inch-thick vines clustering an enormous tree with hanging roots from its spiderlike branches. "It's like the island itself is a walking obstruction case."

Bella walked over to her vehicle, feeling the humidity permeating off the seat and trying to soak through her pants. The cool clamminess of the cloth on her skin made Bella squirm. Already, her other nemesis—the jungle—was sending out a warning that this case would have many unforeseeable challenges. Bella would have to keep her guard up. Many dangers lay ahead.

As they went to leave and head back to Honolulu, Rachel rolled down her window as Bella started her car and turned on the air conditioning. "Billy just called. The bug squad and techs have checked everything from top to bottom. They just finished up with the cars. We'll drop that clunker of yours back at the airport and get you a real FBI vehicle back at the shop. In other words, our fortress of security has had all six bugs removed, and we are once again a bastion of secrecy."

"Really? A bastion of secrecy?" Bella rolled her window up and shook her head. "And you teased me about 'modus operandi.'"

———·———

Hawaiian FBI Building
Enterprise Street
Oahu, Hawaii

Two hours later the agents made it back to Enterprise Street and the Hawaiian field office of the FBI. Bella had seen the glimmering glass building earlier when they had passed, but up close the crystalline bullet- and bomb-proof windows were impressive. The architecture and the structure had all the vibe of high technology with the solid steel frame, slanted corrugated steel roof, and precise office spacing. On her way to the team boardroom, she noticed that many of the agents were as slick and polished as the glass protecting them. Rugged chins and determined faces of professionals who had spent countless hours, just as Bella had, tracking down the most dangerous people on the planet. The team that Bella met was just as professional and competent as her team back in Colorado. She would be able to get a lot of work done with such an efficient ensemble.

"Agent Walker, you do remember Agent Makani?" Rachel gestured to the semiathletic, bronze-skinned Hawaiian man.

Bella smiled and shook Billy's hand. "Why, Agent Gentry, of course. Was it the side of the mountain in the mud, Agent Makani? Or the side of the mountain in the rain and... the mud?"

"I would say it was the mud, the rain, and the finger god, Agent Walker," Billy replied with a mischievous smile. He was the one who had to transport the finger from the side of the hill back to the lab.

"You folks and your colorful names, Billy. Where are the rest of them?" Bella was ready to start reviewing and going over the other finger gods and bodies with the coroner.

"Well, after this formal introduction, I'll take you to see them."

A brown-haired man with chestnut eyes and a stocky build extended his hand to introduce himself. "Aloha. I'm Special Agent Thomas Joseph O'Reilly, but you can call me TJ."

Bella shook TJ's hand and introduced herself with a polite smile. His iron grip felt as coarse as sandpaper. "Special Agent Bella Walker. Forens—"

"Oh, finally! The forensic expert has finally arrived after what… months? What took you so long?" Bella bristled at TJ's interruption, but by the spark in his eyes and overemphatic gestures, she realized he was joking. "Did you know Rachel filled out and sent three requests to you?"

"Well, they say the wheels of justice sometimes turn slow." Bella nodded over to Rachel to get the formal presentation moving forward.

"That they do, Agent Walker," chimed in TJ as he took his own seat. "That they do."

Rachel spent an hour going over the recent crime scene, the position of the victims, and some of the evidence. It was at the top of the second hour that she nodded to Bella to walk up and meet the team formally. Bella always hated these pompous, formal meetings. She thought of them as a waste of time. But with the possibility of a compromised agent, she *really* hated this moment.

"Agents, I'm honored you requested my help. As many of you know—or maybe not—the paperwork sometimes takes a little time between offices here and on the mainland. But rest assured, I'm here now." Bella scanned the audience and noted each agent in the room. She looked down at the podium for a moment, pretending to gather her thoughts. But in reality, she was making a mental note to herself of each of them. One of the people in this room had leaked the informant's information and gotten them killed. She had to test them early and see if she could flush them out.

"I must add that while we have had a few setbacks with the tragic death of the informants and your beautiful weather washing away a lot of clues, I feel certain with this great team that justice will be served, and we will catch this monster soon." Bella methodically scanned each team member on her final statement. "We're just lucky that we have more CIs that I can talk with to help us."

Bella noted Billy Makani kind of flinched on the latter. From a side glance, she saw Rachel's mouth tremble—but that could be because Bella had just given false information. More curiously, an unidentified agent in the back of the room dropped his head for an instant, shaking it in disgust. TJ O'Reilly turned methodically and studied the agent, then turned back and grinned at Bella. He cocked his head and narrowed one of his eyes to study her, then looked back at another unidentified agent who was stifling a laugh.

Bella turned and whispered to a perplexed Rachel as the crowd of agents began clapping at the good news. "I'll explain it all to you later."

"It was a nice try, but I tried this before to flush them out," Rachel leaned in and whispered back.

"Then why are they cheering and clapping if they know I'm pulling their legs?" Confused, Bella looked back at the agents who were disbanding and leaving the room to go back to work.

Rachel put her hands up apologetically and shrugged. "You gave them an opportunity to pull a gag on you? Or maybe to break up this clown show and go to lunch?"

Bella face palmed her head and groaned. *So much for first impressions,* she thought.

CHAPTER SIX

FOUR GRUELING HOURS LATER, WITH THE BRIMSTONE SMELL OF decay permeating her clothes and the acrid chemical smell of form-aldehyde giving her the fiercest of headaches, Bella examined each of the victims in the morgue alongside the corner.

With gloved hands, Bella leaned in and pointed. "Doctor Diehl, what could cut so smoothly without powdering the vertebrae or leaving barely a fragment? Could that be a machete?"

Dr. Ted Diehl inspected it carefully and turned back to her. "The bladework is quite impressive. No, it wasn't a machete—too awkward and clumsy a stroke for lopping off a human head. Also, I ruled out an ax, with the minor fracturing of the bone and hardly any fragments." He rubbed his face with his shirt sleeve and paused a minute to look over one of the decapitated corpses. "It's as if someone used the sharpest blade on the planet ... or a laser."

"Based on your experience, what's your guess?" Bella walked over to look at two more of the decapitated corpses. "I know you have more analysis to do. I'm just trying to form an idea of possible weapons. I believe it may give us another clue as to who killed them."

"If this were Ireland or Scotland, I'd say a claymore—a Scottish claymore or broadsword. One swipe with that beast of a sword and the head drops like pulling the wings off a dragonfly." Diehl pursed his lips and narrowed his stare, concentrating. "But this is Hawaii. The sharpest ax we have still would cut jaggedly and leave fragments throughout the slice."

"Do you know of any Scottish clans that may be roaming the hills of the North Shore dealing in Hawaiian war god trade?" Bella asked.

"Can't say any come to mind," he chuckled. "Is there anything else I can help you with?"

"What about cutting off each pinky finger of the left hand?" Bella asked. "Do you know of any Hawaiian rituals or outfits that do that?"

"That's where I was researching when you and the team dropped in. I haven't heard or read of any local murderers or cults doing that. I'll investigate other possible groups," he sighed and covered one of the decapitated heads, "but they would have to have incredible strength to wield the weaponry that did that."

Two more long hours of reviewing pictures of the locations and more case files had Bella rubbing her eyes and temples again. A second pass over the files had indeed opened up more possible follow-ups. The complexity of even the victim selections was growing in her psyche, and she was beginning to correlate how they were chosen. Bella was starting to see a pattern, though the motives still eluded her. She ran it through her head over and over until Rachel knocked on her desk. Bella blinked and looked up. She hadn't even heard her come in.

"Hey, why don't you take a breather? You look awful."

"Gee, thanks," Bella muttered. "I'm going to take these eight boxes and go over them tonight. You cool with that?"

"I knew you'd pull an all-nighter the minute we got you to these files. You can take all ten or more if you like. Just sign them out, and I'll get Billy and TJ to help put them into your car." Rachel waved for the three agents to assist her, but Bella grabbed her hand and shoved it down. "What are you—"

"I'll handle them myself," Bella whispered pointedly. "Especially since we don't know who the leak is."

Rachel grumbled. "This mole situation really is a pain, Bella. I can't trust anybody? Is what you're saying? Not even Billy?"

"*You* may trust him, but *I* don't know him," Bella countered. "Sorry."

Rachel sighed and nodded in surrender. "Well, at least let me help."

Bella allowed it and grabbed a couple of file boxes herself. "I know it's a bad situation. I've been there when a fellow agent turned rogue or worse for money. Who knows what the motives are with this situation? All we do know is that someone got some people helping us killed, bugged our vehicles and offices, and is most likely still in the building right now. And it goes without saying, they know we are on to them."

"When you put it that way, it makes perfect sense. But these are people I've known for years. Which makes it all the more difficult. But I've seen the surveillance equipment they installed. I've seen the CIs murdered." She walked with Bella out to processing and then to the car in the parking lot. "Someone who I've eaten lunch with, played softball with, and most likely invited into my home, has gone bad."

After processing and checking out ten boxes of evidence and loading them into her vehicle, Bella drove to her bungalow, completely worn out. Yawning and cracking her stiff neck, Bella made the fifteen-minute drive almost in a fog of thoughts. As she pulled up through the automatic gate, Bella sighed with relief to be away from the FBI office. Too many shenanigans were afoot in the ranks back at the office.

One by one, she begrudgingly carried each bulky box. It would be a pain lugging them back and forth by herself, but it was the only way she could do any work on the case without wondering whether she was directly placing herself in the sights of a traitor.

The sun was setting in a spectacular shade of crimson on the beach just south of Bella's bungalow. But the driven agent didn't stop to notice it too much. Nor did she pause long enough to take in the beauty of darting hummingbirds in the tropical flowers by her window. As she lifted yet another evidence box to the table to rifle through, she thought the birds had become more of a distracting nuisance than a wondrous joy.

How does anyone get any work done with all these distractions? she thought. *I mean, I love birds, but that must be the twentieth hummingbird to whizz by.*

After having rummaged through eight of the boxes, Bella stood to stretch her back and give herself a needed break from the case. Maybe she'd go take a dip in the pool. Maybe the sauna or hot tub would clear her head. Either would do the trick after a light jog down by the beach. But before any of these excursions, Bella had to follow up on Thor.

The mighty and majestic Thor was her Alaskan husky. And Thor was also the best friend Bella had ever had. His eyes held all the glacial blue of ice, his sable black fur held all the warmth of the most comfortable bed, and his loyalty and love to her without question had gotten her through some of the most painful times in her life. It was to Thor, and only Thor, that she confided her deepest regrets without judgment. And her beloved protector, if she was threatened, flattened his ears and growled a warning of menace to anyone trying to hurt her. What better friend could anyone ask for?

She dressed in her running attire—black leggings, a simple T-shirt, athletic socks, and running shoes—then jogged down to the beach to make her call home among the white dunes.

"Pizza Palooza. Home of the three-inch thick Bigfoot Pizza. No Bigfoot used in the pizza. How can I help you?"

"Funny, Justin." Bella tried not to laugh. Her good friend Justin always had a way of coming up with the silliest names for his latest pizza pie. "Where's my dog?"

"Last report from the Canadian Mounties was he crossed the Canadian border with a wolf pack. He said send his dog food to the Canadian Mounted Police, eh." Justin exaggerated with an accent to embellish the joke.

In the same instant Bella was sarcastically saying, "Really?" she heard Thor bark in the background. The bark grew louder as Justin placed the phone by Thor's snout.

"Well, at least someone misses me. I miss you too, boy." The dog barked and howled with joy. This was something the two of them had done for years when Bella had to work. And Justin had always been the intermediary and guardian while Bella went on assignment.

"Dare I ask, how's Hawaii?" Bella could hear a slight something in his voice. Was it fear, worry, or concern for her safety? He always had a weird way about him when she went on assignment. But then again, Justin had seen Bella at her worst—sobbing in a bloody ball after having been stabbed by the Harbinger.

"So the illustrious owner of the largest pizzeria in Telluride wants to know about Hawaii? Why? Are you going to open up a shop here too?"

"Big Kahuna Pizza will be the name. Pineapple and mega-anchovies with thin-sliced spam on the pie. I bet we sell out in the first hour." He mischievously chuckled on the other end of the phone.

"I think I'll barf now." Bella hated the smell of anchovies, but she hated the smell and texture of spam even more. "You were, however, spot on about all the spam fast food places. Who knew it was a booming business here?"

"I did try to give you as much intel about Oahu as I could remember. Spam, pineapple, and righteous North Shore waves were the best I could recall. That was one place I hated to leave when I was deployed." She could hear Justin moving a metal bowl of something as he spoke.

Unlike the faux-Canadian accent, his surfer's drawl was completely natural, though it was more Californian than Hawaiian.

Bella looked down the coral sand coast out at rolling waves. "It's really beautiful here. So many flowers and the greenest of greens everywhere. If I hadn't had to climb down a slope down into a valley, I might never have gotten the real Hawaiian tour."

"In all that rain too." Bella had forgotten what Justin's most eerie specialty had been in the Navy. In a former life, Justin was one of the best weather forecasters and intelligence experts for his SEAL team. Though his job had been medic, he had an uncanny ability to predict weather and outcomes. His uncanny abilities to just know things had earned him the coveted nickname the Conjure Man. "Evidence collecting in that jungle menagerie is a mess even on a good day, I bet."

"You know we never talk about work, right?" Bella continued her walk along the pristine beach, looking up as the celestial stars made their ascent. A crescent moon was following in their path. "I couldn't tell you anyway."

"Well, the way I remember it, we did work together once. Though, I'd never want to go through one of your FBI interrogations again. I'd rather go through BUDs than be mind-warped by your brass." Justin was reminding Bella of the night he found her after her encounter with the Harbinger on Mt. Rainier.

Years ago, as the fire raged on Mt. Rainier and Bella lay on her back in a pool of blood, another shadow moved between the trees toward her. She knew it couldn't be the Harbinger. He was unconscious—possibly dead—on the ground just a few yards away. No, this shadow darted among the fires lighting the forest from the IEDs that had gone off. He carried a hunting rifle in his right hand ready to fire. In her delirious state, Bella found it odd for a federal agent. But the shadow who ripped his own camouflaged shirt for a bandage to stop Bella's bleeding hadn't been an agent. He'd been a former special forces man who was taking a break from the world up in the mountains. Little did Hospital Corpsman Second Class Justin Trestle know he'd stumbled inadvertently into another war: Bella's war with the Harbinger.

"I totally get that. Anyway, this one is a slippery slope, Justin." Bella wanted to tell him more, but there was still a mole in the Hawaiian office. A mole who was most likely nearby, contemplating his next moves and trying to figure out how much Bella knew.

"Let me guess. Corruption, interoffice politics, your friend still trying to compete with you years after the Academy. Oh, and did I mention the corruption? Just another day on the beautiful islands." Bella heard him moving some pans and tossing what had to be a big glop of dough on them.

"I get why they call you the Conjure Man now. How do you know these things?" Bella stopped and turned back down the beach. Without realizing it while talking with Justin, she had trekked two miles. It'd be a long haul back up to the house.

"Some call what I have a gift, Bella. For me, it is a bona fide curse. I promise you I hate the insight and the knowing more than you can know." She heard the distinct pop of a jar opening and a liquid being poured. Most likely the secret pizza sauce that Bella, after three years, still had not discovered the secret to. She had yet to get Justin to relent after all her charms.

To talk about other things than the case, Bella went over the sauce's ingredients. "Tomato, oregano, apple cider vinegar, and—"

"Lots of love, Bella. It's that simple!" Justin howled with laughter on the other end of the line. This had been their inside joke for years. "But seriously, you watch your back out there. Even the feds have their virtues and vices. A lot of people making money illegally. You ruffle feathers or stop their cash flow, they might say aloha to you and your services."

"Point taken, and that's the slope we are facing." She considered it a moment and decided she had no choice but to tip her hand a little. "Henry got word that they shelved Rachel Gentry's request for me three times. Besides Rachel, I feel like no one wants me here." If someone was surveilling their phones or her, this wouldn't be any new information. Heck, for all she knew, the whole island already knew everything about the investigation.

"No offense, but you need better friends." Justin's voice was firm and warning. He knew more than he should about the Hawaiian field office. If Bella had to guess, Justin knew of the bugs and possibly the who. But how to ask him without tipping off the inside guy?

"Any chance you can leave Thor with Bugsy Carpenter?" Bella asked in the sweetest and most endearing voice that she could.

"Uh-oh, I don't like the sound of this. When you are too sweet, you need something. Usually, against my better judgment."

"You got me," Bella admitted. She'd have to devise new tricks to get him to leave his business to his mom and pop for a week or more.

"Come on, Bella. You have an entire office of FBI agents. I'm a retired sailor running a pizza shop."

"We've been down this road before, pizza guy. You and Thor are the only people I ever trust these days. And yes, Thor is a person and not a dog." Bella stretched her legs. "But you have behaved like a dog on occasion, or must I remind you?"

"You lead with that to get me to leave my prospering new business? You want me to tag along and play amateur sleuth, and you call me a *dog*? Hmmm, I guess I'm loyal, so I cherish the compliment." And just like a dog, he'd come running to help. He always did.

"I promise things will be different this time." Bella finally came up the stairs in the back of the house and made a spontaneous decision to hop into the pool to cool off a little. "You won't be relegated to staying out of sight of the FBI this time."

"Which you promise every time I show up to help. I end up staying at the safe location or the out-of-pocket hotel until we can figure out the baddies," Justin countered. "I can offer all the assistance you need from my phone in beautiful Telluride." Bella could tell Justin was feeling guilty. She had him wavering to commit.

"This one is tricky, like I said. Too many self-interests and misdirects, Conjure Man. They could have me here for months if I don't think outside the box." Bella walked inside and looked at the stacks of files she had perused while adding, "I'll cover your hotel if it comes to that."

"You had me at hello." She could hear him laughing and Thor howling. "You'll have to break it to Thor though. Last time he stayed at Bugsy's apartment he got some serious fleas."

Bella had taken a few months off recovering from the vicious stab to her side. While many of her friends had offered her assistance and even to help get her on her feet, Bella had opted to be alone—apart from her parents, who would never let their baby girl heal up on her own. Bandages were changed regularly, and medicines were taken accordingly.

The curious part was the daily follow-up by Justin. Despite an exhaustive interrogation of why he was on the mountain that night, Justin had survived the worst accusations against him. In the end, the FBI thanked him for rescuing Bella and gave him a nice letter of thanks.

And Justin, being Justin, had used the FBI thank-you letter to light Bella's fireplace. That had been the first time he had made her laugh. And through the years, it wouldn't be the last. Even though they had yet to become a couple, some of Bella's happiest times in life had been her recovery hikes up in the mountains and pizza night with him.

Bella rubbed her temples. Justin was starting to grate on her nerves by not giving her the definitive yes she needed. "Seriously, Justin, are you that lame? 'You had me at hello' has to be the cheesiest one yet. Will you stop messing around and get over here to help me?"

He sighed. "It'll be different this time?"

"I promise," she replied.

Justin sighed. "Fine. You owe me a spam burger."

"Deal."

CHAPTER SEVEN

I T WAS NEARING TWO IN THE MORNING, AND THE CRESCENT MOON was high up in the night sky as Bella yawned at a table facing the beach. It had been hours since her conversation with Justin, and after an exhaustive comb of all the evidence yet again, Bella stretched her arms and decided it was time to sleep. Those hours fighting fatigue and back cramps had been productive for her. She had managed to better organize and discern more clearly each of the evidence boxes, meticulously analyzing each photo, each report, and some of the collected clothing along with objects that had been recovered from the scenes.

Pushing from the table and its boxes, Bella trudged in a bewildered daze to her bedroom and fell face-first into the down-covered mattress and a dreamless sleep.

At seven the next morning, Bella heard a car pulling up—most likely Rachel or Billy. She was fully dressed and drinking a steaming cup of Rachel's own family blend when the knock came on the door.

"I have to hand it to you, Rachel, this stuff is way better than the junk they have at the office," Bella said as she opened the door to her friend.

"Oh, I know. Consider me spoiled, but I can't even drink the stuff. I bring it from home if I have to."

Bella welcomed her inside and jerked a thumb back at the boxes. "I guess we'll need a minute to lug these back to the office."

"It's the only reason I'm here." Rachel walked in and proceeded to grab two boxes stacked on top of each other. "Did you find anything I might have missed?"

"There are some new developments. I may have a better understanding of our killers." Bella nodded and grabbed her own two boxes to place into the car. She looked out to the rise of a golden sun and felt the cool, humid fog dampening her shirt. "We'll get these to the office, check them back into the evidence room, and then debrief with the team."

"Sounds like a plan," Rachel replied with a tinge of giddiness. "I knew you'd be a huge help. I'm super excited to see what you found."

Bella shut the trunk of her cruiser, then turned and ran back to the bungalow to lock up. She double-checked every door and then turned back to her car to find Rachel still waiting for her.

"Bella, wait a minute. You do know why I pushed so hard to get you out here, right?"

"Yes." Bella didn't want to give too much away. At this point, every FBI agent, including her friend, might be working with or for the murderer.

"You aren't showing your hand much." Rachel took a deep breath. "So, tell me exactly why you believe I requested you."

"You need to clean house. And for some reason, you are obsessed with the idea that I can help you do that."

Rachel cracked her neck and then shook her head in disbelief. "It's not an obsession. It's a fact. I know you've been in my shoes up in Colorado. Especially in the weeks following the Blue-Eyed Banshee case. Didn't you identify and nab three dirty agents on that one?"

Bella opened the door and climbed into her cruiser but paused before closing the door. She stared sternly at Rachel who was wiping her glistening brow. "I got lucky on that case, Rachel. There was no mystery or secret formula. You review the evidence, follow the leads, chase your tail in a circle sometimes, and maybe—just maybe—evidence aligns with your theories."

"And a former intelligence guy with the SEALs just happens into your life. Spare me the bull, Bella. I know you had outside help." Rachel gave a devilish smile to Bella. Bella was a little rattled that Rachel knew about Justin. Bella would have to be doubly cautious out here.

Bella's eyes narrowed, and her face tightened. "You've been investigating my personal life a lot, Rachel. That's usually not what a real friend does."

Rachel put out her hands defensively. "Now, don't get upset. My whole life I've had to watch out for people always angling on me or my family for money and favors because of our businesses. I vet all my friends and the people I plan on working with. It's just what we Steins do."

"So, use your family's influence and its personal army of investigators to dig into who the mole or moles are." Bella rubbed her temple. This case and all its intrigues were wearing on her. "Yeah, I know all about the personal security outfit your daddy employs. Vesuvius. Justin called them rank amateurs with a big bankroll. We knew you were prying into our affairs long before you told me. But thanks for admitting it."

"Ouch, my friend. That was harsh, even for you," Rachel said with a wince. "I had to know you weren't losing it like some of your colleagues in the Colorado office had rumored. I swear I didn't want to go probing into your private life. Though the guy is a good match for you."

"We're just friends. My life gets too complicated for anything more with Justin." Bella shut the door and didn't even wait for Rachel to get into her car before she peeled out of the driveway.

Bella needed this fifteen-minute drive to cool the rage she had right now. Her friend had used all her family's old money and security teams to intrude into Bella's life. That kind of prying from a family of coffee plantation owners was bound to dig up her past. But worse, she had done a deep dive into someone that she truly cared about. That was way out of line for a colleague, much less a purported friend. It was like after all these years, Rachel was still trying to compete with her.

She rolled her window down and took in the fragrant morning breeze as her thoughts swirled.

Rachel had no right to do that. I've been above board since we met. She went digging into Justin's past and mine for more than just a cursory check. I feel a little Sun Tzu spying went down. What is it they say about knowing your enemy and yourself? Yeah, of course, you will always win.

There was a tense pervading silence between Bella and the entire Hawaiian FBI team for most of the morning. Bella remained distant and icily cold to most as she recounted her findings. In the last seventy-two hours on Oahu, she had dealt with this field office shelving requests to have her on the case. She'd been shuffled from hotel to bungalow and not given a chance to jump into the case right away. There had been open espionage within its ranks leading to murders. And her own friend had spied on her and Justin's lives back in Colorado.

One thing was becoming alarmingly clear as the ocean waters of Hanauma Bay. Someone—most likely her formal Quantico rival Rachel Gentry—was trying to sabotage her own work to disgrace Bella. It was the very definition of cutting off your nose to spite your face. But enough was enough. Bella had no desire to wade into a cesspool of criminality and corruption. She'd help today, then shuck the rest and leave.

After the sixth meeting on the evidence files, Billy and the others got up to file out, but Rachel gestured for Bella to stay in her seat. She was irritated, but complied as Rachel followed the group, whispered something to Billy, and shut the office door behind him.

"Subtle," was the only thing Bella said.

Rachel took the chair across from her and took a nervous, steadying breath. "I'm sorry for what I did, Bella. But tell me, if I'd been… struggling, the way you seem to have been, wouldn't you want to know if I was still on top of my game?"

"No. I draw the line at spying on friends and their… friends." Bella gritted her teeth, trying not to say anything more. The less Rachel knew of Bella and Justin's relationship, the better for everyone. "Look, you did it. There's nothing you can do to correct it. You had your reasons, and I have mine. But to be clear, you aren't fooling me."

Rachel leaned back and put her hands on her desk, gazing at Bella with a fixed stare of disbelief. "I'm the one who requested your help, Bella. I begged for you to come here and help me catch a bad guy. Why would I sabotage my own case out of pettiness from years ago?"

"Professional envy or paranoia are good reasons. But you and I can agree there. That's been the question I kept asking myself, Rachel." Bella saw Rachel's mouth open in shock. They had never been this candid about their professional rivalry before. "I know whatever it is, your heart was in the right place. I'm leaning toward you trying to protect your family, Rachel. Why else would you have been so stupid and tried to surveil the Conjure Man?"

Rachel laughed nervously and clapped her hands together. "The Conjure Man?"

Bella slapped her leg and grinned. "I know, it's a funny nickname for the goofball. That's Justin Trestle for you FBI up-tights. But when you go to him for help, he will creep you out with that gift of his."

"Alright, truce for now?"

"Fine." She had to admit that she probably could have done a better job of being a friend too. Maybe Rachel was right—maybe she had been more off her game than she'd thought. But in any case, now was not the time to hash that out. They had a case to solve.

"Anyway, I'm craving sushi after putting my foot in my mouth with you. How about raw fish for an apology?"

They got up and left the room to enter the larger bullpen where TJ, Billy, and a few other agents rapidly turned back to their workstations as if to pretend they hadn't been spying on them.

"Agent Gentry, that sounds divine." Bella grabbed her purse on the way out the door. She cast one brief glance back at Rachel's office and the conference room. Then, shaking her head at the bewildering amount of data they had covered in just a few hours, headed out the door to eat.

It took ten minutes to get to Kami Kaze Restaurant off Nimitz Highway. The restaurant itself was situated not far from the white sands of beautiful Nimitz Beach. Parking, of course, was a little delayed, with all the patrons wanting to clamber in for a meal. Deciding to bring five from her team in the Lincoln, Rachel dropped off Bella and the scant team members in front of Kami Kaze while she fought for a parking spot. A few minutes later, she met Bella and everyone inside.

Bella noted from the jump that this was not your ordinary sushi joint like back home. "They have octopus and live fish in the tanks by the sushi bar. That's unbelievable."

Rachel grinned. "Yeah, if you're squeamish to watching a fish get cut up or an octopus, skip the ringside sushi bar."

Billy had arranged for the team to have a table for ten as a few more agents showed up from other cases. At first, Bella couldn't figure out why so many had shown up for just your average lunch. On a good day, she might have a sit-down with three or four of her colleagues. But then the table got even larger as a few more piled in. Then Bella knew exactly what was going on.

Rachel stood and nodded to a senior agent that carried the same tired eyes as Henry did back home. He stuck out his hand to shake Bella's. "Agent Walker, nice to meet you. I'm Special Agent in Charge Charlton Harris. I'm sorry we didn't get introduced earlier this week, as I've been quite busy."

"Pleasure." She didn't want to say much more than that. Had this been the man to turn down the three requests for her help?

They shook politely, and then Harris turned to address the growing crowd of twenty agents. "Yes, this is Bella Walker from the Harbinger Killer Case, agents. I see we keep getting more of you showing up, so I figured I'd get the pleasantries out of the way. Agent Walker, these colleagues of ours are fans of your work. Would you like to entertain us, if ever briefly?"

Bella became red-faced and out of sorts at being put on the spot. She stood and bowed to the group. A young, blond-haired agent in a pressed black suit raised his hand as if he were back at the Academy. "Did you really get stabbed by the Harbinger?"

Bella winced, and her face grew taut. "I did."

A young woman in her early twenties with short raven hair stood to ask Bella another question. "And he had IEDs up and down Mt. Rainier?"

"Yes. Several agents were k—" Bella paused and put her head down. Her mouth twitched as she bit down on her tongue.

The woman went wide-eyed and put her hand to her mouth as if seeming to remember how insensitive her question was. "I'm sorry for your losses."

Inside her mind, a raging storm of thoughts went through Bella's spinning head.

They always say that when one of us is killed. It's the polite thing to say. It's the professional thing to say. But do these people realize that today, tomorrow, or someday soon, they'll be in the same boat. And maybe, just maybe, if there is some karma in the universe, they'll get the same stupid questions.

Bella sat down, and the other agents, sensing she was done, backed off their questions.

Rachel leaned in and whispered, "Those two are always hobnobbing for the spotlight with SAC Harris."

Bella studied each agent looking and pointing in her direction. "Those ambitious types are in every office. I've kind of gotten used to it. Their questions were benign compared to some. We sure do try to tear down our fellow agents and second-guess each other too much."

"You seem okay, Bella. But I've noticed that drive of yours—the fire to be the number one in everything—seems to have cooled." Rachel seemed to be trying to squelch the blaze that had roared in their earlier exchange.

"Fresh mountain air does wonders to satiate ambition," Bella told her. "You gain perspective on how insignificant you are in the grand design of our planet and the universe. That's what I learned from life after the Harbinger." Bella sighed and took a sip of a lemon water placed by her right hand.

"I can see something has made you more at ease. But then again, you did read through twenty files yesterday and last night, so I know you haven't slowed one bit," Rachel cracked with a nudge to Bella's ribs.

For a minute Bella smiled, then looked off through a window at the busy Nimitz Street full of people. Then she grimaced. "Come clean on who you're protecting. I don't have to say his name, do I?"

Rachel turned her head ever so slightly and leaned in murmuring, "Look, I'll get to who I'm protecting when we get a minute. But for now, we need to focus on the present issue. The reason I needed to call you for help is because of what happened to the responding officer at the first crime scene. Honolulu PD's Perry Leilani. Perry's a great guy. Been on the streets for years." Rachel took a minute to sip her spiced tea. "He and his partner Tanori Omosito were called out to the Waianae site. They split up after calling in the murders to secure the scene with police tape. They were setting up the last leg of the perimeter. It was just the moment that Tanori looked up at a ravine after hearing something. He turned back and Perry had disappeared."

"Gone?"

"Gone. As in, likely taken. And whoever did it left no trace."

Bella considered it all for a moment. "We have a cluster of ritualistic murders. People bugging the FBI without impunity. A group—I'm truly of the belief it's a group now—covering tracks and kidnapping HPD cops. Heck, some of the group you can bet are sitting at this table in FBI sheep's clothing." Bella clenched her fists under the table to the point they were about to bleed when she released her grip and sighed. "This is an absolute mess, Rachel."

Ten minutes and two glasses of lemon water later, Bella's first Hawaiian sushi arrived. She had opted for the onion-spiced lobster cha-wanmushi, which lit her tongue alive with its buttery sauce and tender lobster. Then she, Billy, and TJ shared an ahi marinara with a ginger vinaigrette that made the seared tuna dissolve sweetly as she ate it with a course of braised vegetables and peppers.

The food was delicious, and it did wonders for Bella's mood. She could understand the pressure that Rachel was under, having experienced it many times herself. And despite their tension, she *did* consider her a friend, so she decided to throw out an olive branch or two during the meal. Or a seaweed branch, as it were. As they ate and laughed over old times at Quantico and life in general, Bella couldn't help but catch a glance at Hawaiian news reports on the TV. "Rachel, is that a thing out here?"

Rachel looked at the same television and the story unfolding of arrests of a high-dollar smuggling ring. She scratched the side of her head and rubbed her temple.

"Stealing genuine Hawaiian artifacts? Absolutely. People are willing to pay millions of dollars for legitimate goods. Though there are a lot of imported and exported fakes that get swindled by people too."

"But there's a curse," Billy chimed in. "Pele's wrath will fall on anyone who removes sacred items from her islands—even the rocks or her tears. Bad luck will come to those people. I'm sure of it."

Bella chuckled. "Sounds like something out of one of those old pirate novels. Robert Louis Stevenson."

Rachel's eyes lit up. "Now that's the bookworm Bella I remember. This whole chain of islands has its pirates, its curses, plundered gold, and ancient history. You'd love it here."

"My Aunt Natalie read me every book Stevenson had on pirates, treasure, and Dr. Jekyll. She was kind of cryptic about something with him and our family too. I wish I could remember what she said."

"Well, if you want to know anything about Robert Louis Stevenson in painful detail, might I suggest the great Algernon Magnum and his store The Salty Pirate." She pointed out the window in the direction of a small store with a cheerful sign called The Salty Pirate.

Bella chuckled at the cartoon depiction of a pirate flag and the fake parrot on top of it. "Now that looks like something I've got to check out. It looks like a Barnes and Noble for pirates."

Their check paid, Rachel and Bella got up and began filing out with a few of the agents while more stayed behind. "Algernon Magnum? Now there's quite the name."

"You say that now, Bella." Rachel turned and gave a wicked grin and bad imitation of a pirate's voice. "Alas, mate, wait until you meet him."

CHAPTER EIGHT

R ACHEL PAUSED THE GROUP AS THEY FILED INTO THE PARKING LOT to talk with Billy. "Billy, do you want to get the car running? I'm going to walk Agent Walker over and introduce her to the owner of The Salty Pirate. We shouldn't be too long."

"Yeah, yeah," he said as he caught the keys that Rachel tossed him. "You mean the old fella who thinks he's a pirate? Good luck with that one, Bella."

"No one is ever ready to meet Algernon Magnum. And that's on his off days when he believes the Tiki god Kaulu has hidden his reading glasses," Rachel replied. "He's relatively harmless, Bella."

"Well, we better get a move on, or those won't be the only Hawaiian gods that'll come down on us," Bella said, pointing to the storm brewing from the east.

"Aye aye, cap'n," Rachel joked.

With TJ and Billy waiting in the car, Bella and Rachel made haste across the slowed traffic on Nimitz to cross, reaching The Salty Pirate.

The store seemed much livelier than Bella had expected. Jimmy Buffet seemed to be rambling a song about being the son of a sailor as they opened the wooden door into the place. As they pulled the door, instead of the usual chime or ring announcing their entry, a squawking parrot screeched, "Welcome aboard, me hearties!"

Bella couldn't help but giggle. Then she looked at the walls adorned with pirate memorabilia from beautiful paintings to carved wooden ships and murals. "This has quite a nostalgia to it, Rachel. I'm glad you brought me over."

"Well, you needed to take in some of the fun that Oahu has to offer. Besides, don't thank me yet. You haven't met the man who put all this together." Rachel pointed to a detailed recreation of a pirate's street that could have rivaled Pirate's Alley back in the French Quarter of New Orleans. "I expect you might recognize the collection of books in the right corner."

"It's all of Robert Louis Stevenson's books in first editions! It's incredible!" Bella moved swiftly to the collection as if she were finding a lost friend. Just seeing the books brought back many happy childhood memories with her family. "Is the Hawaiian folklore just as detailed?"

A voice with all the qualities of a salty sea dog bellowed, "Our library is the most comprehensive on all the islands of Hawaii, lass. Not even the University of Oahu can rival our collection."

"That's a bold statement, sir. Most universities in Hawaii would challenge that, professor." Rachel cupped both hands around her mouth to taunt the voice.

A towering, weathered frame of a man walked from around the other side of the bookshelf. He had a reddish-gray mustache, eyes the color of the deepest ocean, gray-streaked red hair pulled back in a ponytail, and skin tanned from a lifetime of sailing the seas. He spoke in that same squawking rasp toward Rachel. "I see you haven't changed in your obstinance of hearsay rather than actual facts, Rachel Gentry."

"You old coot. I see you still think you're a pirate." Rachel embraced the man with a laugh. "Agent Bella Walker, this is the infamous Professor Algernon Magnum, an expert in Hawaiian lore and maritime history."

"My dear, I'll always be a pirate first and a coot second." Algernon walked up to put out his hand to introduce himself. "Young lady, I must say it is a profound pleasure."

"Likewise, Professor Magnum." Bella nodded and shook Algernon's hand.

Algernon put up his hands and swished them forward in a mock protest. "Oh, nonsense on the Professor Magnum. Call me Algernon."

Then he stared for a moment taking the measure of Bella. He squinted again and shook his head while scratching his beard. "Have we met on the open seas sailing to Maui, Agent Walker?"

Bella crossed her arms and answered, "I can honestly say no. This is my first visit to Hawaii."

"Wait, Agent Bella Walker from the Harbinger Killer and Blue-Eyed Banshee cases!" Bella wanted to groan as Algernon said the words. Could she go anywhere without hearing either of those scoundrels' names linked with hers? "You are one lucky lady to catch both those monsters. I imagine you're here to help Rachel with the current creature on our beautiful island?"

Bella looked at Rachel and then back to Algernon with a nod. "Yes. There's some kind of Hawaiian ritualistic theory I'm reviewing."

"There's only one creature you need to stop. Kaulu is his name. He is the foulest of tricksters, and at times, violent and destructive!" Algernon got a little animated, raising his hands in the air dramatically. "Of course, it makes for good fiction battling a god," he chuckled. "We know it's people and their free will that commit the real atrocities."

"That they do," Bella replied, chuckling at the man's act. But even as she did, she studied him with a careful eye.

This is one highly shrewd man. For a moment, I believed he was insane. There's that fine line that Aunt Natalie always warned me of when hunting maniacs. Intelligence and insanity seem to balance between that line. Just as good and evil do.

Algernon moved to rearrange a shelf across from the Robert Louis Stevenson collection. "Is it possible that I could trouble you for an autograph to place on our growing wall of fame?"

"I guess we could oblige a pirate of the seven seas." Then Bella added as she took out a pen, "My team and I were lucky to catch either of those dangerous men. Though luck kind of runs in the family." Bella looked around the store trying to change the subject. "That's quite the collection of Robert Louis Stevenson you have there. My Aunt Natalie would read those to me—"

Algernon clapped his hands together and squawked. "That's what has been troubling me. You *are* the niece of Natalie Roberts! I see the auburn curls, the porcelain features, and those emerald eyes that used to make my knees wobble as if they were caught in a tempest!"

"You knew Dr. Roberts?" Rachel's eyes narrowed, and her mouth hung ajar.

"How could you possibly have known Aunt Natalie, Algernon? She never came to the island that I'm aware of," Bella said skeptically.

"On the contrary, Agent Walker. Your aunt worked several cases out here." Algernon turned and shrugged in Rachel's direction before continuing. "But one case out on Big Island, she never solved."

Bella ran her hand through her hair. "If I'm to believe you—"

"Believe me or not, I knew Natty—my nickname for her—and when she wanted to follow up on your ancestry with Robert Louis Stevenson, well look behind you." Algernon huffed and pointed to the vast collection of all the author's books.

Bella's face reddened to the color of a rose. Then her skin went taut with anger. "Look, I can't prove right now if what you're saying is the truth, Mr. Magnum. But I can guarantee if you are lying to me, or pulling the wool over my eyes, I won't be happy. Until we can resolve this, I'm leaving. My aunt would have told us if she had visited Hawaii."

Bella stomped her feet and pushed open the wooden door as she stormed out of the store.

"I'm sorry, Algernon. She gets sensitive about her aunt," said Rachel, before she walked out to find Bella. "Her family never keeps secrets."

Algernon went to the Robert Louis Stevenson shelf and pulled a photograph out from between the pages of the book Treasure Island. It was yellowed and faded with time, but it was unmistakably a young couple embracing by a wrecked pirate ship. The man had sun-bleached red hair and a ponytail. The woman had glowing auburn curls and green eyes. "Wait, Bella! Rachel, tell her to come back! I can prove all of it."

He grimaced and groaned as he placed the picture back on the wall by the Robert Louis Stevenson collection.

Now you've really done it, Magnum. You had better call Natty to get ahead of all the trouble that will be coming.

"Bella, are you okay?" Rachel had found her a block down preparing to cross over Nimitz and back to the parking lot.

"I'm fine, now. That guy is a few bricks shy of a full load." The traffic had paused long enough for them to cross. Bella sighed and sprinted with Rachel in tow who looked puzzled. "I think the elevator in his brain doesn't go all the way to the top. Aunt Natalie would have confided in me if she had been here."

Rachel stepped up onto the sidewalk and kept pace with her. "Maybe your aunt wanted this mystery all to herself, Bella. We give up so much of our privacy to others sometimes. Maybe after being in the spotlight for so long, she wanted a getaway where she wouldn't have to explain every detail to everyone. Maybe it was a special assignment to check into the Bureau. There were a lot of shenanigans back in the day, you know."

"From what I'm seeing and hearing, there still are," Bella muttered. She stopped walking and looked at the car where TJ was laughing with Billy about something. "But, yeah, it's possible Aunt Natalie needed a break from everything. I can totally understand. You see too much, you hear too much, the world goes sideways, and you just want to forget everything and get away. Maybe she just wanted to try a normal life for a while."

Rachel winced. "Ouch. You know how to stab deep when you want to. Did you learn that from the Harbinger?"

"Funny, Rachel. But I'm sorry for the low jab. I know you have enough to worry about in your department. It doesn't go well for the lead investigator when the criminal can bug your office and buy your agents." Bella rubbed her right brow with her hand. "We need to squash that mole soon."

"More importantly, I have never known Algernon Magnum to ever react like he did. He has his exuberant moments for sure. He'll be a little goofy and lean into the ancient lore. But for the most part, he's a stand-up guy."

They finally approached the car, and Billy got out to let Rachel in the driver's seat. Bella got in on the passenger side of the backseat with Billy while TJ continued to sit in the front. "Maybe he can prove what he's saying, Rachel. But for now, we need to get back to work."

It was around eight in the evening when Bella drove up to the bungalow and parked. The last couple of hours tracking down possible leads and reviewing more case files had been tiring. She needed a run and a swim in the pool to clear her head. Then she swore that she would go back over fifteen of the evidence files tonight before bed.

Rachel's Lincoln pulled up with Billy and TJ not far behind in a candy-apple-red Jeep ranger. Rachel rolled down her window. "Change of plans, Bella."

"What is it now?" Bella asked, cracking her neck and stretching.

Rachel rolled up the window as Bella got into the front passenger seat. "I'll tell you everything when we stop for a quick bite at The Spamster."

"Are you kidding? No way I'm eating a spam burger!" Everyone laughed.

The Spamster could have been a McDonald's or Burger King restaurant with its art deco design, large colorful sign, and red seating. A UFO adorned its signage with a fluorescent logo. Underneath was the curious brand logo that proudly boasted, *"Our spam burgers are out of this world!"*

Inside everyone sat at a large, red booth with their selected orders. Despite protests, Bella did order the signature spam burger with all the toppings, and she had to begrudgingly admit that it wasn't bad. Not that she would ever go out of her way to order something like this. "So, what's our lead?"

Billy nodded to Rachel, sipped his Sprite, and began. "Would you believe… it's a half-senile, blind woman who escaped her assisted living center on the North Shore two nights ago?"

"Are you serious? You are, aren't you?"

"As a heart attack. The guards who chased her down were the ones who called in the scene."

"So, why aren't we interviewing them?"

"They didn't see anything, apparently," Billy shrugged. "They just said she kept repeating to call the police."

Bella's eyes went wide with disbelief. She wanted to put her head down and groan. "Even if she could see, how would we get a statement from her? Even if we did, the district attorney would laugh us out of his office."

"I said the same thing, Bella," TJ chimed in, wiping his mouth with a napkin. "But Agents Gentry and Makani outrank me. So here we are."

"Let me get this straight. You want us to go visit this elderly woman in the middle of the night and get a statement?" Bella couldn't believe what she was hearing. She looked at all three agents sitting in the booth and shrugged. "One more question before we go wake up someone's grandma."

"Shoot." Rachel stood to drop her trash into a bin.

"Why are we taking all four of us?" Bella looked at each of them as she asked. "Seems a waste of manpower."

"Exactly what I thought too." Rachel nodded, pointing to Billy and TJ to head out. "See you two clowns in the morning."

"You just wanted dinner with us, didn't you?" Billy laughed as he got up.

"Don't push it, Makani." Rachel smiled sweetly, but her voice held an edge to it. He laughed and waved as he and TJ headed out to his Jeep.

"This is probably a wild goose chase, just so you know," Bella remarked as they climbed into the Lincoln.

"Oh, a hundred percent. But it was a last-minute lead, and it's better than nothing."

"I guess the ride could help clear my head. Why not?"

"That's the spirit, Agent Walker." Rachel turned on the lights and proceeded to drive out into the darkness of the jungle road headed north.

Hidden Gardens Assisted Living was as much a nursing home as the Taj Mahal was just a house. Right off the back, Bella noted considerable differences in the place from any assisted living or nursing home she had ever seen. It started with the massive waterfall running right through the middle of the horseshoe-shaped, two-story compound. It continued as they walked the long halls decorated tastefully with paintings and Hawaiian artifacts and as they approached the guarded doors surrounded by every type of fragrant flower the islands had to offer. The hallway was resplendent with the aroma of bananas, fine perfume, and curiously, chocolate.

Puzzled by the fragrance, Bella paused and sniffed it more closely. "Why does that little white flower smell like chocolate?"

"Because it's a chocolate orchid. There are orchids in Hawaii that smell like chocolate, raspberry, and many sweet flavors. And now I'm craving chocolate, Bella. Thank you very much."

"If it makes you feel any better, I'm craving ice cream." Then she gave Rachel a wicked smile. "With tons of chocolate a mile high."

"Well, maybe we'll pick up some after this," Rachel offered. They laughed as they entered the office of the director of the facility, Donald Kalea.

Donald Kalea could have been a television evangelist with his overly tanned orange skin, brilliant pearl teeth, and bleached white hair. "Agents, I'm sorry to say, but this is unacceptable. Waking one of our elderly patrons up at this hour is absurd."

Bella and Rachel were sitting in identical plush leather chairs across from the man. Rachel cut a look to Bella and leaned in with her hands together. "I agree, Mr. Kalea. But if we can have five minutes with Mrs. Noelani, we promise to not bother you again. I'm sure she won't be able to say much anyway with her decline."

"Senility is not a decline, Agent Gentry. She is still quite sharp, as can be witnessed by her escape past the guards. That is the reason you're here, isn't it?"

Rachel nodded. "Yes. We believe she may be a witness to a case we're investigating."

A clock somewhere in the office ticked incessantly as Donald clasped his hands together. Bella glanced around the immaculately clean director's office. Again, there were intricate and detailed paintings of Hawaiian lore. One was a volcano with villagers moving to shelter. Another depicted sailing ships from the eighteenth century docked off the coast of a Hawaiian shore. Another painting was a little creepy: it was a highly detailed acrylic with crimson, violet, and emerald-colored feathers adorning a burnished mask. To Bella, it looked just like the crude statues from the crime scene.

"That's one scary mask, Mr. Kalea. What exactly is it?" From a side glance, she saw Rachel look up and recognize the painting too.

Donald pointed to the painting and stood up to discuss it more with Bella. He seemed quite excited to explain its meaning. "That is the terrifying war god Ku. The flaming weapon in his hand is a mace. The mace is quite interesting."

Rachel leaned back in her chair. She turned to face the painting and added, "How so? It certainly is creepy."

"That was the point, Agent Gentry. The mace is most certainly a horrific device without all the flames… and souls it possesses." Bella watched as Donald stared in admiration of the weapon. He was becoming as unnerving as the painting. "The ancient Hawaiians believed that Ku's mace kept the souls of those he had slain."

"That's frightening to think a weapon could take a soul." Bella put her hand to her mouth pretending to be in awe of Donald Kalea's intellectual prowess in Hawaiian lore. As Donald turned to talk of other antiquities in the room, Bella winked at Rachel to make a move.

"Mr. Kalea, we should be heading out. Any chance we can have a five-minute chat with Mrs. Noelani just to check her off our list?" Rachel was pouring on the extra sweet pleasantries and smile.

"Well, if it will clear things up for the FBI, I don't see why a five-minute chat could hurt." He gave a grin and flashed his pearly white teeth. They were so brilliantly white that Bella would later swear that they were glowing.

"Thank, you Mr. Kalea." Both agents thanked him as he escorted them a hallway over and two doors down on the right to Mrs. Pualani Noelani's room. It was on their walk that Bella observed more lurid paintings of various Hawaiian deities. Or at least they looked like deities of some sort. From winged beasts to twisting reptiles, each one left an indelible impression on her. Also, curiously, she took in more scattered Hawaiian artifacts and antiquities, scrutinizing each closely.

Donald knocked before entering Mrs. Noelani's room. Since her escape, an attendant had been posted to keep watch that she did not try to escape into the forest again.

"Julia, it's Mr. Kalea." A middle-aged woman with tired eyes, a haggard face, and tossed brown hair greeted them at the door of the room.

"Sir, it's kind of late for visitors." Julia rubbed her tired eyes and looked at Bella and Rachel, then at the FBI badges they presented. "What's the FBI want with Mrs. Noelani, anyway?"

Bella moved to the door and smiled. "It's just a question or two to clear up a little incident we had up on the mountains. Shouldn't take more than a minute."

Julia leaned outside and whispered, "She's in her bed pretending to be asleep. Be careful, she may try to take off again."

Donald groaned and rubbed his forehead. "That woman is a real pain, I tell you. I'll advise security. If you need anything else, just let me know." Then he hurried off.

Rachel and Bella followed Julia into the room. "Is she really blind?" Bella had to ask. From her observations as Mrs. Noelani opened and then closed her eyes pretending to sleep, the woman didn't look blind.

Julia pulled both women to a nearby window and pointed to the jungle outside Mrs. Noelani's window. "The staff doctor says she's legally blind—macular degeneration of the eyes from blood thinners. But to be honest, I think she faked her testing and ability to see. She's a conniving lady, and I'm almost certain she duped the technician when they did the eye charting and slit lamps. No way a blind woman with her alleged impairment escapes past two seasoned security guards. And even more incredible, she managed to walk five miles in the dark to see the sunrise on the beach."

"Did you say 'see' the sunrise on the beach?" Rachel looked at Mrs. Noelani, then back to Julia shaking her head.

"Those were her exact words to Mr. Kalea when he was thinking of calling her family to come get her."

"Sounds like a real piece of work," Rachel chuckled. "I like her."

"One more question before we ask her a couple of questions." Bella glanced around at more Hawaiian paintings and wooden masks in the room. Julia nodded. "How long has Donald Kalea been director here?"

Agnes grabbed her chin and concentrated. "Well… let's see. Mrs. Noelani got here in January two years ago. And he arrived a month before she did in December. So, I'm thinking just over two years ago."

Bella made a note and looked over at Rachel. They both shrugged together and proceeded to Mrs. Noelani's bed. They noted an intricately designed quilt pulled over an equally intricate silk nightgown. Bella ascertained that Mrs. Noelani was slightly obese with tangles of gray hair covering her face.

"Mrs. Noelani, I'm Agent Walker, and this is Agent Gentry. We have a few questions." There was no response. The elderly woman pretended to snore. "Mrs. Noelani, that's not very nice to pretend to sleep."

Mrs. Noelani sat up and scolded, "It's not very nice to wake up a lady in the middle of the night."

Bella noted the woman seemed to stare directly into her eyes. She returned the favor. "Pretending to be ill and hiding out in an assisted living center isn't very nice either."

The trickster woman winced. "It's not illegal, Agent Walker. And my eyesight has been tested. Unless you've become a doctor too." Mrs. Noelani rolled back over irritably. "Were you going to ask questions or not?"

"We'd like to ask about your escape attempt the other night," Rachel started. "What exactly was it you saw that prompted a call for the police?"

All the irritation fled the old woman's face and was replaced by a despondent grief. "My baby boy. Kai. I told him no good would come messing with them."

Bella and Rachel shared a look. "Messing with who?"

Mrs. Noelani raised both hands in a shrug. "I don't know. Bad fellows. The kind that do the terrible things they did to my grandson."

"Mrs. Noelani, we are sorry for your loss." Bella didn't know what else to say in the moment. Anything else, she thought, would've been disingenuous. "But were you able to… see what happened?"

She chuckled caustically, bitterly, out of grief. "I may not be blind, but I can't exactly see like a hawk these days either. No, I just had a feeling. I can't explain it. So I went to go find where I felt it."

"A feeling?" Rachel asked.

"A feeling like the island spoke to me," Mrs. Noelani explained. "Like I had to go see the sunrise. And I just knew something had happened to my poor Kai."

She took a deep breath and lowered her shoulders, shedding a tear. She dug below her mattress and pulled out a photograph. She looked down and handed the picture to Rachel who proceeded to show Bella. "Please, Agents. Please find out who did this to my boy."

Bella looked at the picture with widened eyes. In the picture, there was a smiling Hawaiian boy who seemed so proud. There hadn't been an official identification yet, but she already knew exactly who it was. Kai Noelani was standing in the same valley where they would find him headless days later.

In the picture, he was holding an intricately carved statue at least three feet in height and a foot wide. It was a Hawaiian war god.

CHAPTER NINE

T HEY WEREN'T ABLE TO GET MUCH MORE OUT OF MRS. NOELANI, SO they thanked her and headed back through the facility. Again, they passed the sparking waterfall at the centerpiece of the assisted living center.

Bella was glued to her phone, zooming in closely on the photo of Mrs. Noelani's photo she'd taken as Rachel unlocked her Lincoln and both women climbed in to leave.

"Any luck?"

"Nothing yet. This young boy doesn't seem like the criminal type." Bella studied the smiling boy wearing a Spongebob T-shirt while holding the ugly statue.

They headed east on Kamehameha Highway, then south on H1 back to Oahu. "Most of these poor kids—and make no mistake that Hawaii is an impoverished economy—get caught up in all sorts of trouble. A local gangster probably offered him a few bucks to scout his backyard to find relics. Then the same crook will auction the piece in a private auction for millions. I tell you, Bella, it is a vicious cycle when these kids get caught up in the drug and artifact trade. Some scoundrel always finds a way to take advantage of desperate people."

"That they do." Bella took a deep sigh, then glanced over. "It's a shame that it has to be that way."

"What does that mean?" Rachel turned, squinting. Bella could tell that her words might have bristled her friend. "Don't hint at it. Just say what's on your mind."

"Your family—your *father* has encouraged this." Bella had been waiting for Rachel to admonish her complicity in the artifacts trade. "I know buying the stolen artifacts isn't the same as stealing them. But encouraging the market doesn't make him clean either."

"Wow. My father gets a deal on a priceless mask. Pays above and beyond its worth from a reputable dealer, but he's complicit in a crime?" Rachel looked out the window angrily. "That's like saying every time you buy a cheap pair of pants from Amazon or any number of websites that you support forced child labor too."

Bella grimaced and put her hands out defensively. "Well, I—"

"Come down off your pedestal, Saint Walker. The world is what it is sometimes. The goods we buy to show off or make our lives easier aren't coming out of Willy Wonka's chocolate factory or a genie's lamp." Rachel paused and then pulled into a gas station to fill up. "And now I'm *really* craving chocolate!"

Bella rolled down her window as Rachel stomped over to the pump. "So, you do see the hypocrisy at play here, then."

"Yeah, I've heard this type of rhetoric my whole life. Bella Walker, the queen of purity and chaste behavior. You never had a family secret or fell short of society's moral standards?" Rachel stared at Bella and shook her head while pumping the gas. As she studied Bella's response, Bella looked around at the unlit darkness of the jungle and the growing fog.

"I grew up on the outskirts of New Orleans, Rachel. Every virtue and vice surrounded me." She took in a breath of the misted, cool air. "I'm not judging you or your family. I just find the dealings a little suspicious. I wouldn't want you to compromise your role as an investigator… or for there be an appearance that you are compromised in your duties."

"So, your daddy running off-the-books surgery for Mad Dog Caspari didn't compromise your family?"

Bella's eyes went wide in shock. Rachel really had gone all out in her investigation of Bella. It was definitely for a purpose. And Bella was seeing the full design now.

Rachel scoffed and turned away into the store for her prized chocolate, leaving Bella there to contemplate what had just happened.

Rachel got me here to disgrace me, no doubt. She turned over every stone and dug up every lurid detail about my family, my friends, and me to leverage the dirt against me should I kick up something on her. Which she figured she had to do when she dug into Justin's past.

But then, why does a woman like Rachel get into the law enforcement business in the first place? Certainly, it's not to uphold the law. Is it for the good of her family? Or… to protect them at any cost using the FBI as her own personal security guard service?

But therein lies the enigma of the Stein family. The latter makes no sense. Her family has one of the best private security outfits in the world. And plenty of money to obtain the best detectives, as she just proved to me.

As Rachel walked out of the store with a bag of chocolate, Bella's head was spinning, and her mind had more thoughts sifting through it than grains of sand in an hourglass. Each grain a piece of a greater puzzle. A puzzle that seemed as ever-shifting as the sands.

Rachel tossed a Mauna Lau chocolate bar to Bella. "This will make you wish you had never eaten a Hershey's bar."

Bella was tired of the cryptic game they were playing. The whiplash back and forth from friend to rival back to friend. "So, you investigated every detail of my life, my family, our family businesses, and my friends. What's your endgame, Rachel? You easily could have solved this case with your private security force. Why am I really here?"

"It's simple. You were requested by the lead agent on an FBI case to help solve a series of murders." Rachel turned the key to start the car and proceeded on the long drive back onto H1. "And, no matter what you find out, you solve this case and never once spare my feelings or anyone else's, for that matter."

"I see. So, you do want to catch these people. Despite the cost to your family." Bella glanced at Rachel with sympathy. As she watched Rachel wincing at her own words, Bella recalled similar feelings not so long ago. And Rachel, using her army of private security, had unfortunately dug up that painful event in Bella's life. A time, not so long ago, when the fabric of what she thought she knew of her family—her own parents—had been rattled to the core. When Bella herself had to test the validity and culpability of people she loved dearly. And in doing so, had almost lost both.

Confusion, misdirection, and rage had all defined her emotions during the murky Blue-Eyed Banshee case. A case that wasn't as dangerous or harrowing as the Harbinger, but much more painful to Bella personally. "Well, now that's out the way, I think I'll try the chocolate."

Rachel finally smiled. "Like I said, you'll never eat another Hershey bar again."

When they had almost arrived back in town, Bella looked at the snapshot of Mrs. Noelani's grandson again. She expanded and zoomed into the picture, lost in thought. There had to be something more to the war god than theft—some detail or belief that made obtaining and displaying replicas of them with body parts so valued. Maybe it wasn't so much the item or finding them. Maybe it was a message being sent out to rivals and law enforcement.

"We'll have to really delve into some artifact research here." Rachel gave Bella a side glance. If there was ever any doubt that Rachel relished seeing her in discomfort or even pain, Bella could conclude with certainty that her rival and friend championed it. "I know this—"

"Can it, Rachel. I know we have to go back and see Algernon." Bella rolled her eyes at Rachel. "Besides, I have an autograph to give."

CHAPTER TEN

THE NEXT MORNING, BEFORE THE SUN ROSE AS A GOLDEN ORB ON the distant horizon, Bella went for a run down on Nimitz Beach. She started as always with the creaking and cracking that comes with a precursory stretch of her arms, legs, and hips to prepare for the jarring and uneven landscapes of the dunes and beach. Once her stretching was done, she secured a chilled water bottle to her waist pack and headed out.

Running like the wind, she maneuvered between the outstretches of beach naupaka and vitex with their clusters of white and purple flowers. Onward down the dunes to the beach, she caught a glimpse of pink beach morning glory and brilliant yellow puncture vine in the dwindling celestial light. Finally reaching the glow of the talcum powder sands, Bella increased her pace from a jog to a full sprint down the winding and flat picturesque shores. After six undaunting and precarious miles, Bella slowed to a crawl to take in the morning sunrise by a rocky inlet.

The deep crimson and orange outcrop lit up like molten lava in the first rays of the morning sun. Bella took in their blazing beauty with the awe of a child in a dream. She stared further at her surroundings, realizing cascading blue waves were crashing below on the precipice where she stood, each crash sending up diamond-like droplets of sea spray. Some of those gems landed on her jogging clothes. As the sun continued its ascent, the morning rays lit the dried spray and sweat droplets causing them to shimmer.

Bella couldn't resist the temptation to wander and explore the twisting rock formations housing all manner of lava tubes and caves. On her second winding turn of one of the caves, Bella spied a curious oddity lodged between two jagged rocks. As glasslike waves poured over the object—a heavily barnacled, wooden hull—Bella looked down farther along the rugged red coast, wondering how the crashed vessel had ended up this far into a cave.

Wiping sweat, chilled by the early morning sea winds, Bella speculated.

The formations of barnacles are so dense. This shipwreck has been down here a while. And its location is so remote; it must have been stuck in this cave for at least a hundred or more years. It certainly is quite the find. I sure would like to investigate it further. But I'd need ropes and tanks to do that. And I'm not keen on either.

By nine, she had showered, gotten dressed, and stumbled into her morning cup of Stein Coffee. On her second cup, she called Rachel and told her she was going to talk with Algernon.

"Behave this time, Bella." Bella could hear people moving around in the background as Rachel added, "I know he got under your skin with the whole Aunt Natalie thing. Maybe he's telling the truth."

"An old sailor like that, telling the truth? Now I've heard everything."

Bella once again pulled open the ornate wooden door of The Salty Pirate, heard the squawk of the parrot welcoming her, and walked into the establishment. She proceeded to rekindle her childhood memories of Robert Louis Stevenson. The shelves held many more curiosities, including even ships' records from the eighteenth century or before. Her growing curiosity about the intrigues of this store and the man who owned it was piqued.

She had made two steps in the direction of the prized books when Algernon coughed behind her. "I see you're back for another round of accusations and insults, Agent Walker."

"If you mean tangling with braggarts and liars, then yes. Are you ready to parley this round and confess your transgressions, you salty dog?" Bella gave a wide, sheepish grin to Algernon, then watched as the man went to the Robert Louis Stevenson collection in a huff.

He pulled three books from the shelf. One was *Treasure Island*, the other *Kidnapped*, and the third *The Black Arrow*. From each, he pulled a photo and a letter. Then Algernon pressed a panel behind a pirate statue that opened the bookshelf panel to a hidden room. He walked inside and came out moments later with a leathered book with gilded lettering. The book said 'Memories.' As he walked out of the room, the shelves slid back into their place, hiding the secret room.

"Just when I thought things couldn't get weirder with you, Mr. Magnum." Bella lifted her brows and put her left hand to her head rubbing a growing headache.

"Oh, you ain't seen nothing yet."

He handed her the stack and waited patiently as Bella looked over the aged, yellowed notes of Aunt Natalie. She felt embarrassed and red-faced, as if she were peeking over a curtain into a very private couple's life. She pushed back a tear reading some of the content within one of the letters, the information which she'd have to process later and follow up on long after her current case was solved. But if the letters hadn't broken her heart, the pictures of her Aunt Natalie living a happy, normal life far away from the rigors of her fame, certainly did.

"I'm truly sorry for my behavior, Algernon. You had no reason to lie." Bella turned to leave the store with her head hung low in shame.

"No need. It's not what you were expecting when you came to Hawaii, I imagine." He put a hand on Bella's shoulder and patted it gently. "Enough of all of this. How can I help you?"

Bella frowned. "Why would you help me? Especially after the way I acted toward you."

Algernon leaned his head down and stared with his ocean-blue eyes. He put his hands together in a kind of prayer. "Because you need help, lass. These islands have many wonderful and dark mysteries within them. You'll need help with the complexity of some of the island's secrets. Unless you want to spend years chasing your tail like I did before I asked for help."

Bella took out her phone and showed him the picture of Kai Noelani—grandson of Pualani Noelani—the now-deceased boy. "He was caught up in something out on this valley. Someone cut off his head with five others and placed bad mock-ups of Hawaiian war god statues in front of them."

Algernon sighed heavily. "Oh dear, it is starting again. You know, thirty years ago, Pat Garrick and the HPD had trouble getting anyone to come forward." He ran his fingers through his beard. "That's the official version of their reporting, anyway. And the ones who were brave to come forward only disappeared. That was quite the curiosity."

"So, which Tiki god is it?" Bella looked and pointed over at the Hawaiian mythological collections in The Salty Pirate's left corner.

"None of them." Algernon's voice was vacant and distant as he replaced the Robert Louis Stevenson books on the shelf.

"What do you mean, it's none of them?" Bella put her hands up in protest. "That's a Hawaiian war god, right?"

"There are four war gods. Ku, Kanaloa, Kane, and Lono. The one in the picture is obviously Ku." Algernon raised his brow and shook his head. "But nothing about these murders is Hawaiian except the landscape."

Bella was getting ready to ask more questions when her phone rang. "Excuse me, Algernon, I have to take this."

Algernon nodded as Bella walked outside. "No problem, Bella. I need to dust the middle section—Viking lore—anyway. Please excuse me as well."

Bella walked outside the store into the blaze of a midday sun. Squinting her eyes to adjust, she put on sunglasses and answered her phone. Billy Makani seemed exhausted as if he had run up several flights of stairs. "Bella? Rachel's out of cell phone range, or she would have called."

"What's going on?" Bella walked hurriedly to her car, already assuming the worst if Rachel couldn't call.

She heard him take a deep breath. He must have sprinted quite a stretch up or down the mountain, but she wasn't prepared for what he was about to say.

"Another kill site but at a different mountain. Three victims."

Bella opened her car door and climbed inside. "I'm on my way."

CHAPTER ELEVEN

WHEN BELLA ARRIVED AT THE SOUTHERN BASE OF THE KO'OLAU Mountain Range, she instantly knew why Billy had sounded so winded. A throng of HPD police cars, FBI vehicles, and most notably, a familiar white Lincoln were gathered around the famous Haiku Stairs, or the 'Stairway to Heaven.' With blue lights strobing and headlights blinding her, Bella trudged her way up the steps, edging her way through the police forensic technicians once again bagging evidence and deputies securing the nearby trail.

She waved to Billy, who was still perspiring from his descent and leaning against a boulder. "You look a little tired."

He jerked a thumb up to the upper climes of the Moanalua Valley, some four miles away. "Hope you brought your hiking boots, Bella."

"Is that where we're headed?"

"Unfortunately."

"Wonderful."

Strong winds gusted across the trail, causing Bella's red curls to twist in the breeze. Sometimes the kickups caused gravel to spiral up around them. Other times, the winds caused puddles filled with earlier rains to splash up and cover Bella and Billy in grit and grime. When the trail weaved into the valley, tall grasses whipped across sometimes, leaving a nasty sting on her arms and face. But finally, Bella and Billy reached a large, yellow square of police tape set up for the perimeter. And there was Rachel just outside the perimeter scratching her head.

And I thought the last hike down was tough, Bella thought, her heart roaring and lungs burning from the two-thousand-foot elevation. *How do they get any investigations done in this place?*

"This is starting to seem like old times, Agent Gentry." Bella walked up pushing back her tangled hair. "What do we have?"

Rachel shrugged as a forensic technician walked behind them in a blue Tyvek suit with a bag in hand. "Second verse, same as the first. All three decapitated and sitting as if praying."

"War god statues and left fingers missing?" Again, Bella knew the answer but wanted confirmation. Rachel and Billy both nodded. "Does HPD have any leads this round? Or will we be back to nobody talking?"

Rachel looked over to Bella and leaned in. "We have something to follow up on. I want to be cautious with this lead."

TJ O'Reilly came staggering up, covered from head to toe in reddish mud. Bella noted on his feet he wore expensive dress shoes rather than Bureau-issued hiking boots. Everyone looked at him shaking their heads. Billy chuckled. "I'd say to watch your step, TJ, but it seems a bit late for that."

"Alright, we better get to it," Rachel declared. "I don't want the weather to catch us off guard again." Everyone nodded. Their nemesis—weather—could strike at any time.

Each of the team went methodically in a grid search combing the scene. With the winds picking up velocity, Bella and the team moved more swiftly on the third and fourth pass through the seventy-foot by one-hundred-foot square. Gum wrappers, an old belt, and even a ragged, filthy, black shirt with 'Metallica' on its front, were found, identified, photographed, and bagged. Whether it was related to the current crime scene or another was anyone's guess.

"Rachel? Bella? Y'all might want to look at this," came Billy's voice. Bella turned to see him near one of the locations of the victims' bodies. He had bent to one knee and was bringing a bag out of his pocket. Bella saw him collect something shiny.

"Hey, hold on before you bag that!" Rachel shouted from a spot on the right upper side of the valley. "We need a picture and location marker, Billy!"

Red-faced, Billy paused. "Crap. I'm sorry. I got carried away with retrieving it."

Bella struggled to move up the valley incline to get to him. It was like every time she pushed herself up she slipped and slid down ten feet. Agonizingly, she pulled up again to the safety and sure footing of the ridge. From the ridge's flatter vantage point, walking became a dream.

TJ had followed up on her left and made good time to reach him without another fall. He moved nimbly and swiftly on his ascent. Bella wondered how such a graceful guy could have slipped on the Moanalua Valley Trail. He yelled jokingly at one point to Bella, "Watch your step, Agent Walker."

Bella waved and continued her trudge across the ridge. "No worries there, Agent O'Reilly. This is quite the view though." Bella looked upon the swaying tall grasses and the intricately twisting banyan lining the tree line surrounding the valley. As another gale blew from the mountain's peak, she saw more trees like fluorescent breadfruit and fragrant eucalyptus bend and creak to the wind's forceful advance. After another gust of wind blew through forcing her to sit and wait it out, Bella knew she needed to make haste, or she might be trapped in her current spot until nightfall.

"Like always, Bella, I'm glad you could finally join us." Rachel grinned and stooped to look at what Billy had found.

"I'm here now. That's what really matters," Bella said, breathless. "But once again the island slowed the response." The team laughed for a minute. Well, everyone but TJ, who shook his head and wiped mud off his face.

Once Rachel had looked over the item—a broken shard of steel with a curious wave pattern in its patina—she took a photo of with with her phone and nodded to Billy. "Now, finish bagging. And make sure to get that to our metallurgical department as soon as possible."

"Got it."

"Have you ever seen a piece of steel like that before, Bella?" Rachel asked while wrapping her windbreaker up tightly to cover her face. The team seemed glad to be heading down from the blustery winds.

Over the howling winds, Bella screamed to answer. "Maybe on a Ginsu knife in one of those commercials. Or was it a lawnmower blade? I forget."

Rachel paused in front of her and turned around. "Bella, could you hold back for a minute?" Rachel waved over three HPD officers who had been assisting the team. TJ turned around, and Billy continued his descent without hearing anyone. "TJ, you head down with Billy. I'm going with these three HPD officers and Agent Walker to check something out."

TJ looked up to the ridge of the Ko'olau Mountain Range, taking note of the rickety, rusted stairs that had been built—and abandoned—long ago. The whole thing stretched for miles and miles. He narrowed his chestnut eyes and laughed laconically at Rachel and Bella.

"You're going up The Stairway to Heaven with highly inexperienced personnel, Agent Gentry. Are you sure you don't want to wait and get specialists up here to check out your tip? People do go missing and die up there."

"Noted, Agent O'Reilly." Rachel waved a hand at him. "No worries, we aren't that foolish. We won't be traversing the trail. We'll see you at the bottom."

Bella followed Rachel and the officers as they made the ascent to the midpoint of Haiku Trail. She trotted up next to Rachel and lowered her voice. "What the heck was that all about? TJ was bordering on insubordination."

"I'd like to say he was being overprotective. But I'd be wrong." Rachel continued walking and shrugged. "You didn't catch anything else in that conversation?"

"Yes." Bella took a breath. She was already winded from the Moanalua Trail hike. This further hike at higher elevations was really wearing her down. "How did he know where we were going?"

Rachel turned and raised a single brow. "That's a question I'll ask him later. I didn't tell anyone about this lead. Not even Billy."

They went ten minutes farther without saying a word. Then, Rachel had everyone pause just before they reached the summit of the Haiku Trail midpoint to rest.

"I managed to get a bar on my phone for a minute. I already texted Billy and SAC Harris to check for bugs," Rachel said.

"Oh, boy, another surveillance check of FBI headquarters. I bet everyone will just love cleaning their rooms again," Bella murmured.

While resting and rubbing her shins, Rachel addressed HPD officers Jerry Thomson, Sal Garrett, and Patty Ryan. "Officers, I'm hoping he's safe and they just tied him up. He's one of the good ones."

"If we're all the way out here, Rachel, you know it's not good." Sergeant Sal Garrett looked up to where they were headed. His face was featureless, with blue-gray eyes the color of hardened granite. When he addressed Rachel, Bella swore his very voice seemed ageless and wise. "Officer Leilani is truly one of the good guys. No one has ever said a bad thing about our Perry. How he makes all of us laugh. Plays a mean ukulele too. Let's hope and pray we find him alive."

Jerry Thomson chuckled and wiped away a tear. "You remember the policemen's benefit last year? He did Don Ho's song 'Tiny Bubbles', and it brought down the house." His black hair was combed back into a pompadour like an aging rocker from the fifties but with much more gray on his temples. His cordwood muscles seemed to tense as he followed Sergeant Garrett's gaze to a twisted banyan tree at the midpoint.

Garrett stood and nodded to Rachel. "Let's just pray he'll be back singing Don Ho again soon. Keep your head in the game. We're walking a dangerous stretch now."

Officer Patty Ryan, who was sitting with a boot off to rub her feet, seemed to be the only optimistic one of the bunch. "He's going to throw his arms around us and tell another of his corny elevator jokes real soon for us."

"I hope he's okay too," Bella added reluctantly. "But keep in mind, whoever kidnapped him, may be setting us all up. We all should be ready for anything." She raised her head to look at Rachel and the large banyan tree that loomed before them.

"She's right, officers." Sarge looked at Rachel and Bella with his stone-cold, granite eyes. "Remember the disappearance of Daylenn 'Moke' Pua. We found his camera and those pictures of the kid hiking up Haiku Trail. The internet sleuths are still blasting his pictures on the internet all over those damn podcasts. Never forget the look of that crazed man that had been following Moke in the photos just before he disappeared. Weirdos and psychopaths frequent this place. Be ready!"

Bella looked into the valley to the eastern side of the Haiku Trail. She was having feelings that had not surfaced since that fateful day on Mount Rainier with the Harbinger. It was her gut sending out messages of impending danger. There was a shaking and shuddering in her knees pleading for her to run away from this misadventure before it was too late.

Bella studied the midpoint, stretching her neck and rubbing her side—the same side holding a scar from the Harbinger.

Why am I feeling like this? This intense feeling of déjà vu that I'm about to walk into another ambush and good people will die. Why does this feeling of perpetual dread seem to never leave me?

They approached the winding, spidery twists of the ancient banyan tree atop Ko'olau Mountain, and the winds seemed to howl with an intensity she hadn't heard since her climbs in the snow-covered Colorado mountains. But here those same mournful cries were with an ocean of jungle surrounding her, not the dry mountain air back home. The team heard the creak of the timeless tree as those same gale-force winds blew through. Large, verdant leaves rustled and ripped while the weather continued. Bella was amazed at how the tree made ropelike strands from its boughs that seemed to tether the eighty-foot circumference of the tree to the rocky soil of the mountain.

"Dear lord!" Bella heard Rachel gasp and bite her fist to stifle a scream.

Bella turned and heard the ever-optimistic Ryan scream as if shot. Then Bella watched as the woman fell to the ground in grief, punching the earth while screaming in angst.

Thomson ran to the tree looking for any way to climb it to unleash a woeful burden the tree was having to bear.

The stone-cold granite eyes of Sergeant Garrett were wet with tears but carried a silent rage as he, too, moved with incredible swiftness to help Thomson.

All this occurred simultaneously as Bella stood stunned. For before her stood the horrific site of men scrambling and falling, trying to climb the banyan tree that had been set high on its mountainous perch for hundreds of years. Yes, screaming officers and crying agents working together to bring down and bring home the hanging body of Officer Perry Leilani.

CHAPTER TWELVE

"WHAT CAN WE DO, RACHEL? WE CAN'T GET CLOSE ENOUGH without risking one of us falling hundreds of feet below." Bella paced and pleaded, trying to reason with Rachel who was just as invested as the HPD officers to get Perry down. They had all had their shot to scale the immense tree and its slippery climb to cut Officer Leilani off the tree's bough, but none had succeeded.

"Whoever did this is inhuman," Rachel raged. "I will not leave him desecrated like this for his family to see on the news." Rachel tried moving around to lock her foot in a midlevel grotto formed naturally by the banyan. She heaved, then pulled herself up another few feet before almost falling back into another slippery recess. "No one hangs one of my friends like a common criminal!"

Officer Ryan had picked herself up off the ground and wiped off her hands. Rubbing her eyes with the sleeve of her shirt, she called up to Rachel. "I admire your determination."

"You mean her desire to fall out of a perfectly good tree and off a cliff," Bella cut in. Kind of sums up my entire time in Hawaii." She put her head down and rubbed both her temples. "She's going to fall right down, and we'll have two good officers taken out by this monster."

Officer Ryan was taken aback, but Bella didn't care. She stormed forward and positioned herself around the back of the tree. Before ascending, she made sure her gun and handcuffs were secure. She did not want to have to explain how she had lost both up on Haiku Trail. With those items secured, she made sure she had her service knife ready for when she reached the rope and cut Officer Leilani down. But she'd make sure before performing the cut that Sarge Garrett and his team would have the body secured to pull him onto the trail. There would be no sense to cut Perry down if they'd just be dropping him down into a distant ravine or worse below.

"Officer Ryan, you get vines or whatever secured around him to catch or pull him to the trail. Otherwise, when I cut him down, he could fall, be further damaged, or lost."

The HPD officer, a little out of it, shook her head and asked, "How can you damage him anymore? He's dead."

Bella thought of explaining how Leilani's body was now evidence in a murder investigation. That letting him drop might damage the evidence and allow his killer—if there was a trial for this monster—to walk free. Then she thought better of it due to the nature of the officer's emotional state in the current moment.

Bella had chosen the right part of the banyan tree to ascent more rapidly as Rachel struggled to reach the next two feet and onto the bough. Moving swiftly through a strand of banyan roots, Bella pulled on them to test their strength as she used them to guide and pull her body over an enormous, twisting, octopus-like bow that blocked her from reaching the extended branch that Perry's rope was tied to. Once tested, Bella took a long careful breath to think about her moves after she reached Officer Leilani. Before she advanced, she needed to make sure that Officer Ryan had advised her colleagues to secure Perry's body.

"Sarge, are you down there? Thomson, Ryan, can you hear me?" Bella crouched and, sitting on a fin-shaped branch, awaited their answer. She wiped the sweat off her hands, face, and forehead. She certainly didn't want a slippery hand losing grip on a vine or root over a thousand-foot drop below.

"Agent Walker? Wow, you got all the way over!" Officer Thomson looked up and whistled. "Sarge found a stash of old parachutes on the back side of the tree. The para-cord is in excellent condition."

"It might be better if you tied the cord to his waist if you can, Agent." Sergeant Garrett came from around the base of the tree with a thick roll of black rope on his shoulder. "Wait, Gentry, are you still in the middle of the tree?"

"I was just about to say, Bella would have a tough time dropping the para-cord around Perry's waist and then pulling it up to tie him off for the fall." Rachel slapped something—most likely a bug—then continued. "Bella, if we work together, you get a stick or something, and I tie to it from my vantage point. Then we just run the tied stick around him, then I tie a slipknot or two to secure him."

"It should work." Then Bella groaned. "If he isn't too decomposed."

If his body gets pulled in two, it'll be a horrific mess.

Rachel seemed to be thinking the same thing as she called up to Bella. "We need to try and gently drop him down. We don't know how long he's been up here. If you can cinch him down with a second para-cord, that would help considerably."

"On it."

Bella moved and scrambled over the twisted mesh of banyan roots that seemed almost impenetrable. She used her titanium knife to hack through the basket-weaved root system impeding her. After half an hour, and between the twisting and creaking of the wind-swept tree, Bella went over onto the enormous branch holding the body. Inching ever carefully, dragging the needed branch to secure the para-cord, she stooped and crawled out onto the branch.

She looked down and immediately regretted it. There was at least a five-hundred-foot drop to the canyon below. To steady herself, she grabbed dangling banyan branches and roots to support her as she slowly proceeded to the hanged man. After fifteen minutes that seemed an eternity, Bella finally reached him.

"Well, Bella?" Bella knew by Rachel's cryptic tone what she meant. "How long, best guess?"

"Three days. But I'm not in the best position to know for sure." Bella stared down and gave a nod to Rachel.

As the wind picked up a bit, Bella stooped low to the branch for balance and a better grip. She looked out to the dwindling daylight on Mount Ko'olau.

To have brought him up here, Perry had to have been alive. They wouldn't have been able to drag or carry a body on those rusted stairs only to hang it in this tree in the middle of nowhere.

Bella and Rachel had a moment or two where either could have fallen. Bella almost lost the branch on one occasion and the para-cord on another as it got caught on Perry's body a time or two. But providence and luck finally prevailed, and they got him to the trailhead. Once Perry was secured, Bella hiked down to find a satellite signal to text and call. She stumbled and staggered after two miles down the Haiku Stairs to call for assistance from HPD and the FBI. Following her call, and hours of waiting for the winds to die down, a rescue helicopter arrived just before dusk and carried Perry Leilani home.

The hike back down Haiku Trail and Moanalua Trail was somber and quiet for all, with the only noise being the howling, ghostly winds.

Bella moved slowly and deliberately the next morning. She definitely would be skipping her morning run. It was five o'clock, and she moved to the hot tub and sauna to work out the inevitable kinks from climbing a banyan tree on top of a mountain. The heat helped, and the morning swim loosened the rest of her aching muscles and joints. She was almost able to move without cramps to the coffee pot when TJ O'Reilly called.

"Tarzana, I hope you are okay on this fine morning." His voice sounded smug and gloating.

"Is there a reason you called, Agent O'Reilly?" Bella wasn't in the mood. Her back and legs were starting to spasm again. She'd need another round of the sauna and hot tub for sure.

"Sorry. That was a rough day for everyone." TJ seemed sincere. Maybe he was just a blockhead and not an inconsiderate jerk. "HPD wanted a sit down to go over a few things with you and the team on the trail. I'm guessing it's a customary follow-up."

"And why didn't Agent Gentry call me? This is a little curious that a rookie is calling me about an internal investigation with the FBI and HPD." Bella could hear TJ tapping his fingers on his desk. Then she heard him move something in his office.

"Agent Gentry has already had two meetings this morning. Once again, I'm assuming she was surprised you weren't here yet." Bella gritted her teeth and clenched her fists. The old rivalry for showing up Rachel must be back in play.

"Tell her I'm on my way," she sighed.

Bella stretched her thighs trying to relieve the returning knots in her muscles then grabbed a bottle of water and ibuprofen to reduce any more inflammation while she dressed, groaning the whole time. Why couldn't Rachel just be normal and take a moment to heal up?

Bella circled the block three times on South Beretania waiting to find a parking spot at the Honolulu Police Department headquarters. While waiting, she took in the towering trees in front of the building and the occasional colorful bird resting in its branches. Her windows were down, and the breeze was gentle. It was a far cry from the nightmare she and the team had endured bringing one HPD's own back home for burial.

The instant an HPD cruiser left to go out on a call, Bella took the moment to finally park and go inside the relic of Hawaiian law enforcement—or as Rachel was so fond of saying—the bastion of safety.

"What took you so long?" Rachel smiled and handed her a much-needed coffee.

Bella took the cinnamon cream latte and sipped slowly. "What is your secret, Rachel? Because all my tricks to heal up after those climbs yesterday pale in comparison. Or rather have failed miserably."

"Coconut and fish oil. No ibuprofen—it's hard on the liver, you know." Rachel smiled and pointed to the HPD chief's office.

A tired Hawaiian man with fists the size of bowling balls waved Bella and Rachel into his office. As the ladies entered, he pointed a calloused, powerful hand to an officer to shut the door. "Aloha. Chief Israel Como," he started, shaking Bella's hand. "Welcome to HPD, Agent Walker. I wish it were under better circumstances. I wanted to thank you both personally for helping my team bring..."

Bella watched Chief Como pause to compose himself before he finished. "Thank you sincerely for bringing Officer Leilani down from the mountain."

"We felt obligated to get him down." Rachel sat straight and rubbed her hands together. She glanced briefly into Chief Como's eyes, then put her head down.

"Nonsense on the obligation, Rachel. Most FBI agents and HPD would have left him there and had specialists fly up to extract him. I know why you risked your neck, so cut the formality for once." Chief Como put both his massive arms on his desk and leaned in to stare with his black, obsidian eyes. His eyes seemed to see through Rachel.

"It was Perry, Israel. What was I supposed to do? No one should go out like that alone."

Bella was caught off guard by Rachel's response. It was obvious there had been some history between the late officer and the FBI agent. What that history was, Bella could only speculate.

Chief Como ran his mammoth hand across the top of his bald head. "You do the job. I know your SAC won't tell you this Rachel. And Lord knows I'm not your boss. But since I *do* care, you don't go climbing trees on the side of Haiku Trail when the victim is long dead. I gave my sergeant and his officers a serious reprimand for allowing you and Agent Walker to climb that dangerous tree—without climbing gear or anything close to a buddy system, I might add. I'm sure your boss will tan your hides, too, for being so reckless."

"Why are we here, Chief Como?" Bella had her hand against her chin in thought. She knew every word Chief Como had said had been his heart. The man appeared to care about people.

Chief Como sat straight and stood up. He walked over to a window in his office and put out his arms and hands. "This island has so much allure and beauty. But, at the same time, so much darkness and evil." He put his head and hands down then closed his eyes briefly as if in prayer. "Perry was destined for some kind of trouble out here. I've been doing this job fifteen years, and you just know the ones who are going to get hurt. But I never thought Perry would get taken out like that. It enrages me." Chief Como slammed his right fist into his left palm with a force that easily could have smashed a coconut. Or a skull.

"What kind of trouble, Israel?" Rachel was on her feet and patting his shoulder. "What did he get into that made these evil men do that to him?"

Chief Como turned to his right and looked down at Rachel. Then he glanced at Bella. "He did his job. Evil men do not like cops that do their job and uphold the law."

"Is there anything else you can tell us to help catch these scoundrels?" Bella could see the man wanted to say more. The death of Perry had crossed a line.

He looked at Bella with his shiny, black eyes that softened a minute. "You took down monsters and corruption in your own department. You, of all people, Bella Walker, know the score when you drop your guard. You get more than a crack on the chin. You would have found a kindred soul had you met Perry. He never backed down when someone broke the law. Regardless of who they were."

For a moment, Chief Como's eyes fixed on Rachel. Then he turned his head back out to the blue Hawaiian sky. "The bad rendition war god statues are distributed by a guy who runs a hotel on Big Island. Rachel… can help you with the name."

"Oh. I can?" Rachel's face went red and tightened. As Bella looked at her, she put her head down and walked out of Chief Como's office hurriedly.

"Thank you for your time, Chief Como," Bella said quickly, then turned on her heel to catch up with Rachel.

CHAPTER THIRTEEN

"**D**O YOU WANT TO TELL ME WHAT THAT WAS ALL ABOUT?" BELLA grabbed Rachel's arm and turned her around.

"You heard him. We have to set up flights for Big Island. I'm going to call the travel agent to get us over there now." Rachel pulled her arm back and went to dial her phone.

"I heard him say you know who makes these war god statues. How did you leave out that critical piece of information in our investigation? What kind of games are you playing, Rachel?" Bella pointed a finger in her face. "If you are compromised, you need to tell me and recuse yourself from this case."

Rachel walked out of the HPD building and around the corner to explain. "I told you from the start: I want you to do your job. You arrest whomever has decapitated those victims on the mountains and hanged Perry." She took a deep breath and prepared once again to call. "If you think I'm botching my own investigation to protect my family, you are dead wrong."

"Funny choice of words in a murder investigation involving compromised agents and cops. If I'm wrong, or make a mistake, I'll be as dead as Perry. I get it." Bella stormed off to cool down, then she turned to see Rachel right behind her.

"This guy that Chief Como thinks might be involved … I was following up with all my resources—my personal army you called it—to see if he's involved. I will tell you more when I know more on Big Island." She pointed to a bench and asked Bella to sit.

"Rachel, you had better not be involved. I promise you I'll throw the book at you despite our friendship." Bella leaned in and ran her hands through her red curls.

"I know."

It was three o'clock in the afternoon, and Bella needed a break. She was munching idly on a pack of cheese crackers and rubbing her eyes when Billy burst into the temporary office set up for her.

"Hey, I got a call from a bar near the last scene. Do you want me to take TJ or Agent Sue Namara and follow up on it?"

"No, I need a break from these boxes. I'll go with you." Bella stood and grabbed her purse. "But you can drive. My feet are still cramping from our hike. Please tell me we won't be mountain climbing today."

He chuckled. "In Hawaii, I can never promise that." Billy kept Bella's office door open as she walked past. Then he shut it and followed her to her cruiser.

On the drive over to the bar, Bella yawned, cracked her neck, and said, "So, tell me about this lead."

"Well, according to the proprietor of this bar—Silas Cowell, who runs The Sneaky Tiki—a group of strangers that no one recognized came into the place celebrating."

"That's not unusual, Billy. Especially in a bar."

"It's kind of suspect when you come in as they did," Billy explained. "They were celebrating on a weekday. And not just any day, mind you, Agent Walker. It was the day Perry Leilani went missing and most likely was killed. And the bartender had some pretty interesting things to say."

Bella performed one more cursory review of the previous interviews. Maybe there was something to this lead after all.

They pulled on the rusted outer door of The Sneaky Tiki, and Bella heard it creak on its worn hinges. Inside, she noted several small, round, black tables positioned for ease of movement, each surrounded by equally black, wooden chairs. The place had all the flair and pompousness of a Las Vegas-styled casino, a classy but casual motif. The Sneaky Tiki had certainly lived up to the sneaky part with its hidden away grandeur.

"Is that him?" Bella pointed to the bartender. Billy nodded that it was as they walked up to the sleek mahogany bar. A vintage jukebox just to one side was glowing with an array of rainbow colors and blasting Elvis Presley's "Trouble." The bartender winked and looked her up and down with a smile.

The smile changed when Bella smiled back and showed her badge. Then Silas saw Billy and groaned. "I already told the FBI and the cops everything I know. You guys are bad for business."

Bella began, "Well, you'll have to put up with it. Agent Walker." Bella shook her head in Billy's direction. "I know you already met with Agent Makani. But we needed a follow-up. I want to discuss with you the strangers that came in a few nights ago."

"Fine, but if I lose business from all this police harassment, I'm going to complain." He huffed under his breath and pointed to a table in the left corner of the room next to the jukebox. "These guys came in for a drink to celebrate. It was late in the evening, and the TV was on. I was getting the hot wings and fried spam fingers ready for the big game—New Zealand versus France."

Bella frowned. "What game is that?"

Silas leveled her with a deadpan look. "Rugby. Anyway, just before kickoff, they showed up laughing and cursing up a storm. Then they really started grunting and howling like in an actual huddle when the missing cop's picture was posted on the screen."

"Was this the cop?" Bella pulled out a picture of Perry Leilani. Silas nodded. "What was it that struck you as odd about them?"

Silas grabbed a Sprite and offered Bella an orange Fanta and gave Billy a Barq's root beer. "It was a group of men all dressed in bush fatigues. There were three Japanese men, a British gentleman who whined about the decline of the monarchy, and I believe an American who could have been Brad Pitt's twin. That's *Interview-with-the-Vampire* Brad Pitt and not the burned out dude in that awful movie *Babadook*."

"I do believe the awful movie was *Babylon*. Anything else you can remember?" Bella pretended to scribble in her notepad while sipping her orange-flavored drink. She nudged Billy while glancing to see if anyone in the bar was paying her any mind. No one seemed to care.

Silas put a lime in a glass and poured his Sprite into it. He toasted Bella and Billy then continued. "The men stayed to themselves, drank their drinks and then left."

"Any ideas or impression of who was in charge?" Bella knew it was a reach. If these had been the men responsible—which was starting to sound unlikely—they might all be the leader if they were hired mercenaries.

Silas nodded leaned in on his bar and took a gulp of his Sprite. "No. I'm sorry I couldn't be more helpful."

"One more question." Bella saw Silas bristle. She figured he thought he was free and clear on any more questioning. "Does anyone else come in here by themselves or with a group dressed in bush fatigues?"

"Like I said, Agent, these guys were strangers. Strangers that dress funny and don't talk to anyone go on my radar to call HPD. And if they really put off a creepy vibe, I call Rachel Gentry." Bella's stomach churned hearing Rachel's name being spouted by the less-than-reputable bartender. She'd have to follow up with Rachel again about her arrangement and dealings with Silas Cowell.

Bella finished drinking her Fanta and scanned The Sneaky Tiki one more time.

Silas is probably one of her many CIs. With an island this crooked and corrupt, you need as many eyes as you can to keep watch.

"Thanks for the drinks, Mr. Cowell." Bella and Billy turned to leave.

Silas grumbled and then coughed with his hand out. "The sodas are eight bucks a piece. It's not cheap getting them shipped to an island in the Pacific."

Bella leaned in and stared in disbelief. Then gave him a twenty. "Keep the change. If you—

Silas winked with a devilish smile, "I know the drill, Agent Walker. I've worked a long time with my... colleagues."

Bella and Billy walked out of The Sneaky Tiki without saying a word. Billy unlocked their doors and both agents climbed in. Bella shook her head and slapped the interior of the car's armrest. Billy gave her a side glance.

"Do you want to talk about it, Agent Walker?"

He turned on the radio and the song "Tiny Bubbles" was in midchorus. Billy tightened his lips angrily and shut it off immediately.

"FBI special agent, or CIA operative running traffic or a sting?" Bella looked over at Billy who gave a half smile and rubbed his left temple.

"In Hawaii, take your pick. Silas was taking it easy on you." Billy rubbed his chin and massaged the left side of his neck remembering something. "When Rachel sent me out to 'interrogate' him for the first time a year ago, he wasn't as friendly. The guy can take a punch, I'll tell you that much."

"So, was this a waste of time? Is she having me run in circles chasing my tail to show off?" Bella hadn't wanted to let on to what was transpiring between them. Telling Rachel's partner that there was trouble between them was sure to kick off another argument with Rachel soon. Which was fine with Bella. She'd had more than enough of this case.

Billy took a breath and sighed. "No, it wasn't a waste of time, Ag—"

"Bella. You call me Bella. You earned it with what you've dealt with over the last couple of years," Bella interrupted.

Billy had made it back to FBI HQ and went to park. He cut the engine, but before he got out, he turned and spoke softly. "Bella, she wants to catch whoever this is. Agent Gentry knows more than she's letting on for a reason. But she always does the right thing, even if it costs her everything. If she hasn't told you something—from my experience—it's because she wants to protect you and keep you safe."

"Safe from what, Billy?" Bella frowned and processed what he was saying.

Climbing out of the car, both agents headed back inside. Billy paused, and Bella turned and glanced. He seemed he wanted to say more, so Bella hand gestured for him to do so. "Like I said, take your pick. We got the local gangs who have their ruthlessness. I found that out as a poor kid growing up near Kenai. I fought one group of thugs for refusing to join their gang. Even bested and beat their leader and made him swear to never come back selling drugs to my village. In retaliation, they burnt my family's home to the ground. My grandma was inside."

Bella gasped. "I'm sorry. That's awful."

He shrugged as if it didn't bother him anymore. "I wanted revenge for the man that had killed my Nana. I was twelve, you see. My grandma was my world. I joined a more ruthless outfit and squared. But I absolutely hated myself after. At the lowest point of my life, I fell back to my village's religion—God, and I swore to leave that feared gang—the Yakuza. But once you are blood-bound to them, you never leave. So, I joined the greatest gang of them all and arrested the people who would have done a lot worse to my family, my peaceful village, and my beautiful island. I joined the FBI."

"Dear lord!" Bella's head swirled as she became dizzy. That feeling of impending doom that she'd had during the Harbinger assault was back. She tried to focus, but her thoughts scattered at endless perilous possibilities. What Billy Makani had just revealed in an earnest attempt to explain why he had joined the FBI was damning for the agent. He had been a member of an international terrorist organization known for countless atrocities—Yakuza!

How many of these criminals were inside the Hawaiian FBI? How would Bella deal with such a nefarious organization known for its international surveillance, trafficking, drug rings, and murder—a gang so evil and vile that they forced self-mutilation or suicide when a member fell out of line?

"Billy, you, me, SAC Harris, and Rachel have to talk."

"Hey, folks!" Rachel walked up with a smile on her face and showed everyone's flights on her phone. "Are we ready to head to Big Island?"

CHAPTER FOURTEEN

"**H**E DISCLOSED HIS TROUBLED YOUTH WITH THE SCREENING office, Bella. The selection board for the Academy also vetted him. What more do you want me to say?" Rachel leaned back in her leather chair.

Bella glanced down the hall where Billy sat with his elbows on his knees and his head down. "Explain to me how he managed to get a cushy job in Hawaii—his home state I might add—when agents usually are assigned to different locations around the country. Besides you, he's the only other exception I've come across."

"It's obvious my family has strong affiliations with the FBI, Bella. Sorry that we don't all excel at everything and have to use the gifts we have been given." Rachel pushed back her chair from her desk and stood up. "Billy has lived a life neither of us could ever understand. He scored tremendous marks in all his training. If he wasn't Hawaiian, and knew every culture religion, every locale better than any Google search or map, I'm sure they would have assigned him somewhere else. He has been an invaluable resource. Besides, Agent Walker of the *Colorado* field office, he's *my* problem. Not yours."

"If my new theory pans out, he'll definitely be our problem." Bella stood to leave. "I'm thinking after the Big Island follow-up, I'll head out. You seem to work things differently than I'm used to."

"You're leaving over Billy Makani?" Rachel crossed her arms and angled her.

Bella unloaded her misgivings and didn't pull any punches. "It's everything, Rachel. From squaring-off today with your little friend at The Sneaky Tiki to this agent with a checkered past. Then there's your daddy's involvement in the smuggling and how it aff—"

"Now, hold on. You crossed a line there. My dad runs a hotel chain with fine antiques. He runs the largest coffee plantation in all of the Hawaiian islands. He doesn't need to smuggle." Rachel walked over to Bella, her face a mask of rage. "Even for you, that was too far."

Bella held her ground. She'd faced killers before. She wouldn't back down now. "Did I hurt your feelings, Agent Gentry? My apologies for trying to keep you out of a massive FBI scandal and possible jail. The bugs were one way to undermine your leadership. Buying artifacts on the Hawaiian black market will really charm the brass at the inquiry."

Rachel whispered back seething in an icy rage. "You fool. You are too damn determined to see the worst of any situation and too regimented and by the book to see the old tactics they taught us don't work in an unconventional setting like… Hawaii." She pinned Bella with a steely gaze. "You can't recognize that I set up an outside sting, risking my father's life, to stop these smugglers."

Bella felt the size six shoe on her foot lodged into her mouth. She had no place to hide, and she dared not drop her head in shame. "Rachel, I'm—"

"Shut up, Bella. Not another apology, not another condescending word. If you want to go back to Colorado, you just go now. I don't need your antagonism anymore. You'd swear that we were competing like the childish fools we were in Quantico."

"You're the one who saw fit to dig around in my personal life," Bella fired back. "You call me here for help and then immediately drop that on me?"

"That was because I was worried about you, Bella. Because you haven't been yourself, and you know it. And I need your help."

Bella didn't know what to say, so she said nothing.

"This isn't a game, Agent Walker. If we screw this up, people I love will die!"

With that, she stormed out of her office and left Bella standing there in silence.

A slight knock on the door brought her out of her thoughts. "Everything okay?"

She looked up to see TJ standing there with a concerned look on his face. "I'm fine. It's just been a long afternoon," she admitted.

He nodded slowly. "The boss can get downright brutal. We've all been there when she rips us a new one for being a fool."

Bella chuckled silently. "I guess now I know how it feels. See you in a few hours."

He nodded, and Bella walked out to her car to drive off and head to the bungalow. It wouldn't take her too long to pack an overnight bag ... if Rachel still needed her help.

On the drive to Nimitz Beach, she thought about calling Rachel. Then decided against it. Rachel needed a little time to cool off. Maybe by the time Bella had everything ready, she'd call to apologize and get back to the case.

She sat for a long time in the car, ruminating on everything that had happened. This had been the last thing she'd wanted to happen when visiting her old friend. Sure, they'd had a friendly competition back at the Academy, but that was all it had ever been—friendly. Or so she'd thought.

She sighed and leaned her head against the window, watching the beautiful, orange sun playing against the sparkling waters.

I suppose this island has some way of revealing the truths we'd rather keep hidden.

She finally cut the engine and got out of the car. Suddenly, she heard a sound from inside the bungalow. Like someone had opened and then closed one of the doors.

Her heart immediately leaped to her throat, and she put her hand on her weapon. Somebody was inside the supposedly secure bungalow. Her mind raced with theories: Was this Rachel, coming to put another crazy twist or turn in their relationship? Was it Billy, about to confront her for her distrust of his past? Or was this something more nefarious: A killer coming to squash the case and leave her strung up just like Perry Leilani?

She forced the thoughts away, held her gun out in front of her, and slowly climbed the steps. Footsteps came from inside, confirming Bella's fear that there was definitely someone inside. As quietly as she could, she slipped the key into the lock and clicked it open. With one hand on the doorknob and the other on her gun, she rushed in and thrust it in front of her.

"FBI! Freeze or I *will* shoot!" she bellowed into the darkness ...

…only to see a shirtless man with a towel wrapped around his waist standing in the kitchen, halfway through a peanut butter and jelly sandwich.

"Hey, Bella," he said through a thick bite of peanut butter and with a wave of his fingers.

She lowered her gun and pinched the bridge of her nose. "Put a shirt on, Justin. And you need to quit doing that!"

Justin Trestle laughed heartily, his voice carrying all the calmness of a North Shore surfer. "Sorry. Nice pool, by the way."

———•———

"So let me get this straight, Billy Makani is Yakuza?" Justin asked. After the adrenaline had worn off and Bella had thoroughly admonished him, she finally sat down for dinner with him at the kitchen table.

"He was when he was sixteen."

Justin wiped his mouth thoughtfully. "They don't just let you out of the Yakuza. It's not a frat party or your average gang." He moved from the table and placed his paper plate into the trash can near the fridge. "More like a trained mercenary group that's been around a thousand years. Relentless, unmerciful, and masters of espionage."

Justin grabbed a bottle of water from the fridge and gave a smirk. "Now that's a stocked fridge, Bella. Rachel surely spared no expense. When are we throwing the luau, or as I like to call it, the Big Kahuna Kalua Party?"

"In your dreams, Big Kahuna." Bella also moved from the table and placed her paper plate into the garbage. Then she swatted Justin on the back of the head. "You are a mature and responsible business owner these days, may I remind you. Whose taxes, after years of international misadventure, were finally straightened out by me."

"Point taken. I shall refrain from the devilish behavior that has so often soured my soul and my relationships." Justin rolled his eyes with a fake frown.

"Exactly, Mr. Trestle. Until you show me that you will stay responsible, we are staying the best of friends. You dig, mister?"

He chuckled. "I will abide by the terms of our friendship, Ms. Walker. But I must protest to the responsibility and chastity that you have had me endure for, what is it now, four years?" Bella narrowed her eyes, and the action was enough to cause Justin to put his hands up. "I call a truce. We seem to have more perilous adventures ahead, from what you told me."

Bella followed his glance to see Rachel's vehicle driving up with Billy Makani in the back seat on the driver's side. His face and eyes registered concern. TJ O'Reilly was in the back seat on the passenger's side, but he seemed calm and excited about the trip. A third agent, most likely Susan Namara, waved nervously to Bella as Rachel parked.

Justin had moved out of view into the shadows next to Bella. "Just like old times, Bella. I stay out of sight and out of the FBI's mind. Especially with this clown show. Agent Makani looks like he carries the weight of the world on his shoulders. You drove a pile driver into that brain of his for sure." Bella could feel the warmth of Justin's voice as he whispered, "You be careful, okay?"

"Are you sure you don't want to tag along in the shadows and protect me?" Bella smiled and saw Justin's shadow had already moved out the back sliding door. "I hate when you do that too!"

But he'd already sent her a text.

Justin: If he's sincere about getting out of that nest of vipers, the FBI would be damn fools to not have enlisted him and kept Billy Makani in Hawaii.

Justin: Keep an eye on him and Rachel for sure though. Those deaths you mentioned… both Hawaiian agents should have recognized the who.

The team arrived barely thirty minutes before the flight. The check-in and security checks went smoothly for the FBI investigators, naturally. As they moved single file and boarded the plane, Bella couldn't help but hope Justin would be fine.

Just before she turned off her phone for the flight, she fired off a text in response.

Bella: You better stay low-key and not draw any attention to yourself. I know you want to wrap this one up quickly, but it may take a little longer than we planned, knucklehead.

Rachel, sitting in the seat next to her, leaned back and was about to take a nap when she opened her right eye. "This businessman you'll meet has been a friend of my father's for fifty years, Bella. When we meet with him, keep that in perspective. Many players are not going to be happy when we take him and others off the board."

"And you are going after this particular antiquities and artifact smuggler for the greater good of all Hawaii?" Bella looked out the window as the plane began to gain speed and depart.

"Now you get what I've been saying." Rachel closed her eyes and smiled.

THE GIRL IN PARADISE

Bella rubbed her right temple and pushed back a curl. "Why do I get the feeling we'll be capturing one devil, only to have another more ruthless take his place?" she murmured while staring out at the vastness of the blue ocean.

The view as the sun set was spectacular. The ocean glimmered like molten gold, and the islands shone like bright emerald jewels against the endless expanse of sea. The waves seemed like pearl ripples shimmering below the golden rays. All of it was so beautiful and captivated her with a sense of wonder.

But then she recalled the dark side of those verdant islands and shimmering waves: decapitated bodies left as tributes to the Hawaiian war gods. She recalled, as she massaged her cramping legs, pulling down a murdered police officer from a twisted windblown tree. His only crime was doing his job to protect and serve the Hawaiian community. His reward was to be mercilessly hung on The Stairway to Heaven atop haunted mountains.

The mountains, with their vast histories of violence and death, surely carried vengeful wraiths and all manner of phantoms pleading for justice—a justice that Bella and her team desperately needed to deliver to bring peace to their innocent, tormented souls.

Barely forty-five minutes after they'd taken off, they cruised in for an uneventful landing. Bella's anticipation was at a fever pitch to move forward and start their investigation. But while her spirit to track down the murderers was strong, her body, beaten down by grueling hikes and climbs, needed rest. She took a long stretch to relieve the muscle cramps in her legs and feet before climbing out of the plane.

"You still stiff from Haiku Stairs, huh?" Rachel winked as she grabbed her luggage from the overhead plane bin. She grabbed Bella's small jump bag as well. "I'll give you the fish oil gel capsules and get you a tub of coconut oil. You'll be running twenty miles after taking those."

"I hope so. I'm thinking this is all part of the acclimatization to the altitudes though." Bella winced and grabbed her bag from Rachel while exiting the plane.

TJ was waiting for them with his rolling suitcase at the gate. He'd gotten off the plane first and headed straight for the rental car desk. "You called for the cars, Agent Gentry? The guy at the desk said no one from the FBI travel service had called."

"Travel arrangements have been met, Agent O'Reilly. Follow me, folks." Rachel led Bella and everyone out the front door of the Kona

Airport to a stretch limousine. A chauffeur was standing beside a passenger door toward the back of the limo.

"It's a pleasure to have you home, Mrs. Gentry," said the driver, a tall, bronze-skinned man in his fifties with powdery white hair. He was dressed to the nines in a well-tailored suit, and his voice was soft and musical. His features—jaw, chin, and brow—seemed chiseled out of iron rock. He politely tipped his hat and opened the door for Rachel. "Will you be meeting up with Mr. Gentry this evening?"

"It's great to see you, Arthur," Rachel smiled. She turned to Bella and the team, who were all in shock, and motioned them into the limousine. "Why, yes, I shall see my beloved. I know Shane has missed me dearly."

"Where should we place your colleagues?" Arthur turned his eyes toward Bella, Billy, TJ, and Susan. "Might I suggest Saul's place again?"

"That would be splendid, my dear friend. Splendid indeed." Bella shook her head at all of Rachel's posturing and formality. She had never seen Rachel in her aristocratic world. Bella was finding all of it quite intriguing. "Did you bring all of Father's literature on Hawaiian lore for Agent Walker?"

"Of course, ma'am. We have the books inside next to her glass of sparkling water, coconut oil, and fish oil capsules," Arthur announced as he closed the door to the limousine and returned to the driver's seat.

Bella smirked at Rachel as she dropped the fish oil and coconut capsule into her glass of sparkling water. "Thank you. I feel so much better now."

"The masseuse will meet with you an hour after you check in. After one of those brutal realignment sessions, you may hate me. But you'll be a brand-new agent ready to go." Rachel nodded and took a sip of her own sparkling water.

Billy, who had been sulking and quiet most of the trip, tapped Rachel's leg. "What exactly is Saul's place, Agent Gentry?"

Rachel stared into each agent's eyes. "On Kona Island, Billy and team, you can call me Rachel around my folks and the hotel. When we are on assignment, we are all FBI agents again. We've been going through a lot. I figured we needed a little team building while out on this assignment." That seemed to placate the crowd, and they relaxed a little. "Any questions before I drop you off at The Flamed Heart Resort?"

Bella had one question she needed to get out to the team in this moment when everyone was about to let their guards down. It had been a nagging question she had gone over and over since talking with Justin.

As Arthur slowed the limousine to a stall, Bella launched it. "I have one question."

Billy rolled his eyes. Rachel said, "Oh boy." Susan Namara seemed puzzled and wide-eyed. But TJ rubbed his chin in intrigue.

"Go ahead, Bella. Proceed with caution," Rachel told her.

As Arthur opened the door to let Bella and the team out, Bella climbed out and stood looking at each of them, trying to figure out which one of her colleagues might possibly be working for a killer. "When were you folks going to tell me that these decapitations were a Yakuza hit?"

CHAPTER FIFTEEN

THE FLAMED HEART RESORT STOOD TOWERING AND AGELESS before them. Bella marveled at the immense doors and lava rock threshold that had been polished to the fineness of mirrored glass. She couldn't help but stare in wonder at the nostalgic grandeur of the place.

Established on Kona before Hawaii had even become a state, the décor seemed to transcend time. From its intricately carved wooden Hawaiian scenes to the lavish paintings and tapestry depicting early life on the island, all held their own charms and mysteries with each viewing. Even the very floors held a hidden mystique from the countless wanderers in and out of the resort doors.

From what she caught in her glances of the pictures at the front desk and throughout her walk to her room, the resort still hosted everyone from billionaires to celebrities in various fields of sports and entertainment. There had even been several television and movies filmed on the lush tropical grounds and inviting pools with patrons hugging or holding hands with the likes of Tom Selleck and Elvis Presley. The latter picture

THE GIRL IN PARADISE

reminded Bella of her dad's horrible rendition of "Suspicious Minds" with his over-the-top flipped shirt collar.

"Well, I'll leave you to your own devices, Bella." Rachel hadn't said a word since Bella had name-dropped the Yakuza as suspects. Bella figured she couldn't say much—not that Bella would believe it. Therefore, after this round of interviews and investigation, Bella resolved that she and Justin were bouncing out of this mess of a case.

"Thank you, Rachel. I'll go over the lore of the war god stuff anyway." Bella couldn't resist sarcastically kicking up that particular waste of time at her. "I know it was a useless lead—"

"Look, you don't know the score pushing there." Rachel looked at her sternly then turned to gaze out at a cascading waterfall. Both watched the falling water running alongside the resort and into the sea. "The Yakuza's reach into the community, politics, and law enforcement is immense, Bella. You scorch-earth one of these viper's nests, two more rise out of the jungle to strike."

Bella shrugged her shoulders, grimaced, and put her head down as she slowly pulled her suitcase to her room. "I guess we do like the veteran FBI agents used to do: we investigate and fill out the forms, then stick our heads in the sand and enjoy our lives in paradise. Ignorance is bliss, right?"

"That's not fair, Bella. I'm not ignoring the issues and neither is our team. We just need to be cautious about our ways. These killers don't just go after the person that crosses them. Like the cartels, they instill absolute fear. They kill off families. Kids. And pesky agents too." Rachel walked up to explain just as Bella pressed the elevator button to ascend to her room. "We'll talk about all of this up at the plantation when I get a minute. Far away from the team, okay?"

"Sounds good to me, Agent Gentry." Bella was keeping it icy and formal. Rachel, with all her misdirection and schemes, had earned that much. Bella would have a full-scale probe launched at the end of this wacky case; that was becoming more of a certainty.

All the drama of the last few days was finally catching up to Bella. She had taken a moment to pull herself out of the case and look around the joyous mood surrounding the resort. Yes, Bella regaled in the smiles and the exuberance of the place. She noted the laughter of patrons caught up in the moments of pure delight on the elevators as they dove and frolicked in the pool below, and the intimacy of couples headed to and from their rooms.

But now, in the silence of her room, watching the bright moon sending glimmering light over the ocean, hearing the tumultuous sounds of crashing waves against the black crags of the shore, she felt just as chaotic. Her thoughts were swirling, moving, rising, falling… only to repeat all over again.

She went and sat at a small desk near the balcony window to start checking out the books on Hawaiian folklore Rachel had given her. She put a closed fist to her temple and rested her head against it as she went over the lore again of Ku, the trickster, the first of the primary war gods.

Billy had enlightened her to the fact that there were actually thousands of gods called *akua* and just as many war deities. Now that the case had become that much more complex, she almost felt like she was wasting time. But maybe she would get a better understanding of the message being sent by the murders.

She yawned and blinked heavily to keep her eyes open while studying all the stories of Ku, Kanaloa, Kane, and Lono. It was interesting, sure, but she didn't know what to make of any of it. She wasn't sure how relevant any of this was to the case.

But then an answer started to form. She checked fluctuating auction prices for stolen Hawaiian art pieces and artifacts, remembering Rachel's carefree attitude toward the black market trade of artifacts. It seemed as common as buying a pound of coffee for a businessman or any hopeful entrepreneur to secure these items. And there was the legal trade just ripe for a crime syndicate—an organization that trafficked in slavery, guns, drugs, and even tech. Artifact stealing and selling to the highest bidder was too lucrative for the Yakuza to pass up. So, now the only question was, who was their broker or middleman? Who was the guy cleaning up the sales for all these private auctions?

Bella turned off her lamp and grabbed a bottle of sparkling water from the room's fridge. She twisted it open with a crack and raised the bottle, thankful for the refreshing taste. She turned with the bottle in hand and went out to the balcony to stare at the moonlit, rolling seas, wondering where Justin might be on Oahu. And more importantly, what skeletons had he discovered in the closet of each of the Hawaiian FBI agents. And most importantly for everyone's safety, who had the Yakuza compromised and how?

Bella heard a resounding knock at her resort room door that broke her train of thought. A second knock had her saying, "Just a minute."

She squinted with her left eye through the door's peephole and was surprised to see TJ in a brilliantly blue Hawaiian shirt. The flamboyant attire was adorned with hibiscus and parrot printing that almost blinded Bella with its colors. She glanced down at her watch. It was nearly eight o'clock. Not necessarily too late for a visitor—especially a colleague—but not exactly early either.

"TJ, it's almost eight," she grumbled through the door. "We have a big day tomorrow. What's so important that you aren't resting?"

"I found some stuff you need to look at," he told her. "It's some invoices and sales receipts. Can we go over them downstairs at the bar? I'll wait for you down there." He cracked a smile. "Anything in particular you want to drink from the Squeaky Tiki?"

"Is that really the name of the bar?" Bella shook her head. "I'll have a sparkling water with a twist of lime. And you, Agent, will have the same. No benders or drinks while on assignment."

"You got it. I'll be as pure as an altar boy. Can you see my angelic halo through the peephole?" TJ smiled broadly and made a mocking halo with his hands over his flowing brown hair then did a comedic turn.

"I see your halo alright, TJ," she chuckled. "It's supported by your devilish horns, mister."

She finally opened the door to follow TJ down to the lobby. He was just turning a corner when, out of nowhere, he was hit by a phantom hand that seemed to come out of the shadows. Then the same two hands leaned over apologetically and picked the man up as if he were a feather twisting in the wind. Bella was stunned at the force of the man that had leveled the tall and athletic agent.

"My apologies, sir. I was running down to get my kid a Mauna Loa candy bar," said the man, whose face she couldn't see as it was obscured by a red hoodie.

TJ was a little bemused but gathered himself. "Oh, you're good, man. Sorry about that."

The man nodded and headed off in the other direction. Bella followed his retreat with her gaze. She was pretty sure the man was not going to get his kid a candy bar. But there was a certainty in her mind that the powerful hands and frame of the gentleman who toppled the oak that was TJ O'Reilly did have a familiarity to them. His bad British accent pretty much gave his identity away.

So Justin had made it to the Big Island. Good to know.

As Bella approached, she could see that he was obviously troubled by something. "Well? Out with it."

He sighed, then looked out over the pool. "This is bad, Bella. And I already know you're on the fence about leaving the case."

Bella touched the tall man's gripped right forearm to chide him to talk. "Whether I leave or not, remains to be seen. I never quit an assignment if it makes you feel any better. Rachel should've told you that. I might posture and scream as I go. But if I leave a case, it's because I got tossed off it by the upper brass. Sometimes the greater good of the FBI conflicts with the actual truth. And with many of my investigations I discover embarrassing things the Bureau usually doesn't want to leak out. Regardless of their archaic guidelines, I always endeavor to find the truth. Even if management pulls my leash off the case."

"But what do we do now?" TJ put his head down.

She said the only logical thing. "It's simple enough, TJ. We bring the evidence you have to Rachel and go from there as a team."

"That's the thing. The evidence *involves* Rachel. Well, actually it involves her parents, Rita and Morris Stein."

Somehow, Bella wasn't surprised at that, and she nodded for him to continue.

"I found purchasing receipts from one of his companies for Hawaiian artifacts. Coincidentally or not, with the names of several of the decapitated victims involved in each transaction as a sort of trust." Bella could almost hear Agent O'Reilly gulp in disgust at having to tell her. Then he put his head down, sulking in shame.

"Well, don't that beat all," she replied. So, this was what Rachel had been keeping from her. But what was the angle with the Yakuza? That was the real question. Did Rachel possibly know the man leading this group of killers?

"Regardless of how this goes down, TJ, per protocol, you have to let the lead agent know your findings." Bella closed the file TJ had shown her. Then she had him put the computer drives of digital evidence into her hands as well. The feel of them was rigid and cold as she secured them. "Where did you have these stored, in a frozen meat locker? Wait here one minute while I call her. Go ahead and get Billy and Sue here too. I want everything above board."

An hour later, a groggy Rachel walked up with a tall, handsome man who could have been the very image of a young Clint Eastwood. His glowing blue eyes seemed to exude an unswaying force locked in on Rachel's eyes. The two held all the adoration toward each other of a newlywed couple. Rachel leaned in and whispered something to the cowboy just as he leaned down to listen and smiled. Then the couple walked up to the gathered agents. Rachel's eyes narrowed on each of them curiously. Bella could only imagine what Rachel was thinking in the moment.

"Before we begin, Bella, this is Shane Gentry of the Saddle-Sore Ranch. Shane, this is the woman who stood us up at our wedding." Bella's face went flush with embarrassment.

"Pleasure to meet you, Bella. I heard that you would've probably preferred Battle Ax's wedding to what you went through." Shane gave Bella the friendliest and most welcoming of grins. Bella was sure he'd get all of Rachel's wrath later for that comment.

"You aren't whistling Dixie there. That one took the wind out of me." And Bella meant every word. Especially when her lung had been punctured in the final takedown of the villain. "My apologies to both of you." Bella glanced to the side and saw Billy and Susan nod while she talked with Shane. But curiously, TJ seemed to bite his cheek and wince.

"I'll be by the pool, Rachel. Pleasure to meet you, Bella." He leaned in and gave Rachel a kiss on her cheek. "Let me know when we can leave."

Rachel nodded, then walked over to the large table in the corner of the hotel's beach viewing area where everyone was gathered. She sat down and looked at each agent again carefully. "Out with it. What's the new information you found?"

To keep Rachel's rage in check, for she knew this behind-her-back tactic by TJ would infuriate and possibly leave her a little out of sorts, Bella began carefully. "We've been reviewing some financial documents related to the case."

"And?"

"We found invoices linked to Morris and Rita Stein." With her head turned away from the rest of the team to address Rachel, Bella winked with her right eye. "They have the names of the victims on sales of artifacts to one of his businesses."

Rachel nodded to Bella's wink and furrowed her brow. "That's troubling. Team, we will have to investigate this lead. I will recuse myself from the interview and that part of the investigation. Anything—"

"You need to bow out altogether, you know," Billy cut in. "You could be compromised, Agent Gentry." Then he lifted his eyes and turned his head and said a phrase that puzzled Bella at the time. "*Alae'ula kaikua'ana.*"

Bella made a note of Billy's words. She'd follow up on the meaning later.

"Agent Makani, your objections will be taken into consideration. I know we were sending you and TJ out to interview the witnesses near Pololu Valley. But in light of this new evidence, I'll follow up with TJ." Rachel turned to Bella. "Since you are the senior investigator—though with everything that has occurred, not my first choice—I'll have you and Billy go to Stein Plantation. Susan, you back—"

"I thought Billy and I were the team, Agent Gentry," TJ interrupted. It was very uncharacteristic of his easy-going personality. "You're punishing me because you know I found the invoices."

Rachel, obviously taken aback, leaned forward with a steel stare. "That's not the case, Agent O'Reilly. In fact, I was just going to promote you to junior lead. In your new promotion, you'll be going with me to Pololu Valley. We have some witnesses near the beach. Bring bug spray, good boots, and plenty of water for our hike tomorrow."

"Bella, you can see that I'm being punished, right?" TJ pushed his chair back angrily as Rachel remained cool.

"I'll follow up with you later, TJ," Bella said.

Rachel put her hands together, then looked up with an emotionless stare. "Do you have anything else you'd like to say, Agent O'Reilly? It's not too late to get another agent out here."

"No, ma'am." TJ sighed and sat back down with his gaze straight ahead. "My apologies for my disappointment and anger." He took a deep breath and slowly let it out. "For the greater good of the Bureau."

"Exactly, Agent. That's the spirit." Rachel nodded at each of them and then stood. She went to turn away and walk out to her husband. But for just a moment, Rachel paused and glanced back. "Does anyone have anything else?"

No one at the table looked up or said a word. Bella rubbed her temples and thought, *that will be an interesting ride tomorrow with a guy whose career I tried to end. Equally puzzling is why Rachel tolerates TJ's outburst in front of the team. Anyone else, including me, would've written him up and sent him home. It's certainly curious. We had better check up on him later.*

Not long after the meeting, Bella found Billy and TJ in the elegant oyster restaurant. Hearing laughter between them, she spied the two eating the largest oyster platters she had ever seen. There were several empty glasses by TJ's plate as well, almost as if he'd ordered three or four drinks at once so he wouldn't have to bother going up to the bar for them. "Good evening, gentlemen."

Billy's face tightened as he put down his fork. "Good evening, Agent Walker."

TJ's mood seemed more jovial and festive despite his earlier encounter with Rachel. The alcohol had certainly helped. He stabbed his fork into a thick, gelatinous oyster and offered one to Bella. "Have a seat. You should order this oyster plate. They really know how to fry 'em around here."

Bella smiled radiantly. She was really trying to turn on the charm and ease the tension between the team. "If I were a fan of oysters, I'd most certainly eat a few. I'm more of a gumbo gal though. What about you, Billy?"

"I think I lost my appetite, Agent Walker." Billy pushed back and left money on the table for TJ to pay for his meal. "I'll see you in the morning. We have to go interview and possibly interrogate one of the wealthiest men on the Hawaiian Islands."

"I remember," she replied, trying to lighten the mood, but Billy walked off without so much as a smile.

"Guess we should hit the hay, huh?" she asked TJ, suddenly feeling very tired.

"Well, someone's got to take care of Billy's plate," TJ said, already leaning forward to inspect the leftovers. "And besides. Wouldn't you prefer to hang out a bit?" he asked.

There was a glint in his eye and a crooked grin on his face that could only mean one thing. And he was even so bold as to place his hand on Bella's thigh. "Accidentally," she was sure.

The thought of sliding deep-fried oysters down her gullet at this hour made Bella feel sick—and his hand on her thigh nearly made her lash out in rage right then and there. She scooched away from him, letting his hand slip into the air, and smiled diplomatically. "You get on that. I guess I'll head back to the room."

"Suit yourself," he said through a mouthful of batter.

CHAPTER SIXTEEN

B ACK IN HER ROOM, BELLA THOROUGHLY REVIEWED THE NEW information TJ had provided and tried to square it with the puzzle that was still hazily forming. Their only lead had been the procurement of the war god relics at the sites, and that was pretty much a direct line of evidence leading straight to Rita and Morris Stein.

Bella groaned and looked out the window at the rolling seas. So many questions on top of questions. How did the Steins factor into this, anyway? Were they connected to the Yakuza? A family with that kind of money wouldn't be trading in small-time stolen goods unless there was a reason. Some debt owed? Some type of contract with the Yakuza that he had to follow or they'd kill him?

Bella shook her head. That wouldn't be enough to scare a man like Morris Stein. Or a threat to his family? That might do it. And it might explain why Rachel had been so eager to bring her here in the first place, when the two had clearly not been on the best of terms.

She lay down, but her racing thoughts wouldn't let up. She closed her eyes and took deep breaths for what felt like a few hours—and groaned when she glanced at the clock and found that only fifteen minutes had passed. What little she did sleep had her tossing and turning fitfully, and then, as the clock passed midnight, she got up with a rage and screamed.

Something ominous was coming. She could feel it twisting up through her stomach and choking out her lungs, just as she had felt it the night when everything went sideways during The Harbinger take-down. She was missing something big, and when it erupted, she would be just as helpless as before. The growing dread this round, however, was focused on Rachel Gentry. Something was wrong with Rachel and her family. Could it have been a growing, subconscious feeling predicated by all the wacky angles of this case? Was Bella projecting her own previous failures from the Harbinger or Blue-Eyed Banshee cases?

Maybe it was both.

She got up and got a drink of water. As the cool water refreshed her mind and palate, she walked out on the balcony to clear her troubled head. The case, with all its theatrics and logistical challenges, was wearing her down.

She'd barely been out there for a couple minutes when her cell phone buzzed. It wasn't a good omen when that happened this late at night, especially while Bella and her team were working on an active case. "Agent Walker."

"Sorry to wake you, Agent Walker. I'm Officer Ted Gamora. We were given this number by one of your agents. I believe an Agent Makani." Bella was already not liking where this was going.

"Go on, Officer Gamora." She paused to get out her pen and a note-pad to jot down information, then moved to her closet in haste. She'd need her field clothes for wherever they were going. Most likely to investigate the latest homicide, if their luck was anything to go by.

"Well, Agent Gentry was supposed to meet with me and my part-ner a couple of hours ago. But she never showed for our meeting. If this was any other agent, I'd expect them to cancel especially just landing on Kona. But Rachel Gentry never cancels on us. She always shows up."

A meeting at this hour? Bella kept her voice as calm as she could as the ruminations flew through her mind. "I'll follow up with my team, and we will get back to you."

"That sounds good, Agent Walker. Call us if you need anything." Bella got a shiver up her spine. Where could Rachel be? Why would she have met with Kona PD at such a late hour, anyway?

Bella called Rachel's phone first, but it just went straight to voice mail and nothing more. Bella left a message, but her dread began to grow. Rachel was usually pretty good about picking up. But if she were on a case, or up in the mountains, the phone might not be picking up.

She didn't have Shane's number to follow up. But she did have Rachel's residence at the plantation. Hopefully, her call wouldn't cause a stir. The phone rang twice, and a gruff male voice—most like one of the many security screeners—answered. "Stein Coffee."

"This is Agent Walker with the FBI. I'm trying to locate Rachel." Bella could hear papers shuffling in the background and the man sipping his coffee before answering.

"Usually when she's in town, Agent Walker, she's with her husband." There was a pause on the phone as the guard must have been going over his logbook. "She has two meetings tonight. One she called in and canceled with Kona Police Department. Wow, she never cancels any of her appointments. It's a curious one, I tell you."

Bella, getting frustrated with the security technician vented, "Look, we got a call from KPD. She didn't call in, or no one told Officer Gamora. They called us."

The security guard kept calm and seemed to be tapping on a computer. He agreed with Bella. "I can see where being woken up in the middle of the night can be tiresome, Agent Walker."

You aren't only a consummate professional, young man. You must be moonlighting as a comedian, Bella wanted to say, but bit her tongue.

"Where's the other meeting that she went to?" Bella stubbed her toe on the corner of the couch as she tried to dress. She stifled a scream in pain.

Bella could hear the man again flipping through pages and typing on the computer. "It's cryptic, but here goes. It says S.M. RSVP S.T." The security professional grumbled, "I'm going to have to reprimand my guy on this, Agent Walker. We tell them all the time to write out the meetings with no shorthand."

"Well, thank you, anyway. I'd advise Shane if I were you," Bella warned. Then she heard the man groan and hung up the phone.

Armed basically with nothing, Bella knew she had to wake up her people for a search. Bella shook her head angrily and started calling the team.

She sighed and called Billy first. She heard him hit his head on something. Or possibly he'd hit the alarm clock. "Bella, it's one in the morning. What gives?"

"Rachel was supposed to meet with Kona PD two hours ago. She never showed, and now we can't contact her and don't know where she is." Bella was flat and calm. She knew the ramifications of getting too emotional. If she rattled Billy, he'd certainly fly into a fury to find her. "Any ideas where she'd be?"

"She should be with Shane at the plantation."

"Already tried that. They don't know where she is either."

Billy yawned, and Bella could hear him fumbling to get dressed. "But she called this meeting with KPD. It was to follow up on some witnesses that she's keeping close to the chest," he explained.

"If she were to meet with someone, where's her usual meeting place?" Bella was already heading out the door awaiting Billy's answer to begin her search.

Bella could hear the door opening to his room. She couldn't believe he'd gotten ready that quickly. "She usually meets them at the restaurant. But it's closed now, along with the viewing corner, her second place to gather people. Maybe… the lounge. Even when they should be closed, it manages to stay open for Rachel."

It took three calls for TJ to pick up, and when he did she could practically smell the alcohol wafting off him all the way through the phone.

"Meet us downstairs, TJ," Bella told him.

"You—huh?" he slurred. Somewhere in the background, she heard a squawking, almost as if someone else was in the room talking to TJ. She couldn't quite make it out, but it sounded like a woman's voice.

She sighed. "Sleep it off, TJ. We'll convene in the morning."

She would have to talk with TJ about getting drunk and picking up women while they had a job to do. She was glad she hadn't stayed out at the bar with him or who knows how they might have ended up?

Susan Namara picked up her phone on the first ring, and after being told the situation, she said, "Yes, Agent Walker, oh no. Do we have any idea where she could be?" Bella advised her to meet them down at The Squeaky Tiki. "That's a horrible name for a resort bar."

"That's what I've been saying," Bella grumbled.

For some reason, Bella looked over the cryptic message in her notepad for Rachel's other meeting. Obviously, she knew what RSVP meant. That was the French phrase *repondez s'il vous plaît*, or *reply, if it pleases you*. But the S.M. and the S.T. could be anything. A location? Not like that could have helped. It could be anywhere from a mountain to a resort or any one of the Stein and Gentry ventures on Kona. Was the meeting relevant to the case? How could Bella possibly even know that information?

But what she did know was that Rachel had been delayed long enough to call off a meeting with the local PD... something she rarely did.

"So what's the plan?" Billy was the first to ask when they had gathered in the lobby with Susan.

"I was thinking we call in a missing person and start a grid search of the entirety of Big Island," Bella said with a straight face.

"Funny, Agent Walker. We'd probably lose the search team searching for her on a grid that big. Most likely in the first cave," Billy replied.

"Yeah, I was worried you were serious, Agent Walker. No one has conducted that big a grid search in a couple of weeks," Agent Namara agreed, yawning and rubbing her eyes.

"I figured we'd start in the obvious place and work from there. The security guard at the plantation gave me this weird note for a meeting she was having tonight." Bella showed Billy and Susan the log entry from the security technician. "Any guesses? I may have to call in the Hawaiian field office if we don't find her soon."

Billy smiled like a Cheshire cat at the note and then up at chairs lining The Squeaky Tiki. Bella turned around to see what made him smile so smugly. Then she felt the pinpricks of absolute rage and disgust at what she was seeing.

Agent Rachel Stein Gentry was laughing it up while sitting close to a gentleman at the bar. He was a man who had the blackest hair Bella had ever seen, the color of obsidian and shoulder length on the man's head. His face seemed leathered and tanned from years of good living in Hawaii. His teeth seemed the whitest pearl like the color on a white guitar pick or piano key. And the way his hands moved so animatedly reminded Bella of a circus barker revving the crowd up for the next show.

Pacing, trying to keep her temper in check, Bella interrupted the two. "Rachel, it's so good to run into you at this time of the night."

Rachel seemed caught off guard and narrowed her eyes at Billy and Susan, who both put their hands up apologetically. "Bella, I can see it's been too long. It seems just yesterday we went on our hikes up in the mountains."

"So, this is your hiking friend that stood you up at the wedding?" the man with the greased obsidian hair and black eyes replied with a wide grin. Bella figured they were the best teeth that money could buy. "Rachel still fumes about that with Morris and me." He slapped his right leg on his silk suit pants. "There's a reason Shane calls her Battle Ax."

The stranger produced a bronze hand three times the size of her own. "Bella, I'm so glad to finally meet you. I'm Saul Manning. Owner of this fine establishment. I've been a friend of the Stein family for over forty years. This little lady is my godchild."

Bella glanced at the two drinks before them, shaking her head.

Saul caught Bella's glance. "Before you go thinking bad of us, I never drink. And Rachel only tee-totals when she's with Shane. That's a mint coconut water in my glass and she's got a pineapple, ginger, and coconut juice concoction. She says it's the secret to her staying young."

Bella smiled. "And here I was thinking we'd find you back out on the Haiku Stairs, Rachel. Police were looking all over for you."

More curiously, Saul nearly spit his mint coconut water. Something Bella had said hit deep. The man's brow seemed to suddenly sweat, and Saul wiped it several times before bellowing a warning. "You girls stay away from that trail. It's a dangerous place." He studied Bella and Rachel carefully before continuing. "The stairs are rusted and falling apart. They have had people go missing up there. And I heard recently they found a cop hung up there. Bella, if Rachel hasn't warned you, I will. Hawaii is an extraordinarily beautiful place with many incredible places to explore. But it can be equally deadly. Especially on the Haiku Stairs. Stay off that ridge. It's a cursed place for sure."

"We're the ones who found the cop, Saul," Bella replied. "Surprised that Rachel herself didn't mention that to you?"

Rachel gave a nod to Billy and Susan while Saul leaned in to adjust himself on his chair. Bella figured it must be to close out the tab by the way Billy moved over to The Squeaky Tiki's register. "Saul, I must get back to Shane. We have a new head of cattle arriving in the morning."

"Yep, he mentioned they would finally arrive, now that the cattle truck is fixed. I tell you, Rachel, farming is a rough life. While I wish I'd gone that route long ago—pineapples or even coffee—I'll take the head-aches of this hotel to any of it." He gave a proud smile that nearly blinded Bella, then laughed. "Besides, I always have a room."

Back up in Bella's room, Rachel paced and shouted. "What the heck were you thinking, Bella? You have probably caused the activation of a thousand security protocols with that one call to my dad's place. Or kicked off something far worse."

Bella sat on her bed with her arms crossed. "You didn't answer your phone, Rachel. KPD was concerned. Officer Ga—"

"Ted never checks the logbook or follows up with his dispatch," she snapped. "I can't tell you how many times he's been fussed for it by his chief. But in his defense, the dispatcher is usually catching a nap. I know it's not very efficient over there at KPD sometimes. But the guys are top-notch, Bella." Rachel tilted her head and rubbed her face. Then she squinted her eyes suspiciously over to Bella, Billy, and Susan who shrugged. "And Billy, you of all people should have let her know before she made a fool of herself."

"Well, you kind of went missing a bit, Rachel. Then we all saw you with that businessman, and everyone was relieved." Billy stood putting his hands out apologetically. "This case has been bonkers. Everyone is a little more watchful than usual. You must see that?"

"Get out!" Rachel huffed one more time, guiding Billy and Susan out of Bella's room. "Everyone goes to bed now. We leave at nine o'clock in the morning." She paused before letting everyone leave. "One more thing. Where's TJ?"

Bella looked at the ground and whistled nervously. Rachel groaned, "Oh dear lord. Out with it, everyone. What do you folks need to tell me now?"

CHAPTER SEVENTEEN

IT WAS ALREADY PAST THREE IN THE MORNING WHEN BELLA FELL back on the bed, mentally and physically exhausted. More days like these would hasten her decision to retire early from the FBI.

She lay in the stillness of her moonlit room going over the details of the last few hours. Then she compared them to everything she had accumulated and analyzed in the last few days. The patterns were finally arranging themselves. It started with the murders and the way the victims had been executed. Now that she wasn't chasing her tail believing this the work of a local cult, the pieces fit better for the other: organized crime.

Clenching and unclenching her hands while lying relaxed on the bed, Bella focused her mind. She reflected on her mentor Henry's absolutes of any murder case. He believed the reasons to murder fell into three categories which many times overlapped: financial gain, to usurp power, or for control—either of a person, group of people, or business. In this case, it was obvious the ringleader murdered for financial gain.

But the antiquities and artifact markets for the Yakuza didn't make sense. Usually, they go for high revenue and fast return. Unless...

Bella sat up and wondered out loud, "They are cleaning their dirty money. But why stolen relics? Why not a h—" She paused and looked at the room in her resort. Then face palmed her forehead and groaned.

With the answers in front of her as obvious as the sleuth's nose on her face, Bella could finally see the angles and hurdles that Rachel had been navigating. No way would she ever want to have her colleague's life. Especially right now. How Rachel would weather this storm when the clouds cleared would certainly be a mystery.

Despite tossing and turning most of the night after last night's events, Bella awoke to a brilliant morning sun at seven-thirty. She sat up, stretched, and began her morning routine of a hot shower, a lathering toothbrushing, and then the most aromatic coffee she could find in the resort. As she walked into the resort's premiere coffee shop—Stein's Gold Cup—she saw a trio of familiar faces looking extremely exhausted. With one, in particular, wearing a black eye and grumbling.

"Good morning, agents." Bella tried to sound perky and upbeat, but it came out rather snarky.

Billy took a gulp of his coffee and put his hands around his large-sized cup. "Morning, Bella. I speak for everyone when I say I'll be glad when this one is over."

Hearing the wrenching twist of stiffened muscles moving and creaking in the corner of the coffee booth, TJ leaned forward to concur, "I second that." Then Bella noted greater details of the purplish shiner to his right eye. "This has been a pretty rough one."

"Dare I ask how you got the black eye, TJ?" From what Bella could recall, the hooded man—no doubt a former SEAL who most likely went by the call sign Conjure Man—hadn't hit TJ in the face. But it was dark in the initial takedown of the bullish man.

"A guy running to get a candy bar for his kid sucker punched me earlier." Bella couldn't believe it either. For one, had Justin punched TJ as he just alleged, the FBI agent would have been in the hospital—and it was *before* they'd gone downstairs. In fact, they'd had the whole meeting with Rachel, and he'd been drinking at the bar afterward and had been fine. Why lie about that?

"And it came to blows?" she asked offhandedly.

TJ seemed to realize his blunder a bit too late but nodded. "Yeah, it was a miscommunication on his part. But not a big deal. Didn't hurt much at first, but I guess it was more serious than I thought."

All Bella could think as she looked at the battered man was that if he was willing to lie about this, what else was he capable of? And he was wincing and bruised all over in pain.

Unless Justin went back and worked him over for information and just plain cruel fun—which is definitely a possibility especially after he saw this fool try to come on to me—this guy got beaten pretty badly.

Bella turned from the group. She went up and ordered a mocha latte coffee with extra heavy cream, and while she waited, she pulled out her phone. Nothing from Justin yet, but she decided to shoot off a text anyway.

Bella: *Need to talk today.*

She stared at the phone for a long moment, enough to see that the message was clearly read by the recipient—but no response came. Once the barista brought her brew, she shook powdered cocoa on the foamed topping, then went and sat in a chair beside her team's booth. As she sipped her third round from the brew, Bella heard Rachel's chipper voice declare, "Well, Agent O'Reilly, there's a sight for sore eyes."

The team laughed as TJ just sulked and smiled wearily. "Funny."

"Is everyone ready for a fun day on Big Island?" When no one said a word, Rachel smiled. "I can tell by your enthusiasm this will be an epic day. Let's go, TJ."

TJ staggered out of the resort with Susan watching in case he fell or staggered too far in the wrong direction. Billy got up as well, nodding to Rachel and then Bella. "I'll get the car. I'm sure you two have a few things to discuss."

"Thanks, Billy."

"I guess it goes without saying it was quite a night. What happened to TJ after he made the moves on you?" Rachel had a wicked, knowing smile.

Bella rubbed her chin then took another sip of her coffee. "You heard about that?"

"Of course, I heard about that. That's a grade-A dog limping to our car. None of the loyalty of a dog and all the swagger of being in constant heat." She studied Bella carefully, narrowing her eyes and pursing her lips. "It's funny that a random father getting a candy bar for his kid could work him over that quickly."

"You honestly don't buy that story, do you, Rachel? He got worked over by somebody long after the father had left. And the 'father' didn't sucker punch him either. It was more of a calculated pivoted thrust toward his mid-section to stun." Bella returned an innocent glance.

"Is there someone around here I need to know about?" Rachel moved closer and sat down at the table. She rested her chin on her propped right hand across from Bella. "Your guardian angel, so to speak? I don't need him ripping out all my informants' gears to snag lowlifes."

"You mean you don't want your godfather to get hurt." Bella nearly sneered in disgust saying the words. "That ship's done sailed, Rachel. He's in with the worst of the worst. The Yakuza rarely let a guy like Saul Manning sail off into the sunset."

Rachel put her hands out defensively. "Is that what you believe, Bella? Then why keep working this case with me? I could care less about what happens to that sleazeball. My concern is they come after my parents in the blowback. We never wanted to do any business with them. Saul, that scoundrel, made several shell companies. He lied to Dad and Mom that the Yakuza were going to kill him. And because they got involved, these monsters decided they wanted a bigger score. If my family doesn't play by Saul and the Yakuza's rules, they'll kill the Stein and Gentry legacy— my entire family."

Bella sat there in stunned silence. She had no place to once again hide in shame. She had been so wrong about Rachel. Her whole behavior since they met had been one of begrudging obligation to her family. It was as clear as all the other clues falling into place. Bella had been right that Rachel was using the Hawaiian FBI office as her own personal bodyguard service—but not out of want. Out of a desperate need to save her family, her friends, and most certainly, the innocent people of Hawaii who had suffered countless, horrific crimes by these Yakuza thugs.

"Well, say something Bella." Rachel's words seemed to have a controlled rage in and of themselves.

"Sorry seems to be the only word in order, Rachel. I never had to live with this kind of threat in my life. Your decision to join the Bureau has been a persistent puzzle… especially with the security team your father put together."

"If you only knew the half of it." Rachel interrupted with a growl.

"Anyway, your security is pretty good." She smiled to ease Rachel's tense mood. "Pretty good was my security exp—"

"You mean boyfriend, Bella. Just quit being you. Call him your boyfriend, for Christ's sake!" Rachel took a deep breath and continued. "Your eyes light up every time I bring him up. You get all giggly when you talk about mountain hikes with him. He found you out after the Harbinger case and then uprooted his life to move to Telluride, Colorado. He left that thriving pizza business right after you called him—yeah, I heard about that too. He's somewhere out there camped out across the jungles of Hawaii for you. Now, if that's not a dedicated boyfriend, husband, or whatever, I don't know what is. So, stop acting like one of these weirdo kids these days that can't commit to anything but a video game."

"It's complicated with Justin and me, Rachel. We have our baggage, you know." Bella put her head down and looked at the caramel swirls in her coffee.

"Everyone has baggage in their lives, Bella. You bring it into the relationship and sort the trash out, then work with what you have to build a life. We all have our mommy and daddy issues, personal hang-ups, and quirks that make each of us unique." Rachel crossed her arms and leaned back with a knowing nod. "I know this much. If you don't carry forward and just be happy in the short amount of time we all have, you'll spend your last days always in the worst of situations imaginable."

Curious, Bella lifted her head and stared at Rachel intensely with her emerald eyes. "Oh, yeah, Rachel. What's that exactly?"

"What if…" Rachel sadly said. Her words carried a chill in them. Their very meaning seemed distant, cold, to a point they sent a shiver down Bella's spine. "The dreaded 'what if' of what my life could have been, as I close my eyes to the finality of it all. You and I have seen the 'what if.' You and I watched partners and friends pass on too soon. We've seen many people leave this world alone or unaccomplished in what they truly wanted. What if I had married him? What if she had said yes to our project to build a hospital? What if I had the courage to tell my family to buzz off and married that poor cowboy without two cents to his name?"

Rachel grabbed Bella's hands and smiled with sparkling eyes too wise for her age—eyes that seemed to know all the mysteries of the celestial stars. "You ditch the what if. You forget the damn handcuffs that were designed to shame you, break your heart, and kill you with a life of misery. You climb the mountains of oblivion to a new life and an ever-richer one. You stare the devil's tempest down and roar until its destructive storm is obliterated by a chill breeze. And whether you live days, weeks, months, or years in happiness and bliss… you cherish it all as a life well-lived."

"Are you going to put that on a Hallmark card or your obituary, Rachel Gentry?" Bella pulled her hands away, slapping both down on the table in a howl of roaring laughter. Tears fell from her eyes as she continued to bellow laugh at her friend. "The mountains of oblivion, ha-ha-ha!"

"Maybe both, Bella." Rachel shook her head and laughed with her.

After a few minutes with both their heads and stomachs cramping from the much-needed laughs, Rachel got up to leave. "It's time to put these murderers behind bars." She glanced back. "Take it easy on Billy. He's still shook up that you turned on him."

"Well, Rachel, as I'm learning, the mistakes we make sometimes push us to a level of greatness beyond our comprehension." Bella beamed, feeling for the first time in a while like the two were becoming real friends.

Rachel returned the grin. "Now, that's the spirit."

Then Bella stared out to the dark, forbidding mountains in the distance of Kona. "Or the same mistakes push us into a nightmarish level of darkness that is also beyond our comprehension."

Rachel put her hands up and walked out to one of the two all-terrain SUVs that the team would be using. "Now that sounds like the nutcase that let the Harbinger stab her so she could bring him down." She tsked and shook her head. "I'm seriously wondering how messed up your mind truly is."

CHAPTER EIGHTEEN

WITH MULTIPLE SITES OF INTEREST TO CHECK OUT, THE TEAM split in two. Rachel and TJ headed north to follow up on the shop where the crude war gods had been made. They weren't expecting much, and besides, the war gods weren't the target. What Rachel was really going after was the whereabouts of the supply and distribution chain of the Yakuza. An outfit with the powerful reach of the Yakuza needed to enlist locals in many of their exploits. They also needed places of anonymity. But most important to a smuggling ring, they needed a place to entertain and auction to clients. What better place than a pottery store that was also a seafood icehouse?

Situated on the western tip of the town of Pololu, The Dragon Trade Collectibles and Seafood House was discreet, well off the highway system, and even had ocean access for landing water planes or bringing in ships. The location could easily house an army of trained mercenaries and Yakuza soldiers. The locals could be recruited, bought off, or killed without law enforcement raising a brow.

On the western side of Big Island, Bella, Susan, and Billy headed to follow up on more than a lead. This interview would assess how deep into the Yakuza the Steins were. Their interview would be at Stein Coffee itself, which was situated on the northwestern corner of Big Island near Waimea. The place encompassed nearly three thousand acres for agriculture and cattle farming. One thousand acres of land were devoted to the coffee and pineapple plantations for the Stein dynasty, while the other two thousand acres were dedicated to the ranch. On its fertile farmlands were the best wagyu beef cattle in the world. All three were extremely lucrative businesses that required their own army of plantation and cattle hands—plus a portion of land set aside for the security teams. By field reports, and Bella's personal records, this was the best private army of trained security professionals that money could buy to guard billionaire Morris Stein, his wife Rita, and the family at all times.

"Tell me again, Bella, why does Rachel work for the FBI?" Billy Makani whistled as they drove up to a heavily fortified guard shack and tower. Concertina wire and fencing ran the perimeter of the farm and ranch lands as far as the eyes could see. "Just the security of this place cost more than half the island communities put together."

Bella leaned forward in the SUV and stared through the fence waiting on security to check them in and escort them to the main house. "It does boggle the mind. Why would she take a lowly public servant job when she has an empire like this? Maybe we're missing something bigger in this picture."

Susan Namara seemed nervous in the back seat. Bella glanced back and saw the young agent fidgeting with her manicured nails. Then, as her nervous anxiety grew, Susan would run her left hand through the strands of her blonde hair. "I'll be glad when we get this one over with. Extremely rich people make me nervous."

"Agent Namara, it goes without saying to get a grip. This is an official visit to interview suspects. Fall back to your training when in doubt. Besides, we'll be handling the interviews while you take notes."

Susan fixed her hazel eyes on Bella and nodded, calming down. "That's fine by me. This is a powerful family whose daughter just happens to be my boss. I highly doubt anyone in this family is involved in such underhanded murders and thefts. The Steins don't look like they need the money."

"No, probably not, Agent Namara." And for once, as the security guard ushered their SUV on through, Bella agreed with Susan Namara on something.

A blazing white Hawaiian sun blistered the crimson road in the team's drive to the main house. It was a winding, twisting road that went on for several miles past endless rows of forest-green stalks of pineapples. But as Bella spied farther into the hundreds of miles of green, she caught sight of another crop that Rachel had forgotten to mention. There were equally hundreds of miles of fifteen-to-twenty-foot high purple sugar cane. The sight stunned Bella for a moment and at the same time drew on some of her nostalgia for the endless miles of much smaller cane back in Louisiana—back when Daddy and Momma would ride all over the state, passing the massive rows of endless green.

"I didn't know they grew sugar cane too," she mused aloud. Bella rolled down the window and tried to touch the hanging leaves. Then she remembered how razor-sharp the leaves could be and stopped.

Billy glanced over and grinned. It was the first time he'd actually smiled at her since she called for an investigation of him. "And cocoa and a ton of macadamia nuts. They charge more for the macadamia nuts than the coffee. I think it's like a dollar more, but still."

"Wow! When you think you have too much going on in your life, agents, just look around. How does she keep it all separate without one business overlapping with another and her day job?"

"To hear her tell it, she has no interest in this place. That's why her dad and husband run it," Bella said. But Bella could guarantee that one day, Rachel would have to step up in her real world—this plantation and ranch life—and walk away from all the mystery and fun of the Federal Bureau of Investigation.

Billy drove the last mile of the crimson road that wound up to a house that could have been set on any of the banks of the Mississippi River back in Louisiana. With its towering white columns supporting a giant upper balcony veranda, Bella had her second nostalgic memory of Louisiana. Back then she recalled a dinner comedy at Oak Alley Plantation where the great Dr. John Doucet, Professor of Neurosciences LSU, would put on his pirate Jean Lafitte-inspired play *Turn Coats*. She had belly laughed for days at the over-the-top performances by the cast. Now, she'd have to give her own performance to the owners of the house and this empire of agriculture and antiquities.

"So, is there any plan when we get there, Bella?" Billy seemed a little out of sorts. He seemed to be having his own jitters. The repeating of her name, the tapping on the driver's wheel, and his continued wide-eyed glances were all his tells. Bella figured he'd be an easy read in a poker game.

But in this particular game, with so much at stake—careers, lives, fortunes, and murder—Bella needed him to keep his head in the game. "It goes without saying that this guy will be as shrewd as they come. Just put it out of your mind that he's Rachel's family. No small talk, no forced tactics on this guy, and for certain don't let him off the hook. Too many people have died unnecessarily. This man may have the keys to topple the Yakuza crime organization. You do remember what they are capable of?"

Billy nodded and kept his eyes fixed forward intently. "How can I ever forget that." It was a statement, not a question.

Well, there's act one of the drama with Morris and Rita Stein, Bella assessed. *You can bet their security is surveilling us and is informing him. I'm showing my hand before we arrive by using poor Billy Makani. Let's hope the rookie catches on to what I'm doing when we have the actual face-to-face with Morris and Rita.*

"And Agent Makani, if you persist in putting down your fellow agents and harassing poor Susan, we will be discussing your demotion real soon!" Bella acted enraged and gave a furious glance at Billy. Bella saw Susan trying to speak in his defense. "Not another word from you either, Agent Namara. I know you were complicit in the exchange."

Billy slapped the wheel and winked. Susan saw the wink and was naturally confused. Then she looked at the truck in front of them and behind them. Upon seeing the communication antennas on the trucks and the roof of the house, she gasped. "Oh, dear. This is going to be quite interesting."

A lumbering man who seemed to sway like an endless purple cane field walked out onto the porch with a cowboy hat on. He lifted his hat slightly and studied Bella and her team with a set of crystal blue eyes as they got out of their SUV. He surveyed the men on both sides of the team and nodded to Bella, Billy, and Susan. Without saying a word, he turned and walked inside his massive home. Bella and the team were ushered in.

A burly man with a thick red beard and forearms as thick as tree trunks, moved in next to Bella and the team pointing to the opened front door. "This way, ladies and gentleman. Mr. Stein is a busy man, so try not to keep him too long."

Bella didn't flinch. "We'll keep him as long as we need to, sir. And I trust Mrs. Stein will be here as well?"

Another security agent, who could have been Justin Trestle's twin brother, nodded. "Of course, Agent Walker. You'll get the full cooperation of the family."

They walked up a marble set of stairs onto the porch of the massive plantation. It could easily have been a football field in size, perfect for a ball or grand dance. Onward they were led through a ten-foot-wide and twelve-foot-high front door of the blackest hardwood. As they walked into the home, and from behind her, Bella heard several tropical birds in the ancient trees surrounding the place.

They were escorted into an opulent room with the finest emerald embroidered wallpaper and many antiquities and art pieces; the team spied an immense guest couch that was three feet in height and at least thirty feet in length. The fine leather of the couch was studded with brilliant brass—or maybe even gold—tacks.

The swaying cowboy who had stood watching them on the porch was now leaning back in the finest red chair Bella had ever seen, his legs and armed both crossed. Right next to the stranger was an elegant woman with an uncanny resemblance to Rachel, with lustrous brown hair and deep brown eyes. She could have been a plantation belle in any number of New Orleans' homes. She probably had been, not too long ago.

With a drawl that could have been from Texas or Georgia, the cowboy spoke while continuing to keep his arms crossed. "I'm Morris Stein, and I welcome you to my little farm. This here is my wife, Rita. It goes without saying, agents, you're wasting valuable time. If you could kindly get to your questions so I can get my family back to work, that'd be right appreciated."

"I'm Agent Walker, Mr. and Mrs. Stein." Bella kept eye contact directly with both Steins. She gave a sparse, polite smile. "I'll start—"

"You're the girl who declined being a bridesmaid for my Rachel at her wedding. She's still steamed about that." Morris didn't waste any time throwing off her questions.

"I was in the middle of a case," Bella replied, trying to regroup her thoughts to question Morris. She had to be careful and stay on point. He was already trying to twist her up with Rachel.

Morris launched another mind jab to ruffle her feathers. "Yeah, I heard about your investigative techniques. Letting a butcher stab you so you can draw him out is a little odd, Agent Walker. I'd have shot him the minute I saw him."

Bella's blood was boiling. Had Rachel told him that intimate detail? Probably not—but nothing was out of the question in this wacky case. She took a breath to reset herself. "I did what I had to do to bring down one of the worst serial killers in history, Mr. Stein." She let her words hang just a minute then with an icy menace. "I'm not afraid of risking my life to make sure innocent people won't suffer anymore. And I made sure of that by breaking every bone in his face with my fists."

Billy Makani gulped, one of the security guys went wide-eyed, and Susan Namara put her hand to her mouth. But Morris Stein kept his face flat. Bella hoped he'd gotten the message loud and clear.

"Hah-ha-ha, Agent Walker. You are every bit the spitfire we've been told. Can you believe, that Rita?" Morris unfolded his arms and held his wife's hand with a smirk.

Rita leaned in from her equally impressive, crimson-embroidered chair. Her brown eyes seemed to see right through her. "Yes, dear, I'd say she's kicked off several ruckuses in her career. I can see why you and that hurricane of a daughter of mine are friends."

Bella felt the tension between them easing. But with these two shrewd people, it would be a chess match for sure. "So why did you get involved in this antiquities business? Why go to an auction and buy artifacts? You don't look like you need the money."

"We don't involve ourselves in the Hawaiian relics trade, Agent Walker. Most of it got buried in the land for a good reason, you see. Besides, there must be a thousand curses on those nasty things ... curses that this family doesn't need." Surprisingly to Bella, Rita answered the question with a stern stare.

"Yet, we have these invoices with your names on them." Bella produced the documents to show Morris and Rita. "If these are fake, then we will be leaving now."

"The business logo and the invoice came from one of a thousand companies we own." Morris pulled out of a nearby drawer a few business binders and a laptop. He gave the binders to Billy and Susan and the laptop he turned on for Bella. "Here's my signature and Rita's on these. And the laptop keeps that fancy encryption signature on the other businesses—hotels, restaurants, and what all. Search all you want, but I guarantee you won't find anything of the sort."

Two hours of interviewing Rachel's family provided all the necessary information the team needed. The signatures were assessed and proven to be horrible forgeries. Even the invoice numbers and electronic signatures had elements of sophisticated spamming and hacking. Anyone with a trained eye could see that the trail was cold on the couple.

"We appreciate this, Mr. Stein," Bella said.

Billy Makani bowed while adding, "It goes without saying that the charitable work, the schools and hospitals you built, are a blessing. Thank you sincerely for all your help."

Morris put out an accusing finger that seemed as hardened and calloused as a weathered knife. "Well, the way you treat women, and your fellow agents, your community needs it. I've never had respect for a man who berates and hits a woman."

Bella grimaced and winked back at Susan and Billy. "Mr. and Mrs. Klein, about Agent Makani's behavior to Susan, I must explain." She brought up the ruse they'd done in the car, and Morris laughed heartily.

"You outfoxed us, Agent Bella Walker. Well played by you and this delightful group of agents. We have needed some great entertainment out here on the islands."

Bella grinned sheepishly, but it didn't reach her eyes.

He gave up the game too easy. We are missing something.

CHAPTER NINETEEN

As Bella and Billy had gotten up after their third cup of the finest and freshest Stein coffee, Susan had poured herself another small cup for the road. That was when Bella cut her a subtle look, and Susan returned it with an imperceptible nod of her own. Looking up innocently enough, she asked, "So, with all the big questions out of the way, Mr. And Mrs.—"

Rita interrupted bringing her own porcelain cup to her mouth, "Call us Rita and Morris, my dear. You have earned it with all the great work you do."

Susan nodded and gave a broad grin. She put her cup of coffee down on its saucer next to an oaken table. "Thank you, Rita and Morris. I guess the last question we have is what's your affiliation with Saul Manning? He seems to be on a lot of these other invoices in your businesses."

Billy's face went taut, but Bella had already been watching closely for their reactions. It was the question Bella had wanted to start with. The pleasantries and the niceties wearing on Bella's focus had managed to thwart their efforts and get them off track. This was the reason she'd brought an entire team.

Morris's smile evaporated like the steam on his coffee. "Call Herman Redmond, Mr. Stewart," he directed the red-bearded guard. Morris looked at Rita grimly and turned back to Bella and the team. "I think our attorney should be here for anything else, agents. He'll be on his way shortly."

The tension was back in the room. Morris again leaned back in his chair with his arms and legs crossed rubbing his right temple. Rita had her hands together and her head down in a slight prayer. While waiting with the concerned couple, Bella looked at the incredible frescoes on the room's ceiling. Each was an exact recreation of the art of the famous Sistine Chapel. The brushwork and the gilding were flawless. Bella traced cherubs around various saints. She saw winged angels and possibly a devil, darting in and above as the last rays of Hawaiian sun from the window sent heavenly rays to set them alight. It was at odds with the rest of the décor in the room, but somehow it worked.

After twenty more minutes of sitting, Bella and everyone stood to stretch. Morris and Rita also stood with them, and each looked at their watches. Morris scratched the stubble on his chin. He then leaned in and whispered something to Rita before turning to face Bella, Billy, and Susan.

Morris straightened his denim shirt and pointed to the barbecue pit in the backyard. Three of his cowboys that had just walked in nodded without a word and headed to the black pit. "Well, while waiting for Herman, I suppose we should prepare a meal for all of you. It's the polite thing to do."

"I think we'll come back. We've intruded enough on you today." Bella nodded for Billy and Susan to pack up to leave.

Morris pointed to a massive building next door out the window. The place looked like a mini version of the Stein plantation. "Bella, that's nonsense. You are our guests. Herman won't mind the work. I keep him on retainer twenty-four hours a day and seven days a week for dustups like this. Besides, if we go too late, we have the best rooms money can buy."

"This could go easier if you just clear the air on Saul Manning." Bella nodded for them to sit down. She was going to try a new tactic. Maybe it would work. Or maybe they would tell her to take a hike. Either way, she had no intention of wasting any more time here.

Morris resumed his chair and crossed position, and Rita sat down beside him. The plan was simple. She'd hammer home the truth and pray for the best.

"I'll level with you, Morris and Rita. We already met Saul Manning." Bella saw Morris flinch and Rita glance up, concerned. "Yes, it wasn't planned. I also know a lot more that I'm not saying. So, lawyer up if you want. Herman is going to get paid, and we are going to go digging a lot deeper into your forty-year friendship. Which, from what I gathered, isn't all that friendly."

"Rachel told her, Morris. Can't you see? Even our own daughter knows the man's poison." Rita broke her silence and wiped a tear while looking at her husband. "You can't hide what he's done. This isn't the old days anymore. He's changed."

"No, you're right." Morris patted his wife's hand and smiled with his eyes watering. Bella felt as disgusted with herself as was possible. She had forced Morris's hand by pleading to Rita's moral culpability. "I tried for years to get Saul to go legit. You see, he's one of those arrogant types that thinks he always knows best and has every angle figured out. But people always get swindled or hurt in his schemes."

"So, how did he hook you into all of this?" Now that he was talking, Bella pushed to learn more.

Morris raised his brows and side-glanced at his wife. "First off, I'm not the one he snagged. I'm the one trying to squash this venture before we get too involved."

Bella scratched her head. But then it all made sense. The real truth had crashed down like a towering waterfall into a dark valley. "Rita, why did you get involved with buying and auctioning Hawaiian relics?"

"For better or worse, I trusted him," Rita said. "Saul wasn't always a bad man. A little unusual, sure, but we were all close once. But in the last few years, some of the associations he's made… he convinced me that he was going to get Rachel and Shane in some kind of trouble, Bella. I know it's stupid to think that now." Rita curled her hands in her lap and then continued. "She's an FBI agent, for goodness' sake. And he'd said her career would be over once they framed her and Shane. Arrested, their precious ranch would have been sold at a police auction."

"Rachel would have been too smart to get framed. As for the cattle ranch—which is exploding with sales—we own the deeds, Rita." Morris shook his head. "I don't know what the hell got into Saul, but he's become a sidewinding polecat of a man. I don't do business with him anymore except through Herman, you know that. He swindles all his friends." Morris stood and huffed as he went to the window to cool off. "So, he tries to get the cattle sick or rustle some through our Fort Knox of a fence. We'd have handled it."

Rita slowly and sadly looked up. "Well, you know since the tumor—"

"Not in front of them, Rita. We don't need their sympathy." Morris pointed directly at Bella. "They are here to throw the book at us. Especially that one."

"We came here for the truth, sir. I can assure you that no one wants to throw the book at you. We do want to lock up Saul Manning and his Yakuza—"

"Did you just say Yakuza, young lady?"

Bella nodded to a pale-faced Morris, who cursed under his breath.

"What in the blazes has that fool gone and done now?"

"You didn't know? No. Why would that scumbag tell you that?" Bella looked over at Billy, remembering how he had gotten out of the Yakuza syndicate. Then she looked back at both Rita and Morris who by now were on their feet, worry written plain as day on their faces. "The people involved in the various auctions—auctions that we believe were coordinated by Saul Manning—have all met untimely deaths. The buyers of the original goods and the people recovering them get murdered. Then Saul and his enforcers resell most of them to higher bidders."

"Rita would have never done this before the brain tumor. They got the thing with the gamma knife. But she's had terrible headaches since. The medication to stop the pain, well… it makes her loopy. That bastard took advantage of my wife's illness." Morris gripped Rita's hand and gritted his teeth in an obvious rage.

"No more questions. I'm sorry for everything. Tell your lawyer that you were under duress when I pushed you to say anything." Bella nodded to Billy and Susan again that it was time to go.

"Thank you for your time, Morris and Rita." Billy seemed on the verge of tears as well. "He's an evil man, to do what he did, Morris. That's no friend."

"Yes, he is a slithering viper. But once upon a time, Billy, he was a poor kid who just wanted people to respect him." Morris gave Billy a knowing glance. "You managed to get out of the Yakuza, I hear. If you ever tire of the Bureau, come and see me."

Bella's mouth went wide open. Billy leaned back in disbelief.

"This case's craziness never stops," said Susan, shaking her head and heading out the door.

"He knew the whole time we were pulling his leg in the introduction, huh?" Billy was still shaking his head as they drove on the main highway back to the resort. He slapped the wheel. "He knew, Bella!"

"He was six moves ahead of us in there. Rita was ten." Bella saw Susan's puzzled face and Billy's smirk. "We'll follow up with Rachel when we get back. I'd never want to play poker with those two wolves. They played us big time."

"How so? Was everything they said back there a lie?" Agent Namara rubbed her temple trying to grasp all that had occurred.

Bella looked back to Susan and explained. "From what I watched happen in there, yes and no. But the best liars, politicians, and swindlers usually add some level of truth to their lies. Was there a brain tumor? Rita probably had one and it was cured. But is there a medicine out there to make her belligerent to sign contracts? Again, there is. So, it would be safe to assume that the on-retainer, high-powered lawyer could null and void the contracts. So that was the first chink in their armor."

"What was the rest? Because right now my head is spinning that they played us." Susan sat back and placed her hands on the side of her head, then cracked her neck.

"Well, they were perfectly willing to chat our ears up on anything but the subject of Saul Manning. Then Morris looked at Rita and wanted to lawyer up. But I believe that was a ruse. Especially right after he tried to distract me with a barbecue and room at their place. He probably knew I'd refuse—which we did per FBI policy. But that was the point. He put pressure on me to wrap things up today and get me to press him on Saul Manning. They both worked us to tell them what we knew."

"Dear lord, Bella. I handed them the keys to the castle. I asked about Saul Manning." Susan hit her seat with her palms in frustration.

"No, it was the right question to ask." Billy glanced back in his mirror. "Their gears are turning on how much we know about Saul. How far down the rabbit hole did Rachel go to get everything she could on the Yakuza connection? They'll either clam up and cut ties with Saul or bring the hammer down on him to keep him quiet. Either way, if they do anything… we'll pounce."

"Or unleash Rachel on them." Bella added, thinking about everything in her conversations with Rachel over the years. As best as Bella could remember, Rachel was always angered by her parents' latest caper. "For Morris Stein to say the man had swindled all his friends, I almost laughed in his face."

"But I keep circling back to the why. Why would the Steins risk their fortune? What do they gain by hooking up with a terrorist outfit like that? They have all the money and power that anyone could ever have." Billy slowed as they approached The Flamed Heart Resort and parked up in the valet section.

"Maybe they got bored and wanted to kick things up." Susan offered. "Instead of buying more yachts and race cars, they buy stolen relics and artifacts from organized crime. Wait, now that I've said it out loud to y'all, it sounds ridiculous."

"Let's save the scenarios and speculation until we've gone over everything with Agent Gentry," Bella said as they entered the lobby. "But I will say, I must hand it to them; it was well played. They learned that we know about their connection to Saul Manning. Also, that we know about Saul and their ties to the Yakuza. But the most brilliant part was Morris's rage-bait saying he hates Saul Manning. No one keeps a guy they hate around for forty years and makes him a godfather of their child. And reminding you, Billy, of your previous ties to the Yakuza—"

"I see that the interview of my beloved parents went well." Rachel was sitting on a couch in the lobby as Bella and the team walked by.

"Yeah, they're a bunch of crooks. No offense ma'am." Susan was the first to answer.

"Those kind, considerate, hard-working cowboys? And you wonder why I didn't join the family business," Rachel replied.

Bella sat down next to her and didn't pull any punches. "How involved are they? We all know that was an act with them."

"Did you notice that my father couldn't dismiss his own security team? Or that Mother couldn't leave the room without one of them following everywhere? Do you understand what that scumbag Saul Manning has done?" Rachel had tears in her eyes as she sat back and looked at each of them. "Of course not. You guys got an act alright. It was the performance of their lives."

"So, Saul has taken control of your parent's finances and their lives?" Bella was rubbing her head. So many secrets within secrets and twists within turns.

"But he's on limited time with his power and control. I'm pretty sure he's ruffled enough feathers." Rachel shook her head. "Anyway, we need to get back to the field office with what we have."

Bella went up to her, pleading with her hands. "But your parents, Rachel. We should get a team in there to take back the place."

Rachel stood and grabbed her suitcase by her leg. "They're safe for now. As long as the Yakuza feel they are playing ball, they are safe. Heck, they'd rather Dad be in charge. He doesn't aggravate and embarrass them."

"What about your husband?" Billy watched Rachel's jittery response with concern.

"Shane is in the same boat. If he handles his cattle and stays out of their way, he's safe." Rachel sighed and stared at everyone. "I chartered us a plane. Go on and check out and let's get out of here."

Bella hurriedly ran up to her room, tossed her things into her go-bag, and headed down. She went to grab a coffee to sip while they waited to leave. As best she figured, she could drink half of her coffee before they boarded the plane. She noted Rachel was sitting with her own cup across from a lobby wall of Hawaiian relics.

Rachel pointed to the wall in the lobby as she and Bella sat sipping their coffee. "All of these you can bet are stolen or fakes. How many innocent people got swindled or lost their lives over these wooden pieces of junk? I truly wonder if people and their need for greed and power will ever change."

"Maybe one day, Rachel." Bella slugged her friend playfully. "But then we'd be out of a job."

The drive took approximately fifteen minutes to get to Kona Airport. The FBI-chartered small jet looked warm and inviting to all. Bella could almost smell the newness of the leathered seats in the pristine plane as it sat waiting for the team to climb aboard. Bella glanced at the somewhat happy faces of her team. She noticed TJ wasn't smiling so much. He seemed to still be bruised up and might have a slight limp. That would explain why he was so far behind.

But then Bella felt a wave of heat like she did at the beach when she'd run in from a wave. In the same instant, a force hit her from behind like a punch to the gut, followed by a feeling of weightlessness as she was launched into the air. She tumbled and fell several feet away on the hard tarmac. Her head spun, and blood dripped from somewhere as a deafening roar and roll of flames washed over her. Bella tried to get up, but her legs nearly gave out from under her.

"Rachel!" she yelled. "Billy!"

Their warm and inviting chartered jet had exploded.

CHAPTER TWENTY

BELLA SAT ON THE BACK BUMPER OF A RICKETY AMBULANCE AS A paramedic placed a bandage on a small scratch on her scalp. Her eyes never left the scene where the plane had blown up. She watched the last swirls of black smoke rising into the air as the firefighting teams finished extinguishing the fire, spraying foams of various colors and consistencies in a lopping splash to the burned plane.

Bella rubbed her ash-filled brow and groaned. All that soapy foam would make the area smell more like a laundromat than a plane runway for the next couple of weeks.

Then an icy feeling ran down her spine. Shuddering, taking in the enormity and meaning of the destruction, it finally hit her.

We came pretty close to being retired permanently. Someone is going through an awful lot of trouble and exposure to shut down our case. There must be a lot of money on the table this round.

Fortunately, the entire team got away with nothing worse than a few scrapes and bruises. A piece of debris had hit Susan in the ankle, and

Billy's shoulder had gotten pretty banged up from where he'd hit the deck; but otherwise, everyone was okay. She was glad for little miracles.

An FAA investigator walked up with a clipboard in hand. Bella continued to study him as he walked up with a deliberate but casual stride. He was a tall, reedy man, with short-cropped black hair. Throughout the firefighting, she had watched him working alongside the fire teams dousing, then inspecting each inch of the wreckage. From what she could gather from his gestures, he'd been through way too many crash investigations.

He extended his hand to formally introduce himself. "Agent, I'm Lieutenant Ricky Sawada with the FAA. I've been assigned to investigate your small mishap."

Bella extended her hand and nodded accordingly. "Special Agent Bella Walker. I wish we were meeting under better circumstances."

He smiled broadly. His hair still looked damped from the firefighting, but then the candle smell of surfboard wax and the scent of the ocean emanating off him told a completely different tale. If she had to guess, he was a surfer. It was probably a needed escape after dealing with plane crashes and mishaps all day long.

"It goes without saying that your team was lucky."

"I totally agree," Bella said as the fire near the right rear fuselage belched a last orange flame, then was extinguished by the purple foam. "Any ideas what caused the blast?"

"Normally, I'd say we are still investigating. But the idiots that put in the incendiary devices were quite sloppy. A kid with a regular chemistry kit could've done it." Lieutenant Sawada studied Bella for a minute, then continued. "This was done by hack amateurs. Have you made anyone angry lately?"

Bella snorted. "You don't know the half of it."

"Well, then, what about the case you are working? Any suspects emboldened and dangerous enough to try and set a bomb to kill FBI agents?" Sawada jerked a thumb back to the smoldering remnants of the plane. "In my experience, only high-level crime organizations, terrorists, and the desperately angry try that."

It could very easily have been the Yakuza, of course. Bella had known that from the split second after the blast. But she didn't want to go through the issue of having to explain the details—and she certainly didn't need the interference of the FAA in their case.

"Our case is Hawaiian artifact smuggling, Lieutenant. That could be any of the hotels with a beef because we're digging too deep into their business. Maybe check with The Flamingo in Oahu or The Grand Hawaiian."

Sawada nodded. "I get it, Agent Walker. You know, I could tie you and the team up in long hours of interviews. But that would just buy time for the bomber to make tracks and run off. I'd rather not do that."

"Thanks for the professional courtesy." She gave a grimace and stared knowingly. "We're close to shutting them down. Otherwise, they wouldn't have blown up our plane."

"The thing I can't get over is why would it be so sloppy?" Sawada wondered aloud. "If an organization was going to even attempt this, why do it with such traceable materials? Gets me thinking that this was more personal. Smaller scale."

"Far be it from me to know the inner workings of the criminal mind, Lieutenant. I just catch 'em," Bella shrugged. "I'd proceed with caution, though. It may be a red herring. Something to lure you out."

A light of recognition glinted in his eyes. "Is there something about this case that you're not telling me, Agent Walker?"

She smiled diplomatically. "Just… be careful. This case has had so many rocky twists and turns."

"That's been my life for forty years, working crashes in Hawaii." He gave a big grin and put out his right hand with his fist closed. He stuck his thumb up and little pinky out shaking them in a classic Hawaiian shaka, then said, "It's why I spend most of the days I have left surfing, Agent Walker. Mahalo."

"Mahalo," Bella replied. Sawada gave her a wave and went back to the investigation site.

"Well, Agent Walker, what a day!" Rachel walked up with soot on her white blouse and a large rip in her black suit jacket. "I'm looking forward to a hot bath after all this smoke. Preferably back on Oahu. Flights are booked and ready to go."

"Let's hope there's no bombs this time," Bella cracked, drawing a laugh from Rachel. "It goes without saying that this was an inside, amateur job, you know."

"Yeah, I got the memo from Lieutenant Sawada too. As my daddy would say, 'We got some rat killing to do.'" Rachel tried to growl like her bear of a father. But the utterance sounded more shrill than coarse.

"Don't… ever… do… that again, Agent Gentry." Bella held her ears with a wince. "I'd rather hear nails on a chalkboard."

Three hours later, after the pat-downs of security checks, the stamping of boarding passes to enter the plane, and laughs with the new flight's boarding team, Rachel, Bella, Billy, Susan, and TJ sat on the plane ready to take off. No one said a word. And no one slept a wink on the flight back to Oahu. Even in their respective vehicles driving to the FBI field office, no one bothered to begin a conversation.

Bella, who rode with Rachel, looked out the window of the cruiser thinking, *It's extremely difficult to talk to anyone in our group right now. Especially when I'm pretty sure one of us tried to kill off our team.*

"Bella, did you say something?" Rachel broke Bella's train of thought.

"No." Bella rubbed her temples and put her head down. "I was mumbling under my breath.

Rachel glanced and nodded. "I've had the same mumblings myself. It comes with being around turncoat scumbags who try to kill us."

"Who planted the bomb?" Bella glanced back with her emerald eyes. "My first guess would be Billy with his Yakuza background. Maybe they leaned on him with his family." Bella didn't waste a minute as she scratched dust off her slacks. "But that doesn't feel right."

"Too sloppy for a Yakuza hit. But not out of the realm of possibility." They pulled into the parking area of the FBI office and parked. Rachel turned and put her hands out to further explain. "This bomb attempt reeks of a desperate individual trying to fix a bad mistake in a hurry."

"That's what I was thinking," Bella nodded. "That leaves TJ and Susan left to review."

Rachel gave her a wry grin. "So, I'm not included with those horrible swindling parents of mine?"

"You were the first person on my list—especially with the crummy parents and bad godfather." Both women grinned at Bella's jest.

"Susan has turned up pretty clean. She did get caught cheating at a poker game this morning at The Flamed Heart Resort's casino." Rachel chuckled at Bella's puzzled face. "She was card counting at the time someone would have been trying to rig the bomb on our jet."

"That's not what puzzled me. The fact that she had the brain power to card count is a stunning new development. Susan has never, in the very short time I've known her, struck me as a casino gal," Bella noted as Rachel opened her door to get out. Her friend whistled lowly and nervously. Bella rolled her eyes. "Of course, you talked her into a quick game."

"Guilty as charged. Boy howdy, you are so insightful into the criminal machinations of the elusive card counter. Next, you'll solve the identity of the assailant who gave TJ the massive beatdown. You know, the dad that went to get his kid a Mauna Loa candy bar."

Bella didn't even want to dignify that with a response, so she just raised an eyebrow.

Rachel put up her hands defensively. "I saw the black eye, the bruises as he went to place an ice pack on them, and the set swollen fingers. Justin really—"

"Justin just bumped into the guy. A strike to the upper chest, at most. Somebody else worked over our fine young Agent O'Reilly." Rachel and Bella narrowed their eyes. Rachel's hands clenched tightly.

"We have someone who performed sloppy bomb work. An agent—with numerous sloppy casework files and a mountain of disciplinary action reports—beaten to the point he was almost limping. And, if I remember correctly, Bella, he was the farthest behind us going toward the plane. Am I wrong on that point?" Rachel paced, then growled.

Bella pulled her suitcase out of Rachel's trunk. "He was five hundred feet behind us. Yes, he also seemed to increase his limp as we neared the plane. In fact, I noted that his behavior was definitely strange. It adds up the more I think about his interactions with everyone over the last few days."

"I probably can help you ladies, if you aren't too busy chasing your tails." A tall man with the chiseled frame of an Adonis—golden hair, ocean blue eyes, and bronze tan—casually called over to Bella and Rachel in the fleeting rays of the late-afternoon sun. "I can tell you pretty much everything."

"Oh, you can?" Bella asked with a furrowed brow. "How about you tell us the why before I haul you in."

The golden hair man shrugged and answered. "The murders are by the Yakuza. They are moving stolen artifacts through Saul Manning to clean the goods for shipping to hotels and museums. But more importantly to the FBI, they are cleaning laundered money by diversifying their billions of dollars of drug money into legitimate ventures. You know like forcing innocent—or not-so-innocent—farmers to take their money as startup investment."

"Is there anything else, good citizen?" Rachel angled her head suspiciously.

The man pointed a single finger at Rachel. "Why, yes, there is, Agent Gentry. You are Agent Gentry?" Rachel nodded to confirm she was. "Run the Yakuza and that scumbag Saul Manning out of your family's plantation. And for the love of God, fire your security team when the smoke clears."

Both women leaned their heads back wide-eyed. Then Rachel composed herself, "In my office, mister, right now!"

CHAPTER TWENTY-ONE

T HE TRIO WALKED BRISKLY INTO RACHEL'S OFFICE. BELLA CLOSED
the door behind them, its glass rattling as the door shut.

"Out with it. Who are you? And how do you know so much about
this case?" Rachel was in a full lather, pacing and studying the stranger.
She gave the golden-haired man a menacing stare.

He put his hands out coolly. "I'm Jacques Collins. I run Kanaloa Dive
Tours back on Big Island. My boat is docked in Kona."

Rachel stopped her stride and leaned against her office window. She
gave the man a narrow, intense glance. Bella at the opposite window did
the same. "Well, since you already know who I am, I'll also introduce you
to Agent Walker."

Jacques grinned. "A pleasure, *madame*."

"Charmed," she replied, not feeling particularly charmed at all.

Rachel gestured for him to take a seat, and he did so. She and Bella
remained standing. "Okay, Jacques with Kanaloa Dive Tours, why are
you on the island of Oahu at the FBI office with such an incredible tale?"

"I was contacted by a guy the name of Turtle Poole. Real friendly guy—one of the best clients I ever had on a dive tour. Anyway, I told him about my troubles with the treasure business of late, and he told me to contact you directly."

Rachel flicked her eyes at Bella before returning her attention to Jacques. "What kind of troubles are you talking about?"

"Well, before I ran the dive tours, I used to be sought out by private antiquity dealers for special... procurements."

"Procurements?" Bella prodded skeptically.

He flashed a smile that undoubtedly worked on many a young woman out on the beach—but wouldn't work on her. "This is going to take a while. Do you have any coffee?"

Rachel called for Billy to get her some coffee. "Agent Makani has gone home for the day," Susan answered from his desk phone. "I'll get the coffee for you though."

"Thanks, Susan." Rachel hung up the office phone and nodded. "Go on, Jacques."

Bella interrupted just as he was starting his tale again. "So, by procure you mean you dig up relics and artifacts up in the mountains?"

"No, ma'am. I am in the honored trade of treasure hunting. I got suckered by Saul Manning into this heinous, disorganized cluster of a deal to auction some of my recovered items." Jacques put his head in his hands and groaned. Then all the cool, surfer-boy chill evaporated from him and he sobbed dejectedly. "All of my beach buddies are dead! Saul Manning got all of them killed with his stupid con."

Bella shook her head in disbelief. She could almost guess how Saul caused their deaths. But they had to hear who the friends were and how it happened. "Jacques, tell us who your friends were and what happened."

Jacques sat up in his chair with tears rolling down his cheeks. He took a deep breath, composed himself, then continued. "Well, Tommy Reville and his wife Beverly had heard of this high roller with a hotel chain looking for people to dig up in the mountains. They got some local kids, like my friend Kai, who knew where to dig. The others were Mattster and Kiwi. They were the nicest couple and always there for me before I landed on my feet with the scuba boat. Anyway, they had a couple of others, but I can't remember their names. It was a simple gig to just dig the stuff up or find a cave system where a stockpile might be. You washed the items with this special rinse and packed them away."

"And did you go on this dig?" Bella asked.

He shook his head, haunted by the memories floating behind his eyes. "No. No, I'd heard... something was off. I felt like something was wrong. I didn't trust Saul. I knew he was in it for something more than the treasure. That man doesn't live by the island code—I can tell you that. How much money does the man have to have? How many more people…" he trailed off and let out a rattling breath.

Rachel leaned in to touch his trembling shoulder. "Go on, Jacques."

"But as it always happens with these deals on this rock pile, someone got greedy." Jacques huffed under his breath and then pointed out to the mountains. "Then someone got hustled. And all my friends got killed."

"So, your friends tried to con the Yakuza?" Bella was trying to get the distraught man to focus.

"No, my friends didn't believe in conning and hustling. They were just like me on that. We bonded on treasure hunting and finding cool things."

"And you weren't afraid of the curse of Pele?" Bella asked.

Jacques wiped his eyes with a silent chuckle and looked out the window. "That's just a story to scare the tourists off," he said. "Nobody really believes that sort of thing."

"So why do it?"

"None of us really cared about the money much. It was the thrill of finding a lost civilization. Of researching and excavating a lost god statue like Ku or Kanaloa. Then came the adrenaline rush of trying to auction with the rich, conniving clients—like it was a high-stakes poker game. Of course, how were we to know how high the stakes truly were? No one thought that people would get killed once they outbid alleged business-men. Had we known they were Yakuza thugs, we'd have bailed."

"Why do you think Saul Manning had them killed?" Rachel leaned forward on her desk.

The moment that Jacques was about to explain, Susan opened the door with the coffees—then, realizing her mistake of barging into a witness interview, tried to scurry away. Bella nodded and motioned the red-faced and embarrassed Susan in with the coffees for everyone.

Jacque took his coffee and added two spoons of sugar and a splash of cream. Taking a sip, he continued. "This is great coffee, Agent Gentry. I'm sorry, what was the question again?"

Rachel took a sip of her own black coffee. "Why do you think Saul Manning had them killed?"

"Well," Jacques took a gulp, "my treasure-hunting friends watched how he was running the antiquities and relics business at a loss. He started skimming and pocketing the Yakuza money rather than pay for the shipping, truck fuel, and boxing costs. That was problem one with us. Then the word got out to the collectors of some of his goods. Many of these collectors had been friends of mine since I was a kid. Saul tried selling fakes to my friend Kevin Kiger, a massive money guy, and that was it. Kevin pulled out of the auctions and any dealings with Saul. And all the previous collectors followed suit. When they backed out of the war god statue deal, they were murdered."

"Dear lord!" Rachel hissed. "I knew the man was bottom-dwelling scum. But I never pegged him for being a murderer." Rachel stood and swigged down the rest of her coffee. "Bella, you know what this means?"

"I'm going to earn more flying miles to Kona?" Bella looked to the office ceiling and shook her head.

"Even better. We're going to arrest my godfather." Rachel moved briskly to leave, almost forgetting about Jacques Collins.

"We have some paperwork to fill out before we fly off," Bella reminded Rachel. "This will be specifically involving Mr. Collins needing a quiet place to stay." Bella pointed to Jacques who had begun to stand.

Rachel turned and walked back to her desk. She motioned for Jacques to sit and waved Susan to her office. "Jacques, with all you told us and the evidence we have accrued, you're going to need protection from the Yakuza. You've become a key witness in testifying against Saul Manning. Do you understand what that means? We'll have to put you in protective custody."

"What will happen to my dive shop while I'm in a safe house?" Jacques rubbed the right side of his face and sat dazed.

"Let's worry about the scuba tours and shop after Saul Manning is put away, okay?" Bella chimed in, and Jacques looked at both nervously and nodded.

"Oh, one more thing." Jacques reached into the pocket of his white pullover.

"What's that, Jacques?" Bella stepped up to ask.

"Turtle told me to give this to Agent Walker. He said you could split it with TJ?" Bella gritted her teeth, wishing there was someplace she could hide, especially in the presence of a laughing Rachel Gentry. For the item that Jacques Collins had been asked to give Bella was a Mauna Loa chocolate bar.

CHAPTER TWENTY-TWO

B ELLA TOOK THE FIFTEEN-MINUTE DRIVE TO THE BUNGALOW IN stride. She was extra cautious steering her cruiser home. Fatigue—even on such a short journey—was her nemesis, and she was aware of the many agents through the years who hadn't paid heed and got in wrecks—or worse—falling asleep at the wheel. The surge of her body's own adrenaline was waning after the last twenty-four hours. And the glimmering afternoon sun that blinded her bloodshot eyes wasn't help-ing. The golden glow weighed heavily on her eyelids.

Before she knew it, Bella had pulled up the driveway, sluggishly climbed the stairs, and collapsed headfirst into her bed to sleep. Within the throes of deep sleep, Bella dreamed of crashing waves and towering emerald mountains.

"Agent Walker, it seems like just yesterday we were having a plane fire together," cracked Rachel as she strode into the office the next morning.

"That it does, Agent Gentry. So, are we ready?" Bella rubbed her eyes and yawned. She felt relatively refreshed but still had barely managed five hours of sleep.

Rachel called the team to report back. While reviewing case files with the new information provided by Jacques, they put each on speakerphone in Rachel's office.

The first call was to Billy Makani, who sounded like he was at the beach as Bella heard the roar of a wave in the background. "We need to bring in a few more agents if we're going back to arrest Saul Manning," he pointed out. "You can bet he won't go quietly or peacefully with us."

Rachel grinned like a Cheshire cat. She couldn't resist her team motivator. "Now that's the spirit, Billy. We'll see you in a few. Pick the best of the best to go with us. Tell the new members—we'll need ten or more—that the new plane will be bomb free."

The second call was to TJ. Naturally, the call went to voicemail, but both agents were certain he'd be coming back in the next hour. His life might depend on it.

Thirty minutes from the time Rachel had called his phone, TJ walked into Bella's temporary office. "So, what's so important that we're going back to Big Island? I thought we had a bomb investigation to follow up on with the FAA?"

Bella kept her face entirely straight. "We have had a great development. Can you believe two witnesses have come forward identifying the bomber that almost killed all of us?" She watched TJ wince and tense up, and it wasn't from his injuries. Of course, she wasn't about to tell him *she* was one of the witnesses.

"There were people in the flight hangar besides the crew?" There was a slight stutter and stammer in his voice. "Those check-in logs are pretty accurate. Are you sure they got into the hangar without signing in? We could be getting taken for a ride by these alleged witnesses."

"Maybe. But I never said they saw the bomber in the flight hanger. But from the logs that Lieutenant Sawada gave me, the bomber is pretty much going to be getting picked up any minute now." She could see her ploy was working. The agent rubbed his brow of sweat and pursed his lips.

The phone rang in Bella's office, and TJ jumped at the noise. Bella studied him intently without showing her hand.

This guy is really spooked. He's nuttier than a squirrel with his jitters. What's got him so jumpy and terrified? This kind of crazed fear right now is certainly not about getting arrested.

Bella turned to face out her window. She looked at a swaying palm tree as she answered the phone. "This is Agent Walker. How can I help you?"

The grave and exhausted voice of Special Agent in Charge Wilson Dutton replied while taking a gulp of something. "How's your vacation in all that warm and tropical splendor?"

Bella sighed, continuing to look at the palm tree. However, she remained aware of TJ in her peripheral vision. The attempted bomber appeared out of sorts while continuing to stay in her office. "I've had better weeks hiking in the mountains. Hawaii isn't as tranquil as you'd believe, SAC Dutton."

He chuckled. "I've heard the place can get downright explosive, Bella. You know those 'vacation' luaus with all that fire and heat can really throw you for a loop." Of course, Wilson had to poke fun about the bombing, and he obviously knew Bella wasn't on vacation. The story of an attempted bombing of FBI agents had spread like wildfire through every office in the Bureau. "How's the coffee princess and her Hawaiian minions?"

"Agent Gentry has had a taxing week as well. Her family's coffee and sugarcane businesses have been receiving some very interesting investors." Again, Bella glanced briefly at TJ. The compromised agent seemed to almost heave from nervousness and apparent nausea.

"They pretty much grow everything, huh? Bring me a couple of bags of macadamia nuts when you fly home."

"Am I being recalled home from my vacation, SAC Dutton?" Bella already knew the answer. Wilson would never have called her otherwise. Bella looked back outside as the ocean breeze lightly swayed the green palms. "What's the real reason you called, besides ordering me home?"

"Well, I heard you might be tired of all that fun in the sun. Besides I need that fancy brain of yours back up in the ice and mountains. We promise that your colleagues won't try to kill you back home."

How Dutton had already gotten that private tidbit of undisclosed information was grating on Bella's nerves. Bella would have to have a heart-to-heart with Rachel on professional disclosure. But more concerning, he had said it loud enough for the obviously eavesdropping TJ to hear it.

"I thought that was a standard promise to not kill each other when you worked for the Bureau, boss. Besides, why should I cut this thrilling vacation short? Leaving, just as I'm about to close this one, could cause quite the scandal, I'm sure." Bella grinned and squinted looking at her reflection in the glass.

Bella could hear the creaking of Wilson's aged, leather chair. He was almost certainly leaning forward onto his desk, resting his elbows—a gesture Bella had seen countless times when he needed to get something off his chest. "A new maniac is in town. He's killed six around the Denver area. It's all women with their bodies left in carved ice."

Bella turned from the window to her desk. TJ O'Reilly had run out the door.

Undeterred by his sudden departure, Bella asked another question. "Why does this new case sound similar? A lot of these psychos use ice to throw off the timeline. Heck, didn't the Ice Man use this very method?"

"With the exception of murder and bodies frozen, it's not even close to that dead maniac. These are young girls—runaways. Press is calling him the Snow Ghost. He deep freezes them in a block of ice then carves the ice into... well, the creepiest ice ghosts you'll ever see. I swear I don't think I'll ever be able to get the images out of my head, Bella. I've already canceled my reading of *A Christmas Carol* for the Christmas play this year."

Bella rubbed both her temples from an oncoming headache. Why couldn't Dutton get another seasoned veteran to handle that? He would want to shut the new case quickly to avoid a panic. But she couldn't just up and leave in the middle of an investigation, especially when she was so close to catching the mastermind.

Wilson coughed then lowered his voice in a whisper. "Bella, I'll level with you. This one reminds me of your Harbinger. It has the same creepy vibes."

Bella went for a Hail Mary. "Give me five days to close this one out, SAC Dutton. I promise I'll jet after five, regardless of where we're at."

Dutton growled and mumbled under his breath. "You're kidding if you think I'll give you five days. You have one, Agent Walker."

"How about four?" she practically pleaded.

"No." Bella heard her boss stand up. No doubt he was pacing to calm down. This was a dicey situation. While Wilson Dutton was a fair boss, he didn't tolerate insubordination. There was a long pause between them. Then Wilson relented, "I'll give you three days. Ask for any more, and I'll order you home today."

"Thank you, SAC Dutton." Bella breathed a sigh of relief and leaned back in her chair. She saw Rachel walking into her office with a furrowed brow.

"So," he continued, "what's this latest case's title going to be when the requests come in for your book? You know, the epic one for when you retire out there." Bella could hear SAC Dutton opening and reaching into his office fridge. The popping of an opened soda led her to believe Wilson was having his customary lemon soda.

"Most likely it'll be *Tears of Pele*," Bella answered. "Like those little rocks all over the islands."

"Now, that's a pretty cool title. But you do know those are blasted volcanic rock and not tears?" SAC Dutton laughed at his own statement. "Blasted! I can't believe I came up with that! You get it?"

"It's a working title, SAC Dutton. Years down the road when I retire," Bella grumbled.

"Oh, Bella, one more thing." Bella became concerned that he might have changed his mind about the three days. It was hard to tell between the bellows of his laughter.

"Yes, SAC Dutton?" Bella asked as she stood to update Rachel and leave her office.

SAC Dutton chuckled, and Bella heard a slap—most likely his hand on his desk. "If I had been you in this situation, and my boss had ordered me to leave a case I was close to solving, I'd have put the brakes on his order. If it was me leaving eighty-degree weather, tropical drinks, blue waves, and sunshine, only to run back to a windy, rocky hellhole to hunt an ice-carving serial killer, I'd have told him to shove his order. Then my last business would have been requesting a transfer to remain permanently in Hawaii."

"As always, SAC Dutton, thank you for your outstanding advice. I may take it to heart."

Bella hung up, and Rachel moved briskly. She led Bella and the new team immediately out of the office to their cars. "There's no time to waste. I booked immediate flights, and we needed to board ten minutes ago. They're holding the plane. Where's TJ?"

"I saw him running out of Bella's office and out of the building," said Billy as they piled into the car. "I figured he forgot something back at his house."

"Yeah, he forgot something, alright. But we can't wait for him."

"Why the rush, Agent Gentry?" asked one of the new agents, a moderately stocky man with a Georgia drawl.

As Rachel drove up to the main airport hub to park, she looked at everyone intensely with a grin. "Well, Agent Dwyer, it seems our case's number one suspect—Saul Manning—has run for the hills. Well, scratch that. He's run for the mountains on the northwestern slope of Big Island and disappeared."

CHAPTER TWENTY-THREE

"**E**VERYONE LISTEN UP. WE DON'T HAVE MUCH TIME, AND WE HAVE a lot of information to cover," Rachel said as the plane took off. She motioned Bella up to the front of the plane while she passed out case files.

Bella looked at the eight agents in the plane comprising the new team. There wasn't time for a formal introduction, but Bella did them anyway. It was always part of her routine to know the names of the agents going with her to risk their lives. "Not that we have much time for a formal introduction, but I believe knowing your names is still just as important as the information I'm about to share with you."

Bella took a moment to look at each agent before continuing. "I'll start by saying to the new folks, I'm Agent Bella Walker. I'm a forensics specialist based out of Colorado, requested by your field office. Now, starting from the left and going clockwise, let me know who you are, where you worked before Hawaii, and how long you've been with the FBI."

Billy Makani was to her left and began his introduction. "I'm Agent Billy Makani, my fellow colleagues." Everyone laughed. Bella rolled her eyes. "I'm a Hawaiian field agent of two years."

"Thank you, Agent Makani." Bella nodded to the next person beside Billy. "Next."

"Um, hi. I'm Susan Namara," said Susan nervously. "I'm from Seattle. This is my first year in the Bureau." A round of greetings went around the room, and she looked to the next person.

A tall man with brown eyes and a thin mustache nodded. Then he announced himself with a roaring Texas drawl. "I'm Agent Keith Benton. Transferred here three years ago from North Dakota. Been with the Bureau eight years. I can say after three years on Oahu, I have gotten the chill of those blustery Dakota winds out of my bones."

"Thank you, Agent Benton. Colorado has those iced winds too." Bella sighed and nodded to the next agent.

The short and stocky brown-haired agent from the airport introduced herself. "I'm Agent Paige Rivera. I've been in the FBI for eight years as well. I transferred from New York six years ago after I caught The Leech Killer." Bella's blood ran cold. The Leech had been one of the most vicious, cannibalistic murderers that the FBI had ever encountered. Rivera had been beaten senseless by the brute and almost put on the killer's menu herself. Bella noted that everyone stared, transfixed. Including herself.

Rachel put her head down humbly. "I couldn't figure out why an agent with your service record was working out here. It makes total sense now." She took in a breath and shook her head. "Agent Rivera, it is an honor to have you on the team."

Bella nodded to the next agent. He was a powerfully built, tall man in his mid-twenties with sky-blue eyes and curly raven-black hair. "I'm Agent Jay Francis. I've been with the Bureau for just over four years. Hawaii has been my assignment the whole time."

A blond, brown-eyed gentleman in his late thirties who looked like a prize fighter went next. "I'm Jason St. Michael, originally out of the French Quarter's field office where I worked for ten years. I transferred here two years ago to get the hell out of New Orleans."

"I second that!" The Georgian George Dwyer concurred. The stocky agent, who looked like he could wrangle cattle all day rather than rustle up crooks, introduced himself: "I'm Agent George Dwyer, originally from the great state of Georgia. I have worked alongside many of you, in many other places over the last couple decades. Keith, we nearly froze to death on that Wind River case chasing Bobby Hawkins. The alligators down in Bayou Teche nearly ate Jason and me while we tracked Jack Garou. And Agent Walker, I transferred here after working with you on Harbinger."

"I thank all of you for your service." Bella pointed to the screen and ran her presentation promptly. "I couldn't ask for a better team."

It was no bull either. These were some of the best of the best. And now they were taking on some of the vilest criminals in the world.

"Saul Manning is priority number one. He's as unscrupulous as they come." Bella brought up a picture of Saul as a young man with a younger Morris Stein working on a construction site in Hawaii. "He began as a hardworking, poor kid in the construction yards and quickly climbed up the ladder of success. He had the charisma and the cunning of a wolf to build multiple hotels and restaurants, make investments, and really get himself enmeshed all across the Hawaiian islands. Why he got involved in the stolen relics trade and aligned himself with the Yakuza ... is one of those great mysteries."

"It's no mystery, Agent Walker." Agent Dwyer leaned back in his chair and crossed his arms. "He jumped into that knife pit a long time ago. It's just recently that the Yakuza are finally calling in their favor to launder money through his businesses."

"That's what I also read, Agent Dwyer. Critical details buried away in some field reports from the eighties. And it was confirmed by some of the locals."

Bella thought, *George Dwyer is as seasoned a veteran as they come. He picked up on that clue right out of the blocks. I hate to say it, but he should be running lead on this case.*

George uncrossed his arms and pointed out Rachel's father. "The other guy, his former friend and associate, is Morris Stein. Apparently, they had a falling out once Saul got into cahoots with organized crime. Morris hates drugs, drug dealers, and anything of the sort."

"Which is troubling now, Agent Dwyer." Agent Rivera rubbed her chin and squinted. "Morris is using a security outfit that Saul Manning put together two years after he aligned with the Yakuza. Unless—"

"Unless what?" Billy looked over to Agent Rivera and shrugged.

"I bet we are looking at this all wrong." Paige flipped a page in an older file and looked back at another old field office record before continuing. "That's a policing force that Saul uses to intimidate and control his marks. In this case—whether out of jealousy or just plain greed—Saul has decided he wants to take the Steins' empire from them. It's a matter of time before they have—"

Rachel interrupted, "It's time to go, folks. We can discuss all the possible scenarios after we have that scumbag in custody. Also, as you have guessed already, we will be arresting Saul's security team that has infiltrated Stein Plantation and is holding the family hostage."

Everything was falling into place now: the fight with SAC Harris, the chess match with Morris and his wife pretending to be in control of their plantation, and even the eccentric behavior of Rachel around the man who was trying to steal her family's fortune. But why had a powerfully rich man like Saul Manning gone to such destructive lengths to involve and destroy his friends?

Bella thought more on the question as they boarded the plane headed to Kona: *there's a reason for Saul's hostile takeover. And there's no doubt this is going to get hostile quickly once we move in to arrest Saul and his thugs.*

Now it was Rachel's turn to take over. "There won't be much time for a history recap. Agent Makani, give a full history of the Yakuza to our team. Keep it short and sweet."

Billy seemed hesitant at first but nodded. "What can I add that hasn't already been said about the Yakuza crime syndicate? For one, I know what they can do. Their motto is *gokudo:* 'the extreme path.' And that they are extreme in their handling of enemies is an understatement. As many of you know, as a young and stupid man, I had joined them for vengeance. I left them knowing they may one day make me pay dearly. They are as ruthless as any cartel and just as heartless and cunning as the mafia. Their reach is long on the Hawaiian Islands. Again, as many of you have already seen."

The room nodded and murmured in agreement.

"They are a transnational, organized crime syndicate that has operated since the seventeenth century when they originated from the *Kabukimono*—samurai gangs of feudal Japan. Their numbers have dwindled since the sixties, when it hit a peak of two hundred thousand members; but make no mistake, they're no less of a threat," Billy continued. "This particular group—the *Namikawa-kai*, have been running and gunning since the beginning of the nineteenth century, and they've had operations in Hawaii for decades. The gang recently changed their name on Big Island to The Tears of the Dragon, and their leader, Akihiko Tamaro, has made all members swear allegiance to him as The Bright Prince."

"The ego on some of these gang leaders never ceases to amaze me," Agent Rivera muttered.

"I know, right?" Bella asked. "And we don't help the situation some-times by giving the baddies cool names on the case files insuring their infamy." Bella nodded and looked out to the vehicles. It was time to head out for sure. "But our target doesn't want to run guns and drugs any-more. In recent years, they've branched out into the lucrative practice of *sokaiya*."

"Wow, extortion through brute force and violence toward investors or rich clientele. Or, in this case, the high-stakes antiquities trade," Agent Dwyer said.

Bella nodded. "Right on the money, Agent Dwyer. Anyway, Akihiko Tamaro—or as he's known, Ace—is the leader we're hunting after Saul Manning. He's a vile, bloodthirsty killer. According to Agent Makani's report on him two years ago, he beheaded his boss Tanaka Orima and his second and third in charge, Akimitsu Matsuo and Fukase Sanzo."

Agent St. Michael poised a question that Bella already had a possible answer to. "Are you sure Ace directly murdered those guys? He always uses underlings or someone untouchable who owes him a favor. I guess it's part of his ego not to do the murdering directly."

"That's correct." Rachel gave a stern stare to each agent as she asked, "Since we are on the subject of Ace and his minions, has anyone seen or heard from Agent TJ O'Reilly since three this afternoon?"

Bella watched as some of the veteran agents like Benton, Dwyer, and Rivera got the meaning. Billy seemed to get what was implied too. "We had a mole in the department. This compromised agent got people killed. He's already taking false information to his real boss. Everyone, be on guard for anything."

"That's pretty much the FBI motto, right agents?" Agent Dwyer joked.

The plane finally landed and as they unbuckled their seat belts, the nervous energy in the room was crackling. As soon as they were able to stand, Rachel barked their orders.

"Let's move, people. No time to waste."

They rushed out of the plane and straight onto the tarmac. A station had been set up just before the fleet of vehicles that was waiting for them. Every team member checked their batons, bulletproof vests, utility knives, and firearms. Each Velcro strap was assessed, each boot was noted for wear, and any additional items the team might need were added.

"Team one—Dwyer that's you and your gang— head to Stein Plantation and arrest Saul's men and protect my parents at all costs! Team two, let's go arrest Saul Manning!"

They filed quickly into their SUVs and sped off, tailed by several interagency police cruisers with red and blue lights strobing away.

"Good luck, everyone," Bella whispered.

CHAPTER TWENTY-FOUR

BELLA SAT IN THE BACK SEAT OF TEAM TWO'S VEHICLE. IN THE PAS-
senger front seat was Rachel, who stared intensely at a distant storm
heading their way fast from the horizon. Sitting next to Bella as she
adjusted her gun holster were Agent Paige Rivera in the middle spot, and
Billy, who sat behind the driver. Billy seemed a little on edge. He'd looked
down and made several cursory checks of his firearm. Neither he nor
Bella needed to do so, but they had checked several times out of habit
anyway. No one said a word.

The vehicle twisted around a nameless, red dirt road up the side
of Waimea Mountain. Halfway up, Bella noted the pitter-patter of rain
splashing the windshield. Of course, the storm had to hit just as they
were only minutes from a possible scuffle. After another ten minutes,
someone coughed, breaking Bella's train of thought as their vehicle
climbed toward the summit and dark mountain road of Waimea.

Bella looked out into the darkness of the jungle and sighed deeply.

One way or another, we capture Saul Manning and arrest all his cronies. And I truly hope Rachel's family is okay.

A crackle on the radio broke the silence, and the KPD deputy driving them responded briefly before turning to Rachel. Sergeant Mahina had a kind, round face and forearms as big as his thighs. "Agent Gentry, we have ground SWAT surrounding the perimeter and helicopters in the lower climes keeping a watch. I spread my men around the camp near Waimea Falls. The only thing I couldn't do was get your surveillance drones and choppers in place. The winds were gusting, and we certainly would have lost the drones. Plus, with a thirty-mile-an-hour blowdown from the thunderstorms approaching, trying to get a chopper in there would have been impossible."

"Thanks anyway, Sergeant. We will not take any unnecessary risks with this slimy *puhi*." Rachel tapped the dashboard and pointed to the imminent storm. The winds were already tossing branches and debris on the road. Everyone could hear the branches banging on the roof of the vehicle.

"According to Joe Merchen, Saul paid cash to rent this place from him. Joe thought it strange since he knew who Saul was. He took the money, then called us figuring something wasn't right." Mahina waved to a man sitting in his beach chair watching the parade of cop cars pass by, a beer in one hand and a guitar in the other. He waved to them and whistled. "That's Joe. He's a bit of an oddball but a good guy."

"I can see that, Sergeant," Bella mumbled shaking her head.

Mahina pulled the SUV next to an armada of parked police and SWAT vehicles. "We're at the staging area, two miles from the cabin. Whenever you are ready, Agent Gentry, we roll."

"Why wait? He's had enough time." Rachel was flat and emotionless. "We're done talking and planning. Tell everyone who's staged to get this crook to roll out. Be mindful of IEDs, ambushes, and traps."

"Sounds great to me!" Sergeant got on the radio and advised the staged teams to move forward for the arrest. Bella could hear the lieutenant and supervisors scrambling to activate each group to close in.

"It's time to play in the rain, ladies and gentlemen. I hope you brought rain gear." Rachel gave a wicked grin knowing no one had. Everyone shook their heads. "Too bad. Let's go."

The rain fell in thick sheets, soaking everyone instantly in its cold drench. Bella hadn't encountered rains like this since leaving Louisiana. As everyone clicked on the assigned head lamps lent to them by KPD, Bella realized the lights themselves in this downpour were almost useless. The rain still blinded them as they trudged through the mud and streams of water on their ascent. As they wandered farther and the torrent grew, mini waterfalls would appear or cross their path, knocking some off their feet in its wake.

Four hundred yards from the cabin, Bella could see flash-bangs going off, lighting the dark sky in furtive bursts. She could even smell the sulfurous smoke of red flares lit to illuminate the dark and disorient their enemy. Between the rain, the rivers of water, low rolling smoke, and the red flares, Bella could've sworn she was part of a military unit in a dense jungle rather than arresting an organized crime boss.

"Dear lord, we may have been looking at this all wrong." Bella heard Rachel groan up at the summit of Saul's cabin. Sliding and scrambling, Bella reached the summit to see what was going on.

Red flares were scattered around the perimeter of the cabin, shining red in the rain. SWAT and police units also circled and closed the distance around the cabin. Bella watched from behind the red-lit cabin as a towering waterfall cascaded onto black rocks near another lit flare. It was by this waterfall, in the halo of red light, that Bella saw Rachel standing next to a weird-shaped, colorful rock. But as Bella's eyes adjusted, and she closed the distance in the rain and flare light, her headlamp illuminated the rock next to Rachel.

The strangely colored rock wasn't a rock. It was a headless body wrapped in a black oriental robe with a crying dragon as its emblem on the back. A crude war god lay at the base of the headless body. There was no doubt in Bella's mind that this murder victim's left pinky finger would be inside—another Yakuza hit. No doubt this was once again the work of Saul Manning and his Yakuza enforcers.

But then Bella knelt down, shocked… a little. As she came around to where Rachel and some of the FBI team were standing, Bella looked at the waxen face of the victim's head. She noted the drops of rain falling off the sheen of oiled black hair. She saw the mouth with porcelain white teeth and the gray, lifeless eyes that had once held such arrogance and menace.

The headless victim was Saul Manning.

"This was well played by Ace," Rachel said to Bella grimly. "Well played indeed."

"We sent the other team into an ambush, you know." Bella tried to reason with Rachel who seemed out of sorts. "Your parents—"

"My parents are safe and far away from Saul's thugs. I'm pretty sure Ace will tie up that loose end too." Bella was puzzled beyond words. She could tell Rachel picked up on it. "I called while you were sliding down the mountain. SWAT and everyone breached without incident. In fact, Saul's security teams had all fled."

As if on cue, George Dwyer came out from the rain to join them. "No sign of anyone," he reported. "Our team's already rendezvousing with the KPD down there."

"Why the sudden pivot of The Bright Prince from extorting your parents? Too much heat or what?" Bella wiped the rain out of her eyes to see Rachel's response.

"I have no idea. Maybe this loudmouth before us overplayed his hand. Maybe Ace has found a better solution than this braggart's schemes— plans that probably cost him countless hours and money trying to fix some of Saul's stupid moves." Rachel pointed to Saul's body as a crime scene team hurried to cover up the body and preserve evidence.

"We can't back down, Rachel. I know you want to now—"

"My family will never be safe on this island if Ace is in charge. I will never feel safe if The Tears of the Dragon run Hawaii." Rachel shook out her hair and stomped mud off her feet. "All these moves he's made are without consent from Japan."

"I agree. The Yakuza fly under the radar. Any flamboyance by an out-lier like Tamaro is shunned. We take him down and most likely do the Yakuza a favor." Agent Dwyer almost spat saying the statement. "Not that I ever want to do that group of scumbags any favors. Just look at what that fool O'Reilly's dealing with now."

"You know, too, Agent Dwyer?" Bella's mouth was open in shock. Rachel put her head down as well.

"Of course, I knew. Hell, all of us have known the fool was up to something. Like you, we played him and played him. But I never ever thought he'd have the guts to bug our offices three times."

"You mean twice, Agent Dwyer," Bella corrected him. Then furrowed her brow when Rachel again looked the other way pretending to be scan-ning the crime scene with her headlamp off. "Rachel! Three times? Why didn't you tell me?"

"After you got chummy with the fool—yes, everyone knows about that—we decided to test you." Rachel turned and gave Bella a cold stare. Bella realized it was a lie. But why would Rachel lie?

"Agent Dwyer and Agent Rivera, could you excuse us? I need to have a chat with my colleague." Bella's temper was at a boil, and her nose flared with fury. This chat might end in fists and knees if Rachel was doing what Bella hoped she wasn't.

George wiped his face and turned to leave. "I'll go follow up with forensics." Rivera simply gave a nod, and both left.

"Tread carefully in your explanation, Rachel." Bella hissed. Her heart was thundering in her chest with anger and disbelief.

"You can't go after my parents, Bella. And you would once you started digging. Saul set them up and pinned so much of his dirty business on them. It would be impossible not to." Rachel turned and put her hands out apologetically. "Things aren't always black and white. Some cases and some people are shades of g—"

"That's a bunch of bull and you know it. Your parents got bored and greedy. This time it was money laundering, antiquities, and stolen relics. Then it went to high-stakes auctions with rich friends in these secluded hideouts, or whatever you do for kicks. Where does the thrill end in all this?" Bella took a breath and rubbed her head. "Oh, yeah, chess matches with organized crime!"

"What do you want?" Rachel's voice was cold and distant.

"You're going to resign after this case, Agent Gentry. You have too many conflicts of interest." Bella stormed off into the chilled rain to cool off. Before she realized it, she was back at the SUV. She climbed in waiting for the rest of the very drenched team.

After fifteen minutes of waiting, with her head cleared, Bella decided to walk back and finish reviewing the deluge of a crime scene. Fortunately, she'd found a rain poncho and waterproof gloves in the back of the vehicle.

Rachel walked up to Bella after she had made her third pass rechecking and reviewing the kill site. "Resign, huh?"

"Stop, already. I lost my temper. Besides, your office needs rich people who can't be bribed." Bella couldn't resist the verbal jab. Rachel's antics throughout this case had given her several headaches.

"I deserved that. Especially after the TJ comments. The island politics and corruption really wear you out after a while." Rachel sighed and bent down to pick up a curious item. It was a pizza key ring with a small note attached inside a ziploc bag. "Was there something you wanted to tell me, Agent Walker?"

"I think my intelligence guy is warning us. Something big is going down. We need to get out of here now. Get Sergeant Mahina or someone now!" Bella ran to the porch of the deceased man's cabin to get a better view of the note out of the rain. Bella read through Justin's horrible scribble:

Ace Tamaro (Real Brains—Sorry for pun.) He moved operations to Oahu. I followed him up here on Big Island thinking I had pinned down The Tears of the Dragon's hideout—wrong. I didn't dare send you a text with Rachel bugging your office to frame you (Parents!).

Surprised that Saul Manning lost his head. I was counting on him to hand grenade their whole operation with his mouth.

But he's a cut above the rest—JT.

P.S. get back to Oahu before Ace. He's planning on shooting holes… in your case.

Bella yelled to Rachel, Billy, and the team as they maneuvered to the comfort of the SUV. "Jacques Collins is in danger!"

Rachel, who was watching her step back down toward their SUV, squinted her left brow in disbelief. "Bella, he's in the safe house. I placed him myself into protective custody, if you recall."

"Who watched us put him into protective custody?" Bella hurried down to catch up. She almost slipped on the drenched mountain trail.

Rachel closed her fist and yelled in a rage. "He wouldn't dare!" Then she started calling the safe house as Bella followed in tow with everyone. "No answer. Officer, I need to get a phone call out to the FBI field office in Oahu yesterday! Actually, we all need to get back to Oahu."

"Agent Gentry, it's been a long night. We should take a moment before we go running out of here guns ablaze," George said, somehow looking calm and collected despite shivering and being covered in mud and rain.

"Noted, Agent Dwyer." Rachel waved the KPD officer escorts and remaining FBI agents to the SUV. "And I promise you, there's nothing I'd rather do than go run to check on my mom, dad, and husband if we had time for a Big Island stand down. But the key witness to our case may already be dead. I want to at least try to get our boots on the ground to catch these killers if they have moved on Jacques Collins at an FBI safe house. If we can't protect witnesses in our own backyard, no witness will ever come forward again."

After four hours in the rain and mud on the side of another mountain, the team headed in haste back to Kona Airport. Now in the vehicle warming from the rain, Bella could feel the aches and pains of the last forty-eight hours catching up to her. She was sure Billy, Susan, and Rachel definitely felt the same. But the adrenaline of everything happening was surging and keeping everyone quite awake.

Barely an hour and a half later, between the boarding, flight, and run to Rachel's car for an even faster drive to the safe house, Bella felt she was in a surrealistic blur of a nightmare—a helpless and hopeless nightmare where she could only hope and pray that their key witness had not become another casualty in this battle with the Yakuza.

Rachel's phone rang with several calls from HPD on the drive that took too long. But she immediately picked up SAC Charlton Harris's call. "Rachel, we got there as you asked. It's unbelievable what happened. Blood everywhere. TJ O'Reilly is fugitive number one if he helped that Yakuza dirtbag do this. I'll see he's taken down for killing his own!"

Just as they arrived at the Kapolei FBI safe house amidst a blazing fire and an army of officers and federal agents, Rachel conveyed everyone's concern. "Let's hope and pray Jacques Collins is still with us."

Now the team was amongst the personnel swarming the burning house that was supposed to protect their key witness. Bella just felt numb from everything. Her eyes squinted at the blazing fire that was being extinguished by the fire department. Strobe lights further caused her to wince and be blinded by the ramifications of it all, and just as SAC Harris had warned, there was blood everywhere.

Then in the distance away from the destruction, she saw an ominous sight: four black body bags. Agents had died on Rachel's watch. Not that it was her fault. How could anyone have known how rogue TJ O'Reilly had gone working for the Yakuza? Who would believe a once brilliant agent had been compromised to this level of incomprehensible murder?

Bella watched the flames light up the eyes of George Dwyer, Billy Makani, and Paige Rivera. Susan had found them in tears, her head shaking angrily. George grumbled. And Paige kept calm and surveyed the scene. Hoses were spread out by several fire teams spraying foam to douse the flames. Other firefighters were bringing in more hoses, and one team had breaching equipment. To the right of the blaze, three hundred feet from the house, Bella caught a closer glance at the blood-covered body bags. Bella and the team put their heads down for a moment guessing in angst who was inside.

In the heat of the moment, George Dwyer, recognizing that Rachel was overwhelmed and exhausted, took charge. "No time to grieve, team. We must find Jacques Collins at all costs. Rachel… Rachel," his eyes narrowed with a steel gaze at Rachel.

George took Rachel's hand. "This isn't your fault. We got a rogue agent that stabbed us all in the back. We are going to deal with TJ O'Reilly old school, boss."

"George, this is too much," Bella whispered, putting a hand on his shoulder to calm him. She lowered her head. She was having flashbacks of the Harbinger all over again. She loathed this feeling of chaos and helplessness.

Agent Dwyer's next words were calm, controlled, but most of all charged with fury. Bella swore she'd never want to get in his crosshairs. "All of this is overwhelming. But we will find Agent O'Reilly and all these dirtbags that killed our friends. And I'm pretty sure once Keith, Rachel,

Paige, and myself have a chat with our beloved SAC, he'll gladly buy us a beer when we do square this."

The team spread out, guns drawn, with two agents to each team. They moved away from the inferno that was once the safe house, each team spidering and navigating through yards and inhospitable jungle and terrain. From the side of the house, they swept out into the jungle that headed in one direction, to the valley below.

Rachel had recovered her senses. She took Billy with her to search with George and Bella. Susan followed with Keith Benton, who had made it back just in time to help.

Rachel issued a stern warning as they proceeded into the jungle landscape to search with officers assisting. "Watch for traps, pits, and lava tubes. Flashlights and guns will be your best friends out here." Everyone nodded.

One hour into the search, Bella and George had treacherously navigated near a dense jungle with caves. Bella scanned no fewer than a hundred different caves in just a tenth of an acre of their search. "How will we ever find him in all those caves? How did so many caves form like that?" Bella whispered.

George whispered back in the immense darkness. "These are the dormant lava tubes that Agent Gentry warned us about. Figures we'd get the raw end of the stick on the search." He paused and raised his hand pointing into the upper climes. "But if I was being chased by the Yakuza, I'd have run this way too."

After another half hour navigating a particularly rocky and tube-riddled ascent, Bella's ears caught the strangest, ghostly sound. At first, she thought it was the shrill howl of the wind through the mountains. "Help me! Please, someone, I've been shot!" Bella couldn't believe what she was hearing. It was a pleading, garbled voice in absolute terror. A voice that seemed to echo beneath and around her.

"George—" Before Bella could finish, George Dwyer had moved like the wind and radioed coordinates for helicopter rescue and paramedics to meet him at the mouth of a specific lava tube on Kapolei. Bella struggled to catch up, climbing over massive boulders to reach George. Exhaustion had finally reared its ugly head, and Bella had to pause and rest before she reached George.

She took in a gasp of breath and leaned back looking up at the white, twinkling stars for the briefest moment.

Agent Dwyer is just up another hundred yards by the tube. How he found the right tube with someone in it is quite extraordinary. There must be over a hundred of these things surrounding us.

I know we need to get to whomever is hurt. But George scrambled up to that lava tube not knowing if it was a trap. And he's up there without backup, which is a major mistake.

He's a good agent, but his emotions get the better of him. Like someone else I used to know.

Bella continued her climb to the tube, lumbering carefully over large, black lava rocks and shards of razor-sharp obsidian. A banged shin here and a scratch there reminded Bella how treacherous this run and climb into a lava tube could be. Adjusting the beam on her small, handheld flashlight to watch more carefully for rockslides, Bella continued to follow behind. After five minutes and another reverberating cry for help within the tube, she suddenly lost sight of George's flashlight. Looking down on the ancient, volcanic ground beneath her feet, she noticed a trail of blood heading up into the largest network of Kapolei's lava tube system. Grunting and groaning at the additional climb, she trudged on.

While continuing to follow the blood trail, and twenty minutes after George Dwyer's request, Honolulu Rescue's helicopter arrived. Bella heard the whir of the chopper blades, then saw its lights which lit up her area briefly. Grabbing moss-covered boulders to assist her climb, Bella glanced up to see Agent Dwyer coordinating a landing zone. By then she was sixty yards away from the landed chopper and the medics racing with George into the dormant lava tube. She followed carefully—she didn't need a twisted ankle to add to her growing aches and pains.

Ten feet from the opening of the enormous tube, Bella's right foot tripped over a rock, and she fell with both knees onto the jagged rock. That would have been enough pain and aggravation for the night, but then suddenly the ground beneath Bella's feet gave way, dropping her below. Before she could even breathe, she plunged uncontrollably several feet down, and her flashlight skittered down the wall. Her hands scrambled to grab something to break her fall, and eventually, she got lucky and fell across a thick web of tree roots. Slightly stunned, she realized she'd narrowly escaped certain death!

She took a deep breath dangling from the roots, sat up, and looked up at the brilliant moonlit night sky far above her head. She cast one more grateful glance up to the celestial heavens, took another breath, and moved to climb down into the darkness below. Lit by the dimmest glare of moonlight, Bella managed to pull herself across the root bridge carefully, trying not to shake the tree roots too much. Edging slowly, with sweat pouring from her arms and forehead into the darkness, she felt for the oozing, slippery safety of the tube's side wall. She secured a hand on a root to guide her down to the base of an adjacent tube.

Darkness engulfed everything, and for a moment, Bella doubted moving forward. Listening and praying she was somewhere close to Agent Dwyer, Bella heard voices echoing all around as she had earlier. It was only because of the distant shimmer of flashlights to her right that Bella was able to navigate her way to George and the paramedics.

"It's about time you showed up!" George grinned, breathing heavily and wiping sweat from his brow. He looked at Bella, who had come from a different lava tube below the team. He curiously studied the dirt and gravel covering Bella from head to toe. Then his eyes widened in alarm realizing what had happened. His face tightened as he looked at the cathedral ceiling of the tube. "It was nice of you to drop in."

Bella didn't miss a beat, "Anytime, Agent Dwyer. But you took off without your backup, mister. Not cool. That could have been you taking flight lessons tonight."

Bella knocked dirt out of her hair as she watched the paramedics work on the man they had found. She stood back with George watching one paramedic bent down rendering aid with a bandage to a profusely bleeding wound. The unidentified man groaned his thanks, then reached up his arm, casting strange shadows on the tube's rocky wall. Bella thought the shadows for a moment looked like a rabbit or Pac-Man.

Then she heard a slight chuckle from the tall, bleeding man wrapped in bandages being placed on a rescue board. In the darkness, trying to assess with George how the gentleman got this far into the lava tube without a flashlight, Bella heard the following question from the same pleading voice. "Doc, do you think I'm going to make it?"

Bella had thought she was lucky to survive a fall into a lava tube at night without a flashlight. But as she witnessed the paramedics carry a blood-drenched Jacques Collins out of the lava tube to the chopper, she shook her head in amazement.

She was still bewildered as she and George made their way back down the mountain. The treasure diver had evaded the Yakuza through two miles of the jungle after suffering at least three gunshot wounds. To live, the man had scrambled across razor-sharp barren rock and up into treacherous mountain terrain.

As Bella climbed into the FBI cruiser to head home, her back, arms, and knees throbbed. She was covered in scratches. Everyone noticed her disarray, but no one said a word on the drive to drop her off at the bungalow.

Making the slow walk inside to a hot shower and a cool bed, several thoughts still bombarded her fatigued brain. But while her mind had stayed focused in the calming chaos of the Yakuza attack on the FBI, it was Bella's emotions that had remained bewildered by what she had seen tracking down the lost Jacques Collins with Agent Dwyer. The horrifically injured man—whose undaunting and indomitable will to live saved him from a fate worse than death itself—had been found. For certain, he'd risked everything—his career, his life, and possibly even a lonely death in the vast abyss of the lava tube. He'd dragged his dying body into that enormous, lightless pit of volcanic earth without a flashlight knowing he could become another lost statistic of the lava tubes. Obviously, the fear of capture, the terror of being shot again, and the vicious beheading blade of the Yakuza drove the man to such daring heights.

If Jacques Collins hadn't cried out in the pitch-black darkness of that tube, he would have been lost to the ages. If Bella and George hadn't been near to hear him, he would have remained nestled in the darkness, covered in all manner of scurrying cave dwellers. If George Dwyer hadn't had extensive knowledge of search and rescue in lava tubes, Jacques Collins—the echoing shrill howl that Bella had thought was a ghostly wind—might have become another haunted mystery of Hawaii.

Somehow, it was like the island itself had a way of placing them all in the right place, at the right time.

CHAPTER TWENTY-FIVE

RILLIANT WHITE LIGHT CASCADED THROUGH THE PARTIALLY closed wooden blinds of Bella's room. The rays struck her refreshed face with soothing warmth. She rolled over on her pillow and smelled the aromatic, smoky scent of roasted coffee.

Bella jumped up out of bed with a start. She hadn't made any coffee. Turning to get out of bed in a mad dash, she saw a familiar sight as she opened the door. A calm man with rugged good lucks had just set down a tray. It held two cups of hot coffee at a table next to a massive window overlooking the beach.

"Good morning, Agent Walker." Justin gave a wry smile and sat down. He offered her a cup. "A much-needed beverage after such a restful evening."

"Justin, sometimes you kick up too much of a ruckus." Bella took the cup from his hands and leaned in to give him a kiss on the cheek. "But I will always keep you around for the coffee."

"Indeed, southern belle. So, what's on the agenda today in this fine city? Shall I book a dive trip? Or would you rather scale the Stairway to Heaven? I hear the view is to die for." Justin took a sip of his coffee and smiled wickedly. "Or we could go spelunking?"

"Spelunk—whatever the heck you said—mister, is off limits." Bella groaned. "I'd like to skip caves for a while."

Justin slid over several bandages already prepped with antibiotic ointment and two ibuprofen tablets with a small glass of water. Then he smiled sheepishly. "Is there anything else I can get for you … fallen angel?"

Bella's eyes went wide. He knew about her fall. She hadn't told anyone yet. The only person who knew was George. "You are incorrigible, Justin Trestle." Bella looked at her elbow. She placed one of the medicated bandages on the scrape. "Offering cave hiking after I fell through a lava tube … is … not … funny."

"Yet, you once again have defied the odds—which are pretty high—running into a lava tube untrained, Miss Walker. Next time, wait for backup."

Bella huffed. "I *was* the backup. George just ran off without me."

Justin tsked. "Good old George 'of the Jungle.' Sounds like him." Justin took another sip of his coffee and placed the mug on the table, looking out to the sun rising above the rolling sea. "How far did you fall?"

"You seem quite concerned," Bella noted.

He put his arms up in protest. "I'm always concerned when you go out on these cases. But it is also pretty cool to hear about your near-death experiences too."

Bella glared at him with a look that would have made anyone else wither—but it only made Justin crack up.

"Very funny." She took a sip of coffee, overwhelmed by the drink's flavor. One of these days she'd have to get the actual recipe from the fool.

"We all made mistakes once, Bella. I thought I could save the world in another life. But these days I spend my time bandaging you up … and saving your life." Justin's eyes locked on Bella's, and his words carried an icy chill.

"What does that mean, Justin?" He waved her off, ignoring the question, but she didn't let up. "Tell me right now what you did, or I'll let Rachel know."

He sighed. "Your friend who's in bed with the Yakuza. You know they never forget or forgive transgressions."

Bella furrowed her brow and leaned in for an answer. "Talk," she growled.

"Fine, three Yakuza were tailing you and 'George of the Jungle.' Y'all were so wrapped up in everything, and you were beyond exhausted, that you didn't check your six. The first raised up his fine rifle with the best night-vision scope money could buy for a Remington 700. George was about to be dusted as he was landing the chopper."

"Oh, dear lord. What happened to the second and third?" Bella paused, thinking and rubbing her temple. "Wait a minute. How was the first—"

Justin sipped his coffee and squinted both his eyes in the sip. "After all the years we've been together, are you finally going to start asking for details?"

"Just the basic how in case there's blowback. I don't need the specific method, Conjure Man." Bella pushed back a strand of her hair. She still felt dirty grit in it from the fall.

"The first was a choke out and throw down a tube. East side of Kapolei. The second and third were service-issue knife—not giving the specifics. Also tossed down a tube to the northeast side of Kapolei." Justin stood and cracked his back and neck. "I think I'll go take a swim in that beautiful ocean. You want to tag along?"

"That would be an epic day, Justin. But duty calls." Bella walked out onto the back patio and took in the morning sun with him.

"Of course. I imagine you'll go to the hospital to follow up on Jacques Collins first. Then I think a sit-down with Rachel to clear the air on all her tricks. I tell you, Bella, you need better friends." Justin ran off to the beach for a swim.

"You think!" Bella laughed. Then she shuddered as he dove into the waves. "Justin, please watch out for tiger sharks!"

Bella took another hot shower, sighing as the steam loosened up the knotted muscles of her neck and legs. She also got the last remnants of the tar-like grit out of her hair. Once she'd showered, and feeling the ibuprofen working, she dressed and headed over to the glimmering FBI office. She made a beeline to Rachel's office before the team went to visit Jacques.

"Agent Walker, don't you look uplifted," Rachel joked. Of course, George had blabbed.

"Thank you, Agent Gentry. Gravity can have its moments." Bella shrugged, knowing Rachel would want more details.

Rachel leaned back in her office chair and crossed her arms. "Go on. It's not every day I get to review a fallen lava tube survivor's experience."

Bella lifted her eyes to the ceiling and huffed. "There's not much to tell. I was running after Geo—"

Rachel put her hand on her chin and studied Bella. "Your first mistake was following that fool. How he didn't fall through as well is one of life's great mysteries. You both should have waited for experts, or at the least, backup."

"I had backup. Well, sort of." Bella put her head down and whistled.

"You had better be talking about *spiritual* backup, Agent Walker." Rachel huffed and grimaced. Bella realized she wasn't going to let it go. "Great, what did the Conjure Man do this time?"

"Well, depending on your belief system in a divine power—God, for instance—let's say there was an intervention." Bella put out her hands defensively and sat down across from Rachel with her most innocent smile. "And three Yakuza went to meet him."

"When I requested a forensics expert to help me out here, I didn't envision conversations where I'd be discussing fallen angels and the devil. And you certainly know this particular devil." Rachel rubbed her head and took two aspirin. Bella figured she must have one heck of a headache. "On that note, let's gather up Billy and George of the Jungle and go see Lazarus, Miss Fallen Angel."

Bella went rigid and was a little shocked hearing the reference. Rachel might know more than she'd been letting on about Bella and Justin's talks. "That's the second time I've heard that phrase today."

"Oh, really? You may not know all that you think you know of your friends sometimes, Bella." Rachel stood and grinned, which, coming from Rachel, was a little disconcerting.

"You and my boyfriend play some very curious games," Bella said as they walked outside to the parking garage.

"We each are looking out for you, in our own way. You can believe that much. Even if I can't stand his caveman methods of resolution sometimes."

"Yes, I've had that conversation with him to reign it in on occasion." Bella nodded. Billy and George ran up to climb into the SUV as well.

"Okay, which one of you put the George of the Jungle toy on my desk?" grumbled George as he clicked on his seat belt.

"It wasn't me." Bella shrugged and looked out toward Nimitz Beach. She had an idea who the culprit was. He was a tall, powerfully built beast who'd saved both their lives last night—the same guy out swimming miles from the shore in the Hawaiian surf—and hopefully not getting hunted by tiger sharks.

Rachel pulled up to the side of Queen's Medical Center where the paramedics had dropped off Jacques Collins for treatment the night before. Police cruisers and FBI agents were strategically placed guarding the hospital in the event of another attempt by the Yakuza to kill Jacques—which was highly unlikely now that all agencies were involved in a manhunt for the ringleader. Walking beneath the swaying banyan and palm trees surrounding the hospital, Bella felt like she was walking into an old hotel or museum rather than a hospital.

As Bella walked through the sliding doors to proceed inside, she turned to Billy. "Any word on the whereabouts of our 'colleague?'"

Billy shook his head. "Not at home, not at a friend's, the neighbors haven't seen him, phone won't pick up, and tracing is useless. I even went to visit our friend at the dive bar for a follow-up. The only stranger he'd seen all week was this Reacher-sized buffoon looking for good coffee?"

Bella grimaced and Rachel laughed uncontrollably. "I guess that answers the question."

"What's so funny about the description?" Billy was left scratching his head.

Rachel glanced at Billy as the team made their way toward reception. "Oh, it was envisioning a six-foot, five-inch-tall special forces guy in a Hawaiian shirt, asking for coffee, while wearing sunglasses. Then picturing the brute drinking the coffee and saying, 'Details matter.'"

Billy's eyes narrowed with skepticism. "I never said he was wearing a Hawaiian shirt and sunglasses, Agent Gentry. How'd you know that detail?"

Agent Dwyer came to the rescue before Billy inquired further. "Woman's intuition, my fine young agent. And I'd leave your inquiries there."

Billy made an O with his lips and cast a knowing nod to Bella, George, and Rachel. "I get exactly what you guys are saying. No worries about the follow-up. But the three Yakuza by Kapolei—"

"Such a tragedy, Agent Makani," Bella interrupted. She cocked her head, faking concern. "Those lava tubes can be… deadly."

"Oh, can I ask?" Billy asked.

Rachel nodded as they climbed into the elevator.

"The guy in the Hawaiian shirt? He took out three guys at night armed to the nines with rifles, pistols, and night vision. Wow! The bureau needs more friends like that."

"Wait, Agent Gentry, three Yakuza operatives were taken out at Kapolei? When was this?" George's eyes realized the ramifications of the deaths.

"Last night, Agent Dwyer, when you ran off without your backup into a lava tube. Luckily you had a guardian angel." Rachel gave him a stern stare. "I understand emotions were high, George. But luckily everything rolled our way... with outside help."

"Should I ask the name of the help?" George mumbled as the elevator doors opened to the third floor.

Bella ignored the question. George, not getting an answer, got the answer he needed. "Of course."

Five doors down on the left, with two FBI guards at the door and HPD officers at the fire exit and elevators, they found Jacques Collins asleep in his room. A window in the room was half shuttered. The monitors were beeping, and intravenous lines were attached to Jacques's arms. A tube connected to a ventilator was assisting his breathing.

Rachel knocked, and the doctor reviewing his charts looked up. "Can I help you, agents?"

Rachel badged him. "I'm Agent Gentry, these are Agents Walker, Dwyer, and Makani. We came to talk to Jacques. We are trying to piece together what happened. How's he doing?"

"I'm Dr. Abundo. We were able to get all three bullets removed— right lung, right arm, and left leg." The doctor paused and pointed to each bandage that still covered up the woudns. "Luckily for him, they missed the major arteries. The lung was a concern, but it's patched."

"Is he in any state to talk to us?" Bella asked.

Dr. Abundo shook his head. "He lost a lot of blood, and we had to sedate him. He was lucky to make it. With enough rest, he should be alright, but I wouldn't expect him to wake up for a few hours."

"Damn," Rachel whispered.

"You know, just before going in for surgery, he demanded me to write a note to the FBI." Dr. Abundo pulled a note from his pocket and gave it to Rachel.

The note said the following:

To Agent Gentry and the FBI,

Thank you for finding me. I knew when I agreed to testify that this might happen. But never like this. In the darkness of the tube, I realized how foolish I'd been with my life. I was warned by my friend Kai—he's probably dead now—how dangerous our friendship had become with the Yakuza. But the money to get the dive shop was all I saw. The greatest treasure—friendship— was right there. I couldn't just be happy with that. Anyway, Akihiko Tamaro is their leader. Should I die, I want to be clear. His people shot me when I ran to escape.

Also, The Tears of the Dragon compound moved to Waialua on an unnamed road north of Makua Cave. I'm sorry I didn't tell you sooner.

"Billy, George, we need to go now. Bella, advise HPD and all local police agencies of the location and set up perimeters."

"On it," Bella replied as they headed out of the hospital.

Two hours later, with all roads in and around Makua Cave blocked off and officers staged to assault the area, Bella and the team arrived to meet with the leadership of the SWAT and police teams.

Rachel sighed and began her heartfelt speech. "Gentlemen and ladies, we've dealt with this group's criminality for too long. I know I do not stand alone in wanting to arrest and crush these monsters permanently. But please do not let emotions get the better of you. It could be a fatal mistake. Err on the side of caution and safety. Stay with your backup and stay with your units until each section is cleared. Remember, always check your six. Any questions?"

Everyone nodded in agreement. Most questions were relegated to location logistics and times to reach the respective search sectors. Rachel turned the meeting over to each of the lieutenants and commanders of the various police teams.

The teams fanned out, cautiously and carefully making their way across the rock and jungle-swept landscape to the north of the Makua Caves.

But a surprise was awaiting them as they breached the Yakuza location. The sound of an irate and screaming Chief Como summed up the mission: the compound was empty.

CHAPTER TWENTY-SIX

Hawaiian FBI Building
Enterprise Street
Oahu, Hawaii

BELLA STUMBLED INTO THE FBI OFFICE EARLY THE NEXT DAY WITH a hot coffee already in hand. Rachel was sitting scribbling some notes in a small planner in the conference room. SAC Harris was looking out the window at the beach's morning sunrise. The morning glow cast long shadows off his face.

"Good morning, Agent Walker. Good morning, Agent Gentry. Do you know why we are here just as the sun's come up on this glorious island?" SAC Charlton Harris turned from the beach view to cast a stern stare at both Bella and Rachel.

"How did The Tears of the Dragon know we were coming to arrest them?" Rachel said. "Who is the most likely candidate to have tipped them off?" She leaned back in the office chair she was sitting in, squeezing the chair's arms tightly before speaking further. "You know who probably did it, SAC Harris. It saddens me that we were all betrayed by TJ. But I'm still trying to figure out how he got the information to leak it."

"It's no secret when you have over a hundred people involved." He shrugged. "But unlike you, I'm not saddened, Agent Gentry. I'm furious that an agent of our prestigious department decided to join killers and thieves. I'm angry that this scum wasn't vetted properly at Quantico and washed out of the Bureau years ago." SAC Harris turned back to look at the sprawling white sands of the beach. "He was on departmental probation for reckless behavior and insubordination more times than I care to remember. We should have done what the Academy didn't do: ran that rogue agent out of the FBI."

The debacle at the Tears of the Dragon raid had been all the talk with the agents. Arguments had been overheard between Rachel, HPD, SWAT, and SAC Harris on who had leaked information to tip off the Yakuza. SAC Harris had his suspicions on the who, as did everyone else. It was looking more likely than ever to Bella that Thomas Joseph O'Reilly had been the culprit.

"How did he get access to that particular piece of classified information?" SAC Harris paced angrily and stared at both women in a rage. "Better yet, why haven't we arrested and hauled him in? It's an island, for goodness' sake. It can't be that difficult to find him on it."

Rachel put out her hands defensively to explain. "SAC Harris, he's aligned himself with the Yakuza. Disappearing on an island and evading capture is their expertise. I have a team scouring all four corners of the island for our rogue agent and his friends. He'll eventually pop up somewhere. TJ has a penchant for getting into trouble."

"He must have called in and pretended that he was still on the team. Naturally, he showed up at the office demanding an update," Harris said. "Agent Namara thought everything was cool and he was back on the case with us. She said he was terribly convincing. Anyway, Agent O'Reilly got the heads up on when our raid was going down. But here's the kicker: that was only minutes before we breached. There's no way Ace Tamaro had time to get everything and everyone out that fast."

Bella nodded. "But our former idiot colleague made a catastrophic, career-ending mistake when decided to call Ace Tamora on his FBI-issued phone."

SAC Harris slowly sat, never taking his eyes from Rachel and Bella. "He leaked the safe house location of Jacques Collins, didn't he?"

Rachel nodded, tapping her fingers on the boardroom table. "He had the audacity to use his service-issued phone to call the Yakuza once with the directions to the Kapolei safe house. When we ran a trace on the phone on the receiving end, it was traced to a burner. But when we dug further, we found out that this burner phone was part of a thousand phones bought by a shell company for The Tears of the Dragon. Referencing Agent O'Reilly's phone records shows as much. There were five calls in total."

"He's a ruthless murderer now, Agent Gentry. Don't ever call that backstabber an agent again." SAC Harris slammed a fist on the table in a rage, then put his head down ashamed. "Nothing cuts quite as deep, or hurts so painfully, as being betrayed by someone you trusted."

Rachel and Bella stood to head out as Rachel said, "We'll find him, boss. We'll turn over every rock on Oahu and beyond if we have to. TJ will pay for what he's done."

SAC Harris lifted his head and pushed back from the boardroom table. "That's good to hear, Agent Gentry. You catch this dirtbag and make sure to bring him in alive if you can." He paused a minute and took a tired breath. "I'm pretty sure a lot of grieving and angry FBI agents who lost friends at Kapolei won't want that to occur. Hell, maybe we get lucky. The Yakuza are pretty good at tying up loose ends."

Two hours after the meeting with SAC Harris, Bella was going over maps and possible places the Yakuza could have moved their operations. She, Paige, George, and Billy had spent time checking all the area's cave systems and lava tube networks. Each had proximity and potential to have been turned into escape routes and new hideouts for The Tears of the Dragon.

Billy rubbed his eyes as he looked over the maps. "It's a question of *when* they were tipped off."

"I agree," Paige offered. "To move the stuff—trucks, guns, supply containers, and such—as they did and not be seen on the roads would take an elaborate system of discretion. They have the fear factor to intimidate witnesses to not talk on their side, naturally. But for no one, no drone, or no satellite imagery to detect a convoy of Yakuza equipment? That's incredible." Paige leaned back in another seat opposite Billy and George. She shook her head in disbelief.

George leaned in and put his hands together. He pointed to the cave moving toward the east then to the ocean surrounding Oahu. "It must be the caves. There's no other way. Even if they tried to boat their equipment, personnel, and containers, there would have been delays. Plus, they would have needed really big boats to move the stuff. Someone yachting, fishing, or scuba diving would have spotted them. Despite their ability to intimidate or kill witnesses, there's no chance they get them all. Then there's the Coast Guard to think about. Why would they risk a gunfight with them? And usually, there's a cutter splashing around performing all those checks of unusual shipments and boats."

Bella considered it for a moment, then walked over to the map posted on the wall. She pointed from Kapolei to Haiku Stairs. "I saw the vast lava tubes and caves over here in Kapolei. They could easily house several armies, housing, and equipment if the right leadership had the know-how and money. Ace has both. So, it's reasonable to think he's put together escape routes and hideouts throughout the island. And if I were betting on his tenacity to evade detection, I'd even venture elsewhere, such as Maui and Big Island."

Rivera nodded. "It absolutely makes perfect sense. So how do we figure out which cave or tube these guys are hiding in?"

Bella shrugged her shoulders and looked up at everyone. "I haven't a clue, team. But I'm getting a good idea of a possible place. I want to dig a little deeper into some old records before I offer up the hideout. But now that we have a window and time when they were tipped off... maybe together we can confirm my hunch on the location. We don't need to raid another empty compound."

"Agent Walker, do you have a minute?" Rachel interrupted Bella and the team's meeting.

Bella furrowed her brow and shook her head. "Not really. We're trying to find Ace Tamaro's hideout."

"SAC Harris wants a follow-up with the Steins and Shane. I need you there to run lead on this. Obviously... I'm conflicted."

Bella knew her outburst the other night would come back to haunt her. And now the time had come.

George, Paige, and Billy chuckled as Bella put her hands in the air and grabbed her purse. Nodding to the team to continue their predictive models for The Tears of the Dragon hideout, Bella groaned, "Me and my big mouth."

Rachel continued her broad smile and followed Bella out to the car. "That's the spirit, Agent Walker."

Walking out of the shimmering glass doors of the FBI building, Bella paused to ask Rachel, "Where are your folks and husband staying? It had better be a safe house, Rachel. That's standard protocol."

Rachel huffed with her hands out apologetically. "They won't listen to me. They keep telling me that their fortified safe room back at the plantation is better than any FBI safe house. Then Dad reminded me of the Kapolei attack. What could I say?" She continued walking toward her Lincoln Town Car.

Exasperated, Bella pleaded and tried to get out of the assignment. "That's why I'm going! You could have gotten Keith or George or even Billy to be the heavy for this and force them to go. In fact, I'd recommend it."

"It benefits you, too, Bella." Rachel clicked her seat belt as Bella did the same.

Puzzled, Bella looked out the window as Rachel turned onto the street and headed to the bungalow. "What am I not picking up on here?"

Rachel batted her eyes and smiled an innocent-looking smile. Bella didn't like the looks of this. When Rachel used such tactics, it usually meant trouble for Bella. "They'll be staying with you until we get their safe house sorted out."

"That's … just … lovely." She rubbed her head before a tension head-ache set in, wondering where Justin's Hawaiian hideout might be. She grinned thinking the time might be right to escape Rachel's three-ring circus and just have a normal vacation.

As they pulled up into the bungalow's driveway, Bella had another wild urge to find the Conjure Man and hide out as far up in the moun-tains as possible. For in the driveway were three black Escalades with six towering bodyguards in full guns, suits, and state-of-the-art communi-cation devices. While impressive to Bella, their presence meant things would be anything but discreet and private. The Steins's time with Bella would certainly be intrusive and her privacy limited.

Bella whistled. "They spared no expense on the new security."

Rachel shrugged. "They never do. Which was why it was so darn frustrating when Saul coerced the other guys and used their own team to kidnap them."

There had been something troubling Bella about the other day when Rachel split up the teams—some item that had sat there like an elephant in the room trumpeting an obvious problem to Bella and the rest of the team. "I have to ask you a question that's been bothering me for a couple of days. I would have brought it up soon—"

"Why didn't I go in guns ablaze and save my folks?" Rachel interrupted.

Bella opened the door and noticed one of the security guards had a familiarity about him. "Well, yeah. If *my* folks were kidnapped or being held against their will by a bunch of turncoat security guards, *I'd* have led that team. Forget the assignment to capture a team of assassins. I prom-ise you that I'd have led the charge to protect my family."

Rachel walked Bella up to the door and nodded to another secu-rity guard that looked familiar. She turned and whispered as she opened the door to go inside. "But, dear Agent Walker, then the trained killers, with a history of family revenge dating back to the samurai, would have escaped. And my family and I would have had a bigger problem."

"Well, they did escape, you know," Bella whispered back as they walked in.

Bella was surprised to see the Steins grilling six steaks covered in gourmet salt and peppercorns. She caught the scent of the meat and heard her stomach embarrassingly groan. Onward she walked and took in the aromas of grilled sweet potatoes in butter along with cinnamon and apples from a cobbler baking in the oven. She was nostalgic as well, recalling that in that same kitchen hours ago, Justin had made her one of his signature omelets and that Arabian green coffee she loved so much.

"Agent Walker, we meet again." Morris gave a kind smile while adding a sprinkle of salt and pepper to the sizzling steaks. "Let me guess, medium rare."

"Those smell yummy. You are correct on the medium rare." Bella sat at the kitchen table across from Rachel and Rita Stein. "Yes, these are far better circumstances, Mr. Stein." Bella gave a slight grin and watched Morris grab three plates to put a steak on each.

"Alright, my dear family—and Bella—steaks are served." Morris grinned proudly and put a plate in front of Rita, Rachel, and Bella. He turned and grabbed another plate and added a fourth steak just as Shane walked in from the beach. "Shane, yours is ready too."

Shane Gentry nodded as he leaned in and gave Rachel a kiss. "Hey, Morris, could you make one more for my new surfing buddy?"

"You have a new surfing buddy?" Morris looked up in disbelief. "I didn't even know you could surf. A cowboy surfer... what is the West coming to?"

"I learned today from this towering giant of a guy. He's a great teacher." Shane waved a hand to a chiseled giant holding a surfboard as big as he was. Bella was surprised to see how easily the giant held the board. "Don't be shy, big fella. Come meet my folks."

"Hello everyone. I'm Justin Trestle. It's nice to meet you." Bella shook her head and bit her lip. She could see Justin was quite embarrassed.

"Justin Trestle, I've heard so much about you." Rachel gave Justin a hawkish, narrow stare.

Shane Gentry looked puzzled at his wife and then at Justin. "How could you know Conjure Man? We just met him, Rachel."

"Shane, my dear husband. You are talking to Justin Trestle—also known in the Navy SEALs as Conjure Man for his uncanny weather and intelligence ability. He had a predictive modeling talent that has beaten the best AI out there." Rachel shrugged then jerked a thumb over at Bella. "He's also got a girlfriend in the FBI."

"Ha-ha-ha, if that don't beat all. You're that guy, aren't you? Bella's shadow dude. The Mauna Loa bar had me laughing for days." Shane's eyes went wide with awe and admiration. "Wait, you took out three of Ace Tamaro's best men. Wow!" Shane gave a big aw-shucks grin and slapped his leg. "I knew there was something about you. Bella, this guy swims like a fish. Can I tell her about the tiger shark?"

"What about the tiger shark?" Bella asked sharply, turning her head toward Justin as he put his head down and winced. She had warned Justin about the sharks. "Shane, I know he won't tell me. So, we are all ears."

"Well, in all my years wrangling cattle and riding the occasional bull whether on the islands or back out west, I have never heard of anyone wrestling a tiger shark and … well, riding the thing like a horse. He's not Conjure Man to me. Justin, my friend, you are a real-life Aquaman." The whole table laughed in an uproar.

Morris wiped tears from his eyes and urged Justin to come sit with the family. "Aquaman, you have definitely earned a steak for that one. You need a job?"

"Private security for the Stein Plantation?" Justin moved to sit at the table as Morris passed him a plate.

"No, as a shark rider! Those cowboys are hard to catch!" Morris and everyone started howling with laughter again.

Bella playfully nudged Justin. "You had to go and ride a shark, again. One of these days you'll mess with the wrong shark."

"One of these days, I suppose," he replied.

An hour after the meal and more laughs, Justin nodded to everyone and said, "I'd better get showered and take a nap. It was a fun day."

"I bet it was." Bella stood to walk him out. "I'll be right back everyone."

"We surfin' tomorrow, Justin?" Shane looked giddy as a schoolboy on his first day of school.

"I'll be out there soon as the rosy fingers of dawn creep up the horizon. You know, I could learn to love this place." Justin looked down and grinned at Bella as he said it. "Do they have any good pizza places?"

"If you can stomach spam on your pizza, then Pie-sland Waves is the place to go," Shane told him. "That's the name of the game out here."

"Uh-oh, Miss Walker and folks. I may have to open a real pizza spot. Lots of pineapple and pepperoni. And we'll serve only the finest spam." Justin beamed proudly and winked at Bella as they walked out.

"How did you get made?" Bella asked after they had walked a length of beach to Justin's condominium. "Wait, this is where you've been staying?"

Bella looked upon a sweeping open glass structure with scenic flowers casting a myriad of colors adorning three fountains and gardens. White satin curtains billowed in the ocean breezes to the open expanse of Justin's living room and foyer. It was certainly not what Bella was expecting.

"I was sitting out on the beach reading up on the history and uses of lava tubes," he said as they entered. "Shane was walking by and said howdy. I offered him a root beer, and we started talking cattle. He said he missed his herd on Big Island, and things went from there. He's a kind man with a lot of chores on his plate—mostly keeping Rachel safe and out of trouble." Justin rolled his eyes as he sat down next to a mini fridge. He offered Bella a lemon water.

"Thank you, Aquaman," Bella said, winking. She took the water and looked out at the shimmering ocean waves. "This sure is a nice view."

He yawned and headed for the bed. "I think I need a nap. Surfing can wear you out quickly."

"You mean shark riding, Mr. Trestle. I didn't forget." Bella paused. "How in the heck does one catch a shark to ride anyway?"

Justin turned with a wicked grin. "A shark rider never tells." Then his face dropped, and he became serious. "Rachel's in over her head. You know that, don't you?"

Bella sighed. "I do. But we all are, Justin. This is a group that's been around for ages. Their understanding of operating large-scale and undetected is far superior to most law enforcement entities. But usually these days, they buy off their trouble. Multiple murders of clients are bad for the overall enterprise."

Justin furrowed his brow and looked out at the waves. "It's bad for The Bright Prince if what he's been doing was unsanctioned … especially now that it has cost the Yakuza money. But propping up a new guy isn't what they're about if the system has been in place and doing well. The way things are looking, I'm pretty sure Ace is on borrowed time. Now would be the time to crush his operation."

Bella rubbed her temples and put her frustrated head down. "But where to look for them? I know they went west. I know—"

Justin interrupted and pointed to the eastern mountains of Hawaii. "The lava tubes on this island are extensive. A person could get lost and never come out. You got lucky in your own experience. The Tears of the Dragon moved from the western side of the island to the east. I'd look for an off-grid place where they might have done a few murders or disappearances. They won't be there for long though. I'm sure Ace will be trying to go back to extorting the Steins or some other wealthy families. He can't stop himself now. He's gotten a taste of the big money in the Yakuza laundering operations."

"I was thinking he would head east too. But I never thought about body dumps and such." Bella paused, then an idea hit her like a lightning bolt. "Perry Leilani."

"The murdered officer?" Justin sat down. "What about him?"

Bella held Justin's hands and stared into his eyes. "His partner told us just before Perry disappeared while securing the war god kill site, he had been investigating some missing persons cases near Haiku Stairs. Then we find his body hanging right there. Do you know what I think?"

"That Ace moved east to his backup base of operations. The heavily covered cave systems, and the fact that the Haiku Stairs is closed under penalty of fines to the public, make it perfect for a Yakuza gang on the run. But—" Justin frowned a moment and leaned in.

"But what, Justin?" Bella shook her head puzzled.

"That would be an incredibly closed-in place if it were surrounded. I'm sure Ace and his men could have blasted side caves to the sea for escape by boat or found a cave system that they modified for escape or airport transports." Justin went and grabbed a map.

Bella thought more about how the FBI would proceed if their guess panned out. "Yeah, it's too bottlenecked in for a shoot-out. It would be a poor long-term base. Too many eyes nearby with the hikers on the other intersecting trails. But if your base of operations had almost been breached by the FBI in a raid, this area will do—at least for a temporary base until you could relocate to a more secluded island." Bella pointed to the map and then Big Island and the rest of the islands in the Hawaiian chain.

Justin stood, rubbed his bowling ball of a head, and glanced in the direction of Haiku Stairs. "The Yakuza don't take unnecessary risks. And they don't usually make mistakes, Bella. Unless The Bright Prince himself is hiding from his own syndicate for screwing up, I don't see him basing his whole operation in the lava tubes beneath the Haiku Stairs."

"Justin, you need to rest. You've been working too hard … shark-wrangling." Bella got back up with a coy grin. Then she leaned in to hug the behemoth of a man and give him a kiss.

Justin pulled back and stared at her. "What's that for?"

Bella gave Justin a sly smile as she saw he was nervous. To Bella, it was a typical Justin moment. He was a brave fool who'd ride a shark.

But when a woman kissed him for saving her life, he'd get as jittery as a teenager on a first date. "You saved my life and George's, dummy. Why did you think I kissed you?" Then in jest she added, "It's not because I like you."

Justin laughed nervously as Bella continued to hug him. "I'd better go rest as my girlfriend ordered. I'd rather wrestle another shark than get her mad."

CHAPTER TWENTY-SEVEN

ELLA TOOK A MOMENT BEFORE WALKING BACK UP THE TRAIL TO
the bungalow, considering the best approach to tell Morris, Rita,
and Shane that they would have to go under protective custody with
the FBI. The why was obvious: The Tears of the Dragon were going to
come after Rachel and her family, no doubt. But the bigger question was,
would the rest of the Yakuza syndicate back their play and attack?

There was a nagging question that she kept circling back to. As she
looked at the crystal blue waves—waves she had yet to splash around in,
Bella went over each question again and again to have all her ducks in a
row when she questioned the Steins.

I must ask Rita and Morris why Saul turned on them. What made him
bring in an organized crime syndicate to extort his alleged friends? It seems
an extreme risk for a multimillionaire hotel chain owner. Why not just hire his
own in-house thugs? What did he hope to get out of extorting them using The
Tears of the Dragon?

And, most importantly, how did Saul coerce all the security to betray their employer?

"Ah, Bella, you're back. Your Justin is quite the character." Morris had a pleasant smile as he sat on a large extended couch in the corner of the room with Rita. Shane was on the opposite one, sitting next to Rachel.

"That he is. But your friend Saul was an interesting one as well. I have a lot—"

"Bella, we can take a little time off from the job." Rachel interrupted. But they had already discussed that this would be their tactic to get her parents to open up.

"Normally I would, Rachel. But the Yakuza tend to not chill out on enemies or former customers. While I have greatly appreciated the hospitality, Rachel and I have a sworn duty to keep you safe and catch these evil men. The questions I ask are necessary." Bella kept a firm tone and studied Morris and Rita. Poor Shane seemed surprised at the abrupt change in Bella. And that was the point. They'd brought Shane in on what they were doing as well.

But Justin's chance meeting with Shane had been a total coincidence.

Morris's face went flat and expressionless. He leaned forward picking his teeth with a toothpick making Bella a little uneasy. "I see. You never quit, do you, Agent Walker? Now I know why you aren't married yet. Poor Justin doesn't realize how married you are to the FBI."

Rita leveled her husband with a stare. "That was uncalled for, Morris. She's got a job to do. And right now, it's to protect us from that fool of a friend of yours—the late, great Saul Manning, whose antics could still get us all killed."

"My apologies, Bella. It's been … a hell of a week. Go on with your questions if it will help you catch these thugs." Morris adjusted in his seat and gestured for her to begin.

Bella sat down in a chair across from them. "Why would your life-long friend turn on you?"

"Jealousy. It's simple enough. Saul wanted what he couldn't have." Bella looked at Morris carefully. But it was the reddened face of Rita that was telling the tale.

"Your wife and your plantation? He wanted your life?" Bella thought she understood.

Morris took a deep sigh. Then he recalled a fight he'd had with Saul two years ago.

"Yes, he wanted to take everything I had … just as, he alleged, I had done to him when we were poor kids. Two years ago, he screamed at me in a drunken rage that Rita should have been his wife and my plantation his home."

Rita put both hands on her knees. "Agent Walker, Morris did steal me away from Saul." Now it was Bella's turn to be red-faced with surprise. "This man walked up to me at a luau while Saul went to grab us some spiced pork plates. He introduced himself as Morris Stein. He told me he was the poorest kid on all the islands of Hawaii, but one day he and Saul would have a big farm together."

Rita stopped a moment. She was having a wonderful recollection of the past when Saul Manning hadn't become the bitter, heartless monster he'd later be—when all three of them danced and sang together as friends ... then she ruined it, in a way, by falling head over heels for Morris.

Saul begged me not to break his heart. But I told him it just wasn't the same magic and butterflies like I had every time I saw Morris. Oh! How he wailed and cried on my shoulder when I broke his heart.

Bella watched as Rita wiped another tear. "The heart wants what the heart wants, Bella. Even after fifty years of a happy marriage, this was the only man for me."

"I understand, but... it bothers me. He had all that accumulated wealth, and yet he sought out the Yakuza to square things with y'all. You can see why it's puzzling," Bella admitted to them as she stood to get a bottle of water. She asked if anyone else wanted water. Shane nodded and Rita. Rachel and Morris passed. They both had their own.

Morris stroked his chin. "Saul never wanted to do the work that was necessary. Big ideas... I'd tell him to stay the course. 'Weather the storm, Saul, and things will roll your way again.' I'd say, 'Storms in life roar in and build or break us.'"

"I'm guessing Saul didn't listen." Rachel interrupted her father, sitting forward on the couch.

"He'd get impatient. *Impulsive.* Always hustling for bigger things, always trying to one-up everyone else. Good traits to have when building up a business, but when you're already at the top… well, it seemed like not even all his success was ever enough. He could never lose. He'd get furious and do whatever it took to win. It frightened me on more than one occasion." Morris rubbed his forehead with a handkerchief from his pocket. "Saul at one point had more money than he or generations of his kids—if he'd settled down to have any—could have spent. But being Saul, he had to pull the pin and grenade everything. He got in with the back-lot gambling casinos… then made stupid deals and even stupider bets that got him in deep with the loan sharks."

"And the Tears of the Dragon gave him an opportunity to keep all his hotels," Bella offered, pushing back her curls and taking a sip of water.

"Yes. All he had to do was bring friends to his hotels—complimentary, of course. And the Yakuza did the rest. Then Saul came up with the antiquities auction idea, likely to feed his gambling issues, since he'd been banned from every casino in Hawaii. You already know how his Yakuza friendship ended."

Bella was seeing a picture unfolding in her mind. But there was a problem with this version of Morris Stein's story. Everything fit too easily and was too smooth a conclusion. Bella was certain he was holding something back. It was a good story… but she couldn't be sure it was the whole story.

She decided to go back to the one piece that kept troubling her. "But how was Saul Manning—your friend, a degenerate gambler, and bad businessman—so charismatic to make all of your security people turn on you?"

Morris shrugged and put his hands up defensively. "I wouldn't know how he pulled that one off, Bella. Maybe his Yakuza buddies threatened their families. More than likely, he bribed all of them."

"Well, it's settled then. If they can bribe private security teams, then we need to put you up in a safe house." Bella couldn't suppress a smirk after seeing the shock on Rachel's face. "Wouldn't you agree, Rachel?"

Rachel stood and went to her mother. She bent down and glanced up at both of her parents. "Mom and Dad, if they can bribe and coerce people like Jerry Dover and Pat Buckner, they can get to anyone. We have a nice—"

Morris shook his head and chuckled. "I saw what happened to the last guy y'all protected in Kapolei. No thanks. If you want agents watching us at our fortress on Big Island, I have no problem with that."

"And the former security teams that fled into the mountains—I bet they could breach that compound faster than a Hawaiian SWAT team. But you have a handle on them, don't you?" Bella narrowed her eyes and walked up to him. "Were you ever in any danger?"

Morris compressed his lips into a tight line. Tension crackled between them like lightning.

"How long have you been friends with the other Yakuza, Morris and Rita? The ones protecting you right now from The Tears of the Dragon?"

"Look, we've had nothing to do with any of that scum, Bella. Why do you think we aren't telling the truth?" Morris was becoming agitated. Maybe he was being honest; maybe he wasn't. Bella glanced at Rita. She was cool and calm. There was a tight grin on her face.

"You haven't told him, Rita?" Bella looked at Rachel and Shane who had bewildered looks on their faces. "You haven't told anyone. What was the endgame here, Mrs. Stein?"

"Bella, George is here with the other agents," Rachel said. "We'd better wrap this up quickly or finish this up at the Stein Plantation safe room."

"Well, out with it, Rita. You're among family." Bella gave Rita a terse grin and crossed her arms.

Rita looked at Morris with loving eyes and grinned sheepishly. Then seeing her charms weren't working, she shrugged. "I was going to tell you, Morris. I swear I was. They are paying seven times what we would make at market for pineapple and macadamia nuts. They need it cleaned—"

Morris's eyes went wide with fear. He jumped up from the couch as if he'd been struck in the face. "Oh, dear lord, Rita! What have you done?"

CHAPTER TWENTY-EIGHT

"**T**HAT WAS BY FAR THE STRANGEST INTERROGATION I'VE EVER been involved in." Bella rubbed her head and glanced at an equally bewildered Rachel.

"For about a minute I thought Momma had brokered a deal with Yakuza thugs. I mean, I had heart palpitations thinking my mother was cleaning money and not macadamia nuts for the mob. Instead, Mauna Loa's supply is way low, and the demand for Big Island macadamia nuts is sky-high. Seven times the going rate that shrewd woman is going to make."

"Only if they are clean!" Bella laughed.

Shane chuckled and pursed his lips in disbelief. "The fact that you two clowns would even believe little old Rita Stein was a money-laundering gangster concerns me deeply."

"We share your concern, honey. Take care of Mom and Dad over there. You're the only man I truly trust." Rachel hugged her husband tightly. "Well, maybe shark boy will be hanging close too."

"I sure hope so, Rachel. I'll need someone to surf with ... and karate chop a few bad guys." Shane nodded to Bella as he walked to get into the FBI transport for the airport. "That's a righteous dude you have there, Bella. Don't wait too long to marry him." Bella got red-faced for the third time in a day and nodded.

Once Shane and her parents were gone, Rachel turned to Bella. "I have the new guys working with the map information you came up with. I was thinking caves and lava tubes too. But I hadn't even thought about the Perry Leilani and missing cases on Haiku Stairs. You came up with that or Conjure Man?"

"Who do you think told me to look for bodies or some weird guys coming into an area?" Bella took a breath and cracked her neck. "I just was able to line up Perry's death, the cases he had been working on, and the number of disappearances. Then it all seemed to fit. But Justin thinks they won't be there long—if they are there at all."

"It's a dense jungle area with a spiderweb of caves that may or may not be intersecting each other," Rachel added. "It would be tough to get logistics in or around the peaks without winches, elevators, buildings, or Connex containers in place. Yeah, he's right, I think. They used it to get to someplace else."

Rachel walked to her vehicle and glanced in the direction of Kapolei and then Haiku Stairs. "Unless ..."

"Unless?"

Rachel opened her car door, then turned back to Bella. "If they have had a falling out with Japan or with the upper Hawaiian Yakuza bosses, they'd need a secluded place to lie low—a place where The Tears of the Dragon could buy time to get back in favor with the Yakuza. In other words, earn millions of dollars to appease them and buy their lives back. But you can bet they'll all lose their left pinky fingers for embarrassing Japan."

Bella rubbed her head and groaned. "Why do they always cut off the pinky fingers? I've never understood that part of the gang."

"Take a few hours to rest and catch up on some sleep, Bella. I think we've all earned it before we wrap this one up soon." Rachel yawned and climbed into her Lincoln, then waved as she left.

Bella turned and walked back inside. She figured that she would have a ton of dishes to wash, but the Steins had cleaned up everything. Bella almost face-palmed, feeling ashamed of thinking the worst of them.

Walking to the chilled bedroom in the back of the bungalow, Bella finally got a well-deserved nap. She dreamed of vast emerald jungles, roaring white waterfalls, and songs from the jungle birds.

She awoke five hours later refreshed and ready to tackle the world. She stretched her arms and back, then climbed out of bed to stare upon a glorious red setting sun. Bella heard the distant rolling waves and the howling winds blasting through the trees and white dunes.

She thought of two things then. One, she wondered if Justin had slept as soundly. And two, were there any more books on the Hawaiian caves? She wasn't ready to face Algernon Magnum after the way she had acted toward him the last time. Obviously, her aunt had kept her other life in Hawaii from everyone. And Bella's nerve was still raw about the secret relationship.

Bella checked out some other listings of bookstores near her on Nimitz and found just the store. It was sure to have the collection of books on lava tubes and cave systems that she needed. Dressed in athletic clothes for her evening run, Bella decided to make a quick drive to Bent Pages. It was just around the corner. She'd pop in and pop out, then maybe go check out that cool wreck she'd spotted the other day.

If she thought The Salty Pirate was extraordinary, Bent Pages blew her mind. As she pulled the door open, colorful, fluorescent green and red dragon heads on both sides of the door roared and bellowed smoke. Bella was instantly stunned and amazed by the store's props. All around her, shelves were stacked high with fantasy literature and medieval myths and legends, each adorned with knights in suits of real armor propped with swords in front of them pointed down to the floor.

Toward the middle shelves, pirate mannequins in full costume guarded Alexandre Dumas collections, and of course Robert Louis Stevenson first editions. But the centerpiece of Bent Pages was its authentic costumed Hawaiian displays with each of the various war gods guarding their respective books.

"This place is amazing," Bella said out loud as she headed straight to books on Hawaii cave and lava tube history.

"Thank you, young lady. Nathan and I work hard to give our customers a genuine experience." A middle-aged woman with kind, brown eyes and an incredibly athletic frame for her age pointed to a taller gentleman who was adjusting the pirate boots on a strangely familiar pirate. The pirate was possibly Blackbeard. Or possibly Algernon Magnum himself.

Bella introduced herself putting out her hand to shake. "I'm Bella. I'm honored to meet you."

The bookstore owner nodded. "I'm Dara Austin, and that's my husband Nathan. But you can just call him Nate. What brings you into Bent Pages?"

"Lava tubes and the history of them." Bella turned to look at ten different books on the subject. Each was organized and labeled by dates sitting on a shelf to her left. Each book had to be four hundred pages or more. To read and research one might take days. She'd have to assign portions of the books to the team to speed things along.

Dara walked over to look at the titles of each of the books. "Are you a spelunker? Because you sure don't look like a caver to me, Bella. No scratches on the shins or heavy callouses on the hands. I bet you're more of a runner."

Bella shrugged. "You got me. I try to avoid caves." Bella paused in the moment. For some reason she couldn't quite explain—maybe Dara reminded her of her own momma back home—she decided to share a little of her misadventure. "I was walking through a lava tube field the other night. It was a real bad experience."

Dara, wide-eyed with a hand to her shocked mouth, exclaimed, "Are you bona fide crazy? That's a good way to get yourself killed! Or worse, on one of those 411 missing person shows like that David Pa... pa... lot..."

"Paulides, honey. It's David Paulides. And trust us, those shows always give me and Dara the chills," the taller gentleman supplied. "Go with a guide, preferably during the daytime. And never go into those tubes when there's been heavy rain."

Dara paused and studied Bella's face and curls. She leaned back and looked Bella up and down with a puzzled stare. "Now that I'm seeing you, it is truly uncanny. Bella... Walker, you look just like her, you know."

Bella was rattled by Dara knowing her last name at first. But then, information seemed to flow like the wind on this island. Algernon Magnum had probably spread the word. "How do you know my last name? I never told you it was Walker." She paused furrowing her brow. "Second, who, may I ask, do I look like?" She was starting to think coming here was a bad idea.

"Let me start with the picture. Then we can sort out the rest." Dara went over to the Robert Louis Stevenson section. Bella's heart began to pick up a beat in growing concern. She started to feel the chilled drops of perspiration on her forehead as Dara grabbed a book from the section, a grin on her face. Then her dread grew as Dara handed her a black and white photo from over a hundred years ago.

"Bella, you could be the spitting image of Margaret Isabella Balfour Stevenson!" Dara and Nate continued the uncomfortable beaming as Bella looked down at the woman's picture in the book.

Bella lifted a brow and remained calm while analyzing the photograph. In truth, she was stunned and taken aback by the image. But to show any surprise might really bring out the couple's stares and more questions that Bella didn't want to answer. "It is an uncanny resemblance, I'll give you that much. But I've had this with other photographs from antiquity such as Louisa May Alcott and the like. I take it she was someone related to Robert Louis Stevenson by the last name."

Dara gave an accusing point of her index finger. Her brow furrowed, and her brown eyes narrowed. "First, young lady, you do not look like Louisa May Alcott. I can't believe you would be so dismissive of your lineage. Anyway, I'll shoot down your gaff right now." Dara huffed as she pointed to Margaret's chin line. Then she had Nate grab a picture of Louisa May Alcott. He fetched it quickly and gave it to Dara for comparison. "Don't you see? Your chin line is too narrow. And your eyes are too hawkish like Robert's. And that fire in your eyes, Louisa May Alcott only wished she had your passion. I would not want you chasing us as an FBI agent."

Now Nate really stood in awe. His wife had thrown out any chance Bella was going to be able to shrug this one off. He said in a solemn, almost reverent tone to Bella, "You must be relentless when you go after a bad guy. Look at her eyes even now, Dara. I'm getting the chills."

Bella fixed a polite smile on her face. "Well, I'd better be going. Thank you for the book. How much do I owe you?" she asked, wanting to get as far away from the bookstore as she could.

"We cannot accept any money from so distinguished a book lover. You consider it a profound gift to aid you in catching those horrible men that have sullied our paradise," Dara replied. "Use your drive, Bella Walker, just like our beloved Natalie, to jail those swine." Bella was rocked and stunned by her words. Dara truly had a way with them.

"Um. Thank you," she replied. She took the book from Dara, held it close to her, crossed in her arms, and ran out of the store in a blur. Outside in her car, Bella rubbed her temples and groaned. With a face flushed in embarrassment as onlookers came up to the couple and they pointed to her, Bella wished that she could be anywhere but Bent Pages.

When she got back to the bungalow, she grabbed her hoodie in case the breezes picked up the chill near the water. She put the book—*The Comprehensive History and Mapping of Hawaiian Lava Tubes*—on a coffee table facing the sand and surf. She peered out to the glimmering night sky and decided the course she'd take. Due to the darkness of the area and how tricky the rock formations would be to traverse, the wrecked wooden ship wouldn't be an option. Besides, she'd had enough of any seafaring mysteries for the time being. It was time to get her mind focused back on the case and away from the constant Hawaiian distractions... and definitely off anything to do with Robert Louis Stevenson.

She stretched, took some deep breaths, and double tied her laces, wondering if she might run into Justin—literally. Nothing aggravated her more when she was in a full sprint and Justin would dust her on a straight run because she had to stop to tie a lace. With everything checked and stretched, Bella ran like the wind down toward the beach and beyond.

Half an hour later, Justin sprinted up beside her, and they raced the shoreline in full sprint. "You've been slacking, lady. What took you so long to get out here?"

"You wouldn't believe it if I told you." Bella shook her head as she picked up her pace. She moved her bent arms to take in more air and lengthened her stride.

"Try me." Justin tried to match her speed. But Bella could see in a side glance he was fatigued.

"Another time. But I'll never look at *Treasure Island* the same way." Then Bella seized the opportunity as Justin shook his head puzzled by her statement. She put a hundred yards between her and Conjure Man.

And, this time, Bella's shoelaces stayed tied.

Two hours later, they walked back up to the bungalow. Bella was refreshed but tired. Throughout her run, not Rachel, nor anyone else from the FBI field office had called. It wasn't that unusual with the way the case had been wearing everyone down. And after the fiasco of the last botched raid on The Tears of the Dragon, everyone was making triple sure that the information disseminated would be one hundred percent accurate. And that included Bella's speculation of the Haiku Stairs being a possible base of operations—which she prayed it wasn't. She'd had enough of lava tubes for a lifetime.

"So, you got the right book this time," Justin stated as Bella gave him a towel to wipe his face.

"Yes, this store had a reference library better than the Hawaiian FBI. It was quite the place, and the owners were a sweet couple." Bella handed Justin a lemon water. She got her own and then sat down across from Justin.

"What did they look like, if you don't mind me asking?" Justin's face went taut and his voice became too casual. Bella was caught off guard by the question.

Puzzled by Justin wanting their description, she answered, narrowing her eyes. "Both are middle-aged. She has brown hair and brown—"

"Brown eyes and in great shape? He's tall and athletic-looking as well?" Justin smiled a wolfish grin and pointed at the window, where the very couple in question were approaching. "I think you have groupies. At least they have the stare of rock band groupies. Is there something important you aren't telling me, Bella Walker? Are you secretly a social media influencer?"

Bella growled a warning and rubbed her left temple. "Can it, Aquaman. I'll tell you about it later. I really need to talk with Rachel about protocol. I bet she told Algernon where I live in Colorado too. Ugh!"

"They seem harmless enough. Maybe they have some more information about our case." Justin kept grinning as he watched Bella squirm. "This is going to be fun ... for me."

Bella watched as Nathan rang the doorbell. By the way they were both dressed, they seemed ready to enter a church, not a Hawaiian bungalow. "Bella, we hope we haven't disturbed you."

"How did you get my address, Nate?" Bella had to get the leaked address out of the way.

"That was simple enough. Agent Gentry has been a dear friend for years. We have helped her on several of her cases, as we have your Aunt Natalie."

Bella glanced at Justin who had a Cheshire cat grin. Bella wanted to slug him. She could almost read his thoughts: *You need better friends.*

"I could already guess that you have, Mr. and Mrs. Austin." Bella cocked her head and looked to the sky.

"And this fine bull is your husband? Rachel said you have been a happy couple for years, Mr. Trestle." Dara nodded politely and grinned. "Oh, where are my manners? I'm Dara and this is my man Nate."

"I'm truly glad to meet you," replied Justin with a classic aw-shucks grin. He extended his hand to shake both of theirs politely.

"So, what was it—" Bella's phone rang interrupting. It was Rachel. Bella excused herself and walked out by the pool to answer the call.

"Does just everyone have your address, Rachel?"

"Relevant parties. The team was going to invite you to a lava tube crash, if you were game. But I see you are entertaining the Austins." Bella could hear Keith, George, Susan, and Billy laughing as they shouted,

"Hey, Fallen Angel. Gravity works! It must have hurt big time when you fell from heaven!"

"Funny. I guess they have some more information." Bella paced the length of the pool looking back to see Justin laughing with Nate and Dara.

"I've known Nate and Dara for quite a while. If there is anybody you can trust on Hawaii, those two are tops in my book. They'd only give the information to you. You made quite the impression on them." Rachel paused to tell Keith to shush, then continued. "I'll follow up with you in the morning."

"Sounds splendid. Tell Shane and the family I said hi." Bella knew Rachel would be checking on her family to ensure they were staying safe. Babysitting her husband and parents was probably giving her headaches.

"Welcome back, honey." Justin had a glimmer of boyish mischief in his eyes. "Have a seat. Nate was giving me an incredible history of the Hawaiian war gods. Nate, this Ku is of particular interest to Bella's case."

"It *should* be of particular concern to her case, Justin. The Tears of the Dragon think of themselves so arrogantly. It's probably why they are on the outs with their prefecture." Dara nodded knowingly to Justin and then to Bella.

"Wow, you were divulged all the particulars of our case, Dara? Nate?" Bella was furious. Giving out particulars to civilians was a massive violation of standard FBI procedures. If Rachel or anyone at the FBI office did so, and the brass found out, it would be more than a slap on the wrists.

"We were given all this information by one of your people." Nate stood and brushed back his hair to explain. "We thought Rachel had sent him to us. But the more he pestered us about antiquities and relics, the more we got concerned. We didn't mind him asking us about Hawaiian history and the lava tubes. But when he kept asking over and over again about the costs of relics," Nate said, pointing in the direction of Haiku Stairs, "I got furious with him and Dara did too. Especially his disrespect of the war gods Ku, Kanaloa, Lono, and Kane. That was the line in the sand he crossed for both of us."

"Why didn't you go immediately to Rachel with this?" Bella narrowed her eyes and leaned in.

"We didn't make the connection of what was going on until after the first murders, Bella," Dara admitted apologetically. "Those poor people beheaded by the Tears of the Dragon in a sloppy rendition of a sacrificial ceremony to Ku was a disgrace. But we both can tell you from years of experience dealing with the Yakuza as business owners, you walk a dangerous slope going up against Yakuza thugs in Hawaii."

Justin sat up in his chair and cracked his neck, then gave the couple a stern stare as he rubbed his chin. "Not that I need to ask, because I can already guess… but who was the agent?"

"I can't remember his name. We get so many people coming in and out of the store. This is frustrating indeed." Dara looked over to Bella apologetically then back to Justin. "Can you remember anything, Nate?" The two winced trying to think of the name.

"It's okay, Nate and Dara. What about what he looked like? Anything ring a bell?"

They shook their heads. Bella knew they were lying. Most likely scared to cross the Yakuza or their bought-and-paid-for agents.

"I know you're scared. I know you could tell us right now," she urged. "Please."

"But we told you; we don't know his name. Only that he said he was with the FBI and knew Agent Gentry." Nate continued to put his hands out defensively. His wife followed suit.

Justin pointed to Nate and Dara to sit. "You came here to tell Bella the agent's name. But the weight of doing that may be too heavy." Justin gripped his fists, and his knuckles cracked like machine gun fire. "The Tears of the Dragon cut heads off of people that they do business with. Keep that in mind. Saul Manning found out, and the people who bought from those black market auctions across the Hawaiian Islands did too. But I'm sure the recent news over by Kapolei scared you silly."

"That scared everyone," Dara said nervously. Bella got the couple some water for their dry, scared mouths.

"Well," Justin began, "scared or not, you need to keep your heads in the game. I'll handle the rest so you don't lose them." Bella almost gulped as Justin pulled both Dara and Nate in by the bottom of their chairs. Then he put their faces to within inches of his own. "You get my drift? Now, quit the act. I know both of you were at the auctions too. I'd hate for Ace to find out."

CHAPTER TWENTY-NINE

"Do you think they'll talk, Justin?" Bella held his hand as they stood on the porch watching the Austins drive off in a hurry.

"I think we rattled those two pretty good. Give them a few hours. I twisted things up in their wheelhouse. Maybe they grow a conscience." Justin sighed. "Rachel couldn't get them to squeal. She turfed them off on you. You know that, right?"

"No doubt on that. They probably played me at the store with the whole Robert Louis Stevenson thing." Bella realized she had inadvertently let the cat out of the bag. "Oh, boy, here it comes!"

"That crazy story is legit? You're the descendant of Robert Louis Stevenson?"

Somehow, it didn't surprise her to know that Justin had heard about it.

"Better question, Mr. Trestle, how did you hear about it? You don't seem too surprised." Bella squinted looking at him intensely while they walked back inside the bungalow.

Justin shrugged and rubbed his brow. "I was following up with an old contact from back in my high sea days of travel. His name's Algernon Magnum. He—"

"Why does everything on this island circle back to Algernon Magnum?" Bella stormed off and went to her room. "I don't have time to go over the details of my alleged—and I do mean *alleged*—ancestor. We have a case to close. Good night."

Bella had her coffee in hand at seven the next morning and was proceeding up the side stairs into the FBI building when she saw the strangest—or not so strange—sight. The Austins were already waiting for her.

"I wasted your time with your husband last night. And I can see he's a man not to be trifled with. Did he really ride a tiger shark?" Nate was fidgeting and overthinking his words. It was obvious he was trying to stall.

Bella pursed her lips and began to scold the couple. "He's not my husband. And you're wasting my time now, Mr. and Mrs. Austin. As it stands, I have you referencing one of our agents in your store. That's an accusation against a man you can't name or identify. Well, you *won't* name and identify. For all I know—"

"We got scared when we saw the picture you had on a desk. It was a crime scene photo with you on a mountain bagging evidence," Nathan began. Bella remembered the wind and how she slid on that Moanalua Valley trail. She recalled the agent in the photo had taken an easier path to reach the crime scene… a path he'd probably taken earlier to help the Yakuza murder innocent people. "He was right next to you smiling."

"We have seen the decapitations before, Bella. We have seen friends and family that crossed the Yakuza and The Tears of the Dragon. They always come down on the snitches and the agents in the end. Can you promise we won't end up like them?" Dara pleaded, her eyes wide. The woman looked like she had aged years overnight.

"I can promise you that Rachel and I, plus everyone at the FBI, will do whatever it takes to keep you safe—starting with putting you under our protection." Bella placed a hand on both their shoulders. "Now, tell me the name and describe him in detail."

"I really believed him when he said he loved Hawaiian history. We both fell for his charm. Quite handsome—he had that Brad Pitt thing going on, didn't he Nate?" Dara looked over to Nate for confirmation.

"I suppose he wasn't hard on the eyes. He would primp in the bookstore mirror like he was going on a TV show or something. And that's when I knew he didn't read books but probably sat on them or something. The way he said words was too funny." Nate shook his head remembering.

"Oh, yes, dear. He called Ku, 'cow,' when he first came into the store. Then there was that bad poem he recited in a bad English accent. He certainly is no Byron, that one." Dara held Nate's hand and gave Bella a wry smile. "We got duped by him, you know. He talked us into coming to one auction saying it was for a preservation society benefit. We should have known better."

"Yes, you should have known. Especially with all your experience with the Yakuza and the history of stolen relics on the islands." Bella exhaled bitterly. "Now, quit stalling. You bought relics and went to the auction. That was a recent sighting, from what Justin's people told me." Bella watched the kind, brown eyes of Dara go wide knowing they were caught in another lie.

Dara went on a rant, which didn't surprise Bella in the least. "Fine. I see you have no soul, Agent Walker. You are putting our lives at risk. You are as relentless as your ancestor for a story. Just like that disgusting Robert Louis Stevenson, you need your fill of literary pain. Sure, we sell his books because they are priceless. But the history of the man would pale to what we have done. Did—"

"Give me the name, or I lock you both up!" Bella interrupted with an angry demand. "Then I put the word out across the island. Once they hear you got locked up, which will get back to your friends with The Tears of the Dragon, you'll get the closest shave of your lives. Then you won't have to worry anymore about being heads above the competition in the stolen relics trade."

Dara and Nate Austin both leaned in and whispered. Bella wasn't surprised who they revealed. It gave her final confirmation of what the team had long known. "It was Thomas O'Reilly. But he'd rather us call him TJ."

CHAPTER THIRTY

THE AUSTINS WERE BROUGHT TO RACHEL GENTRY, CONFIRMING again what they had told Bella. SAC Harris was also in attendance as they went over each time TJ had shown up pestering them at Bent Pages.

"He's been coming to your store for over two years asking questions about relics, and you're just now coming to us?" he asked skeptically. "Seems you have more to tell, don't you?" He looked over to Bella and Rachel before setting his steel eyes back on them. Bella was glad that he seemed to have caught on to their ruse.

Dara took a sip of coffee that had been provided to her in a Styrofoam cup. She brushed back a loose strand of hair and cleared her throat. "Well, sir, he duped—"

"You duped yourselves." Rachel's voice was almost a hiss. Bella could tell she felt betrayed by her former friends. "Algernon warned you not to do it. But you couldn't resist that quick cash to pay off the overhead you were incurring on the new shop. If Nate hadn't gotten that stomach bug on the day of the last auction, convenient I may add, you would have been the eighth and ninth headless bodies we would have found."

"Rachel, how can you say something so cruel?" Dara scolded. Bella shook her head. This was going to get her in much worse trouble.

Bella's and SAC Harris's eyes went wide as Rachel fired right back. "Don't scold me after what you have done, Dara! Don't you dare stand on your pedestal now and lecture me. You have been involved with the very filth that's destroying our island."

"I'm sure the Stein family are bastions of honesty and integrity," Nate grumbled under his breath, looking out the window toward the Hawaiian mountains.

"Oh, I see. Not that I need to explain my family's success to a bunch of crooks, but my parents run successful businesses honestly. So, when something goes south or a new group of thugs shows up, the first thing you and your ilk do is accuse them of criminal ties. Could you two just admit that you are projecting? I can see you won't admit you chose to entangle yourself into a murderous crime syndicate." Rachel took an angry breath and pointed her index finger at both of them accusingly. "News flash: look in the mirror! You *gladly* walked into black market auctions of ancient relics. You chose to wash dirty money for the Yakuza. Now your legacy will be marred forever… not that running a failed bookstore on one of the busiest streets in all of Hawaii is much of a legacy."

Rachel paused, seeing the tears falling down Dara's face and Nate grumbling obscenities in her direction that made even SAC Harris's face flush. "Great, I finally get to see the real Austins."

"Go on, Rachel. It wouldn't be the first time a Stein stepped on a small business with their haughty ways." Nate held his crying wife and leered angrily.

Rachel put her head down and took a deep breath. "One more thing before we put you into custody for money laundering. Your store was a crown jewel to me and the real book lovers of the Hawaiian Islands. It was as mysterious as an ancient museum in the oldest cities and as eclectic as the finest wax museum in Paris. But a failed venture, nonetheless, for whatever reason."

Dara looked up, her eyes aflame with a vengeful fury. "Well, thank you, Rachel Stein. Maybe you can get your daddy and momma to buy it, like they have everything else. Turn it into, as you say, an ancient museum."

"We're done here." Nate Austin angrily grumbled. "Our lawyer will chew you up and spit you out, agents. There'll be a suit for the way you treated us."

"You'll probably beat the wrap, Mr. and Mrs. Austin. The evidence, at best, is your own admission. I'm sure you'll say you were under duress. But all the same, I wouldn't want to be you when the Yakuza find out you snitched and the islanders find out your real business. If you have any bargaining chips, now's the time you come clean." SAC Harris motioned to them both to stand to be processed. "Agent Makani and Dwyer, bring them to be processed."

"We might be able to help on the other auction and processing areas." Dara blurted out as Nate facepalmed and shook his head. "We need to think of our future, Nate. Put us into protective custody somewhere other than Kapolei. You guys really blundered that one. That man is lucky to be alive."

After Dara and Nate were put into protective custody pending a possible formal arrest, SAC Harris met with Rachel and Bella. "They have some very useful information. They are both cooperating fully to see justice for the murder victims."

"Out of the kindness of their hearts, I'm sure." Rachel looked out her window in the distance then back to SAC Harris and Bella. "This job, sometimes… and the people you thought you knew."

"Don't be too hard on yourself, Agent Gentry. I keyed in on one thing about both of them. They have been at this conning game a long time. It just took a very long time for them to get caught." SAC Harris narrowed his stare and slightly bent his head. "It's a shame all the work they put into the place will be a waste."

"That's what frustrates me the most, SAC Harris. They had such a wonderful place." Rachel pursed her lips and put both hands behind her head looking at the ceiling of her office. "Both of those con artists seemed to have an extensive, encyclopedic knowledge of various literature and history. They were better than a Google search when I needed specific details of something for a case. Now I know why they knew so much of the local criminal element. It saddens me that they have so much local literary intelligence, but they can't stay out of trouble."

"It's a double-edged sword dealing with crooks like that," Bella offered. "You need their information, their savvy, and impressions of a particular area and the criminal element working there. But on the other hand, it's a deal with a devil who may be funneling your information, whereabouts, and case direction to the highest bidder of said criminal outfit."

Harris checked his watch. "It's nine o'clock. We have a meeting in ten minutes with HPD, SWAT, and the other agencies over our vanished Tears of the Dragon and, of course, our beloved Thomas Joseph

O'Reilly. It's obvious we will no longer call him an agent of the FBI." He gave a devilish smile to both Rachel and Bella. "I even brought in the Hawaiian parks service who will be our guides, if we're headed where I think we are."

An hour into the meeting, the team went over the details of breaching the mountain of Ko'oalau. George and Keith began with the multiple possible entry points for a vertical assault. Each began with a brief history of the Haiku Stairs and the various abandoned structures that could be potential hideouts for Ace Tamaro and his men.

"Here were several power generating stations set up by the Navy in the forties. The batteries and hardware with the right skills and repair might generate enough power to run a small city. They sure built these to last a long time," Keith said, outlining each area with a laser pointer. "Anyway, as you can see, this won't be easy terrain to view, much less climb. If they are there, helicoptering into each of these areas and these modified caves will be risky. They'll have the rifle advantage to pick us off as the SWAT and police teams rope in."

"We'll be sitting ducks is what you really mean, Agent Benton." Chief Como put his hands together and grimaced. "I don't like it. The climbs on those ridges, provided they're solid and not rifled with lava tubes and caves, will be risky enough. Yakuza lurking in the bushes, in sheltered caves, and down in lava tubes with guns, is practically a suicide mission. What makes you so sure they haven't flown the coop?"

"We don't know, Chief Como." Bella looked up from scribbling notes on a legal pad. "That's the point of the drones. We send them first to scan all the areas in a grid search of Ko'olau Mountain, Haiku Stairs, and the Moanalua Valley. Hopefully, they spot some new structure or activity."

"That sounds great on paper, Agent Walker. But the reality is we don't have enough drones, and there are too many places beneath the mountain to hide." Lieutenant Gamora of Oahu Search and Rescue leaned back in his chair. The bull of a Hawaiian flexed his biceps and leaned in to look at his search formula calculations. "Just following the SAR probability models off the top of my head, we have a thousand potential areas they could be. And that's before adding in the drone grid searches. That number triples when you are talking three specific search locations of thousands of miles."

"How long do you plan on going out there, is my next concern?" Chief Como rubbed his chin. He carefully studied the projector with the map of Ko'olau Mountain, then glanced over to Lieutenant Gamora, who shook his head.

"Unless we land some kind of a miracle, folks, we are looking at a minimum two months." Lieutenant Gamora studied the map with an intense stare.

"That's not too bad, Lieutenant." SAC Harris grinned with relief. "We'll set up tents at the base of Ko'olau, here and here. That—"

Lieutenant Gamora cut him off with a sigh and rubbed his temples. "With all due respect, SAC Harris, that's just the search on one-fourth of Moanalua Valley. Sir, you could spend the next year or two out on all three sites and never see the hide nor hair of Ace and his men. Remember, these guys are masters of deception and hiding."

Harris groaned. "Well, then, what about the entrances to the biggest cave systems? The containers and equipment this gang would be hauling to protect their large sums of cash and the stolen relics would have to be considerable. Bella, what did you dig up?" The team chuckled at SAC Harris's pun.

Bella nodded. "I might have a potential spot to cut the time down. I've been working with a former Naval intelligence expert who's a consultant now. Together—"

"Are you talking about Corpsman Trestle?" Bella nodded to Harris that she was. "Seriously? Your boyfriend hardly qualifies as a lead source for such an extensive FBI and interagency operation."

"The kid's the real deal," George weighed in. "He saved my bacon the other night as I was about to get one in the back. Well, actually three bullets in the back." Rachel and the team nodded their concurrence as well.

SAC Harris's nostrils flared, and his eyes went hawkish. "Great, I have a rogue SEAL on Oahu killing Yakuza at his leisure. He killed those three near Kapolei, didn't he, Agent Walker?"

Bella kept calm, took a breath, and gave SAC Harris a full report—though slightly abridged. "As an innocent bystander, taking a night stroll, Mr. Trestle observed three heavily armed men about to shoot two FBI agents and an injured man—our lead witness—in a lava tube. Corpsman Trestle subdued all three bare-handed, sir. All three of the deceased had extensive criminal records and were wanted internationally for several murders."

"So, when do we pin a medal on him?" Chief Como and the team laughed heartily while Charlton steamed. Bella could tell the man was infuriated by the breach of protocol.

"I should toss his ass in the stockade. But it was an extraordinarily bad night in Kapolei. Agents, great people fell to this plague on our community. So, Agent Walker, tell your *boyfriend* no more shenanigans on my watch," he grumbled. "I had a hell of a time cleaning up his last dumpster fire when he took a night stroll back with the SEALS. He really doesn't like The Tears of the Dragon very much."

"Don't blame him," George cracked, which set off a round of laughter in the room. Even Harris joined in before nodding to Bella.

"Please continue, Agent Walker."

"We studied the topographical maps and all the Hawaiian historical caves and lava tubes." Bella looked over to Sergeant Tanori Omosito, who was sitting by the far back wall. Perry Leilani's former partner appeared to be deep in thought. "Sergeant Omosito, something has bugged me for a few days now. I have been wanting to follow up with you. I guess this is as good a time to do it."

"Agent Walker, we're here to plan an FBI takedown and not review an old case." Chief Como seemed to know what Bella was going to ask. The fact that he spoke up to stall was curious. *Could he have been the one to tip off the Yakuza in the last raid?* Bella thought as she saw the HPD police chief fidgeting with his hands. She glanced at Rachel and SAC Harris and nodded. They saw the peculiar behavior too.

"Chief Como, can I have a word with you in my office?" SAC Harris gave the nervous man a stare that made even George Dwyer edgy. "Agent Makani and Agent Namara, can you join us?"

Both agents nodded and said, "Yes, sir."

The chief of HPD tried to stall to leave. "SAC Harris, I don't think—"

SAC Harris's eyes were like a predatory tiger's. His words seethed in a controlled rage as he loomed over the withdrawn HPD chief. "It isn't a request, Chief Como. Unless you want me to embarrass you in front of your men." SAC Harris nodded to a threatening Billy Makani who opened his suit to reveal his service pistol and handcuffs.

"Sergeant Omosito, wait to answer Agent Walker's question until after we leave." SAC Harris nodded to Bella and then ushered the chief to his office.

Five minutes after SAC Harris and Chief Como had left, Bella asked her question. "The old mountain trail where we found Perry. Why would they hang him there? It's a rough haul just walking up those collapsing stairs. What kind of message were The Tears of the Dragon sending by desecrating his body like that?"

Sergeant Omosito kept his black eyes fixed on Bella. His voice was harsh and bitter. "They are animals. The sooner The Tears of the Dragon are put down, the better. They are rabid dogs that don't follow the rules of even their own nefarious organization." He pointed toward the direction of the Moanalua Valley. "You'd have the gratitude of the Yamaguchi-gumi, and not their ire, for removing them. They are an absolute shameful disgrace to everything it means to be Yakuza."

Bella tried to get Sergeant Omosito to answer the most important question. "But—"

"They are sending a message to their men to stay the course. Obviously, you figured out the why, before asking me," he replied. "There must be dissension in the ranks now that Ace Tamaro has fallen out of favor with Japan." He looked back from the mountains and rested his chin on his right fist.

"Thank you, Sergeant Omositio." Bella and the team nodded to the man. More importantly, Bella had gotten the confirmation she needed to kick off the assault.

"Gentlemen, there's your answer. And, I know I don't have to say this to you fine gentlemen in your departments. As Chief Como is being reminded in his interrogation, discretion is the better part of valor. No leaks to anyone. We'll let everyone know when we go in."

"Thank you, Agent Walker." Rachel stood and looked at each of the interagency department heads. "Discretion is the better part of valor, pretty much sums it up, folks. The Tears of the Dragon are being sold down the river by the Yakuza. Leaking to them we're coming—not that I'm saying any of you would for a quick cash grab—will incur the FBI's wrath. I know that may not bother some of you, but getting in the way of a Yakuza Hawaiian regime change might get you a lot worse."

An unknown officer with HPD reminded Rachel that even the FBI had been compromised. "Agent Gentry, have y'all found your agent? What was his name? Oh, yeah… TJ O'Reilly. Maybe he got a cool haircut… that's to die for." The whole conference room laughed. Bella looked over to see Rachel's face in a fiery, shameful rage.

"Thank you for reminding me, officer. Former Agent O'Reilly is a fugitive at large. He's to be arrested immediately should you run into him. Also consider him armed and dangerous. One more additional note. He knows the Haiku Stairs and the terrain well from his previous investigations and bad reports. Wait for backup if he gives you the slip. Lord only knows what traps he and The Tears of the Dragon have set in there."

The officer smiled a broad smile. Bella could see he was trying to lighten the tense mood in the room. "Officer Evan Dipoli, ma'am. But people call me Kahuna."

Rachel cracked back with a wicked grin, "Obviously, *Little* Kahuna, right?" The conference broke into bellows of laughter just as SAC Harris walked back in.

Charlton saw Little Kahuna standing embarrassed. He looked at the team that had all gone suddenly silent. "Do I want to know, Agent Gentry?"

"Probably not, Big Kahuna." The whole conference room roared in bellows of laughter and slapped Little Kahuna on the back. He gave a nod and grin to Rachel.

Bella stared at the two with a realization, or rather a speculation.

I bet she staged this laughing session with Officer Dipoli to ease the tension between the FBI and the agencies. If she did, it was a good call. But I pray we stopped the main leak to Ace.

CHAPTER THIRTY-ONE

Ko'olau Mountains
Oahu, Hawaii
FBI Base Camp
July 28, 2023

BELLA ADJUSTED HER BULLETPROOF VEST AS SHE SAT AT A LARGE table underneath a large tent for the various teams involved in The Tears of the Dragon compound assault. She double-checked her forty-five, then triple-tied the hood strings on her windbreaker anticipating gale-force winds on top of the mountain. Once she had performed her cursory uniform and equipment checks, she followed up with the respective team leaders. Each team lead had his own area to canvas, and she pointed out each designated region on her color-coded master map.

A man wearing an HPD short-sleeved shirt was holding a drone console. The man in his early fifties jogged up in the middle of the briefing. "Agent Gentry?"

Bella shook her head no. "I'm Agent Walker. And you are?"

"Sergeant Aaron Estrada. I'm the senior lead for HPD's drone and reconnaissance division. We got them field checked and ready to roll. We should have about twenty minutes to survey—providing the wind and weather cooperate." He pointed to the twenty drones strategically placed and marked for launch up toward the Haiku Stairs. "Our drones will get the videos you need. Plus we have some added features to ping on any cell phones that might be getting use—even if it's a satellite phone."

"It'll definitely be safer if we can get the drones up in the mountains. It's too easy for an officer, even an experienced one, to get injured. Thanks for keeping us updated. Agent Gentry is at the next table over there." Bella pointed Sergeant Estrada in Rachel's direction. It'd be Rachel's call when the drones should fly. Bella had enough on her plate as it was getting the teams positioned should they discover anything.

A ragged Chief Como walked up to Bella's table as she was going over details of the breach with some newly arrived military specialists from the Army Rangers and Marine Reconnaissance. "Agent Walker, are we ready for a long couple of weeks?"

"Chief Como, I thought they'd have you processed by now." Bella looked up with menacing eyes and a disdained look. She went right on the attack of the corrupt chief who more than likely had tipped off the Yakuza in the previous attempt to arrest them. Now, Chief Como hadn't been on the base camp site thirty minutes, and he was already fishing on the team's plan. Why hadn't SAC Harris detained the man for further questioning in regard to the leak? And why was he coming to her for the information when he could easily have asked one of his own subordinates?

"What's that supposed to mean, Agent Walker?" Chief Como replied with a puzzled stare. Bella felt that she was missing something obvious.

Bella was furious with the man, knowing he was the source of the leak. More officers and agents could have been injured or killed by the man's selfish actions. "You leaked to Ace Tamaro when we were going to assault his last hideout. Everyone in the conference room saw how you acted. If I were you, I'd be getting a lawyer and leaving the capture of criminals to *real* cops."

"That's enough Agent Walker. Chief Como, don't you have somewhere to be?" SAC Harris strode up and gave a warning gaze to Chief Como, then waved his hands at the nervous chief to leave.

"Yes, SAC Harris. Rein this one in before she gets hurt."

"I'd like to see you try, scumbag!" Bella lunged at the chief, but Harris gripped her leg and wrist like a vice. "*Enough!* He's cooperating, or I'd have put him in cuffs back at the FBI office. Now take a chill pill, Agent Walker. We need the HPD's cooperation to navigate these mountains."

"Sounds to me like you sold your soul to a higher bidder. Pun intended, sir." Bella turned and stormed off to count to ten before she cracked the FBI SAC for his complicity as well.

"It'll all make sense later, Agent Walker. Trust me for once that I know what I'm doing," he bellowed after her as she walked to the tree line to let her boiling temper cool.

Ten minutes later, with her mind refocused, Bella returned to the team's tent to follow the progress of the drones with Rachel. "Well, anything?"

"Marine Reconnaissance, Army Rangers, and HPD SWAT are reporting no signs of human activity from chopper recon. They have noted a thousand caves and lava tubes though. The ground support units from the surrounding islands are also reporting no human habitation, no signs of shelter, and not even a fire." Rachel paused, listening to the radio reports to view the video feed of the drones. "We may be too late again. They may have vanished, just in time."

Sergeant Estrada's gruff voice came over the radio next to Bella. "Looks like the winds are picking up. We have ten more minutes before they really wreak havoc on the drones. I'll have to call it day when that starts to occur."

"No problem, Sergeant Estrada. We wouldn't want to lose another one."

At the HPD table next to Rachel, Bella heard a stressed-out Chief Como groan and belch horrendously.

"My apologies, ladies. My heartburn is kicking up something fierce. Agent Gentry, I think losing a fifty-thousand-dollar drone today might have been the cause." Chief Como belched again and took a swig of a milky substance. Bella figured it was milk of magnesia, but she couldn't be sure.

"Now, Chief Como, I hope your health improves. I know you had one heck of a morning with our beloved SAC. Don't let it go to your… head." Bella had to stifle a laugh as Rachel's words had their effect on the agitated chief.

"Between the cost of manhunt hours, the meetings, and the lost drone, the community is going to want me to retire for sure," he groaned.

"Rachel, have them circle where we found Perry Leilani before they call it," Bella said. Rachel nodded and advised Sergeant Estrada.

Bella watched the men with HPD, specifically Chief Como's response when she said it. Curiously, Chief Como was unmoved by her request or didn't hear Bella make it.

But Sergeant Tanori Omosito bolted rapidly from the tent toward the left side of Ko'olau. Puzzled by the officer running to the middle climes of the mountain, Bella thought he was running to find a better phone signal. Then she panicked thinking the worst: he was running off to warn the Tears of the Dragon.

But then she saw something that made her eyes go wide with dread. Something Sergeant Omosito had deduced that was even more profound.

As the corrupt and haggard Chief Como was tossing his milk of magnesia bottle into a trash bag, Sergeant Omosito screamed into the radio with a feverish pitch of blood-curdling excitement. "The search drone just went down by Perry's tree. Someone just machine-gunned down the drone!"

CHAPTER THIRTY-TWO

BELLA TOOK IN THE SCENE AS SHE KEYED IN HER RADIO. WITH Alpha Team, she bolted from the FBI base camp tent out to four landed helicopters preparing for takeoff. Each chopper would be dropping off their respective assault teams to critical areas of Ko'olau Mountain. Bella's Alpha team would be dropped precariously by the Haiku Stairs to try to locate the hideout entrance by the very tree Officer Leilani had been hung. It would not be an ideal drop-off. There would be no LZ for the helicopter, and the team would have to shimmy in the wind down ropes. Hopefully, the coordinated drop would put them on or near the stairs.

Despite meticulous follow-up on wind and weather that gave the green light for the helicopter breach attempt, there was always uncertainty: there was no way to know with absolute surety how the wind would be blasting that particular ridge of the mountain.

As she climbed into one of four helicopters assigned to the FBI assault, Bella roared a warning to the military and SWAT teams breaching the lava tubes and caves of the mountain.

"Team, proceed with caution! The Tears of the Dragon are possibly inside. Repeat, proceed with caution. Shots fired on drone near the eastern slope of Ko'olau Mountains near the third portion of the Haiku Stairs." Bella repeated her radio warning. She knew that if the Yakuza were in there—and most likely they were—they'd be on high alert. But she also guessed that TJ had more than likely set up a radio system to monitor the team's traffic.

And that would be a big unknown. As they moved toward the Haiku stairs, the SWAT team's leader gave her a last-minute update on radio communication. "Agent Walker, it gets tricky inside these things. Radios and phone communication are often garbled and wonky at best. I'd stay close and not wander too far in the recesses of a lava tube."

"Copy that," Bella replied simply, then looked out as they were moving fast toward the drop. She grimaced with concern, studying the location before she would rope down with SWAT.

Most likely TJ wouldn't know that The Tears of the Dragon had hung Perry on the western side of Ko'olau. Also, since he wasn't there and probably didn't care to check the reports much, Perry was two-thirds up the mountain and one-fourth away from the crumbling Haiku Stairs. Let's hope my trick works. Otherwise, we are walking into an ambush.

Rachel gave a tense smile to Bella. She barked her own distinct warning as she climbed into the second helicopter headed to the western side of Ko'olau Mountain. "It goes without saying, team, should you see former agent Thomas Joseph O'Reilly, proceed with caution and arrest on sight. That goes triple for you, Agent Walker."

"No worries there, Agent Gentry." Bella tried to stifle a sarcastic laugh but failed miserably in her endeavor.

There were three SWAT teams labeled Alpha, Bravo, and Charlie accordingly. Each team was headed by a seasoned veteran. Team leader for Alpha Team was led by the golden-haired, freight truck of a man, Lieutenant Chuck Child, who held the most seniority and mountain breach expertise. They were tasked with Bella to enter the eastern side and stave off any Yakuza trying to backtrack out to the coast.

Bravo Team's Captain Clancy Straub held six years' experience in mountain assaults but six more years of special forces experience in the Army Rangers' Tropic Lightning division where he had retired. He was tasked with Rachel to breach the critical western side of Ko'alu not far from where the drone had been shot down.

Charlie Team's leader, Sergeant Owen, was tasked with George Dwyer to back up Rachel's team. Between the two of them, they had a mountain of experience. All had speculated the most firepower would be on the western side of the mountain with the shape and layout of the terrain being the critical factor in their assessment.

The final team, Delta, contained junior SWAT members. Corporal Wilson Faulkner, who had just made his sixth year with the HPD, led the charge alongside Billy, Paige, Susan, and Keith, to back up Alpha Team. On this side of things, they expected little gunfire.

Adjacent backup teams were the Army Ranger 25th infantry, Tropic Lightning, which had been Captain Straub's former unit. They had brought in two of their own helicopters to deploy a platoon to secure the upper climes of Ko'olau Mountain. And SEAL Team One had brought in three of their own choppers with a platoon of thirty men. The SEALs were tasked with securing the lower climes and coast should their prey escape past all through the extensive network of lava tubes.

Rachel gave a final word over the roar of the helicopter's rotors before the assault began. "Everyone, be safe. Time to make The Tears of the Dragon cry."

And so, the FBI assault on the mountainous compound began.

All nine of the assigned helicopters brought each of their specific teams into safe drop points on Ko'olau Mountain. Heading up, feeling the shift and shake of the powerful choppers battling the strong winds gusting on the mountain's ridge, Bella watched each of the four immediate response teams with their respective FBI agents and team leaders land safely at landing zones near the Haiku Stairs and begin their immediate assault. They approached in a cautious, low formation, aware gunfire could erupt on them at any minute. She witnessed each member using the customary left arm on their teammate with their rifle up and ready. Meticulously they swept and maneuvered rocky terrain down toward several possible bat-riddled cave systems and tubes. Each FBI and SWAT member moved swiftly and quietly, checking the customary six of the other.

Thankfully, throughout the drop of personnel into their various heavily jungled LZs, no helicopters were shot at by the Tears of the Dragon… though one colorful parrot tried to flap in and land in Bella's chopper, to the absolute shock of all.

Moving through a makeshift trail between two ancient banyan trees, Bella caught her SWAT teammate in front of her before he went down. She yanked him back by his vest before he tumbled down a five-hundred-foot ravine.

"Careful, Steve."

Sergeant Steve Alau mouthed a thank-you as they continued their trek. On the second turn, headed across the worn mountain trail, Bella herself nearly had a repeat of falling through another lava tube. This time it was Steve's turn to return the favor, grabbing her poncho like a vise as she lost her footing. She looked down to a bottomless abyss as she dangled over the collapsed ground before regaining her footing. Nodding her own thank-you, they continued, even more diligent and cautious.

After nearly two hours of surveillance and close calls, everyone took a minute to pause and rest. Everyone remained silent and aware of their mountainous jungle surroundings. Bella had been carefully spying the trees, rock crags, and trails for any signs of camera setups, trail cams, or booby traps. Thankfully, unlike many of her other cases, there had been none... so far.

Bella wrote a simple note in her tally book and showed it to the team. The note read the following: *Isn't it odd that there are no small cameras, trail cams, or traps, on this worn trail?*

Lieutenant Child shrugged, as did the rest of the team. Bella furrowed her brow puzzled by all of it.

She took a seat on a nearby boulder and took a swig of water. The humidity and heat of their small two-hour trek had worn her down. She was practically panting like Thor probably was back home. But she couldn't think of Thor or Justin or anything else right now. She had to keep her head in the game. They were so close to catching Ace Tamaro and his men. Rachel and her team should be—

Bella paused. She heard something. It was like the chime of a glass bell. No, like a sleighbell at Christmas time. It happened again; metallic and ringing as she'd been sitting near this tree. Except this ancient banyan tree had a trail going underneath its root system—a worn trail that had other sounds as she got closer to it. Generator engines running, hammers clanging on a pipe possibly, and... voices. Voices in Japanese!

Bella fell back in shock. Lieutenant Child saw her response and moved swiftly to her aid. She quickly put a finger over her lips and pointed. He listened, then turned, as puzzled as she was. There wasn't supposed to be activity on this side of the mountain. Everyone had agreed that Bella and her team were just a glorified backup team. But here they were, with possibly The Tears of the Dragon a hundred yards or less down in the cave system beneath them.

"What do we do?" she whispered.

While everyone looked at the SWAT team leader absolutely perplexed, a shadow in full SEAL team camouflage moved up like a ghost and sat next to the man. He coughed and Child jumped back, dropping his rifle. The look the Conjure Man gave Child was classic Justin. The men were initially stunned that Justin had snuck up on all of them, but then they smirked. Justin's gestures said it all.

Get your head out of your rump and let's finish this!

Bella knew something had to be done. Conflicted herself as Justin pushed the team to get ready and helped Child to his feet, she sighed. This was supposed to be Rachel's arrest, but they'd been outfoxed. That crooked Chief Como must have leaked their information. Against her better judgment and training, they had to risk it.

She traded a look with both men, and they nodded.

The team followed her into the cave in the original formation from earlier. Justin moved into their formation at the end while Child moved back to his lead position. Bella had shifted to the number two position of the SWAT line, which was fine by her. The lead guy always seemed to catch the bullet if things went south in these unexpected scenarios—especially when assaulting a dark-as-night cave or a nasty bat- and bug-filled lava tube.

In the pitch blackness of the lava tube, Bella heard footsteps moving swiftly to her right. She tapped Child's shoulder, and he froze in place. Everyone went to a crouched position and moved to conceal themselves from whomever was coming from their right.

The footsteps seemed to be paused twenty feet in front of them. The quiet in the darkness became deafening as Bella and the team patiently waited to see what the unknown group of men would do.

From her vantage point behind a pile of large black lava rock, Bella could see ten men crouching low, getting into a pincher formation with five men set in the shadows to each side of the lava tube. It was a classic ambush setup occurring just in front of Bella and her team. The shadowed assailants had not seen the team but were clearly set up to ambush them. But then a horrific realization brought an icy chill down her spine, making her tremble.

They knew we were coming. Someone down at base camp tipped them off that we were making our way to them. If we had been another five minutes, we'd have been ambushed.

A familiar voice behind Bella and to her left spoke in unspeakably bad Japanese. *"Anata wa hontō no doragondesu yo ne, desu ka?"*

Gunfire erupted to Bella's left where Justin had called out to identify members of The Tears of the Dragon. It was brilliant and foolhardy.

But Bella didn't have time to chew him out. She identified herself as FBI, watched as the assailants went to fire on her team, and started firing.

Gunfire and angry screams erupted in all directions of the pitch-black tube.

CHAPTER THIRTY-THREE

THE SCENE UNFOLDED IN FAST PULSING STROBES OF BLINDING light and thunderous cracks of gunfire. There were flashes of yellow light from the SWAT team's arsenal assault rifle fire and blinding orange and white light from the Yakuza's AK-47s. Ear-deafening roars came from both. All caused Bella's head to spin as she dodged gunfire and returned her own. The ricochet of bullets could be heard as thuds on the carved rock walls of the obsidian lava tubes. The battle waged between The Tears of the Dragon assailants and Bella's FBI team could have lasted ten minutes or ten seconds. Bella truly couldn't tell.

As the firefight continued between them, Bella crouched behind her limestone and obsidian wall. She fired controlled, tight bursts from her forty-five, hitting two assailants in the legs before ducking back down to cover. She smelled the sulfurous char of gunfire smoke and heard their agonized screams of pain in the darkness. She heard two more Yakuza in the darkness stop shooting. Then Bella suddenly caught their gasping in the darkness. She became sickened as to what was happening to them, knowing full well the source of their demise. Finally shuddering, she heard their groans in the pitch and then the crack of something— possibly bone.

Then two more The Tears of the Dragon rifles fired no more.

The HPD SWAT was wrapping up the firefight rapidly. Child fired a round of three controlled bursts, and then it was down to one rifle firing from the Yakuza.

"Surrender!" Bella called out. "It's over!"

Before the man could even respond, he was surrounded by Justin on one side and Steve on the other, each with their guns pointed directly at his forehead. The man glanced around at the bodies of his fallen comrades and then tossed his rifle to the ground before falling to his knees. The ambush by The Tears of the Dragon was ended. Everyone grouped back together and left the dead to die.

"*Ato nan-ko arimasu ka? Nokori was dokodesu ka?*" Justin asked the handcuffed Yakuza man. His towering frame to the smaller man seemed like something out of a surrealistic fairy tale. Bella thought for the moment that it was like looking at a real-life version of Jack and the Beanstalk, especially with Justin's intense jungle camouflage that made him look like a tree.

The Tears of the Dragon prisoner told them there were twenty left toward the western center tubes. Their compound would be easy to spot with the lighting and markings. Justin picked the man up by the neck and lifted him with one arm above his head. Then he gave a fierce warning to the terrified Yakuza man in Japanese. Bella didn't know what he said to the former killer, but its effects were clear as the man began leading Bella and the team toward the remaining Yakuza.

If accurate, Bella calculated while tripping over a moss-covered stone, they'd surprise and subdue The Bright Prince and The Tears of the Dragon in no less than thirty minutes. If not, they'd be ambushed, and Justin most certainly would break this prisoner's neck.

Justin whispered to everyone before they continued their journey. "Compasses and most electronics don't work well in these tube and cave systems—probably due to the materials being magnetized. Always keep your bearings. Mark a trail for everything. I wouldn't want anyone to endure what I did a few years back, getting lost in one of these. It was one of my creepier nights outdoors, camping in a lava tube."

Bella and everyone nodded in understanding. Justin gave one last look at Bella before directing his Yakuza prisoner to lead on. He knew what terrified her above all else when he'd found her on the frozen mountain so many years ago. He knew Bella, despite all her courage, had a slight claustrophobia of caves. A few minutes or even a half hour in a cave system was fine. But after one hour or more, she started to crack; and Justin had seen her melt down on two occasions. The first had been the night of the terrifying Harbinger assault. And the second was two years ago exploring the vast mines and caves of the Rockies.

Everyone clicked on their headlamps and put them on the brightest setting. Then Justin and the prisoner, whose name was Haru Hiroshi, began the trek across the lava tubes of Ko'alau with Bella and the SWAT team in tow. Though the claustrophobia hadn't reared its ugly head yet, Bella felt the tingling in her hands and the increase in her breathing the farther they went into the cave system.

They passed gemmed, crystalline stalactites and stalagmites that reflected brightly off their lights, which eased the sensation of being buried or caged. Immense darkness or tight scurries into adjacent tunnels and caves sent chills racing down her spine, especially if something dropped on her neck such as a chilly drop of water or a scurrying insect. But the worst was the writhing of worms down her neck or back. In those unhinged moments, Bella had to focus her mind. She'd take a minute and lag behind to take calm, controlled breaths and count to ten. But then, without further hesitation, she'd drive herself onward with her indomitable will to capture the notorious Akihiko Tamaro.

Gunfire erupted one hundred feet in front of the team. More gunfire erupted in what sounded like two hundred feet below them. Then to Bella's left, she heard a terrified woman scream in the darkness. The voice eerily sounded like Rachel Gentry. Everyone moved quickly toward the gunfire to lend support.

Bella regripped her pistol and followed Child's lead to return to SWAT entrant formation. They closed ranks and moved with a pace that made her forget her claustrophobia… for now. As they quickened the pace to a light trot, then jog as more screams and gunfire came from the depths of darkness, Bella scanned the tube, which had now opened up to a dome-like cathedral of an immense cave.

She took only one second to appreciate the natural beauty of the massive stalactites hanging down before the SWAT team slowed their pace to a cautious crawl and crouched together behind a large outcrop of granite and limestone boulders.

Justin was still out in front with his Yakuza prisoner. Out of kindness—and caution—he'd let Haru walk the last one hundred feet. It was the last walk the man would do for the rest of his life. Once they reached the opening of the large expanse of the cavern and were well behind the large boulders of stone, he made a break for it and opened his mouth to shout a warning.

But before he could get out anything, Justin put his enormous arm around the Yakuza killer's mouth and neck. Then, with a quick stomp of his right foot, he snapped the man's right leg, stifling the scream with the girth of his arm. As tears flowed from the pain of a shattered leg, Justin shoved a cloth into the man's mouth with a silent warning: if he put out any more noise, he'd snap more than the man's leg. Then Justin looked back at Bella and the stunned team members. He shrugged to everyone, then tossed the still-crying Haru to the cave floor and continued toward the firefight.

Gunfire and more screams of pain and anger were louder now in the semi-lit tube system. Flickering lights, obviously set up by the gang, trailed down several corridors toward lit-up steel containers with their own lighting and air conditioning. As Bella adjusted to the weird lighting within the cave, she saw construction equipment, bulldozers, excavators, and winches, organized and working on several underground projects. She shook her head in disbelief at the size and scope of the underground compound.

If they'd spent this much time, money, and energy improving the poor Hawaiian communities, they could have turned Honolulu into a paradise. So much poverty on these islands, and for what? For them to get a little richer peddling ancient artifacts?

Another round of gunfire echoed back, and Justin took off into the darkness. Lieutenant Child shook his head angrily and cursed under his breath. "That damn fool must have nine lives. How has he managed to stay alive this long with his shenanigans?"

Bella whispered as they moved toward the gunfight, guns ready for their second battle of the day. "I have often asked myself the same thing through the years."

Child glanced back a minute, puzzled. "You know this clown, Agent Walker? I thought he was a mountain expert with the teams sent to assist us."

Bella whispered a sigh as the SWAT team crouched to ambush the remaining Yakuza. "He's my boyfriend, sir."

The bewildered man fired a controlled burst at two assailants wounding one and taking out the other. Then he groaned before firing. "That's just lovely. How's your honeymoon going?"

Bella fired controlled shots, crippling another of the killers. With a sardonic smile, she answered back, "Funny, Lieutenant. Please, don't give up your day job."

Alpha Team moved quickly and swiftly into the further reaches of the compound. Stunned assailants, positioned to take on Bravo Team, had also been positioned to where Bella and her team were supposed to navigate had they made it past the first ambush. Thankfully, they'd managed to proceed through an alternate tunnel—most likely the one The Tears of the Dragon would have used. Now the team unleashed a fury breaking the back of the dreaded killers. More screams and groans erupted as Conjure Man wreaked havoc on Yakuza necks and skulls. Then more precise rifle bursts along with more screams of rage or pain as the converging Bravo, Charlie, and Delta teams burst forth in the blinding lights and blazing yellow gunfire. More shots and thudded echoes of ricochets as Tropic Lightning and Seal Team One overwhelmed the remaining members. Those platoons demanded a stand down from the Yakuza and an immediate surrender.

They moved in to apprehend the killers, barking out orders, but in the aftereffects of gunshots and flickering generator lights in the glistening cathedral lava tube, Bella couldn't relax just yet. In fact, her dread was growing. She had heard a woman's voice screaming in addition to the gunfire. Now there was just the quiet and roundup of the gang that had caused so much harm. She realized critical elements of their assault were missing. Where were The Bright Prince and TJ O'Reilly? TJ wouldn't leave his top client in the dark to fend for himself against them.

Bella keyed her radio, following a side cave system adjacent to a spacious office. She nodded to Lieutenant Child just as Justin lumbered up to inspect the compound now that the smoke had cleared. "Agent Gentry, come in," she spoke into her radio. "The Tears of the Dragon have been crushed. Repeat. The Tears of the Dragon have been crushed." She knew that Rachel wouldn't be on her radio. Bella had sensed that something had happened to her as sure as she knew TJ wouldn't leave Ace hanging.

The radio clicked and garbled a message. Bella could hear the woman's scream as whoever was operating the radio—certainly not Rachel—was trying to foolishly communicate in the lava tube. "Be…. Bell… can you hear me? I have your friend." More clicks and garbled communication.

The forensics specialist played along. She motioned for Justin and everyone to approach. "I can't really hear you. Wherever you are, Rachel, I'll send all our teams to find you. You must be near the western side." It was a long shot. If TJ—for Ace Tamaro wouldn't have been so stupid to use an FBI radio or any in a lava tube—could key in again, maybe someone would hear a sound or something to clue in.

Justin whispered, "It's a waste of time, Bella. Coordinate everyone to converge and scour in circular sectors to close them off."

Bella grinned. "That's what I'm doing. We got Tropic Lightning surrounding and entering upper clime. Seal Team One is circling them with their platoon. I was just buying time. But if he can give us more—"

"Brilliant, if he doesn't have inner escape networks. Wait, that's TJ. He ain't the brightest bulb in the box." The team laughed, and Steve clapped Justin on the back.

Gunfire erupted beneath the team's feet. Bella started moving to a side tube that wound down like a winding staircase. "We need to move fast. It sounded like it was right below us. Lieutenant, TJ has kidnapped Agent Gentry." Bella then advised the rest of the teams.

The spiraling tube had carved steps that made movement difficult, and as Bella moved into the more confined areas of this particular tube, her claustrophobia kicked in a bit. She felt the all-too-familiar tingling of her fingers and lips. Then came the increased breathing. And as it bordered to unnerve and unhinge Bella, sidelining her just at the final stretch, she heard distant echoes ahead that steeled her nerves.

I must get to Rachel! There's no doubt TJ or Ace will kill her for destroying their plans.

"It's over, TJ. Give yourself up!" Rachel barked in a shrill-like scream as Bella and the SWAT team moved through the narrowing darkness. "Whether you kill me or not, the whole place is surrounded. Surrender now to me. Escape won't be an option today."

After ten minutes, Bella and Alpha Team came to the bottom of the stairs of the spiral tube. The cave system here was just as large as the cathedral above and housed just as much lighting and equipment, to everyone's surprise. Everyone moved in a singular formation to the left of the cave into the shadows, peering to look for TJ and Agent Gentry. Following the left wall with each hand securely fixed on their respective partners, the team glanced and swept in and among the construction equipment and tons of rationed supplies. Forty feet into the second storage tube, Bella heard movement and something else.

In the hazy lit shadows of the lava tube, echoing through the menagerie, Rachel Gentry screamed in the massive cave. Bella's heart plummeted—and then the lights went out.

That had been part of the plan, but that knowledge did nothing to calm her racing heart. Billy and his team had gone through to disable the generator. She could only hope it bought them enough time to take TJ and Ace down.

Darkness ensconced everything and everyone. Bella's ears adjusted before her eyes did. Her heart skipped a beat at the sound of TJ's gunfire erupting, and she had to resist the urge to run in and subdue the rogue agent herself. She wanted to square on whatever had transpired with her friend. Whatever the idiot had done, Rachel, by her pleas and screams, hadn't done well in the exchange. But she kept her outrage in check and reined in her temper before it flamed furiously out of control.

The team paused, waiting to hear TJ make the next move in the dark. Once he did, Alpha, Bravo, and Charlie would pop off a series of flash-bangs and coordinate a simultaneous takedown. They didn't have to wait long before they heard TJ curse. "Great… that's all I need. The generators always die in this hellhole."

The flash-bangs went off, illuminating the cave for barely a moment. Bella got a split-second glimpse of TJ standing over an injured Rachel. Rachel was in a fetal position guarding some type of injury to her abdomen. Unfortunately, the rogue agent had kept his eyes down and covered to avoid being blinded. He ran toward the left of Charlie and immediately disappeared down a side tunnel into the darkness.

Bella pointed to the recessed tunnel and barked, "Don't let him get away! He has a lot to answer for!"

But before they could even catch him, he rounded a corner into the darkness.

CHAPTER THIRTY-FOUR

LIEUTENANT CHILD'S MEN FANNED OUT TO A PROTECTIVE PERIMETER of the complex while Bella moved to check on Rachel.

"About... time," Rachel groaned weakly. She had a small bullet wound to her side, and even despite the pressure she was applying, thin trickles of blood were leaking out between her fingers. Justin jogged over, already snapping on latex gloves and slinging his kit from over his shoulder.

It was quick work on Justin's end, but Bella still couldn't breathe as he inspected Rachel's wounds. The claustrophobia hit her like a hammer, and she suddenly got very dizzy. She took several loud, rattling breaths, trying to calm herself, but all that seemed to do was get her more worked up. Her stomach lurched, and her knees went weak, and her jaw went numb as—

"...the gauze from my pack," someone was saying. It took a second for it to register as Justin's voice. "Bella. *Bella!*" He snapped his fingers, and that finally shook her out of it.

"Get the gauze from my pack," he repeated, his worried expression now focused on her, but she brushed him away. Bella got to her knees and produced the gauze, which he took quickly.

"She should be okay. Luckily the bullet went through and didn't nick her kidney, intestine, or liver. Bandage." Bella looked down and handed him a roll of bandage. "Can you call in a medevac?" he asked. "Are you okay?"

She shot him a look and called for the medevac instead of answering his question. "We need to get her out of here and up to the chopper."

"Rachel, you got lucky that fool couldn't shoot straight." Justin grinned as Rachel grumbled angrily.

"Don't you have something stronger than water for this pain?" she asked. Justin shook his head no. "Fine."

"Lieutenant, we need some type of lift to get her out of this cave to the medevac. Can your guys go look for anything?" Bella asked, pointing to one of several storage containers.

He nodded and ordered two of his men to go look in the storage containers while still being cautious—wanted men were still on the loose. He paused seeing all the blood on Justin's hands and the pool clotted beneath Rachel. "Is she going to be okay?"

Justin nodded to him that she was. "She'll need an IV. I stopped the bleeding, but she needs to get to the hospital."

Five minutes after his order to search for something to transfer Rachel, the team surprisingly brought back a large World War II-era medevac stretcher. The large, bulky, green canvas stretcher gave Justin a chuckle. "Well, I'll be damned. I'll put that one in the WWII Museum, Agent Gentry, when we get done hauling you on it."

Despite her condition, Rachel managed a slight slap to Justin's leg. "Funny, Mr. Trestle."

Bella held Rachel's hand as they transferred her over to the green canvas stretcher, and Rachel stopped her with a determined glare.

"Go get that sucker, Bella. I had him dead to rights. But someone tipped him off. That's the only reason he got the jump on me," she said as Justin lowered an oxygen mask to her face.

"I figured as much when I heard all the shooting. The other Yakuza group would have got us too. Chief Como is going to catch cuffs or bullets for this betrayal."

Rachel swatted away Justin's hands and pulled her mask down briefly. "He won't be the only leak in that department. But dropping him should send a message to the rest. But for getting me shot, Bella, I'll shoot him myself when I get out of the hospital."

"You'll have to stand in line, Rachel," Lieutenant Child seethed as they hurried her out of the cave. He glanced back at Bella. "He almost succeeded in getting my entire SWAT team killed. You can bet Chief Como has already run for the hills knowing everyone lived."

"I'm going to follow them up. You'll be okay down here?" Justin wiped his brow and put on a new pair of latex gloves. He furrowed his brow with concern and gave Bella his intense, knowing stare.

Bella shrugged, batting her innocent girl look, then nodded, "I'm fine. We still have to find The Bright Prince and TJ and get them in cuffs. TJ, the fool he is, will probably lead us right to Ace."

"Maybe so. Watch Ace sneaking back and trying to get out of here in a SWAT uniform. He's a desperate, dangerous man right now." Justin followed Child and two of his men carrying Rachel on the stretcher. And as if to lighten the tense and somber moment for Rachel and everyone, Justin parroted Rachel's favorite saying: "Agent Rachel Gentry is alive due to her former partner's lousy shooting. Now, that's the spirit!"

"Will somebody please shut this man up?" Rachel groaned through the mask as the SWAT team laughed. "Did you know this fool rides tiger sharks when he's bored?"

"Geez, Agent Gentry, you'd think thanks were in order," whined Justin as they ascended the cave. "I'd rather you not shoot a law-abiding citizen working under the guise of a good Samaritan."

Bella grinned at their banter, knowing her friend would be alright, but there was no more time for fun. She tried her radio down in the lava tubes. It seemed to have better reception and transmission. No doubt this was the reason the compound was located in the spot she was standing. She keyed up to see how George and Keith were doing. "Agent Dwyer. Agent Benton. This is Agent Walker. Can you hear me?"

"You're coming in extremely well, Agent Walker." Bella turned to see Keith and George behind her laughing. "Almost like you were right here." They belly laughed some more, and George slapped his leg.

"Funny, guys." Bella bristled and grimaced. "I guess Agent Makani will be on the other side laughing when I call him."

"He should have been here by now." Keith paused and saw the small pool of blood. "Where's Agent Gentry?" Agent Benton went wide-eyed and bent to flash his light on the blood. Then he saw Rachel's badge. "I see she dropped something."

Bella bent down and picked up Rachel's badge. "Someone tipped TJ and the Yakuza off. They knew our plan and where we'd be. He got the jump on her. Luckily no one was killed. Well, except for several members of The Tears of the Dragon. Rachel got lucky O'Reilly's a lousy shot. She should be in the air as we speak on the way to the hospital."

George shrugged and threw up a flippant hand. "The tipster was obviously Chief Como. Even Ray Charles could see he's as dirty as they come. Trying to get your SWAT team killed? That's a new low, even for him." He flashed a light around the cathedral cave system, then finished, "He'd better leave town."

"Where's Agent Makani?" Keith was growing concerned. "The kid is too revved up and punctual to not be here."

"There are probably more storage caves and tubes down here. He might have gotten turned around." Bella was trying to be optimistic, but her own dread was growing. TJ had certainly proven that he would kill his own. "We need to spread out with all the teams. At least two dangerous fugitives are left to catch. We can't let our guard down now."

Keith and George went with their team leads for Bravo and Charlie, and Child returned after handing off Rachel to the chopper. "What's the new plan?"

"Same as before. We sweep each cave and room until we converge and capture them. These are highly dangerous men. They nearly killed one FBI agent and ambushed our teams twice. Be on your highest alert. Watch for tricks, traps, and everything in this wacky lava tube system."

As before, Bella and the SWAT team went into a single file formation with each person putting a left hand on their partners' shoulder. Lead and end personnel were tasked, as was everyone, to check each other's six and look for dangers. They switched on their night vision and proceeded cautiously. Each of the teams would surround, circle, sweep, and converge, looking for The Bright Prince and the traitor. Neither would be an easy capture in this harsh terrain.

But there were some things on their side. Bella almost grinned thinking of the bright side of their final assault on The Tears of the Dragon.

The farther they go down into these tubes and caves, the more likely they run out of flashlight power and possibly even air. And that's provided they had flashlights on them to begin with. From what I recall with TJ, he was relying on the generator system like a dummy. We should find him soon enough.

But Ace Tamaro will be another story. I think he'd crawl all the way into the pits of Hell before giving up. We just must hope for a miracle on that one.

The team did indeed get lucky as they rounded the corner to another large cavern. But it wasn't so fortunate for Billy Makani. In her night vision, Bella could see Billy in a choke hold with a gun to his head. The perpetrator holding the gun was none other than Thomas Joseph O'Reilly.

He twisted Billy around like he was a rag doll and pressed his own forty-five to the young agent's head, screaming, "You should have joined Ace! You were Yakuza once, Billy. You saw what they offer in terms of prestige and power. All the perks—you're a damn fool, you know that?"

Child tapped for everyone to switch off their night vision and prepare to use their flash-bangs and lights to blind TJ as before. But the timing had to be precise. A mistake with the takedown certainly would get Billy Makani killed.

"They kill innocent people who don't play along," Billy spat. "They burned my village and extorted my family and friends. I'd never sell out my soul like you did, TJ. We were f—"

Flash-bangs ignited with a roaring, earsplitting blast. TJ, blinded by the white light of the deterrent grenade, had been caught unaware this time in his argument with Billy. In the same instant, Agent Makani leaned in to break the choke hold and headbutted TJ's gun away from his temple.

There was no time to think. There was no time to react. Bella screamed, "Let him go, TJ!"

———•———

TJ's ears felt as if they were bleeding from the sounds of the percussion grenades. He'd taken a direct blast of light and saw all sorts of red and rainbow swirls staring into it. Blinded, he stupidly loosened his grip just enough for Billy to wrench loose and headbutt his pistol. He thought, *I'll kill you for that, Billy Makani!*

———•———

Bella saw the anger and surprise in TJ's eyes at Billy fighting for his life. He sneered at him and then at her. Bella knew, with nothing left to lose, that the former FBI agent would kill his former comrade.

Bella roared her forty-five in a brilliant blaze that ignited the shadowed darkness of the lava tube.

CHAPTER THIRTY-FIVE

THE STANDARD FBI-ISSUED FORTY-FIVE CALIBER BULLET THAT Bella shot from her M1911A1 traveled with a speed of eight hundred and thirty feet per second. It struck TJ O'Reilly's leg with enough force to rip through the flesh of his upper thigh and shatter his femur into razor-sharp shards of bone, literally knocking the former agent off his feet. Bright red arterial blood poured from the injury.

"Why, you—"

Bella was on him in an instant and slapped him across the face so hard it shut him up immediately. His head lolled back, and Bella popped him again for good measure before she looked down and realized the spurting blood from his leg was in danger of spilling on her and got up.

Seeing that the man might die from the spurting blood, Steve Alau pulled off his belt and applied it to TJ's leg as a tourniquet. The cinching of the tourniquet to stop the immediate bleeding caused the former FBI agent to scream and cry.

"You shot me! Bella Walker, you really shot me!" TJ cried out in disbelief.

"Call a medevac and cuff him." Bella's voice was emotionless and without sympathy for the rogue agent. "After what you and your friends have done to the people of Hawaii and our people today, consider yourself *lucky* it was only your leg." She paused a moment as some of the teams went to look for another stretcher or board to get T.J. to another medevac. "Where's your new boss, TJ?"

"I don't know!" TJ groaned dumbly at the pool of blood around his tourniquet leg. "I can't feel my feet! I'm dying, thanks to you!"

"Next time, don't try to kill your fellow agents," Bella sneered. "Tell me where he is, or the judge is really going to rake you over the coals."

"No dice, Bella. I'm a dead man if I snitch. Better I do my time." TJ winced and rocked while crying in pain.

"Remove the tourniquet," Bella ordered. Sergeant Alau's eyes went wide in disbelief. Bella's own face went into a sinister grin. "You have nothing to live for anyway. Federal agents don't live long in federal prison."

Sergeant Alau shrugged and went to grab his belt. TJ screamed. "Wait! He's two levels over in the east. For the love of God, Bella, please don't let me die down here!"

The SWAT medic arrived, leaned down with his jump bag, and nodded up to Bella. Bella couldn't read the medic's name on his badge. As he applied a better tourniquet and rendered treatment on TJ, the medic looked up angrily. "Is keeping him in handcuffs necessary? He's lost a lot of blood."

"Sir, with that one, you better believe it. Make sure he lives. I want to see him processed myself for what he did to his former FBI friends." Bella shook her head, huffed, and turned away. She was on a mission to end this assault once and for all. Bella Walker was going after The Bright Prince... and she would take him down.

"Left passage clear," came a report. Each of the teams went section by section of the compound clearing each area and capturing any holdouts. Onward, heading east of the main hideout, she and the Alpha Team meticulously swept the remaining sections for the few criminals left. Having subdued most of the gang, Bella and everyone met in the main cave to debrief. FBI and police teams went to interrogate the captured members for a list of who was left. After several tired hours, Agent Dwyer and Agent Rivera had put together a comprehensive final list of who was left to capture. Eight from their list were captured an hour after the list was finalized. After another hour, Bella and her group found the ninth member. With George and Paige now with her group, the gang member—Ace's second in command—was located stuck in a crevice ten feet off the ground.

"Help! I'm being bitten!" he called out in the darkness in perfect English. "Please! It burns!" He continued screaming for help in the darkness. Paige and George were able to grab his feet, and with a hearty pull, yanked the criminal out of his stuck predicament.

"Oh, dear lord!" George yelled as he and Paige jumped back startled. To their absolute horror, the criminal had suffered a horrific event in the darkness of the cave. When they pulled Takuma Miyano from his stuck perch, he was carrying one of the largest centipedes either agent had ever seen. It had its venom-dripping mandibles locked on the poor man's face.

"Man, that's a fate I'd never want to have. In the dark and stuck with something trying to bite your face off." Agent Rivera and Agent Dwyer both shuddered as they pulled the bitten man out of the hole and handcuffed him. Where the scurrying centipede went in the process of pulling him out of the recessed cave, was anyone's guess.

"A centipede stuck to his face! Yikes!" Bella shivered at the thought. "I'm glad you guys found him. If I'd have seen that I'd probably have bug nightmares for weeks."

"Any luck locating the head honcho?" Billy Makani walked up as George went again into describing the centipede in grotesque detail. Billy cringed at hearing the unnerving details of the insect biting the man's face. "I think I'll go look for Ace. You guys just gave me the heebie-jeebies with that one."

"I'll join you, Agent Makani. Feel free to tag along, but no more bug talk. He must be somewhere close. We've gone over every inch of the compound. He's running low on lighting by this time." Bella started back toward the western part of the tube system.

George, catching up and scanning to the north and south of the third section of the supply caves, asked in a whisper, "Are you thinking what I'm thinking Agent Walker?"

"He's backtracking. If I had to guess, Ace Tamaro will try to subdue one of the SWAT guys and take his uniform, then head on out and escape." Bella moved to an angled and slippery chute. She nodded for George, Keith, Paige, and Alpha Team to follow her.

Going halfway down the slippery rocks of granite and limestone, Bella missed a step and rolled to her left into a small puddle of near-freezing cave water. Now soaking wet on her left side, she groaned as Keith went to grab her hand and pull her to her feet. "Just great. Did I ever mention I hate lava tubes?"

"Maybe one other time." George smiled at her, then flashed his light forward to another room of dated equipment and supplies. There were old lighting systems, WWII-era jeeps, lockers, and all sorts of storage crates. "How'd they get all of this down here without being seen?"

"It's one of those great mysteries, I guess." Keith looked around. "There's a switch somewhere. I'll see if these museum relics still operate. I meant the lighting, Agent Dwyer, not you." He laughed as George cursed under his breath with a grin.

Lieutenant Child shrugged. "If this mothballed lighting works, we might get a break. I don't know how much longer we can keep chasing our tails in the dark, Agent Walker."

"Not too much longer now, Lieutenant."

Everything happened in an instant when Keith managed to get the lights to flicker. The first was a moving shadow of a man darting with great agility along the right side wall of the supply cave toward the darkness of a corridor in the same direction. The man was a blur with his catlike nimbleness, and Bella was unable to tell if he was Japanese or something else.

"FBI—stop or we'll shoot!" she called in an authoritative tone. "We have you surrounded!"

That might have been an exaggeration. They had no idea if he could still slip out the back somewhere.

Bella watched as the light flickered just a moment with the brightness of a full day. The dark shadow racing to escape the cave glanced back briefly. It was only a glimpse, but it was enough. While covered in dirt and grime, the appearance was unmistakable. The aquiline nose, the piercing black eyes, the narrow chin, and the raven black hair all confirmed the shadow was indeed the last member to be caught—the ringleader of the Tears of the Dragon gang: Akihiko "Ace" Tamaro.

"Ace, stop or I will shoot you!" Bella screamed in protest at the escaping criminal. In response to her order, she heard the echoes of the man's laughter as he ran off like a night wind through the eternal darkness of the cave.

"That's about right! Alpha Team after him!" Lieutenant Child directed as the men took off to capture the notorious Yakuza member. Bella followed in the pursuit along with a bewildered George, Paige, and Keith.

"Attention, all teams. Tamaro is heading north in section three of the cave," Bella barked into her radio. "Most likely trying to find a way to a tube to reach the coast. Seal Team One be ready! Bravo, Charlie, and Delta teams converge! Repeat, converge!" When no one acknowledged, she growled a protest. "Damn these lava tubes. You never can get a message out when you need to."

"Now that's the spirit, Agent Walker." A winded George Dwyer mockingly announced to Bella while Keith laughed with a tired gasp.

"You are too much sometimes, George," Bella responded back in her own exhausted breath. "We need to stop meeting like this in lava tubes."

Ace ran Bella and the teams another two hundred yards down another chasm of tubes. The air in this particular section was heavy with condensation and unbelievably, as they came into another dome, had its own clouds forming. As they ran on, their flashlights glistened, the towering mists causing mini rainbows throughout their shine.

"I never knew that cave systems or lava tubes could make clouds." Bella almost paused in wonder.

"I've never been down so far into one of them to find out," uttered a fatigued Chuck Child. He had paused to put his hands on his leg to take a breath. "And if you look to your right, you'll see the reason it formed this deep down."

Bella looked with her eyes wide and her mouth ajar. She shivered, feeling the rolls of clouded mist being blown toward her from a cascading underground waterfall of at least a hundred feet in height. She wiped chilled sweat from her brow and shined her light upwards and then back down to see the towering white water of the falls crashing onto boulders at the base. The boulders themselves were part of a vast, raging, underground river that could have been a football field wide. Here the granite and limestone shimmered as the waters swiftly moved past.

"We need to hurry, folks. Ace will be trying to follow this out to the river. Hopefully Seal Team One has this covered." Bella pointed to the winding river and a makeshift trail parallel to the swift, running water.

"Let's hope he didn't have a boat tied off and already took off." George shook his head and tightened his face.

"He didn't," Billy called from the southern trail next to the river. "I got turned around with some of Bravo Team. I followed this with them all the way out from the other side. We looped back and followed it back up. No signs of him."

"We need to circle, everyone. Keep a tight perimeter. He's going to try to backtrack. You can bet on it." Bella pointed to the vast cave near the cascading river. "Agent Makani—"

Billy interrupted and pointed to his radio. "I know. I got that garbled message you tried to send through the lava tubes. I was able to infer what you were screaming and radioed when I got outside the tube." He looked down the river and then back toward the dome-like cave system. "I'll take Bravo Team and continue to scour behind you. Already informed Seal Team One and Tropic Lightning to be watching all the underground waterways too."

"That's great, Billy. Now you're thinking like a Yakuza ringleader." Bella gave him a wicked grin and headed out.

Billy bristled. "Very funny."

The team spread out in the expanse of the darkness of the cave. They would leave literally no rock unturned. It was on a turn around a fifteen-foot-high boulder that a powerful strike to Bella's right side knocked her back, and then a second blow followed it, nearly knocking her off her feet. Someone had kicked her twice in the darkness before she could react. The assailant went for a third kick to the stunned Bella, but she managed to block that kick and regain her bearings and foot placement.

"You take a beating pretty good, for a woman. Who are you, foolish lady? I see you lost your FBI hat when I kicked you," the voice hissed hypnotically. "Do you want it back?"

Bella shined her headlamp, but the figure remained in the shadows, moving like a striking cobra to deliver another flurry of punches. The Bright Prince had somehow recovered her FBI hat and was wearing it as a taunt as he attacked her.

"Nice to meet you, Ace," Bella taunted the man back, then launched a feigned lunge which made her attacker try to counter. When he did, Bella sent a ground sweep, knocking him to the ground, then volleyed another insult to the man's pride to twist him up. "How's it feel to get beaten by a woman?" She took a ragged, burning breath. Her attacker may have broken one of her ribs in his surprise kick. "You're under arrest, Tamaro. Your gang is broken up. Give it up."

She was rewarded for her tenacity with a quick jab to the nose that she couldn't avoid. "I see you are under the delusion that you have beaten me. This is just *one* of my gangs, Agent Walker." Of course, he knew her name. TJ had likely blabbed everything.

"Ace, we captured all of your men. Your bosses in Japan already are not pleased. At best we handcuff you and take you in. You give up critical information about the entire Hawaiian operation. Maybe you get out in fifty years." Bella gave Ace an insidious grin as she kept both her hands up in a defensive position waiting for him to strike.

Ace Tamaro laughed heartily at Bella's offer. "You insult me to think I take a deal like that."

Bella moved to her right as Ace went to throw a punch. "It beats dying, Ace. You know that you're a dead man with the Yakuza for your disloyalty." She threw her own fist this time. Ace countered and grabbed her hand, pulling Bella up close.

"All I have to do is set up a new shop and earn back my losses." He picked up Bella and flipped her onto the rocky ground of the cave. Bella felt the burning and stabbing of shards of rocks as she landed.

"Not if we already put the word out that you snitched. We have people inside your organization in all of the major syndicates." Bella rolled as Ace went to stomp on her head in a rage, and she lashed out her leg which made him trip to his knees.

Both went to stand groggily. Both rounded each other in another barrage of fists and kicks.

"That's not very honorable, Agent Walker. I wouldn't have played so dirty." Bella gasped from the blinding pain of her broken rib. The criminal mastermind saw her gasp and grinned. "This was a lot of fun though. I needed a laugh."

"Bella!" came a voice from behind Ace. It disrupted the tranquil stillness of their battle, which was the point. The Conjure Man lunged forward to tackle the man to the ground. With an arrogant smirk, Ace turned on his heel and quickly dodged Justin's attack.

Now she had him. Bella threw all her force in a right-side front kick to Ace's right knee. He didn't see it coming. It didn't take much to hit Ace's left leg laterally, and he cried out as his kneecap shattered, dropping him back onto a pile of glassy rocks that clinked and tinkled. He tumbled down until he slammed headfirst into the jagged edge of a boulder with a sickening crack. The impact instantly knocked him unconscious, and blood trickled down his face.

"You got your laugh now."

Akihiko Tamaro, The Bright Prince, lay in a pile of Tears of Pele underneath the mountain, blood pooling all around him.

"You know I had him, right?" Bella huffed as Justin walked out of the darkness and turned on his headlamp. "Besides, Mr. Trestle, what took you so long to get back?"

Justin shrugged and put his hands out apologetically. "I got lost."

Bella raised an eyebrow. "You got lost?"

They both laughed with tears falling. Bella gave him a hug and punched his chest. Then she pulled the beast of a man in close in the darkness and kissed him passionately on the lips.

"Wow, is that Ace Tamaro?" Billy Makani walked up as Bella was leaning over to check a pulse and slapping cuffs on him. "You did all that?"

"I got his knee. As for the rest ..." Bella shrugged, "seems like Pele got her revenge after all," she said

"If that's the official story, I'm cool with that," he laughed. He picked up one of the Tears of Pele and closed his eyes. *"'Owaka I ka lani, noke-noke E pele e Pele e,"* he whispered.

CHAPTER THIRTY-SIX

Ko'olau Mountains
Oahu, Hawaii
July 28, 2023

B ELLA SIGHED IN EXHAUSTION AS SHE WATCHED THE WATERS OF the underground river exit out into brilliant sunlight, glistening as fine, white pearls heading south out of the cave system to a cavern opening halfway up Ko'olau Mountain. She'd walked out with some of the team onto the side of the winding mountain. To her surprise, they were right off a traversed trail near a dense tropical forest inhabited by every color of bird. The blue, purple, and red birds were playing and dipping in the quiet pools adjacent to the winding river.

Bella cast her gaze on the sun as she hiked down with the teams. It held all the smoldering red and shimmering molten orange of a late afternoon preparing to set on another day in the emerald paradise of Hawaii. After hours of hiking through the caves, the cool breezes coming from the cave system and the river's lapping waters filled her lungs with something like hope.

On the adjacent ridge, three miles down, there was a sparse open patch of field. It was a somewhat flat and grassy knoll that held just the needed dimensions for a helicopter landing zone. And with the winds somewhat calm on this part of the mountain, Bella took the opportunity to call in a chopper to pick up the equally tired FBI and SWAT teams. The chopper managed to arrive fifteen minutes after her request, and six of her team flew down to base camp. Bella herself waited until all of the teams had gotten to base camp safely. Then she took the last flight of the day down to the camp for a well-earned debriefing.

Walking carefully to the chopper, hearing the whir of the blades and feeling the gusts as it landed, Bella turned one last time in the direction of the lava tubes and caves of Ko'olau. She took in its menace. She took in its grand, alluring beauty, then thought to herself,

That cave and all we just experienced was like this twisting and winding case. It had all the charms with colorful birds and trees. It had all the scenic beauty with that incredible waterfall and river. And there was so much danger walking through that sketchy cave and lava tube system. I don't know if I can go back to Colorado and your average criminals after this experience.

But my boss in Colorado will probably shoot me if I don't. I had better talk with Justin about this one.

As Bella went to secure herself in the helicopter, she glanced out grimly as another chopper flew swiftly in the direction of Straub Medical Center. In that medevac chopper was the former ringleader for The Tears of the Dragon. Bella would later learn from the medical staff that as Ace Tamaro lay on the stretcher, after waking up from his horrific head wound, he cried. As the flight nurse placed a ventilator to help him breathe, streams of tears fell down his face.

But to no one's surprise, no one onboard the chopper or at the hospital shed a tear for him.

The helicopter rattled as Bella made the descent to base camp. She had a moment to take in more of the tropical mystery and beauty of the island: the jagged, verdant cliffs, that towered over the small villages and even the bustling city of Waikiki; the emerald jungles bustling with life; the dazzling waves shining in the sunset as gulls floated above in slow, lazy circles. She even got a brief glimmer in the distance of the FBI building where she had worked over the last couple of weeks.

Then, it all hit her. The one question that had dogged her mind relentlessly since she first learned that the always honest and open Aunt

Natalie had secrets. She could understand her beloved aunt, swirled in the constant fame that came with being a legend, finally finding a place where she could duck out of the spotlight for a while and just be... well... Natalie again. And as an added bonus, solve an alluring family mystery with a dashing, charismatic sailor. Weren't the two of them—both respected FBI agents in their fields, both hounded to solve very public and dangerous cases—very much alike? Only her sailor rode sharks and took down the occasional Yakuza gangster. Okay, maybe there were some differences. Algernon Magnum didn't strike her as the violent type.

But who knows? Maybe the dashing sailor-turned-Robert-Louis-Stevenson fanboy did have a protective side on occasion.

Bella knew something was out of place right now as the helicopter touched down. And it certainly wasn't the helicopter that had gently landed, dropping her off to an awaiting crowd. The team was cheering, and everyone was in a fevered frenzy after handing the Yakuza syndicate a big loss on the Hawaiian Islands today. Bella walked up to the table as SAC Harris clapped and pointed to Bella and then to the rest of the teams with a large smile.

"Well, my fellow FBI agents, members of all our interagency support, and everyone that played a part as one cohesive team," SAC Harris began, "today, we came together as one to crush a vile criminal syndicate: The Tears of the Dragon. Their leader, from what I gathered from agents on site, had a fall trying to take out this lady right here! Say a few, Agent Walker!"

Bella was caught off guard. She was recalling a moment from her childhood when her legendary Aunt Natalie was put on the spot after saving so many back then. Just as Aunt Natalie had been red-faced and tongue-tied at first, now Bella was having the same awkward moment at being thrust into the spotlight.

As SAC Harris gave her a proud grin, Bella gave him a scowl. Then she stepped forward just as the media arrived to set up their shot. She plastered a smile on her face for the cameras as she steeled herself and stepped up to the podium. It was funny. She could take down killers with no problem, and she could throw herself into danger without a second thought, but public speaking? Now that was terrifying.

"The Yakuza group known as the Tears of the Dragon is no more. This was a big win for all departments today, and not just the FBI and the Department of Justice. All of us share this win. The streets and jungles of these beautiful islands are much safer now that these murderers are gone."

Bella reached into her pocket and pulled out one of the Tears of Pele that she had picked up from the scene. She held it up to the cameras, where a flurry of shutters took it in. "These monsters decided they could steal the ancient artifacts of the Hawaiian people. But as any island native knows, Pele herself will curse you if you try. Let it be known to anyone who tries: if you come to this tropical paradise to murder or steal, you will find yourself facing the wrath of Pele—and the FBI."

The crowd of SWAT, military, and all the agencies involved in The Tears of the Dragon assault roared in applause as her face turned as red as the Hawaiian sun she'd watched set earlier that evening.

After everyone had disbanded and left for their offices and homes, Bella walked with her team and climbed into a gray FBI cruiser. As she yawned and rubbed her bruised or maybe broken rib, she noted the tired smiles of Billy, George, Paige, Keith, and SAC Harris. Everyone noted the absence of Rachel.

"Is there any update on Rachel?" Bella asked in general, knowing SAC Harris would be the most likely to answer.

"She'll need a few weeks of rest, but the bullet went entirely through. She's awake and giving the doctors hell, apparently."

Everyone laughed. "She wouldn't be Rachel if she wasn't kicking up some kind of ruckus," said Billy.

George Dwyer howled with laughter and slapped Billy on the back. "You got that right."

For Bella, the incessant need to stay was back again. Maybe this great FBI team's friendship and work ethic was the reason. Maybe the team's camaraderie and laughter were further tethering her to this enchanted place. With all the allure—beautiful beaches, mysterious mountains, and great people—it would be hard to leave. Then there were still the intrigues and mysteries left to solve. The need to search out her own family mystery on this island was drawing Bella in like a siren's song. But it would be foolish to follow up on that urge—to relent and throw caution to the wind and stay in Hawaii forever.

Besides, she had a life back in Colorado with Justin. He had a highly successful pizza business. They had their frigid hikes and skiing to fall back on. She smirked as the team pulled into the parking lot of the FBI field office.

Well, I could trade all the snow for endless fun in the sun and warm hikes around here.

"You all smell like you've been living with bats for a month. I'm ordering all of you home to shower and burn those awful-smelling uniforms," SAC Harris said as everyone climbed out of the SUV. "It goes without saying, team, take the rest of the week off. Especially you, Walker. And get those ribs checked out."

Bella had tried to hide the bruised ribs, but Harris had somehow picked up on it in their exchanges. She nodded and guarded her side. "I'll go right now."

"One more thing, Agent Walker. How would you feel about a transfer?"

Oahu, Hawaii
Straub Medical Center
Emergency Room
July 28, 2023

Billy drove Bella to the emergency room at Straub Medical Center. She didn't wait long, naturally. The medical team put her on oxygen due to the nature of her condition and sent her to get X-rays. A shadow towered over her as she sat on a stretcher waiting to get her chest X-ray.

"You probably bruised them when the dirtbag sucker kicked you in the dark." Justin shrugged and grabbed a chair to sit next to Bella.

"That's what I thought. But it's certainly throbbing pretty good, sir. The guy kicked like a mule." Bella winced and tried to shift herself. "Wait a minute. How'd you get in here?"

"I told them I was your fiancée." Justin gave her a Cheshire cat smile.

"I ought to slug you right now." Bella grimaced as the burning pain in her ribs returned.

Justin put his hands out defensively. "Great, that's the gratitude I get for saving your bacon... again."

Bella groaned as the X-ray tech took her to get the film. "I think I did pretty alright for myself."

"Well, it's better than being stabbed."

"Watch it, mister."

Two hours later, Bella's oxygen mask was removed. Her X-rays showed three hairline fractures to her right ribs. Fortunately, there was no punctured or damaged lung. With strict orders from the ER doctor to rest and take it easy, Bella was discharged into the care of Justin.

"So, they gave you some anti-inflammatories and an order to hang loose, huh?" Justin asked as he wheelchaired Bella out of the hospital. He waved to a teenager waiting out front and tossed the kid his keys.

"Did you just give that kid some car keys?" Bella frowned as she still guarded her bandaged ribs with her right arm. The motion, plus the meds, eased her pain a little.

Justin shrugged and pointed to the kid running out to get Justin's car. "Yeah. Tony Maunalua is a great kid. He'll be a great doctor someday with his work ethic and people skills."

Bella rubbed her left temple in confusion.

Justin has been here just a few days. He has the fanciest condo of anyone on the beach. And now as I leave to go rest at the bungalow… he has a car. This should be quite interesting.

A stretch limousine pulled up in front of the hospital. Bella wondered which Hawaiian celebrity was showing up at the emergency room as she was going home.

Justin, to her surprise, nodded as the driver got out and opened the door for Bella. Inside the limo was a specially modified air foam bed propped up with pillows underneath and around for Bella to rest her arms with limited movement. There was a large bouquet of roses in the center console well away from where Bella would be lying down. And the final touch was a large card stuck in the flowers that read, "Get Well Soon!"

Bella kissed Justin on the lips as he carried her into the limo. "You are something else, Mr. Trestle."

Justin shrugged as he went to close Bella's door. "If it makes you feel any better, I sent Rachel Gentry a *Friends for Dummies* book." Then with a mischievous smile, he added, "And a Mauna Loa chocolate bar."

On her gentle drive home, Bella tried to find the best position to stay comfortable. It was, despite all the effort Justin had put into making her ride home pain-free, nearly impossible not to wince and cry out, feeling every bump in the road with her broken ribs.

At the bungalow, Justin threw out the stops tripling down to make sure he got Bella into her cool room to rest and heal. "I'll be outside the door if you need anything."

"How about a new set of ribs?"

"How about some baby back, baby back ribs from the grill tomorrow?" he replied.

"That sounds nice." Bella wanly smiled and nodded off to sleep. Justin would advise her later that her snores woke the neighbors.

A brilliant, midmorning sun beamed into Bella's room. It had been a long night for the forensics specialist. Justin had pretty much cared for Bella throughout the tumultuous night, especially when she would cry out in pain. And again, he was there when she needed help with medication or a hike to the bathroom.

But now, she was almost awake. Justin was in a chair next to her bed with a tray of coffee cups readily poured. "Did you get the name of the truck?" she croaked.

"The truck, Bella? Did the medicine or lack of sleep make you go loopy?" Puzzled, Justin read the medication bottle and scratched his head.

"No." Bella saw Justin was still perplexed by what she meant. She whispered, as anything more triggered the burning pain and cramping in her side. "The truck that ran me over."

That drew a cheerful snort from him. "You got me." He shook his head and smirked. "You've been hanging out with me too long."

She whispered one more thing, "Did Dutton call?"

"He did. I'm pretty sure he understands." Justin leaned toward Bella with a cup of coffee. She waved him off. There was no way she was moving to do anything, much less drink coffee. The ribs hurt way too much. "When were you going to tell me?" he asked.

Bella was nodding off. She repositioned for comfort to try to sleep. "Tell you what?"

"I was told you got an offer." Justin leaned back and gulped his own coffee with a concerned, furrowed brow.

"We'll talk about it more when I'm feeling better." Bella could see that Justin was looking out the window toward the surf. She wondered briefly, as slumber took her, what he was thinking as he stared at the ocean blue.

SAC Harris called bright and early at eight o'clock the next morning for a follow-up on her condition. Bella groaned as Justin held her phone to her ear. "Doctor Stossel said the X-rays showed three broken ribs but no punctured lung." Bella took a wincing gasp to continue. "He said with that kind of force breaking a rib or three, I was lucky the lung didn't just spontaneously pop too."

"Well, you sound horrible. Take time to heal up. You don't want to aggravate it." He paused on the phone as Bella's head swirled from the medication and pain. "You give any thought to my offer?"

"Sir, we can discuss the offer when my head is clear and I'm feeling better." Bella had exhausted herself just in the brief exchange. She hung up the phone and fell back to sleep yet again. She dreamed of jumping off a ragged cliff into an ocean pool, then awoke with an agonized start remembering something. She looked over at Justin napping and shook her head angrily at him. In the dream, as she'd landed in the water, she had seen below her a shark. The shark was being ridden by Justin.

Three days after the assault on Ko'olau Mountain, Bella was moving with all the grace of a duck on ice. She'd waddle a bit. She'd swoon to move into the kitchen, out by the pool, or living room, then catch herself murmuring insults at herself for re-injuring her ribs. But by the fourth day, she was up to a brisk walk, and after seven days, she was getting into her routine—though, any jogging was out of the question for at least another week.

Throughout the two weeks to rest, Bella called SAC Harris with her medical progress and delayed her answer of whether she'd take the job. She did the same whenever Justin asked. It was a life-changing step that she would not rush into. For one, there was more than herself to think about.

She also, when she was able to, kept up with Rachel's progress. In the first week, it was phone calls. By the second, as she was able to walk around more, it was hospital visits.

"Agent Gentry's room, please," Bella asked the receptionist in the lobby. She noted long bags under the Hawaiian woman's eyes.

"Room 3113." The woman yawned and pointed. "It's the third floor, three doors down on your left."

Bella recalled how Rachel's phone calls had seemed detached and cryptic—as if she wanted to say more about the case but was afraid to do so over the hospital phone. There'd be better follow-up between the agents in person for sure.

Bella walked to the elevator. She pressed the dodgy elevator button three times before it lit to come down. Bella frowned and shook her head. With her luck as of late, she almost expected to get stuck in that ancient relic.

Bella walked the immaculately spotless and white hospital floor to Rachel's room three doors down on the left. She knocked to no response, then opened the door cautiously. There was no one in the room.

"Ah-hum."

Bella turned to her right to see the familiar sight of Rachel's smile on the other bed. "I see you get just as lost in hospitals as you do in caves."

Bella smiled. "I make it a point not to tour them often. Anyway, familiarity breeds contempt."

"I agree. And to think we could have been up at the Alohilani. These linens leave a lot to be desired." Rachel grinned and sat up.

"You both look like you've been through the wringer." Shane stood and gave Bella a very careful hug.

"You should see the other guy." Bella nodded to Rachel knowingly.

Not to be undone, Rachel gave Bella a mischievous smirk. "Bella, do you have a lot of men fall for you? Did you know, Shane, that Ace Tamaro jumped off a boulder to attack her?"

"What can I say? I'm a popular gal," Bella replied. "Even had him on his knees at one point."

Rachel and her husband both let out hearty chuckles at that.

"When do you get to go home?" Bella asked.

"Why, today, Agent Walker. That's why we called you. Shane's just been *dying* to get back out there on the waves with your Aquaman. Did you bring the limo?"

Bella laughed. "Well, don't let me stop you. Just keep him away from the sharks."

EPILOGUE

Oahu, Hawaii
FBI Field Office
August 16, 2023

"ARE YOU SURE YOU WANT TO DO THIS? IT'S NOT TOO LATE TO change your mind." Rachel sat across at her desk and leaned in toward Bella. There was growing concern across her face just as the beams of a morning sun cast a glare into the room, igniting her brown hair.

"I talked it over with SAC Dutton." Bella paused a moment and ran nervous fingers through her auburn curls. "I really wish we could get him over here. We'd have Hawaii cleaned up in a month."

"Dutton is the best of the best, no doubt. But Harris has his charms on occasion. After working in the FBI for thirty years, may we both be less jaded and still diligent in the work though," Rachel added as she stood to look out at the beach and the rolling white waves crashing in.

"You know what I'm going to ask: What about Chief Como?" Bella kept a tight stare and expressionless face as she read Rachel's body language. From what she saw, it wasn't good.

"SAC Harris said it was all too coincidental. But he did assure me that the HPD chief will be scrutinized more carefully." Rachel glanced back at Bella and frowned.

Bella's mouth dropped open in a furious gape. "He nearly got our teams killed! And there was no pushback when he just disappeared in the chaos of wrapping things up? How does that work for law enforcement? Anyone else—"

"Would be in jail with The Tears of the Dragon. Or at a hospital on permanent life support, if I let that cannon-ball vigilante of a boyfriend of yours at him." Rachel turned, took a breath, and looked at the ceiling. "I don't like it either. But apparently, there's more going on with Chief Como and what he knows than we realize."

"It must be a dandy of a tale—especially with all the bodies buried in his backyard." Bella bit the side of her mouth as she lowered her head in disgust. "How does he sleep at night, that one?"

Rachel sneered, hissing her own disgust. "You know, every time I cough, I feel a spasm in my stomach and side. Trust me when I say this: I'm going to square what he did, one day."

"In the meantime…" Bella's words and thoughts trailed off. She had bigger things to face today. This would be a moment of agony and great torture. There was a party celebrating Bella officially joining the Hawaii FBI field office. "Do we really have to throw a luau?"

"It's tradition. Besides, I had an old friend get the best cake out there on all the Hawaiian Islands." Rachel led Bella out of her office to the conference room for Bella's congratulatory party.

"I should have known she'd put you up to selecting the cake." Bella gave a wry grin to Justin and socked him in his arm.

"Like I told her a long time ago: 'Rachel, with all the crooks and cons in your life, you need better friends.'" Justin came up and gave Bella a hug and kiss on the cheek.

"For the record, how long have you known my boyfriend, Agent Gentry?" Bella narrowed her stare suspiciously.

"I don't know, Bella. How long did Justin work for the SEALS in the Pacific?" Rachel shrugged and went to the front of the table with most of the agents present.

"You never told me you knew Rachel before us."

"It never came up. But I did tell you she needed better friends." Justin cocked his head and raised his right brow in acknowledgment.

"If we are going to do this, Justin Trestle, no more secrets." Bella paused as Rachel ushered her to the front of the table to introduce her to the new team. "Do you get my drift, sir?"

"So, you want me over here too?" Justin looked shocked and a little out of sorts.

"Why wouldn't I? You're my boyfriend, aren't you?" Bella walked toward the head of the conference table and left Justin puzzled and bewildered. There would be a lot of operational and logistics planning in his future. Especially moving back to Hawaii.

SAC Charlton Harris lumbered his towering frame into the conference room for the festivities. The man was nearly as tall as Justin, but that's where the similarities ended. "Agent Walker, I'm ecstatic to have you join our team permanently. I haven't been this excited since I brought Agent Gentry onboard to clean up the islands."

Bella took the opportunity to let SAC Harris know she wouldn't be duped. "Maybe we can start an investigation on the man that nearly got our team killed?"

"We can't touch him yet," SAC Harris said. Bella was shocked by his reply. The man leaned in and whispered, "I'll say three initials that will explain why he's not in jail. Are you ready?"

Bella nodded that she was.

"CIA."

A lightning bolt struck through her mind with a massive awakening as to why this case had so many twists and turns. Why, no matter how clear the evidence was to arrest the cowardly chief of HPD, he couldn't be touched.

Chief Como was snitching on a grander and more international scale. But at what cost to the FBI and to America's most powerful surveillance outfit? Bella had to voice her concerns.

"But at what cost, SAC Harris? Are the lives of rank-and-file FBI, SWAT, and military agencies of so little value these days?" She winced as her ribs started to burn from all the talking. "I mean, I get it. If he squeals when a shipment of dirty bombs has arrived in Kona, a new trafficking ring has surfaced in Maui, or China's drop of fake digital currency will flood and bankrupt our markets, it's a major win. But couldn't we do the same surveillance and not sell our souls to this despicable cretin? How about we go old school and spread out undercover agents and confidential informants to achieve the same results?"

"I think it's an excellent idea. Maybe one day you and your team will finish what I started a long time ago." SAC Harris put a hand on Bella's shoulder. "I've grown tired of the constant cycle where we win, then we play ball or lose. And then repeat all over again under a new regime."

Bella nodded her head and stared at the tired SAC. The thought drifted over her as SAC Harris bellowed out their win over the Yakuza and gladly accepted Bella coming onboard.

He's fought time and again with the bureaucracy and the corruption on a level I could never understand. Nor would I ever want to sell my soul to the Devil to want to. Bending here, breaking there, to win one day or lose another. How would anyone not become jaded or cynical?

"Today we bring on a young lady who has brought her relentless expertise and experience to help us crush the Yakuza in Hawaii. I had to ask Agent Walker to join us after witnessing her firsthand charge into a dangerous lava tube system to capture the deadly leader of The Tears of the Dragon. Oh, Bella, I hear The Bright Prince was just smitten." Everyone laughed at SAC Harris's jest. Then as he put his hands out to quiet everyone, he added one more thing: "Most ladies are flattered when a man falls at their feet, Agent Walker. But you literally had one fall for you."

Bella wanted to climb under the table upon hearing the uproars of howling laughter. Instead, she smiled, nodded to everyone, and grabbed some coconut cake, then hastened to the back of the conference room next to a grinning Justin.

"You have to admit it was funny." Justin leaned his body over and put his head next to hers.

"Not, another word, Mr. Trestle." She grinned at him, though, and leaned back, nearly knocking him off his chair. "Eat your cake, knucklehead."

———•———

As a Hawaiian sun was starting to set on the horizon, casting shadows throughout the FBI building, Bella pushed back her chair from her new desk. Her new office was situated two doors down from Rachel Gentry and five doors down from SAC Harris. She was looking at a new case file that was on her desk. The team had named the case 'The Jade Princess.'

As she opened it to read, a picture fell out. It was of some type of party, coincidentally. There were fireworks and presents all around a woman expecting a child. And in the background was a towering beast of a man smiling the widest smile with the expectant mother. None other than Conjure Man himself.

Bella groaned and closed the file. She and Justin needed to have a long talk.

Rachel leaned into her office with a file in her hand. "You got a minute?"

Bella hurriedly closed the file before Rachel could see Justin in the photo. "Sure. What do you have for me?"

Rachel shrugged. She handed over the file, which had been addressed by Algernon Magnum to her. It contained several copies of historical archives, births on the island and abroad, and a detailed lineage from an ancestry site. "Algernon didn't want to upset you, but he just couldn't leave things unturned. He said Natalie would have demanded you know the time and effort that went into finding the truth about your family. The pictures and documents lend credibility to Algernon Magnum's claim that you and Aunt Natalie are descendants of Robert Louis Stevenson."

She marveled at the documents. "He will never let it go. But I'm starting to see why Aunt Natalie cared for him so much. The man is an honest-to-goodness, charismatic swashbuckler." Both laughed. "I'll go over it when I get home. I have plenty of time now to go to The Salty Pirate and annoy Mr. Magnum, now that I'm a resident."

"Oh, that reminds me." Rachel hurried out of Bella's office as she grabbed her purse and keys to leave. Bella turned off her lights and headed into the hallway, waiting at Rachel's door.

Rachel rushed out with a gleaming smile. She handed Bella a wrapped, heavy present. "Promise me you won't open it until you get home. It has sentimental value, and I don't want to cry in front of the troops. Got it, Agent Walker?"

Bella was halfway home when her insatiable curiosity got the better of her. She pulled over near a roaring surf not far from where she had run and found the sunken wooden ship. Leaning against her car's hood, she ripped off the paper as the sea continued to pound the Hawaiian coast. Bella laughed and slapped her leg knowing Rachel had pulled her leg again with a great gag.

For the wrapped present from Rachel Gentry was quite the ancient treasure, of sorts. The gift was from Bella's past—if the ancestral research held. It was one of her famous ancestors who himself had charted many a course under tropical skies. It was *The Strange Case of Dr. Jekyll and Mr. Hyde,* by Robert Louis Stevenson.

"It has sentimental value, alright, Rachel Gentry!" Bella yelled to the surf. With a smirk on her face, she got back into her car and drove home.

AUTHOR'S NOTE

Wow! I can't believe how time flies! This year will mark the fourth year since I've begun writing novels for you, my amazing readers. Safe to say, with everything that has happened in the world it has been the craziest time of my life. Who knew these years would be so full of crazy twists and turns for everyone. With that said, I just want to thank you so much for choosing to continue the ride with me. Writing novels for you has been my place of peace and joy amid the chaos and turmoil. And, I especially want to thank Thomas York for helping me create and write this new series set in Hawaii.

The Girl in Paradise is the first book in the *Bella Walker FBI Mystery Thriller* series.
What are your thoughts about the change of scenery? I thought it was a much-needed addition in the Emma, Dean, and Ava world.
As indie authors it isn't easy to get people to read our work. So, we couldn't be more grateful for your kind words and show of support during these trying years.

You've given us more than enough support by just reading our work, but if you have just a few seconds. We would truly appreciate it if you could take that little time out of your day to write a review for this novel. Just a few words or a few sentences is enough and would truly mean so much to us. Your reviews are the words of affirmation we need to keep writing and striving to be the best writers we can be.

From the bottom of our heart thank you for everything, I hope our words have brought you as much joy as writing for you has to us. Thank you in advance if you have taken the time to write us a review for this novel. You are the best! Here's to many more years of writing for you and many more Emma, Dean, Ava, and Bella novels!

As always, all my love.

Sincerely yours,
A.J. Rivers & Thomas York

P.S. If for some reason you didn't like this book or found typos or other errors, please let me know personally. I do my best to read and respond to every email at mailto:aj@riversthrillers.com

P.P.S. If you would like to stay up-to-date with me and my latest releases I invite you to visit my Linktree page at *www.linktr.ee/a.j.rivers* to subscribe to my newsletter and receive a free copy of my book, Edge of the Woods. You can also follow me on my social media accounts for behind-the-scenes glimpses and sneak peeks of my upcoming projects, or even sign up for text notifications. I can't wait to connect with you!

ALSO BY
A.J. RIVERS

Emma Griffin FBI Mysteries Retro - Limited Series

Book One— The Girl in the Mist*
Book Two— The Girl on Hallow's Eve*
Book Three— The Girl and the Christmas Past*
Book Four— The Girl and the Winter Bones*
Book Five— The Girl on the Retreat

Ava James FBI Mysteries

Book One—The Woman at the Masked Gala*
Book Two—Ava James and the Forgotten Bones*
Book Three —The Couple Next Door*
Book Four — The Cabin on Willow Lake*
Book Five — The Lake House
Book Six — The Ghost of Christmas
Book Seven — The Rescue
Book Eight — Murder in the Moonlight

Dean Steele FBI Mysteries

Book One—The Woman in the Woods

ALSO BY
A.J. RIVERS & THOMAS YORK

Bella Walker FBI Mystery Series

Book One—The Girl in Paradise

Other Standalone Novels
Gone Woman
* Also available in audio

Made in the USA
Middletown, DE
02 April 2025

73690907R00155